Tara Pammi can't remember a moment when she wasn't lost in a book—especially a romance, which was much more exciting than a mathematics textbook at school. Years later, Tara's wild imagination and love for the written word revealed what she really wanted to do. Now she pairs alpha males who think they know everything with strong women who knock that theory *and* them off their feet!

Rebecca Hunter is an award-winning author, reader, traveller, occasional college professor, full-time chocolate lover, and keeper of a very messy desk. Her books have won the National Excellence in Romance Fiction Award, the HOLT Medallion and the VIVIAN Award. She writes witty, passionate stories about complex characters and intriguing destinations for Mills & Boon's Modern line. For reading and writing updates, photos and travel plans, join her newsletter on her website: www.rebeccahunterwriter.com.

Also by Tara Pammi

Her Twin Secret
Vows to a King
His Forgotten Wife
Baby Before Vows

Also by Rebecca Hunter

This is **Rebecca Hunter**'s debut book for
Mills & Boon Modern—we hope that you enjoy it!

Discover more at millsandboon.co.uk.

ITALIAN LIAISONS

TARA PAMMI

REBECCA HUNTER

MILLS & BOON

All rights reserved including the right of reproduction in whole or in part in any form. This edition is published by arrangement with Harlequin Enterprises ULC.

This is a work of fiction. Names, characters, places, locations and incidents are purely fictional and bear no relationship to any real life individuals, living or dead, or to any actual places, business establishments, locations, events or incidents. Any resemblance is entirely coincidental.

Without limiting the exclusive rights of any author, contributor or the publisher of this publication, any unauthorised use of this publication to train generative artificial intelligence (AI) technologies is expressly prohibited. HarperCollins also exercise their rights under Article 4(3) of the Digital Single Market Directive 2019/790 and expressly reserve this publication from the text and data mining exception.

® and TM are trademarks owned and used by the trademark owner and/or its licensee. Trademarks marked with ® are registered with the United Kingdom Patent Office and/or the Office for Harmonisation in the Internal Market and in other countries.

First published in Great Britain 2026 by Mills & Boon, an imprint of HarperCollins*Publishers* Ltd, 1 London Bridge Street, London, SE1 9GF

www.harpercollins.co.uk

HarperCollins*Publishers*, Macken House, 39/40 Mayor Street Upper, Dublin 1, D01 C9W8, Ireland

Italian Liaisons © 2026 Harlequin Enterprises ULC

Italian's Last-Minute Mistress © 2026 Tara Pammi

Convenient Wife Conditions © 2026 Rebecca Hunter

ISBN: 978-0-263-41823-1

03/26

Printed and Bound in the UK using 100% Renewable Electricity at CPI Group (UK) Ltd, Croydon, CR0 4YY

ITALIAN'S LAST-MINUTE MISTRESS

TARA PAMMI

MILLS & BOON

CHAPTER ONE

Sameera Fischer stood in front of the wide marble steps at the entrance to the most beautiful villa on the shores of Lake Como and tried not to hyperventilate.

It was the first time she'd flown across the Atlantic. The first time she'd hopped on a plane to anywhere. The first time she wasn't accompanied by her overprotective parents.

That she'd traveled so far to meet a close friend/ex-boyfriend who had ghosted her for months couldn't muddy her satisfaction at what she had achieved.

Although it was alarming how much Matteo had hidden about his family's standing. Even she, a naïve twenty-three-year-old who'd never left San Francisco before, could tell that the property in front of her would be worth millions, if not more.

The villa shone against the black night, like the lake shimmering behind her, full of magnificent splendor, with the snow-tipped Alps a shadowy outline. The swarm of the designer-wearing crowd and the giant marquee on the grounds said she'd arrived right in the middle of a big-ass party.

Matteo, on one of his visits to San Francisco, had shown her pics, but only bits and pieces. The gardens that he adored but not the lake they led into. His bike but not the bright red

Ferrari parked next to it. The view of Lake Como but not the spot where he'd stood when he'd taken the pic.

From the moment she'd boarded the flight to Milan—on a first-class flight and, then the chauffeured ride to Lake Como—an unsettling realization dawned. Matteo was no lowly manager in the rungs of Ricci International Finances as he'd claimed. Perhaps the fact that his surname was Ricci should have been a clue, but she'd never had reason to believe he'd lie to her…

Her confusion at his ghosting her only deepened.

Four months ago, they'd argued bitterly. No longer eighteen as when they'd met, Sam had realized that their relationship had run its course. Matteo would always remain her first boyfriend and a kind friend who had loved her during a hard time, yet they had nothing in common.

That she'd disappointed him by ending their relationship—after his patience over their long-distance relationship for nearly five years—saddened her. So surprising him by coming here had felt like a great idea. She knew that there was a friendship between them worth saving, even if the relationship was over, and this sudden silence from him worried her because it was so out of character.

Now as she stared at the glittering party, doubts engulfed her. Should she quietly leave? Wait for Matteo to show up in San Francisco again? Would he even come back, after ghosting her?

No, she couldn't give up now. Not on their friendship, not on herself.

This could be the summer where she experienced the world as a normal twenty-three-year-old. One summer where she didn't have to live with the crushing guilt that she'd ruined her parents' life.

One summer where she was bold, adventurous and daring.

* * *

Alessandro Ricci stared out of his bedroom window at his family's villa at the teeming guests and felt a spark of shame. He was the older son, and yet, he was avoiding extended family, important guests, the Bianchis among them and his aunt's extravagant emotions.

The last was what he needed escape from the most. It wasn't enough for his aunt that her son Matteo, Alessandro's half brother, was finally settling down. Oh no, his aunt who had raised Alessandro ever since his mother had died giving birth to him was now bemoaning Alessandro's own single status.

Since she was the one person in the entire world he loved more than anything, he hadn't snarled at her. Instead, he'd chosen to hide.

His presence cast a dark pall at these parties anyway. Especially when it was his thoroughly spoiled, good-for-nothing half brother Matteo's engagement party to the billionaire Bianchi heiress that Alessandro had had to engineer as if he were a bloody pimp. Not that he didn't appreciate the billion-dollar investment it brought to Ricci Finances.

Even after all these years, the gathering today reminded him of his own engagement party eighteen years ago. Of how incredibly happy he had been. How gloriously beautiful Violetta had looked. How arrogantly confident he'd been in his own power that the world was his for the taking.

In the months after he'd lost Violetta, he had hated others' happiness with a violent resentment, like a wounded feral animal. He'd hated the pity and concern, as if they were afraid for him and of him. The next few years, he'd thrown himself into sex with women who knew the score. But the short shelf life of his partners had only encouraged the young women and their mamas in his circle to portray him as a tormented man who needed to be saved by love.

Soon, the isolation had become his armor.

But in the last few months, even his father, a man of few words, had cast him concerned glances. Had started talking about how lost and broken he'd been after Alessandro's mother had died after giving birth to him. That he had saved himself by marrying his wife's younger sister, Maria.

His father didn't know it was too late for Alessandro.

Every day he'd stayed by Violetta's side as she'd tried, and failed, to fight the insidious cancer that had siphoned everything soft and good from him too. Every minute he'd seen of her struggle and lived through the unrelenting powerlessness of it had splintered his heart until nothing was left.

Now, he was far too fond of his own company and excessively critical of everyone else. There was Matteo to produce heirs for the Ricci legacy, and he had his work.

His brother and Angelina Bianchi were a practical match, though there did seem to be some affection between them now. Everyone knew that Angelina had had her heart set on Matteo since she was sixteen. While he'd never admit to it, he understood Matteo's initial resentment toward her.

Angelina had pointed him out to her powerful father, Vittorio Bianchi, as easily as she'd have picked a stud. Then she'd pursued him with a relentless drive that the ruthless businessman in him had to admire. When Matteo had started returning her interest in the last six months, Vittorio had sweetened the merger immediately.

Though, Alessandro hadn't agreed just because of the Bianchis' investment. Angelina had a solid head on her shoulders, was a smart businesswoman who would one day inherit the Bianchi fortune and was exactly the kind of grounding partner Matteo needed.

Hopefully Alessandro wouldn't have to deal any more with Matteo's failed business ventures, the rowdy crowd that mooched off him in return for their adulation, and the debt holes he seemed to fall into. If Angelina could get him involved in Ricci International Finances, Alessandro would have nothing to worry about.

The outline of a young woman standing outside the crowd caught his interest. Dressed in a chunky sweater, skinny jeans and dark boots, she stood out in a sea of laughing, chattering, designer-clad party guests.

The lights around the fountain cast a glow on her face, highlighting the wide, lush lips and a nose too big for her small face. Her skin was a smooth golden brown, lighter than his.

Slowly, she moved toward the wide steps leading to the villa, her long neck tilted up, the strap of her crossbody bag highlighting her slender frame and into the circle of light created by huge floodlights, exactly where she'd be best illuminated.

So that he could get his fill of her... The thought startled him. But not enough to pull his interest away.

The woman's neck moved this way and that as she surveyed the house, like a baby bird hesitant to leave its nest, fingers playing with the hem of her sweater.

Then she sighed, pulled her bag off, tugged at the hem of her sweater before peeling it off her body. A breeze pressed the silky sleeveless blouse with its high ruffled neckline against her, highlighting small breasts, a thin waist and bony hips. With her collarbones jutting out, she bordered on skinny.

A small smile played around her lips. She finger-combed her hair until it fell in waves around her face. The motion tugged her blouse upward, revealing a silky strip of her midriff. Something glinted at her belly button.

Lust was a punch to his stomach. He looked away, wondering what the hell was happening to him. Gawking at a young woman, getting hard at the mere sight of her. It was bare seconds before his gaze returned to her.

Making a pout of her lips, she applied lipstick, straightened her shoulders and started walking up the steps.

There was an innate sensuality to her movements. Something achingly real and courageous in her smile as she fought her nervousness.

He put the tumbler in his hand on the windowsill as he realized why he was drawn to her. He recognized what it took her to shake off her fears and step into the night. To step back into life. It was a step he hadn't taken in eighteen years. Not that he'd wanted to.

She possessed the same hunger for life he had known once.

Suddenly, he was sick of the cloying quietness of his bedroom, the echoing isolation of his own thoughts.

He wanted to be outside where she was, wanted to know what was so precious that she'd fought her doubts. He wanted to taste the magic of that smile on her lips, breathe it in. Steal the very real joy in it.

A fierce longing stabbed through him, reminding him that he was very much alive.

He wanted her, in whatever capacity or form he could have her.

Sam was perusing the shelves in the grand study she'd come across when she heard the heavy double doors open behind her.

When she'd finally dived into the crowd to find Matteo, it had been hard to navigate the gigantic mansion, not counting the grounds and the marquee. For all that she'd hoped that her silk blouse was an upgrade from the worn sweater, she had still stood out. Luckily, she'd wandered inside in search of Matteo and a quieter spot and happened upon this room.

Now that the moment was finally here, she felt a sudden reluctance to face Matteo. Would he appreciate her coming all the way here when he hadn't replied to her texts? Was he still mad at her for being the one to finally end their faltering relationship?

She forced herself to take a few deep breaths. The comforting scent of old books and cigars and leather instantly transported her to her grandfather's cottage she used to visit as a child. The peace and quiet of the room seeped into her skin as she walked around, centering her after the noise of the party outside.

The large mahogany desk with its worn edges, the soft leather chair with the imprint of a body, the well-thumbed pages of several books on classical music and ancient civilizations… The room was full of character. An utter contrast to the extravagant wealth outside.

It was a room that was lived in and loved well—someone's sanctuary. Just like her attic room at her parents' house. It definitely wasn't Matteo's. She rushed out of the cozy reading nook, imagining his surprise. His naughty grin. The familiar comfort of his arms around her. The way he'd always made her laugh…

The man leaning against the doors wasn't Matteo, but the one that belonged to this study.

He held a striking resemblance to Matteo, though. Where Matteo had light brown eyes, dark blond hair and features that bordered on pretty with their lushness, this man was darker, leaner, almost severe. A high forehead, deep-set eyes, sharp bridge of a nose and thin lips with a jawline that she could sharpen her mother's knives on.

Together, his features created an impression of a darkly masculine sensuousness that made her keenly aware of her own skin. Of the wild beat of her heart. Of her pulse racing madly all over her body.

If Matteo was light and charm and laughter, this man was darkness and passion and something she didn't understand. Unlike everyone else in the crowd, he didn't wear a tuxedo. Also unlike everyone else, he didn't need diamond cuff links or designer clothes to call attention to himself.

He stood with his back to the closed doors, ankles crossed, his head tilted to the side, his fathomless dark eyes taking her in greedily. As if he'd been waiting to look at her.

He was tall. So tall that at five nine, if she walked up to him, her mouth would fit at the hollow of his throat exactly. The tight-fitting shirt hugged a leanly muscled torso and made his dull gray eyes pop. Unbuttoned to his chest, it revealed the corded column of his throat, and Sam had the insane urge to lick that hollow...

The sheer naked greed of his expression twisted her breath through her body. As if it was outside of her own control. As if he held it.

He looked at her as if he wanted to inhale her. Even having little experience with sexual chemistry, Sam knew this. As clearly as she knew the hard tug low in her belly was her response to whatever he was putting out.

She wanted to say something to break the spell, and yet she didn't want to step outside of whatever was locking them together in their own gravity. Her body felt new, full of needy claws.

Suddenly, the intensity of his stare died down. From one blink to the next. As if it were that easy for him to turn it off. Breath rushed into her lungs in a wave.

Sam blinked, feeling as if all of her insides had been

splayed out for this stranger to probe. She'd had too many instances in her life where she'd felt small and powerless. But this vulnerability was different.

Embarrassment made heat crawl up her neck. "You're not Matteo," she said, a thread of complaint in her tone.

That thin-lipped mouth flinched in an imperceptible movement. He pushed off from the door, all that violent energy contained. "I'm sorry to disappoint you."

"You belong to this room, though," she added, wanting to mollify him.

"No one has ever said it like that." His gaze took in the study, a tiny flutter of a smile at his mouth. "Point to you."

With each step he took toward her, that awareness slammed into Sam again. It was not unlike the impact she felt when she trained with a punching bag. Except she didn't know where to strike to stop it from coming at her, again and again. "You're mocking me."

He blinked. "I'm not sure I am."

Her middle felt like there was a hook there, relentlessly tugging her toward him. "Why do I have a feeling you're never unsure?"

His lips curved, slashing a dimple in one cheek. But it didn't warm the cold storminess of his eyes. "You're beautiful *and* clever."

"I'm not beautiful," she said, half to fight the effect of his words, half because they weren't true.

She was too skinny, too tall, too angular to be considered beautiful. Not that she didn't like her reflection when she saw it in the mirror. She'd survived too much at too young an age to not appreciate what she had and who she was.

Her eyes were big and wide, sure. There was a certain symmetry to her features that was pleasing, and her cousin said Sam had a body made for modeling. But she'd never been interested in modeling, and since those were ridiculously arbitrary standards society imposed on women, it didn't really make any difference to her. Life had always forced a large dose of reality on her, and she preferred it in this too. With this man, though, her protest stemmed from a place of self-preservation. "I don't like false compliments."

He stopped a couple of feet from her. Again, she had the sense that every step he took was calculated. Raising a brow, he swept that gaze over her with such thorough possessiveness that a lick of heat trailed behind wherever it touched. When it returned to her face, challenge simmered in his eyes.

Her fingers itched to trace the slash of his brows, the sharp planes of his cheekbones. And not all of it was from the perspective of a portrait artist who was drawn to faces with character.

Frustrated at her own sharp reaction, she said, "I'm looking for Matteo."

"Did you ask the staff for him?"

"No, but he knows I'm here."

"How?"

"Are you being thick on purpose?" she asked with a familiarity she couldn't shed.

"I do not believe so," he said, his tone calm in the face of her crankiness. But there was something about his steadiness that felt hollow. As if it were simply an act. "I simply want to know how Matteo knows you're here if you didn't ask for him."

Put like that, his question was fair. "You're right. He might not know that I'm here this exact moment. But he knows that I'm here. In Italy, I mean."

"How?"

"I used the open plane ticket he gave me. The travel agent

would have told him I was on my way. It's how there was a chauffeured car waiting for me at the airport."

"This plane ticket—"

"Why are you interrogating me?"

"You walked—no, *strutted*—into my house as if you were invited, Ms...?"

"Fischer," Sam said, refusing to give him her full name. Because she desperately wanted to hear it on his lips. Really, she was acting strange. "Of course I was invited. I'm not some petty thief," she said, before adding, "Now, please do me the courtesy of telling me who you are."

"Who invited you?"

"You're rude."

"I simply want to understand why you are here, Ms. Fischer."

She rubbed a finger over her temple. "Matteo invited me."

"Tonight?"

"Not specifically. He invited me months ago. It was an open invitation. I decided to surprise him. Now, tell me who you are."

"I'm Alessandro Ricci."

She recognized his name immediately. "You're the CEO of Ricci International Finances. You made that big deal recently with the software company my dad works for in California."

"*Sì.*"

It was all starting to make sense. The extravagant wealth outside. The surname. Ricci International Finances. The resemblance between Alessandro and Matteo...

"And Matteo is...?"

"My younger half brother."

Sam pressed her hand to her neck, backing away. "So Matteo is rich, like you?"

"*Si.*"

Her foot caught on the rug, and the man caught her, even though he'd been several steps away. His hand landed on her lower back. The bare patch of skin between her top and her jeans burned at the abrasive texture of his fingers. Heat from the small contact arced through her, pooling in her lower belly.

How would those fingers feel against more bare skin? Against her aching breasts? Against her belly? Against her—

Jerking away from him, she tried to corral her uneven breath.

Damn it, this man was a stranger *and* Matteo's older brother. A man so far out of her league that he might as well have been the alien overlord in one of her cousin's romance novels.

"You didn't know that Matteo comes from a wealthy family," Mr. Ricci added behind her.

"It's been years since we first met," Sam said automatically. "He did mention Lake Como but not an estate on the shores of it."

"My family owns most of the town."

She turned to face him. "Thanks for clarifying that."

His sharp gaze assessed her relentlessly. "How do you know him?"

"I've answered enough of your questions. I want to see Matteo."

"Not unless you tell me why."

"Or what?" she said, hunger and sudden exhaustion dialing up her frustration. "You'll throw me out?"

"I'm trying to save you from a potentially embarrassing situation."

Laughter burst out of Sam. "You talk just like he said

you do." Matteo had talked about his brother from time to time, but he'd never mentioned his name.

"How is that?"

"Like you know the best for everyone around you. Like arrogance and ruthlessness given shape and form. Like…"

A ghost of a smile floated on his lips. "So you know me?"

"I know of you. The perfect older brother. A cold, ruthless, brilliant man who understands machines better than people," she said, quoting Matteo word for word. She was being an awful guest, and yet something in her wanted to test his steely control.

Mr. Ricci simply watched her. And she realized what she'd thought of as a younger brother's humorous resentment held more than a grain of truth. There *was* a gloss of remoteness to him. As if he stood outside of the world and its inconvenient emotions. Like she'd been for so long.

Was that why they felt such pull toward each other?

"As much as I'd like to deny that I'm the villain Matteo painted, trust me when I say it's better for you if you tell me everything. I do know what's best for you."

"Fine. Matteo and I used to be together."

His frown turned into a full-blown scowl. "How long were you seeing each other?"

"Almost five years. I haven't seen him since we had a fight and broke up four months ago."

"Where did you two meet?"

She glared at him, but the lie came fast. "At a café in SFO."

"And he asked you out?"

"Yes, that's how these things are usually done. One interested person asks the other out," she said dryly.

Her attempt at sarcasm made no dent in his expression. "How old are you, Ms. Fischer?"

For the first time since he'd walked in, she heard cautiousness in his voice. "What does that have to do with anything?"

"Answer my question."

"Twenty-three."

Again, there was that flinch. "So you were eighteen when you two met."

"Eighteen, yes. Matteo was twenty-three," Sam protested hotly. It was the same argument she'd had with her own parents after she'd introduced them. To see her fragile little girl with a man suddenly had sent her mother into a tailspin. "I'm very mature for twenty-three," she said inanely.

Mr. Ricci snorted. Even that was elegant. "What is that you do with that mature brain of yours?"

"I'm a certified professional at annoying arrogant Italian men who treat me like a petty criminal."

He frowned, then blinked, and slowly, a beautiful smile appeared. It tugged one corner of his mouth higher than the other, digging a deep groove in the left cheek. The stark angles of his face softened, giving a glimpse into what lingered beneath the severity. If he flashed a full-blown smile at her, she might faint at the sheer beauty of it. "I'd appreciate your wit better if you answered my questions."

"I'm a portrait artist," Sam said, his reasonable tone dialing up her crankiness.

That scowl returned, and yet when he spoke, his words were silky smooth. Too smooth, in fact. "You're the artist Matteo has been visiting every few months like clockwork for the last few years. You are Sam."

"Yep. Short for Sameera." She tried to not bristle at the distasteful note in his tone as he said her name. "I've traveled a long way to see him."

"You've wasted a long journey, especially if you were thinking of patching things up with him."

"Why?"

Those dark eyes considered her for another long moment. "Matteo is celebrating his engagement tonight. The party you almost crashed is in honor of him and his fiancée and their love."

CHAPTER TWO

Alessandro waited for tears and angry, possessive claims. Now that he knew who she was, the last thing he wanted to do was touch her again. But her golden-brown skin went alarmingly pale.

He reached her just in time. Her thigh hit his as he swung an arm around her waist loosely, giving her space to pull away. She was tall enough in her boots that her breath hit his chin. Every single point of contact of her body against his burned.

"Matteo's engaged," she whispered, then pulled away. She walked through the French doors into his private patio.

Against the glittering lake, she should have paled. Instead, the open emotions on her face made her something to behold. There was a quiet grace about her, even in her distress.

He wanted to hold her, comfort her until she was sparring with him again. He wanted to kiss that mouth until all that remained on her lips was his name. Not his brother's.

He didn't remember a time when he'd wanted someone with this naked, fierce want. All his experiences with Violetta—that first rush of love, that stage of frantic, awkward lovemaking, that fierce need to be around her all the time, to please her, to prove his worth to her had been a lifetime ago.

Forgotten, like blurry black-and-white pictures with echoes of emotions he didn't know anymore.

Dio mio, the first woman to grab his interest in years and she was Matteo's ex. Biting back a curse, he went to the stocked bar. Usually, he limited his alcohol intake to one drink per week.

In the months following Violetta's death, he'd consumed enough to damage his liver for a lifetime. Since drinking himself into an early grave would shatter his father and aunt, he'd channeled that madness into work. Tonight, however, he needed one more than one.

Because this was… *Sam. Matteo's Sam.*

The Sam that Matteo had talked about nonstop for years. The Sam that had made Matteo take unprecedented interest in overseeing their California branch. The Sam that Matteo had been very careful to not betray as a woman, letting everyone assume that Sam was just a close male friend. Why hide her existence from them?

Staring at her phone, the woman shivered.

Leather jacket and drink in hand, he went to her. Relief filled him when she let him drape the jacket over her shoulders, grabbing the edges to pull it close. "Drink this."

Her eyes flared wide. "No, thank you."

A stab of something behind his ribs made him grit his jaw. He disliked how pliable she sounded all of a sudden. "You had a shock. This will help."

"I can't. It messes with my…meds."

Shrugging, he finished the second drink. Even now, her gaze lingered over his throat. She was mourning his brother's betrayal, and yet she watched him with such artless interest.

Alessandro wanted to taunt her for her awareness of him,

but only a weak man attacked when their opponent was reeling.

"Is it Angelina Bianchi?" she said, looking out at the lake.

He studied her profile with greed he couldn't corral. "He told you about her?"

She glared at him. "That you've been pressuring him because it's a good match for the last year, yes. That you constantly push him to do more, yes. That you cast this huge shadow over his life that sometimes he can't breathe, yes."

Laughter burst out of him. Of course Matteo had painted himself as the victim. "Pace yourself, Ms. Fischer. We don't want you to exhaust yourself this early in our acquaintance, *vero*?"

"You're enjoying this, aren't you?"

"I take my words back. You're not clever at all."

She faced him, all fury and disdain. "You don't know me."

The mere hint of her temper, the fight she'd shown him earlier, creeping back into her face made Alessandro push. "Do I need to, when you blame everyone other than the man who two-timed you? And he did two-time you, Sam, because you said you broke up four months ago, but he's been seeing Angelina for at least six months already. You should be glad that your relationship already came to an end!"

"I'm not defending Matteo." Her mouth opened and closed. "I just... I don't like that you're witness to this."

Her blunt honesty took him aback for a second. "Because I refuse to sugarcoat reality?"

"Because you're too eager to pass judgment. Matteo told me that you don't date, you don't socialize. That you might as well be one of the marble busts scattered around the grounds for all the emotion you feel and—" She pressed a hand over her mouth, eyes flaring at her own daring.

"When it comes to me, Matteo told you nothing but truth."

She turned to him, big brown eyes pinning him to the spot. "I'm sorry. It's unfair to attack you. And yes, you're right that Matteo and I finished months ago. You seem to have a knack for aggravating me like no one else." She sighed. "Would a little kindness be too much?"

"Is that what you want, Ms. Fischer? A shoulder to cry on? Would it make you feel better if I took you in my arms and whispered sweet little lies that all of this was a bad dream? A small obstacle in your grand love story?"

"Oh...you *are* unbelievable."

Pushing her hands through her hair, she bundled it into a messy knot. Wavy tendrils defied her efforts, kissing her jaw.

Her breasts rose and fell, and Alessandro was perversely grateful for the color it brought back to her cheeks. He'd rather she think him an unfeeling monster than become the lost waif she'd been minutes ago. Her mouth twisted in an angry snarl as she covered the distance between them. "What I'd prefer is..." she poked him in the chest "...is for the return of my trust back to me."

"Ahhh, that I cannot do," he said clamping his fingers over her wrist. Her fingers folded into a fist, the knuckles pressing against his chest. "But if you would like to use me as a punching bag for life's disappointments, I volunteer. I'm familiar with that role, thanks to Matteo."

Her mouth dropped open, her fist resting against his chest. "That's horrible." Her outrage deflated as fast as it had come. "You're right that Matteo and I finished months ago, and in truth we should have ended long before that. But for him to move on so quickly, and to have started seeing her before we actually ended things... It's not like I can compare to a billionaire heiress."

"Self-deprecation doesn't suit you," he bit out through clenched teeth.

She side-eyed him and sighed. "For an annoying stranger I just met, you are far too right. But it's not self-deprecation. There are a lot of things I couldn't give Matteo, and I accepted it long ago."

Alessandro frowned at the ring of truth in her words. "Ms. Fischer—"

"I'd rather you don't suddenly become warm and cuddly, Mr. Ricci."

"And I'd rather you rage at me again than fall apart. I have a severe allergy to tears."

The sound that escaped her mouth was half cry, half laughter. "Was that a joke?"

Alessandro felt as if he'd achieved a personal milestone, when the doors burst open and closed with a hard thud.

Matteo's gaze swept over them, lingering on Alessandro's jacket over her shoulders.

Ms. Fischer jerked around. A reddish tint crested her cheeks as she wrapped her arms around her midriff in a gesture he recognized as defensive.

"Sam...*cara mia*, you're here," Matteo said. "One of the staff said they saw a woman wandering around looking lost. I recognized you from the description immediately. I'm sorry I haven't been in touch. I have been busy for the last few months."

Ms. Fischer—Alessandro refused to call her Sam even in his mind—stared at Matteo. "Of course you're busy, Matteo, preparing for your engagement. Did you think I'd come up here and cause a scene if you told me? Or is it that you thought I'd never have the guts to leave my parents behind, to live my life as any normal person would?"

Alessandro frowned. It was clear she was throwing Matteo's words back at him.

Matteo raised his hands. "Give me a chance to explain."

His jacket slipped from Ms. Fischer's shoulders as she thrummed with anger. "Nothing to explain. Apparently, as much of a naïve fool that I am, I had the sense to know that our relationship had stagnated. But it was such a hit to your ego that you went and got engaged to your billionaire heiress immediately, right?"

Matteo came to her with urgent strides. Alessandro barely fought the urge to stop his brother from touching her. Instead, he bolted the door.

"How long did you play us both?" Ms. Fischer said. "You even had the gall to mention her to me, but you never had the courage to end things with me even though we both knew it had run its course."

Matteo bent his head toward her. "Sam, I—"

"Go back to your party." Ms. Fischer, it seemed, hid a spine of steel beneath the naïveté.

Alessandro rested his hip against the large desk, his fury now a slow burn. "Listen to her, Matteo."

Matteo whipped around. "Stay out of this."

"Vittorio could have been standing right next to me when you burst in here, you fool. Or any one of Angelina's thuggish cousins."

The flash of fear in Matteo's eyes said he understood the warning. "I should have checked." He cast a glance at Sam, his jaw tight. "Let's talk in private."

"You have lost your mind, as usual," Alessandro said, straightening from the desk. "Do not forget that I'm the only thing standing between you and the Bianchis if they find out about your girlfriend on the other side of the pond. Even if it is over now, they won't like the crossover. You're lucky Ms. Fischer didn't run around the party calling out your name."

"You can't understand," Matteo said with a sneer.

"*No?* You've been playing with both Angelina and Ms. Fischer. And while Ms. Fischer might forgive you, Angelina will not."

"Don't you dare lecture me—"

"I dare?" Alessandro's anger slipped its leash. "You slipped a two-million-dollar ring onto Angelina's fingers not an hour ago."

"I can't explain it. Not that you'll ever understand because you don't have a heart." His brother faced him, his mouth turned into a sneer. It had been always like this: Matteo messed up, and he cleaned up. And yet nothing but resentment festered in his brother's heart for him. "Half an hour in your company and you turned her against me."

"Stop it, Matteo," Ms. Fischer whispered, her expression stricken. "You did this. You've made me doubt our whole relationship, doubt myself."

A knock sounded, a sudden boom amidst their ridiculous standoff. "Matteo, are you in there?" came Angelina's voice.

Ms. Fischer's head jerked in Alessandro's direction, eyes wide.

She trusted *him*. Which meant he could get them all out of this predicament before Vittorio decided his family's honor had been insulted. Or that Matteo needed to be taught a lesson.

"Papà wants to give us our engagement present," called out Angelina.

Another knock came hard on the heels of her voice. "Alessandro? Is Matteo with you?" The voice of Vittorio Bianchi thundered through the hardwood. "My nephew said he saw a woman in your office. Who is it?"

Alessandro cursed. "If he even gets a whiff of you two-timing his daughter," he whispered to Matteo, "Vittorio will break your knees. I am so angry I don't think I'll stand in his way. So go along with what I say." He flicked a glance toward Ms. Fischer. "Come here, Ms. Fischer."

Matteo's glare turned sullen.

Fortunately, Ms. Fischer possessed more common sense than his brother. When she came close enough for him, Alessandro softened his tone. "Let them think you're mine. A certain familiarity will be required." He ignored the possessive satisfaction that ran through him as he made the claim. *Cristo*, he was acting worse than Matteo.

She leaned against the desk like him, leaving too much space between them. "I don't want Matteo to get into trouble." Her lush rose scent made every muscle in him curl with want. "Nor do I want to cause Ms. Bianchi distress."

Alessandro felt a fresh surge of tenderness for her soft heart. Wrapping his arm around her waist, he pulled her close. Instant heat uncurled through his middle, spreading to his limbs. Her waist was tiny, the flare of her hip where his fingers landed a sharp delineation. But there was a lean strength to her that entranced him.

Every inch of him was aware of every point of contact between them. He wanted to deepen it until she could no more think of Matteo than Alessandro could think of another woman.

She was a complication, he reminded himself. A walking, talking disaster waiting to blow up in their faces. The faster he got her out of their lives, the better for everyone involved. Including her.

And yet, he knew, with a deep conviction, that he would do everything in his power to keep her around. At least, until he could figure out what about her fascinated him so.

CHAPTER THREE

ALESSANDRO RICCI WAS the last man she should allow familiarity, Sam reminded herself.

Not that he wanted to be anywhere near her. His austere features spoke eloquently to his distaste at being thrust with her responsibility.

But the corded weight of his arm around her waist, the press of his muscled body holding her up felt like heaven. Made her want to sink into him until her exhaustion fled. Until she felt safe again.

One stolen glance at his granite jawline made her spine straighten. This man was as safe as Matteo was trustworthy.

Matteo, who had got engaged to another woman the moment they had broken up, who had been seeing Angelina Bianchi while Sam had struggled with losing interest in him. Who had probably forgotten her the moment it was over while she had called herself *weak*, *boring*, and *scared*.

She even acknowledged that her hurt came from him doing all those exciting things that she couldn't with Angelina, rather than from him falling in love with her.

Because she was a heart patient who still lived at home at the age of twenty-three, a dull woman among bold, risk-taking twentysomethings. She hadn't finished high school or gone to college or gone even on a sleepover unless it was with her cousin Kavi at her aunt's place, with her mom in the next room.

Now she was in a foreign country where she didn't know another soul. She'd hoped to repair their friendship after their breakup. The entire summer stretched in front of her, static, inert, directionless—the same as it had been for the past decade.

It had taken her so long to break away from the limitations placed on her by her body. From the rut that loneliness had placed her in. From the protective shell of her parents' suffocating love.

Without Matteo's company, where would she go? Could she look after herself? Financially, yes. Living with her parents meant she'd saved every dollar she'd earned from her summer jobs and her portrait commissions. But what would she do in Italy alone? After all the planning and months of fighting her innate fears to get herself here, should she simply turn around and go back?

Her phone pinged.

She was sure it would be a text from her mother, checking she'd arrived safely. Remembering her mother made her spiraling thoughts come to a screeching halt. If her mom discovered that Matteo was engaged, that Sam's trust in him had been misplaced—and that she herself had been right about him—she'd never let Sam live it down. Would never let her forget. She'd jump on the next plane and make an unholy spectacle until Sam had no choice but to leave with her.

Fresh anger surged through her at Matteo.

Even now, with his fiancée on the other side of the door, he was glaring at his brother. Didn't that woman deserve better?

She despised confrontations. She'd always hated being the reason for the constant, emotionally taxing fights her parents had engaged in for so long. The guilt that they were fighting because of her, worried over her health and her future, over her long-term care, over the medical debts they'd accrued had hurt more than the pricks of the hundred needles she'd had to endure.

The thought of Matteo's fiancée, the guests at the party and his family learning about her sent a fresh tremor down her spine.

Instantly, the arm around her waist tightened, long fingers pressing into her hip without hesitation. "You'll be fine, Ms. Fischer," Mr. Ricci whispered, despite his declaration that he didn't do kindness.

Matteo flicked a dark glance at his brother's arm around her waist before he opened the doors. Ms. Bianchi was petite and curvy and vivaciously beautiful in a way that couldn't be achieved solely by designer clothes and expensive makeup. Her gaze immediately fastened on Matteo.

A large, lean man—clearly Vittorio Bianchi—surveyed them, his shrewd gaze not missing Alessandro's arm around Sam's waist. He barked something at Mr. Ricci in Italian.

Mr. Ricci shrugged in return, an arrogant smile ghosting across his lips.

Sam's cheeks burned. No doubt it was about her. And nothing decent either.

Sam breathed out a sigh as the older man left.

"Matteo, what happened?" Angelina said, tangling her arm through his.

Matteo smiled tightly. "Nothing, *cara mia*," he said, switching to English. "I wished to inquire about something with Alessandro."

"And you were shocked to find him in here with a woman?" Angelina said with a tinkling laugh. Her gaze flicked to Sam and cut away. She clearly thought Sam wasn't worth a second look.

Sam didn't know whether to feel relieved or insulted. She didn't know what to feel about anything right now. Least of all, her constant awareness of the man propping her up like a cardboard cutout.

"I know your mother wishes for Alessandro to bring a date to our wedding," Angelina said, laying her palm on Matteo's chest, "but you must trust his judgment, Matteo. If he's hiding this woman, she is not suitable company for us."

A gasp escaped Sam's mouth, a slow burn of anger humming beneath her skin.

But for her casually sexist attitude toward other women, Ms. Bianchi wasn't to blame. That Sam had to listen to it and not even offer a token protest…the fault lay with Matteo for making her face his fiancée as if she were the other woman. It also lay with Mr. Ricci, who let his friends and family talk in such a way about the women in his life.

She'd had enough. When she tried to step away, those fingers gripped the curve of her flesh tight, branding her. Tilting his head down, Mr. Ricci studied her, a mocking slant to his mouth. "Such outrage is not warranted, Ms. Fischer. Remember, you're only *pretending* to be mine."

Sam shivered as his words trickled down her spine like a lover's caress. She placed her palm on his chest, goaded beyond common sense. He was hard and hot against her fingertips. His heart thundering away belied the mockery in his eyes. "You wish I were yours. I do have standards."

His laughter enveloped her, a deep, sensual rumble, as arousing as the man's physicality. This close, she could see the warming of the gray of his eyes. The small scar across his brow. The flare of interest as he said, "And what are those?"

"No liars. And no arrogant, judgmental men who mock others' weaknesses."

The cold frost of his eyes returned. "I never mocked you."

"You aren't as inscrutable as you'd like to believe."

His gaze dipped to her mouth. It was as if one look, one word between them could generate an electric charge that surrounded them. "Or you read me better than anyone has in a long time."

"Shall we join the party, *caro*?" Angelina's loud voice cut across their murmurs.

Looking away from Mr. Ricci felt like fighting gravity.

"You shouldn't keep Vittorio waiting," Mr. Ricci said.

"You two should join us," Matteo retorted.

Sam shook her head.

A glimmer of triumph touched Mr. Ricci's mouth. "I couldn't bear to part with her right now. Go back to your party."

With a dark look at his brother, and not even a glance in her direction, Matteo left, taking his fiancée with him.

Sam jerked away from the man at her side. "I don't appreciate being fought over like a bone between two dogs."

Again those damned double doors closed. His hands tucked into pockets of his trousers, Mr. Ricci considered her. "I don't think anyone has ever called me a dog before. Not even as a boy."

"Probably because you terrified everyone around you."

"You met Angelina, got a glimpse of her father. Do you truly think I bullied you or Matteo just then?"

The openness of his question halted Sam's angry pacing. However much she wanted to blame him, this infuriatingly arrogant man was not at fault. "Fine. Don't use me as a weapon in your ongoing battle with Matteo, then. You knew that he didn't want to leave me here with you, and you still needled him."

"And it is my fault that my brother does not trust you with me?" he asked with such a straight face that Sam wanted to slap the expression off it. "Or that he risks betraying his possessiveness over an ex to Angelina's eyes?"

The discomfort Mr. Ricci caused her was of a different kind. There was something between her and this man. Something she'd never felt with Matteo or any other man.

Sam gathered her sweater, her movements clumsy. Hunger gnawed at her belly, and her head was beginning to pound too.

She threw her handbag over her shoulder and gripped it tightly to steady her fingers. By the time she turned to Mr. Ricci, sudden tears had bubbled up in her throat.

Exhaustion always made her cry. But she had to hold herself together. For some reason, it was paramount that she not show this man any weakness. She'd already betrayed her awareness of him. "If you can have my luggage located by your staff, you can be free of me."

"Now *you* are twisting my words."

"Why are you pulling your punches suddenly? Given the show you put on just now, I'm a problem for you. I need to get out of here. I need to—"

"You're not going anywhere."

"I have an extreme aversion to people telling me what I can or cannot do, Mr. Ricci."

"I don't care if you break out in hives. You look like you're ready to drop, you don't know where you are, much less where to go, and this problem isn't going to be solved by someone taking advantage of you on the streets tonight." His smooth as silk tone dissolved at the end. "Unless you're offering to leave Italy altogether. Right now."

For a split second, Sam considered saying just that. But he wouldn't believe it unless he handed her onto a flight himself. Unlike Matteo, the man was thorough. As for returning home, every inch of her rebelled at the thought.

Other than to salvage her friendship with Matteo, this whole trip had been to prove to her parents and herself that she could handle life. That meant not just physically but emotionally too, including dealing with lying ex-boyfriends and their hot-as-sin brothers.

"I can't," she said.

"Why not?"

"I can't leave without talking to Matteo, after coming this far." It wasn't a complete lie. Matteo had been such a large and constant part of her life for years. Angry as she was with him right now, that ridiculous standoff in front of an audience couldn't be their last meeting. "This vacation is important to me. Even if Matteo and I don't patch up things, I've come too far to simply turn around. I'll make other plans in a few days."

Mr. Ricci leveled a considering look at her. "He's not going to break his engagement."

Was that what he got from her admission? "You won't let him, you mean?" she retorted, just to rile him up. Of course, she'd never had any intention of getting back with Matteo.

He roughly thrust his fingers through his hair. The short haircut couldn't hide the waviness of it.

Sam smiled, wondering if it was the one rebellious element he couldn't control. Slowly, other things came into sharp focus. The grooves around his mouth hinted at tiredness as did the tight lines near his eyes.

One look at Vittorio Bianchi and the flash of fear in Matteo's eyes had told her Mr. Ricci hadn't exaggerated one bit. And while he'd been furious with Matteo, he'd made sure she didn't provoke Angelina's interest.

And yet, Matteo had treated him as if he were the enemy. She'd heard so many stories and tidbits that cast Matteo's older brother as a ruthless, uncaring tyrant who constantly belittled him.

The fairness that was a core part of her disliked that Matteo had played on her sympathetic nature, that she'd made up her mind about this man without knowing him at all. Her pinging awareness of him made everything even murkier.

"What was that smile for?" God, the man watched her like a hawk. "You looked very human just then."

He barked out a laugh, but his eyes betrayed his shock. It drew out a vicious, violent pleasure through her that she could. "Of course I'm human, Ms. Fischer. With all the flaws and desires that entails."

Her beeping watch told her it was time for her meds. While she wasn't ashamed of her condition and all that it entailed, revealing it to Mr. Ricci made her feel exposed. This need to keep a wall between them was a strong compulsion. Which was ridiculous after all the therapy she'd put into feeling normal. "I need water."

A glass of sparkling water appeared within seconds. Accepting it, she turned her body just a bit, which was stupid because he could see what she was up to if he moved an inch, and downed her meds. The bubbles tickled her throat, and her stomach made an embarrassingly loud growl.

She needed food and sleep, fast. Her body had supported her on this first journey, but she had to respect its limits. That was the most important lesson she'd learned in the last few years. "You're right. I can't just storm out of here like some hapless damsel."

His gray eyes gleamed. "I'm happy you realized the inevitability of that."

She barely fought the urge to stick her tongue out at him. "I'd appreciate it if your staff could bring me something to eat, then drive me to the nearest hotel. I promise to eat my meal quietly and leave without grabbing anyone else's attention. You can stop babysitting me."

He began shaking his head even before she'd finished. She planted her hands on her hips, exasperated. "You said you owned the whole goddamned town. Why isn't that possible?"

"I didn't say that it wasn't possible."

"Then, why are you shaking your head?"

"I would like to keep an eye on you. While you clearly possess a lot more sense than Matteo, I can't trust you to go running to him and betray your past to the Bianchis."

"I don't want to get anyone in trouble."

"But you're the one who could get him in trouble, which is why I have to control you."

Sam wanted to continue arguing with him, just for the heck of it, but she was fast losing steam. "Fine. Lock me up, for all I care, and throw away the damn key."

"Do not tempt me, Ms. Fischer."

Her head jerked up.

There was no humor in his eyes as he extended his hand. "Come."

She eyed the double doors of his study with trepidation. "I'm not a fan of big crowds and loud, noisy celebrations. With this party, I'd prefer to avoid any more speculation."

"It's a little late for that. Angelina is a huge gossip. The news of my secret liaison will have already reached my parents and all the cousins. Especially since I never bring my *entertainment* home."

As she watched, he pressed a spot behind one of the bookshelves, and an invisible door opened. A faintly illuminated, narrow corridor emerged in front of them.

Sam nearly jumped in excitement. "You have a secret corridor in your study! Do you know how many times when I was in the hos—how many times I wished to escape like this?" She looked around the high-ceilinged study with new eyes. "What *is* this place, anyway?"

His eyes crinkled at the edges. "The villa used to be a monastery a long time ago. So there are a couple of secret passageways still intact. Not afraid of confined spaces, then?"

"Not at all."

His fingers held her elbow gently as he ushered her in. They couldn't fit side by side. Instantly, he turned to the side, fitting his body around hers. There was something so accommodating about the gesture that Sam stilled, her heart pumping overtime.

"Come, Ms. Fischer. We're both exhausted."

"That was a dirty trick you played earlier," Sam said, following him along the cool, dimly lit corridor. "You could have just said I was a friend."

"Angelina is very possessive of Matteo."

"That's not healthy," she added softly.

Mr. Ricci's grip around her arm tightened. "I'd say justifiably so, given Matteo's extracurricular activities, Ms. Fischer, *no*?"

"If you're going to make a prisoner out of me, you might as well use my name." She saw the shake of his head from behind. "Are you saying no to everything I ask on principle?"

"I have my reasons," he said cryptically. "Will you call me Alessandro, then?"

"I have a good reason to not get familiar with you."

He turned so fast that Sam stumbled into him. In the dim light, every other sense amplified. His hand on her arm, his powerful thighs pressed against hers, the thud of his heart under her fingers. The dark clove scent of him. The warmth of his exhales dancing across her lips. It felt as if she was being swallowed up by him, and the worst part was that she didn't dislike the sensation. Quite the opposite, in fact.

His gaze searched hers. "Enlighten me."

It was a miracle she hadn't the lost the thread of their conversation with so much stimulus. "I won't make the mistake of considering you a friend."

She thought that shapely mouth flinched, but at this point, she didn't trust her senses. The man would hardly care about her opinion of him. Especially when he murmured silkily, "No, you prefer men who lie to you."

"See, that's what I'm saying. Matteo messed up, bigtime. And even I did, I think. But you don't have to rub it in our faces."

He didn't move. "*You* messed up? How?"

"No way am I giving you ammunition against me."

"You don't think you're taking this enemies thing too far?" A thin thread of anger pulsed in his words. "After all, I was the one who rescued you. Did you not notice that my dear brother used the little time challenging me instead of worrying about you? It seems I am the one with your best interests at heart here."

Her exhaustion and the roller coaster of emotions she'd been through made her tongue loose. "Matteo two-timed me, yes. He broke my trust, in more than just him." She swallowed the ache. "But our relationship stagnated long ago. I clung to him instead of making a clean break like I should have long ago. Not a surprise that Matteo took the path of least resistance and went straight into Angelina's waiting arms."

She couldn't simply erase him from her life. No matter what he did, she would always consider him a friend. He'd been there for her at a time in her life when nobody else had, after all. "If there's a chance to fix our bond," she said, knowing she was playing a very dangerous game, "I'll take it. My summer is open anyway."

A flash of pure rage glowed in his eyes, burning away to nothing in a second. The faint shape of a door emerged a few feet ahead of them when he said, "My first impression of you was utterly wrong, then."

Don't ask, Sam. Don't be interested in his opinion.

All the warnings her rational mind blared were useless. "What was your first impression?" she asked in a small voice that echoed in the closed space.

"I thought you were someone who faced the truth however painful it was. Someone who dwelled in reality, instead of false dreams."

He had no idea how close he'd come to the reality of her life.

She *was* a fighter. She'd never had the luxury to live in false dreams.

But this summer was a promise she'd made to herself that she would choose living, however hard and scary that felt. That she'd choose fun and adventure and normalcy. That she'd stretch her wings and fly.

So instead of running away from a broken relationship or from a man who made her feel so much that it terrified her, instead of running back to the safety and security of her parents' love, she was staying.

She was standing on her own.

CHAPTER FOUR

CHOOSING HIS OWN bedroom to keep Ms. Fischer for the night had to be the most insane decision Alessandro had ever made.

Clearly, the stubborn waif wasn't going to change her mind about spending the summer in Milan. Which meant her past with Matteo had more chances of coming out. Which meant his ruse that she was *his mistress* was going to bite him in the ass soon.

Even the prospect of being harassed by his aunt, and the very real risk of Vittorio Bianchi's wrath, couldn't dilute the excitement that filled him at the idea of a few weeks with Ms. Fischer. He felt like a corpse that had been revived for a few days.

When he returned an hour later carrying food, it was to find Ms. Fischer sitting on the upholstered bench at the foot of his bed, clad in pajamas buttoned up all the way to her throat. An overwhelmingly protective urge rose up within him as her head lolled to the side, mouth falling open in a soft snore.

With her hair braided, she looked achingly young. Too young for him to feel that tight heat curling through his muscles.

He pushed a hand through his hair, wondering if years of working ninety-hour weeks, of living his life within rigorously strict boundaries, had finally been broken.

He went to his haunches and gently shook her. "Ms. Fischer? Dinner is here." Cupping her shoulder, he shook her again. "Sameera...wake up." He tapped her jaw with his fingers. "Your stomach sounds like it's eating itself."

Her brown eyes flicked open, warm and soft. The most beautiful smile he'd ever seen curved her mouth. And instantly, he could imagine how she would look waking up next to him after a long night of—*Cristo*, but he was in trouble!

"Only my grandpa called me that," she whispered.

"It's a beautiful name. Did I say it right?"

Her gaze dipped to his mouth. "Better than Matteo ever has."

And just like that, with his brother's name between them, she came awake and alert. Her gaze jerked upward to meet his, the smile and its warmth disappearing instantly.

She straightened her limbs and pushed to her feet. Her brows snapped together. "You have, what...fifty rooms in this house and you bring me to your bedroom? I didn't even realize until I stepped into the shower. At least I had my bag with me, or I'd have come out smelling like...you."

A violent silence followed her irate declaration. She snapped her gaze away from him, but he saw the confused awareness. The thought of her in his shower made desire slam into him afresh. Turning away, he pointed to the lounge. "You should eat," he said, his voice hoarse.

Maybe he was losing his mind finally. It wasn't a far-fetched notion. His lifestyle—his work hours, his isolation—was conducive to madness. His aunt had told him that enough times. Or maybe the part of him that he'd buried with Violetta, the part that liked companionship and affection and people even, was waking up after all these years and he had no idea how to behave anymore. Either way, he felt like he was drowning.

For once, Ms. Fischer followed his command. Slipping into his favorite armchair, she pulled the tray onto her lap.

Alessandro took the sofa opposite hers. Halfway through her dinner, she looked up. A drop of soup clung to her lower lip and she licked it away. The artlessness of the gesture only heightened his response. "Was I supposed to share with you?"

He shook his head. "You haven't touched the sandwich."

"I don't eat red meat."

"Should I have something else brought in?"

A lock of wavy hair escaped her braid and brushed her cheek. "No." She patted her belly. "The cheese, the soup, the salad and the fruit...that's actually the perfect diet for me."

"Diet?" he said, his interest snagged. "Please don't tell me you're one of those women who constantly watches what they eat, Ms. Fischer. You're skinny enough as it is."

She scrunched her nose, running a hand over her body in a self-conscious gesture. "Believe me, I know about the nonexistence of my curves." She burrowed her face into the crook of her elbow, but he heard her mutter, "Especially when you look at me next to Ms. Bianchi."

While there was a confidence about her, her comment made Alessandro wonder. "Explain about your diet."

"Oh, I meant...a Mediterranean diet is good for you. You know, lots of fruits and vegetables and seafood. But no red meat."

"For religious reasons?"

"No. I mean, my mother celebrates Hindu festivals. But she's also very much about everyone finding their own thing."

"And your father?"

"German American."

"So it's—"

"Do you interrogate everyone like this?"

"Only the ones that are a mystery."

"There's no mystery around me."

If she hadn't been shying her gaze away from his, he'd have thought nothing of it. But she did. And it made him want to know everything about her.

"I'm normal. Boring. Safe. Tame. Dull."

Alessandro frowned.

Had no one told her how her brown eyes flared when her temper rose, how her spirit shone out of her when she was challenged, how sensually she moved? "I find you anything but dull. In fact, for the first time in my life, I'm pleasantly surprised by Matteo's taste."

Her fingers stilled around the bowl of fruit. With a boldness that made his heart leap, she tilted her head and smiled up at him with an exaggerated sweetness. "That sounds awfully like a compliment."

"It is."

She fluttered the fingers on both hands in a give-it-to-me gesture. "Don't deny yourself the joy of telling me exactly what you like about me."

A pleasant warmth pooled through him. A sensation he was beginning to associate with her. "Will you give yourself the joy of complimenting me too?"

She cupped her angular chin with her palms and studied him. Her gaze moved over his brows and his nose, landed and skidded away from his mouth. It felt so much like a physical caress that his stomach tightened. "When I find something to like about you, sure."

He threw his head back and laughed, feverish pleasure running through his veins. "*Bene.* I find you…far too interesting." If she wanted more from him, she'd have to ask for it.

She wiped her mouth with a napkin, neatly arranged everything together on the tray before she said, "So why did you bring me to your room?"

"You sound like you doubt my intentions, Ms. Fischer."

"We're back to that, then?" she said. She took a sip of water, her gaze never leaving his. "Did you bring me to your room to rattle Matteo again? Is that wise when you implied earlier that he's a loose cannon right now?"

"Is there reason for him to be rattled that you are in my bedroom?"

Was he asking her outright if she was into him? Was he hitting on her, or testing her?

It had to be the latter. Men like him didn't hit on women like her. And yet...those gray eyes held hers in a dare. The taut vein at his temple said it was no game.

What would he do if she admitted that she was attracted to him, and it was unlike anything she'd ever experienced? If she admitted that with Matteo, it had been safe and fun, whereas with Alessandro...it was a tsunami of sensations.

There was a new stringent awareness of her own body—the pulse at her neck, a tight thrum under her skin, a heaviness in her breasts that had made her cup them in the shower and an aching twinge between her legs that she couldn't get rid of no matter what she tried.

What would he do if she asked him how it felt to be so tuned in to another's breath and body, to be so unbalanced? How did one make sensible decisions in the face of this... overwhelming curiosity to explore what lay beneath?

All she'd wanted was a summer of friendly fun with Matteo. To get away from her parents, to prove to herself that she existed outside of the box she'd lived in all her life. Now she wondered if she could have this man for a summer fling and survive. Dear God, was she actually considering this?

"It's the friction in your relationship that rattles Matteo. Not anything I might or might not do."

Pushing to his feet, he gripped the nape of his neck and moved it this way and that. Had he hoped for a different answer?

He walked around, away from the window with views of the lake. Everything in the bedroom matched him, minimalistic furniture without anything softening it at all. All navies and grays, without a hint of color or warmth. The only personal touch was the grand piano taking pride of place, looking out into the lake, and the shelves and shelves of books.

"Matteo and Angelina have activities planned around the lake to celebrate their engagement. They'll be here for a few days."

Walking around, he opened the bedside drawer and pulled out his charger. It was such a mundane thing, and yet it instantly drew her attention to the large king-size bed with navy blue sheets.

She was going to sleep in his bed, surrounded by the scent of him. Lay her head where he did every night. She'd already touched his things in the bathroom, realizing far too late that it was his. That the whole thing didn't freak her out as much as it should have.

"There's no doubt that Matteo will look for you as soon as Angelina's asleep. My bedroom is the last place he will look. Also, I'm the only one who has a key to it."

"He and I will talk at some point, you know."

Leaning one shoulder against the door, he considered her. "Of course you will. But only after the guests have left. Especially Angelina and her cousins."

"Where will you sleep?"

A wicked smile curved his lips. "It's sweet of you to worry over my comfort."

Sam rolled her eyes. "I'm worried you'll jet-set off to some exotic destination leaving me locked up here."

"I won't go anywhere until I know Matteo is not bringing Vittorio's wrath down on us."

"You'll be working at the villa for the next couple of days?"

His gaze searched her face. "What do you need?"

"Can you please arrange a car for me so that I can visit one of the art museums? That way, I'm out of here from sunup till evening. Obviously, I can't explore the beautiful grounds here without you playing my devoted keeper."

When he simply stared at her, she added, "You can come along and make sure I don't secretly contact Matteo." She couldn't stop the shiver that shook her as she looked around the dark room. "I don't like being cooped up inside."

"I'm not available to you, Ms. Fischer."

She'd expected some kind of pushback, but his bluntness made a dent in her confidence. "Assign me a bodyguard, then. I'm not staying locked up in here. Why should I be your prisoner when I can see all the art Milan has to offer?"

"There's more to it," he said stubbornly.

God, the man was infuriating. If she revealed that she hated being inside—after spending years in and out of hospitals between surgeries, in aftercare, during her parents' work hours with paid nurses—she knew he'd grant her wish. Despite his ruthless exterior, there was kindness in him. But the last thing she wanted was his pity. "How about we make a deal, Mr. Ricci?"

"What kind of a deal?"

"You get me out of here and we can discuss why you're so against Matteo and—"

"You want me to babysit you while you try to persuade me that Matteo, who's even now probably—" his jaw tightened "—with Angelina, that you and he belong together?"

Sam growled. She'd meant they could talk about his relationship with Matteo. Which was clearly more resentful than she'd imagined. Not beg him to help her patch her and Matteo's relationship. "That's not what I meant at all. You're a crude, arrogant—"

"*Buona notte*, Ms. Fischer," he said, leaving and slamming the door behind him.

Sam sat back in the chair, staring at the closed door, his earlier words about Matteo with Angelina barely making a dent in her headspace.

Instead, Mr. Ricci occupied all of it: her awareness, her emotions, even her body's suddenly volatile need for pleasure. At his hands and mouth and that lean, powerful body.

No. She was not going there. Not with a man who'd only mock her for her attraction to him. He'd probably say she was weak or immoral for lusting over her ex's older brother.

She needed Alessandro Ricci in her life like she needed another hole in her heart.

CHAPTER FIVE

SAM SLEPT FOR thirty-six hours straight.

Vague memories drifted through her head of opening the door to Mr. Ricci in the afternoon. The poor man had needed to fetch a change of clothes.

Cheeks heating, she remembered that—in a moment of homesickness—she'd worn her oldest, most threadbare T-shirt that barely covered her panties to bed.

This morning, she'd woken up near dawn, refreshed and her body clock reset to the new time zone, to find multiple texts from Matteo. Every single one raging at Alessandro.

Frustration made her movements jerky as she packed her knapsack for the day's excursion. She was going to sneak out to an art museum in Milan. Following the list on her phone, she shoved in meds, protein bars and salted nuts, even as her mind whirled.

Why hadn't Matteo apologized for two-timing her? How dare he question her about what she and his brother were up to?

Now that she'd met Alessandro, she went over everything that Matteo had ever told her about his brother.

Matteo hadn't lied. The man was exacting, grumpy and crude but brutally honest. Ruthlessly realistic with not a hint of softness or vulnerability. But he had left out the steely core of integrity beneath.

What could dent the ironclad control of a man like that? she wondered with a feverish curiosity. What could disturb the infuriating untouchability he wore like an armor?

Sturdy sneakers in one hand, backpack in the other, she opened the door and came face-to-face with Mr. Ricci again. In a dark navy button down and black slacks, his jet-black hair slicked back, he looked austere. Even the shimmering sunlight couldn't lighten the severity of his looks.

Her breath caught afresh, that wild heat slamming into her middle as he took him in. Unlike Matteo, who spent hours in the gym and even more on his appearance, Mr. Ricci wasn't stocky or overly muscular. He was much taller than his brother and held a lean, wiry strength in his body that made her skin prickle.

A sliver of gray peeked out at one temple, but even that only added to the man's appeal.

Sam stared, fingers itching to find her sketchbook, so that she could capture his aura on paper. To somehow constrain this ruthless, powerful man to two dimensions, to contain him for herself.

A soft gasp escaped her at the sheer folly of the thought.

His gray gaze, in turn, swept over her, taking in her loose braid over her shoulder and her collarbones exposed by the wide neckline of her jumpsuit. "Dare I hope that you're leaving the country, Ms. Fischer?"

With an exaggerated sigh, she handed him her sneakers and made a show of adjusting her belt. His lips twitched as he took the sneakers, but he didn't let the smile bloom. God, the man was a miser with facial expressions.

"In your dreams, Mr. Ricci." Her fingers tingled at the slight contact with his hard chest as she reached for her shoes.

"You keep surprising me, Ms. Fischer," he said, reaching for her heavy backpack. It was such a surprising—and traditional—gesture that Sam let go without thinking.

He turned, motioning for her to follow him along a long, airy corridor. "I thought I would have to wait a few hours before I could escort you to Brera. But it looks like you've been up for a while."

Sam hurried to catch up to him so quickly that she smacked into his side and had the breath knocked out of her middle. His arm came around her waist with the firmness of a metal shackle, but even that couldn't distract her. "Did you say Brera?" she said, butterflies twirling in her belly.

He nodded, his eyes doing that sweeping thing of her face. "If I can trust you to not respond to Matteo's texts or calls just yet."

"I already agreed," Sam said, suddenly aware of the warm weight of his arm around her middle.

She stepped back and looked around. The contrasting quiet of the villa after the noise and crowd from the other night slowly sank in. As if everything else was secondary to her awareness of this man.

The corridor stretched long and cool beneath her flats, flanked by shuttered windows that spilled sunlight across inlaid marble floors. Through the open arches on one side, she caught glimpses of Lake Como glittering between cypress trees, so startlingly blue it looked unreal. Like everything else in this house that smelled faintly of lemon oil, old money and effortless beauty.

"And?" Mr. Ricci said, without missing the slightest cue.

She sighed, hating the feeling of betraying Matteo to this...stranger. "He texted me all day yesterday. Someone also knocked on my door the previous night, but I was in a carb coma after the early dinner and wasn't fully awake."

His jaw tightened at the mention of his brother. "The evening visitor must have been my aunt."

"How do you know it wasn't Matteo?"

"He and Angelina took off for one of those lakeside crawls—bars, boat lounges, something loud, I imagine." His cool, even mildly detached, tone said exactly what he thought of such activities.

"Wait," Sam sputtered, coming to a stop just as they emerged onto the expansive front lounge. "Why would your aunt visit me?"

Mr. Ricci, of course, didn't stop.

Sam followed him down the wide stone steps of the villa, sunlight catching on the ivy-laced balustrade and the pale stucco walls that had likely witnessed centuries of extravagant splendor.

In the courtyard below, a black Mercedes waited—sleek, silent, and somehow more intimidating than flashy—and Sam tried not to gape like a tourist who'd accidentally stepped into a postcard.

"She wants to see what kind of a woman snared my interest," he said, opening the passenger door for her.

Sam inched closer, then stilled. "Why?"

"Because she hasn't seen me with any woman, in any capacity, in a long time." His eyes held hers. This close, the warm bergamot scent of him filled her nostrils. "Apparently, you're going to cause me a lot of trouble, Ms. Fischer."

Sam poked his chest and instantly regretted the action. "You're the one who declared to all and sundry that I was your…girlfriend—*mistress*, whatever your generation calls it."

Mr. Ricci grabbed her hand, his own abrasive against her smooth flesh. A jolt went through her, pooling low in her belly. His brows twitched, as if irritated by her reaction. "I offered to put you on a first-class flight back home."

"And I have already told you that this holiday is important to me." And because the man got her back up so easily, she added, "If you're worried that you'll find me moping around the dark corners of your illustrious villa, don't be. I'll find alternate accommodation soon. And I intend to have fun this holiday, with or without Matteo by my side."

He inched closer, and it was like being pulled into his gravity. "Right, I forgot how interchangeably *your* generation uses partners."

Alessandro did not have experience with being proved wrong, especially when it came to his assessment of people.

His assumption that spending three days with Ms. Fischer would rid him of his juvenile fascination with her had been rendered fully and utterly false.

In three days he'd brought Ms. Fischer to three different museums. On all three occasions, they had run into acquaintances—Angelina's cousins and even Vittorio one afternoon—and he had to play the part of a doting lover to avoid suspicion.

One morning, his aunt and father had waited on them in the courtyard, just to meet his *mysterious captive girlfriend*, as his aunt put it. It should have bothered him no end to play into the fake relationship he had created.

It didn't. If anything, he had liked touching Ms. Fischer under the pretense of an attentive lover, seeing the flush rise in her cheeks, desire dance in her eyes. Her gaze holding his in challenge even as her body quivered at their fake intimacy.

It had taken him mere minutes in the art gallery that first day to realize that she knew art, that she viewed it and absorbed it with a perspective unlike any he'd ever known. She seemed...desperately hungry for life, for any and every experience she could get.

She wasn't like any other twenty-three-year-old he'd ever met. At least not like the crowd that hung around Matteo. She was smart and witty and had no compunction about calling him out on his jaded presumptions.

He had expected a touristy American to treat Milan like a backdrop—snapping selfies in front of canvases, mispronouncing *Caravaggio*, scrolling social media endlessly.

Instead, Ms. Fischer moved through each museum like she was starving for stillness, pausing for so long in front of a single portrait it made even him restless. And when he joined her, she didn't try fill silence with inane chatter, even though the awareness between them thrummed into life. And when she spoke about brushwork or composition, it was with the clarity of someone who wasn't trying to impress him.

His need to understand why she drew him so morphed into an obsession.

How had this woman and Matteo crossed paths? They seemed to belong on different planets. She suited *his* tastes much more than those of his flashy brother and—

The thought stopped his stride, though not his gaze, as he arrived at the upscale café he'd asked the chauffeur to bring her to. Tourists and locals alike waited months for a reservation at the café, drawn by its elegant gilded ceilings that provided a perfect background for their pics.

Curled into a wrought-iron chair at the edge of the chic little spot tucked into a quiet courtyard, Ms. Fischer looked like one of the masterpieces she'd been obsessed with.

A painting in soft motion—sunlight catching the slope of her bare back as she leaned over a sketchbook. Her braid had loosened, sending flyaway tendrils to kiss the fragile line of her jaw. The low waist of her jeans dipped enough to reveal a strip of silky skin when she shifted.

The humming under his skin intensified as he watched her, as did a strange foreboding.

He hadn't been in a relationship since Violetta's death. After discovering his addictive nature when he tried to drown his pain—in drink or sex with strangers—he had effortlessly adopted celibacy as a form of control.

Cristo, he didn't remember the last time he had checked a woman out, much less wanted her with this soul-consuming intensity. And yet, here he was, pulse quickening at the sight of a woman bent over a sketchbook. A woman who was his brother's ex and far too young for him.

His fingers curled into fists at his sides—a pathetic attempt at holding on to control when he was already losing.

Sam looked up just as Alessandro's shadow stretched across the table. No wonder her pulse had been going haywire in the last few minutes.

Tall, lean, dressed in black slacks and a dove-gray shirt rolled up at the sleeves, he looked like the opposite of sun—dark but still blindingly beautiful. Power thrummed under his skin in that quiet, coiled way he had, like the threat of a storm behind glass.

Her breath caught, not because he was simply beautiful—though he was, in that severe, carved-from-marble kind of way—but because he made a long-held wish of hers come true.

It had been three days of losing herself in art. Of walking until her legs ached and her heart pounded with something other than fear, of losing herself in stories that had been told long before she'd been a speck in the scheme of life.

She felt more alive than she had in years.

"Please tell me your appetite for art has been temporarily satisfied, Ms. Fischer." His fingers moved toward her cheek and pulled back jerkily. "You look tired."

A spurt of stupid, grateful joy rose through her too fast to stop. Without thinking, she rose and wrapped her arms around him.

It was a quick hug, her cheek brushing the fabric of his shirt, arms going around his waist, his corded arm caught between her breasts. Over in the blink of an eye. Yet the scent of him—clean, sharp and expensive—coiled through her, making her limbs heavy and aching.

His body stiffened under hers even as his heart thudded violently.

Sam jerked back in a rush, embarrassed heat flooding her cheeks. She'd always been a tactile person, but she had no business touching him like that. Flustered, she moved back toward her chair too fast and almost toppled it.

"Thank you," she said, voice too bright, fiddling with the flaky cannoli on her plate.

"For what?" Alessandro asked, settling into the opposite chair.

"For calling in those favors and getting us access to those private collections," Sam said, heart still pounding. And because she hated feeling like an unsophisticated bumpkin, she added, "I guess there are some perks to being your fake, last-minute mistress. Maybe my vacation would look drastically different if I became a rich Italian's plaything for a while."

She meant it as a joke. When she looked up to meet his eyes, she realized it was anything but. The words hung between them, sharp and strange, like a spark catching in dry grass.

His gray eyes held her in a challenge. "Is that what you're

looking for, now that any chance of making up with Matteo is impossible?"

Sam refused to let him provoke her. Because, for some goddamned reason, he was trying to. "Do you have no memories of being young and reckless and foolish and so achingly in love that nothing mattered?"

A sudden, raw bleakness flared in his eyes that made her stomach tighten. He looked as if he was far away, where she couldn't reach him.

Sam gripped his forearm and shook him. "Alessandro?"

Gripping his neck, he shook his head. "I do remember being in love," he said softly, shocking her anew. A fleeting flash of warmth made his gray eyes pop before they defaulted to blankness. "Feeling as if I couldn't stop smiling. As if the world was a symphony of colors and sensations. But reckless and foolish and out of touch with reality...no. I never had that luxury."

For the first time since they'd met, Sam felt the awareness between them shift and morph, fractured by something so painful that she instinctively hated it. Curiosity about his past and the fear of what she'd find battled it out inside her. "I'm sorry. I didn't mean—"

"I'm not so delicate that your paltry insults wound me, Ms. Fischer." He leaned forward over the table, pinning her under his weighty gaze. "Now I have a question for you."

She waited.

"Did you run away from home?"

Sam sighed. Of course he'd overheard her angry call with her mother yesterday. "I *am* twenty-three so the whole *running away* idea sounds wrong. But yes. How old are you?"

His nostrils flared.

Sam flushed. God, he knew what direction her thoughts were going in.

There was no mockery, no satisfaction when he said, "Thirty-eight."

Instead of serving as a deterrent, his age only made her more curious. Who was the woman he'd been talking about when he said he'd been in love? Why wasn't he with her now? Or perhaps he was in a relationship even as she had filthy dreams about him?

"Do you—" his jaw clenched "—need protection from your parents? Are they abusive?"

"What? Jeez, no." Her laughter cut off at his serious expression. "If anything, they're extra protective. Like pumped-up-on-steroids extra. They love me too much, if we can call it that. Beyond common sense and reason." His continued frown made her elaborate. "I grew up pretty sheltered. This is the first time I've ever traveled without either of them watching over me, checking my every... And I did it without telling them."

"What if Matteo had been—"

"A horrible villain who took advantage of poor old me?" she said, irritation replacing the earlier warmth. "Is there no Off button to you?"

"I'm the one who cleans up his messes."

After three days with him, Sam could see the situation objectively.

Matteo was charming, fun, larger-than-life. But she hadn't missed that he drifted into the easiest paths in life. "I've known Matteo for nearly five years," she said, wanting Alessandro to understand. "Yes, he lied to me. Yes, he started dating Angelina while we were not yet over. Yes, he got engaged to her and didn't even have the decency to tell me. But that doesn't make the entirety of our relationship a lie. I know the distinction."

"Do you? You admit your upbringing was sheltered."

Her temper flared. "Either you respect me enough to know my own mind or you don't. If it's the second, please get out."

Gray eyes gleamed with humor. "I've never been dismissed with such politeness before."

Her anger vanished as fast as it came. "I wonder anyone ever dared dismiss you at all."

He dipped his head, and a thick lock of hair flopped onto his forehead. Combined with his grin, he looked younger, much more relaxed. "So your parents do not know where you are."

God, the man had tunnel vision. "They didn't know until yesterday when I told them on the phone. They didn't know I have a valid passport and a visitor's visa. This trip was my step toward freedom."

Getting everything ready for the trip, calling the hospitals nearby, getting her travel medical insurance sorted, making sure she had enough medication for the trip, shopping for essentials, contacting friends of friends to establish a network of reliable people if the need should arise—all of it had been a big step toward trusting herself. Toward flying out of the safety of her nest. With her next step toward college all mapped out for the summer.

And she'd succeeded too.

She was here. And she hadn't fallen apart at the news of Matteo's engagement.

"Your parents were asking after Matteo on the call," Mr. Ricci prompted, deflating her imaginary fist bump.

Leaning her forearms on the table, she glared at him. "Did you listen to the entire conversation?"

"Your mother's voice was loud."

"She'll rip him to shreds if she finds out he's already

engaged to someone else. The fact that she's six thousand miles away won't make any difference."

"Even without knowing that, she doesn't trust him."

"Do you miss anything?"

"When I'm interested in the subject matter? No."

The truth was that her parents had never warmed up to Matteo. Sam sighed, another knot unraveling in her mind.

Had that been Matteo's appeal—that her parents thoroughly disapproved of him? Was that why she hadn't broken up for years after she realized they weren't romantically compatible?

Her dad liked reliability and steadfastness, which made sense as he was the most dependable guy ever. Her mom thought everyone—except Sam herself, duh—should make a mark in the world with whatever abilities they had.

Matteo had possessed none of the qualities her parents wanted in a partner for their precious daughter. As if there were queues of men lining up to date someone with her history.

But Matteo had made her laugh, had made her feel like a normal girl, had given her hope. He'd been exactly what she'd needed at eighteen, having known nothing of a normal adolescence. Her friends and cousins had moved on—to colleges and new lives and new loves. She'd been too old to go back and finish high school and hadn't had enough credits to go to college, even if she could convince her mom.

She'd felt so isolated and lonely and lost.

She'd survived multiple surgeries, made it through periods of painfully slow recovery, but she'd never learned what it was to live. What to do with her time. How to connect with people.

Until Matteo had walked into the hospital café and flirted so outrageously with her that she'd spent her entire afternoon with him. He'd been the bridge that had pulled her back into her own life. He'd been her hero when she'd desperately needed one. For that alone, she'd always care for him.

She hoped that he'd cherished her friendship too, and not just as a silly diversion to build up his own ego. She needed him to understand that he'd hurt her, yes, but she could forgive him. That she still wanted him in her life.

Which made her insistent attraction to the man studying her so much worse.

"Which part did they not like?" Mr. Ricci asked, with the tenacity of a pit bull.

"Digging for dirt on Matteo is a little beneath you, don't you think?" She scoffed. "Remind me to never introduce you to my parents. Mom especially." There was no doubt in her mind that Alessandro would win them over in a second. Despite the cold remoteness, he was a natural leader, a protector.

"Why not?"

"You and she have too much in common," she said, eyeing him greedily. If she introduced him as her lover, though... Mom would blow her top. The idea sent bubbles of delight through Sam.

"You are an infuriating puzzle made of innocence and strength, Ms. Fischer." His gaze swept over as if he wanted to peel away the surface to see how she was put together. "As your parents, maybe they only see the first."

"But they should know better," she retorted, frustration coiling through her. Even as she was amazed that he saw through to what grated on her so easily. How had he gotten so close to her in three days? What dark magic did he wield? "When life hits you with hard things and you endure them, it makes you tough, ready for things you haven't experienced yet. They expect me to be brave in one thing and then try to shield me from reality in everything else. It doesn't work like that. I can't stay still so that they can feel better."

"Why are they so protective of you?"

He'd drilled down through all of that to come to the one question she didn't want to answer. His gaze stayed on her, waiting.

Sam breathed hard, wondering why she didn't want to tell him the truth. Why it mattered so much that he see her differently than everyone else in her life.

It was foolish. He'd find out sooner or later. She wasn't going to be in his life for long, and anyway she wasn't ashamed. She was a survivor.

But if she told him she'd had multiple heart surgeries by the time she turned eighteen, that she'd spent most of her teens in and out of hospitals, that she'd need medication and frequent checkups for the rest of her life, he'd look at her differently.

He'd treat her like everyone else did. As if she were fragile and needed looking after. As if her mind were also slow, not just her body. As if she were less than a normal person.

Her cousins, to this day, acted wary around her. Tiptoed around their accomplishments as if she couldn't bear to hear them. Were condescending toward her—out of love, yes, but God, it was still infuriating.

Alessandro Ricci, on the other hand, had pushed her when she'd been ready to fall apart. Had made her angry to stop her tears. He'd challenged her notions about herself until she'd no choice but to go toe-to-toe with him.

Would he still talk to her like that if he knew? Or would he pity her too? Would he give her a different version of him—a softer, fake version?

"Ms. Fischer, come back to me."

Sam licked at her lower lip, the resolute look in his eyes

telling her he wasn't going to let this go. And she was equally resolute that he see her as a woman, his equal, an object of desire.

Jesus, *an object of desire*? Why was her mind running away like this? And why was her damned body following as if an affair with this man was even within the realms of possibility?

The shrill ring of his cell phone broke the silence. He held her gaze for an eternity before he answered it.

Like a curtain being pulled shut, that austerity returned to his expression. His torrent of Italian was too rapid for her to follow.

"I have to leave. I will send another chauffeur to pick you up."

Sam nodded, his forbidding expression cutting off her questions.

Shooting to his feet, he turned, then paused. "Why do you think you messed up in your relationship too?"

Sam stared at him, even as her confusion suddenly untangled.

Matteo wanted easy, surface stuff. Forget pain, he didn't even want discomfort. He didn't want messy emotions and digging through one's feelings and assumptions and the raw awareness that could only be found beneath one's fears. The fierce realness of pleasure once you've tasted the worst kind of pain.

A life with her would never be easy or fun. And not just because she'd already tasted the primal fear of losing life itself. But because that fear had also given her an appreciation for things borne out of pain and failure and grief.

Like attraction that went beyond looks. Like the connection between her parents. Like her perception of this man's true nature within seconds of meeting him.

"I didn't understand myself and clung to him for too long," she said, finally seeing past her own insecurities. It wasn't her lack of adventurous spirit. Not her wanting to cling to the safety of her parents' home and love. Not knowing that she'd changed from the eighteen-year-old who'd found Matteo so fascinating. "I used him to feel safe, to feel good about myself."

Alessandro stared at her, unblinking, those gray eyes consuming.

Ask me what I mean, her mind chanted relentlessly.

For a man who'd pushed and prodded her from the moment she'd arrived, he backed off now. The damned man could write a thesis on how to keep her unbalanced.

"*Buona serata*, Sameera."

Sam shivered at the sound of her name on his lips. But he was already gone. "Good night, Alessandro," she whispered to herself.

It was a long time before her thoughts stilled. Before she could stop thinking of how greedy and hungry she was for another moment—quiet or sparring—with Alessandro.

For another conversation.

For another day with that dark, stormy gaze consuming her.

CHAPTER SIX

AFTER BEING ALONE at the villa for two days, Sam began to feel like a hapless heroine in a gothic novel, creeping along its marble-tiled hallways. She hadn't seen either Alessandro or Matteo since the chauffeur had brought her back from the café. Their parents and Angelina and her thuggish cousins, everyone had been gone.

The villa, so breathtaking and boisterous when she'd arrived, now felt cavernous and quiet. As if to add to the dreary ambience, the rain hadn't let up once. Just sheet after endless sheet of gray falling over the lake, blurring the view into something shapeless and cold.

She'd tried asking the staff where Mr. Ricci and the rest of the family were, but they just smiled politely, while bringing her endless meals. In the end, she'd taken to curling up in the armchair in Alessandro's study and sketching him from memory, as if that might conjure him out of thin air.

Worried that the Bianchis might've gotten wind of her or that Matteo was in trouble, she stayed put.

Alessandro didn't owe her anything, of course. Not as his fake mistress. Not as his reckless little brother's ex. Not as an unwanted guest. But two days of radio silence while being stuck at a palatial mansion would make *anyone* cranky.

Watching hour upon hour pass was as painful as waiting for her number to come up for surgery years ago.

What she loathed the most was the needling thought that Alessandro, back in his sophisticated life, had forgotten the naïve, dull, boring Ms. Fischer.

The last of the sun's rays were dancing over the lake when the bedroom door opened to reveal Alessandro.

Dark shadows clung to his eyes as he stilled and stared at her. His gray shirt was rumpled, and his wavy hair was in such disarray that it was clear he'd tugged at it.

Legs trembling, Sam came to her feet just as he said, "Is something wrong, Ms. Fischer? You look troubled."

Usually, she wasn't an overly emotional person. It had been drilled into her that stress could kill her, literally. But this man was like a specially designed aggravation machine. "No, I'm not okay. You left me here, and your staff wouldn't say anything." She fisted her hands. "I expect that from Matteo, not you."

The flare of his nostrils told Sam what she'd just blurted out.

"I apologize. I didn't have your—"

"You must have told yourself the poor fool has neither the choice nor the self-respect to walk away," Sam said, cutting him off.

He reached for her, and she jerked away. "I thought no such thing."

Tears clogged up her throat. "Nothing justifies leaving me here like some rotting vegetable in the fridge. You made fun of me from the moment I showed up—"

"Matteo had an accident."

"What? When? How is he?"

"He was driving his motorbike and took a curve too fast.

He has multiple fractures in his legs, and he hit his head. They worried he'd slip into a coma, but he gained consciousness two hours ago." His exhaustion weighed down the words. "I left the hospital for the first time since they called me at the café."

"Wait, that was the phone call you got? Why didn't you tell me?"

"Sameera, look at me."

She lifted wary eyes to his face. Exhaustion was etched into his sharp features, making him look even more austere than usual. "I couldn't think straight. All they said on the phone was that he had an accident. When I arrived, though..." A groan rattled through him. "I would not have left you alone for so long out of choice. Say you believe me."

She nodded, even though his request was a demand. As if it was imperative that her trust in him wasn't broken. "I thought I got Matteo into trouble with the Bianchis and that you hated me—"

"Shh, *tesoro*. Take a deep breath." His arm came around her waist, and she fell into his embrace, like a puppy starved for attention. He pressed his mouth at her temple, his breath warm on her skin.

Sam thumped at his chest, as if he were her very own punching bag. "Stop ordering me around. I'll push myself into hysterics, if that's what I want."

He fell back against the wall, taking her with him. Her body jostled against his, sending a different kind of shiver down her spine. "You have every right to be angry," he whispered, dry humor coloring his tone. "But I didn't forget about you for a minute. I left the hospital the instant I was free. I needed to explain in person."

Her anger over him had had two whole days to build, but it blew out of her in two seconds flat. "Is he still in danger?"

"He's slipping in and out of consciousness, but there's no risk of him falling into a coma."

She buried her face in his chest, worry twisting her stomach. "Whatever Matteo's faults, he's my friend. My anchor to the world when I..." She swallowed the lump of tears in her throat.

The corded arm around her loosened. Alessandro's hand lifted and hovered over her face, an uncharacteristic hesitation in his eyes. "I'm sorry I made you defensive about your relationship."

Standing so close, Sam felt the tension in his lean body. How his movements were taut and economic when he touched her, as if he didn't want to cross his predetermined limit.

She pushed back and instantly missed the warmth of his body. "How are *you* doing?"

A ghost of a smile tipped up the corner of his mouth. "I'm fine now."

"Will Matteo get back to normal?" That she was asking the question to probe into his heart as much as for info on Matteo was not lost on her. When he gave her that condescending expression she was beginning to know well, she held up a hand. "Not the version you told your parents or Angelina."

"Everyone wants optimism and faith from me. Not you?"

Now that she could see beyond her own distress, now that she was beginning to know the man beneath the remoteness, she saw the strain of the past few days in his eyes, the worry lines digging deep grooves around his mouth. If the truth was painful, she wanted to give him the small comfort of not bearing it alone. "No one should have to shoulder life alone."

His gaze clung to hers. "I'm used to it."

"But I'm here now."

His chin dipping, he looked taken aback. As if she had morphed into someone else right in front of his eyes.

"I've handled hard things in life, Alessandro."

"I'm beginning to see that." He walked past her into the room and opened a bottle of sparkling water. When he raised one in her direction, Sam shook her head.

She watched the play of the muscles at his throat. His tone was flat when he spoke. "Matteo will need at least two more surgeries. Many months of physical therapy to build back strength in his right leg. But yes, he can make a complete recovery."

Sam threw herself at him, joy overriding any sensible caution. "Thank God!"

He caught her, and this time his arms went around her. From chest to abdomen, she was plastered against his powerful body. All that ache in her breasts came back with a twofold intensity. This time, their embrace didn't soothe her. It sparked that hunger that never seemed to be far. He was deliciously hard and lean against her, and all Sam wanted was to press her hips closer, lean her thighs against his until she could feel every inch of him intimately. Until she could provoke his hunger too.

Gentle but firm hands nudged her back. "From enemies to such a warm embrace," he said, clearing his throat, "that's quite a turnaround."

"I never said we were enemies. I admit you're growing on me."

One brow arched in that arrogant face. But that conscious movement couldn't hide the flash of desire in his eyes. For the first time in her life, Sam bemoaned her lack of sophistication when it came to sex and attraction and affairs.

Walking around the lounge, she picked up the loose

sketching paper, books and other stuff she'd scattered about. The bedroom was as much hers now as it was his. "Matteo's been through hard stuff before, right? He told me his asthma had been really bad. That he was teased at school mercilessly for being a small, scrawny kid and you stopped some bully who made his life hell."

"He confided in you?"

"He said he was a runt next to you. But that he overcame…" She sighed. "You're surprised he told me."

"Matteo likes to pretend that he was never weak. He sulks when my aunt reminds him of the almost fatal episode he had once. I think he's even convinced himself that he was always this charming and dynamic."

Sam hugged her sketch pad to her chest. "Is it such a bad thing if you don't want everyone to know your weaknesses?"

"If they make you ashamed, yes," he said, casually picking up her hairclip and her two pencils, before settling into the armchair that had the perfect view of the lake.

Awareness zipped down her spine at how easily this ruthless, powerful man seemed to have accepted her presence—and her innumerable things—in his room. As if she belonged there with him.

"Matteo is ashamed of his physical vulnerabilities and goes to any lengths to make up for them."

She stared, arrested, at the picture he made.

Head thrown back against the chair, long legs sprawled in front of him, with her pink hairclip clasped between elegant fingers, Alessandro was all subdued vitality and masculine perfection. Even with his hair and shirt rumpled, he looked like he belonged on the cover of a magazine.

And she could see how being compared to this man— who was a natural leader—would've bred resentment in Matteo. Being ruthlessly perfect himself, Alessandro would demand the best of everyone. "Does he know that you don't think he has anything to be ashamed of?"

"Does he think I'm a complete monster?" He bit out what sounded like a curse, as if he'd found the answer to his own question. "If anything can defeat Matteo's recovery, it will be himself. Hard work and endurance are not his strong suits."

"He has us to help him with that," she said eagerly. She knew what it felt to not have control of one's body.

His gray eyes flicked open and pinned her to the spot. "Does he have you, Ms. Fischer?" His feet kicked off the ottoman before he added, "To cheer him on?"

Sam could feel her cheeks heating. He had phrased it like that on purpose. She walked around the lounge to the seat opposite him, taking her time before saying, "Yes."

"A prolonged stay will complicate things."

It wasn't quite a warning, and yet there was something in his tone. "Life is full of those pesky complications."

"You will continue to pose as my girlfriend so as not to arouse any suspicion with the Bianchis."

"That sounds like a promotion from mistress. At least in title," she said brazening it out. "Does that mean you can tolerate me now?"

The infuriating man just watched her from under those lashes. "Once my aunt gets her hands on you, you might change your mind. Especially when she realizes you will be the thing that helps her manage her worry about Matteo."

"If I can distract her, I can bear that much."

Leaning forward, his gaze did that thorough sweep of her again, as if he wanted to unravel her and see how she was put together. "I'm beginning to think there's more to my brother than I give him credit for. He gained such loyalty from two intelligent, beautiful women."

"I can absolutely see why he would pit himself against you and come up wanting," she said before she realized it.

Heat poured through her. But she didn't want to take it back.

She wanted to be this girl—no, this woman—who saw a powerful, ruthless man like Alessandro for what he was underneath his remote, aloof armor.

This woman who didn't hide from her own wants.

This woman who boldly challenged a man who would devour her given half the chance. But what if she wanted to be devoured?

What if after everything she'd been through, she'd morphed into a dark, hungry creature who liked grumpy monsters better than charming next-door guys?

Her heart pounded in her chest, her skin felt deliciously taut, and there was that fluttering ache between her thighs… For the first time in her life, she was standing in the arena, instead of watching from the crowd.

Alessandro didn't move a muscle, like a wildcat lounging in its true habitat but tracking every breath and move of its prey. Every inch of him was focused on her. "Because I'm taller, richer and more handsome, *bella*?"

The endearment landed right below her belly like a fishhook, pulling at her entire being. "Matteo is definitely the more handsome one," she said, folding her arms under her breasts, which felt achy and heavy.

"What, then?" The intensity of his gaze made her skin prickle, as if she were standing too close to a flame.

"He knows that, beneath the arrogance and the remoteness, you've got him beat. That you're real, Alessandro. For someone like Matteo, who dwells in illusions, he tells the world and himself you'll always be a threat."

"You're a very dangerous woman, Sameera."

She shrugged, her breath coming in a ragged push. Luckily, she was saved from having to reply by his cell phone.

Her pulse raced as she watched him answer the call, his gaze on her the entire time. He hung up within a few minutes, pocketed his phone and went back to his lounging. With his eyes closed, the dark circles under his eyes looked like bruises.

"When was the last time you went to bed?"

"Are you worried about me?"

"Does *anyone* worry about you?"

"They don't have to."

"That's a very lonely place to be."

His lashes lifted. "You continue to amaze me, *bella*."

"Don't mock my concern. It's genuine."

He dipped his head. "I haven't gone near a bed in three days, no. I did eat, at the hospital café. I had to finalize merger documents for a Japanese company. I grabbed a quick shower at work. Then I went back to the hospital to talk to the specialist. My father is a steady man but my aunt…is falling apart." A soft sigh escaped his lips. It was only when he mentioned his aunt that Sam heard the catch in his voice. "Somehow, I managed to talk her into coming home tonight so that she can rest. Right now, Angelina is with him. As soon as I can muster some energy, I will go back to the hospital and stay with him tonight. The second surgery is scheduled for first thing tomorrow."

"I wish I could stay with him for the night. But hospitals…" she said. "I've had some bad experiences."

"You don't have to."

Sam pushed to her feet, feeling as strung out as she'd felt after the flight. But this exhaustion was less physical and more emotional. Like she'd lived through a year's worth of experiences in a week. "Can I see him tomorrow?"

"*Sì.*"

"You should nap," she said, gathering her painting supplies. "I'll go for a walk."

He flicked a hand in her direction. "*No,* stay."

"You need a break."

"I like your company."

She went a few more steps.

"*Per favore*, Sameera."

She turned around to find that perceptive gaze watching her. "Why do you do that?"

"Say *please*?"

"Call me Sameera in such a…" She blew out a breath. "Why can't you just call me Sam?"

A casual shrug which didn't fool her at all.

"Tell me, Alessandro. Now."

"I like you best like this, *bella*."

The man disarmed her like no one could. "Like how?"

"All fierce and demanding."

Sam swallowed. He lit a fire in her body with a simple sentence, and took up space and familiarity with her as if it were his birthright. From the first moment, he'd given her honesty, realness and himself. "Answer my question."

His chin lifted from his chest. "Sam is his name for you."

Shock made her stare at him for long minutes. There had been distaste but also something so…*possessive, so feral* in that answer. Her breath shallowed. "What?"

"When I hear *Sam*," he continued softly, "I hear it in Matteo's voice. All those years gushing about you. *Sam's great. Sam's wonderful. There's no one like Sam.* I didn't realize you were a woman. But now I know. You are *his* Sam."

You are his *Sam.*

His words echoed through her, raising a hundred questions.

Reaching him, she extended her hand and slightly pushed down on one hard shoulder. The tension in his frame pinged between them, taut and throbbing. Cupping his face, she tilted his jaw just so, and then she reached up to push the lock of hair that fell on his forehead.

His long fingers wrapped around her wrist and held. With one slight shift, he buried his jaw in her palm. His heavy breath made his body shudder. And with her other hand resting on his shoulder, Sam felt every bit of it. Felt the hunger and heat rise in him and envelop her.

Heart pounding, her fingers fluttered, tingling to touch more of him, to trace every angle and plane of his face. His mouth, open and warm, rested against the base of her palm, his breath coasting against the underside of her wrist. Her chest rose and fell, and every muscle in her shivered.

All she wanted was to keep her hand there and sink into his lap. Tug his head down so that she could kiss that mouth. Tell him that she hadn't been Matteo's Sam for a while. Taunt him until he couldn't switch it off anymore. Tempt him until he eased the constant ache she felt at her core.

In the blink of an eye, he let her go, until she was standing by him, her hands dangling by her sides.

"Sameera?"

She jerked away and reached for a glass of water just to give herself something to do. "Hmm?"

"Before Matteo woke up, when the risk of coma was high…it struck me—the source of poison in our relationship—where it had begun. I won't bore you with how it started. Both of us have let the resentment fester. When I saw him at the hospital, I hated that I never even wished to fix it. Never tried to understand things from his perspective." Sam could feel his gaze on her face, but she stubbornly kept hers turned away. "But I love him. If he hadn't recovered—"

"But he did," she said, loudly. "Soon, Matteo will be back to his vital, wonderful self."

"*Sì*, he will. Even if I have to make him take each step." His Adam's apple moved. "See, you and I do have something in common."

"What?" Sam asked, even though she knew what was coming. It was like waiting for the punching bag to hit you back but not knowing when it might happen.

"We both want him to get better. We both love him, *sì*? You will agree then that we can't do anything that would hurt him."

Sam looked at him then, her breath hitching.

It took her an eternity to fix her erratic breathing, to shove away the splintering hurt within her to one corner and lock it up.

When she sat down and began sketching quietly, his eyes closed. For all his brutally honest ways, he'd rejected her in a roundabout way. Stopped her before she made a fool of herself.

Maybe she'd been fooling herself that the pull between them was strong on his side too. Maybe he wasn't into women who threw themselves at him.

Maybe he saw her as an interesting anomaly in Matteo's life and nothing else.

No, he wanted her.

She knew that as well as the unshed tears crowding her eyes as she captured the beautiful lines of his face.

Alessandro stayed still and quiet for how long he had no idea. At least the violent tremors that had taken hold of him earlier had subsided. But he couldn't relax.

Rejecting her, killing the tug of open desire in her eyes, had been the hardest thing he'd ever done. Pushing away from her touch—that he still felt on his jaw like some sort of phantom caress—was like kicking himself when he was already down.

Because after two days of trying to make sense of his world crashing down on him, of coming to terms with his grief and guilt and powerlessness as Matteo lay pale and unconscious in the hospital bed, all he wanted was to lose himself in the compassion in her eyes, in the strength she offered with her words, in the inviting warmth of her body.

She made him forget effortlessly—her fists as they landed on his chest, her body clinging to his offering solace and escape, her words, probing and seeking and giving—everything about her felt like salvation. A relief from the agony of wondering if he'd lose his brother before he could fix their relationship.

But he'd forced himself to remember who she was. He'd rejected her, knowing that he was hurting her. It hurt him a thousandfold to see her retreat. To see the sheen of tears in her eyes. To see her struggle to pull up her armor.

Now the only sounds in the room were the scratch of her pencil against paper and the thundering roar of his own heart in his ears.

Her gaze touched every inch of his face, lingered on his mouth. Even aware that all she saw was a subject, his body still reacted. He was exhausted to the bone, his control in shreds. All he wanted to do was to hold her again, bury his face in her warm neck, pick her up in his arms and take her to bed.

And stay there, for as long as it took to convince her that he wanted her. That he was shaking with need to kiss that soft mouth. That he wanted to make her smile again, wanted her to spar with him again. That he wanted that hand of hers to drift all over him, as she'd been thinking earlier.

Even while he'd been waiting for Matteo to wake up, he hadn't stopped thinking about her. How would she take the news? Would she fall apart? Or would she realize the depth of her feelings for him and want him back?

Selfish as he was, the last scenario had gnawed away at him. The prospect of seeing them back together made him want to throw up. His relief that, while she loved Matteo, she didn't want to be back with him made him shake like a leaf.

There was an inexplicable fragility about her that was a reminder that he did not know all of her. Violetta, before she'd fallen sick, had been bold, vivacious, a lioness of a woman.

But Sameera's strength was more subtle, more nuanced.

It lay in her heart.

Her bold claim that no one should shoulder life alone, that she would hold his hand through this was as painfully real and arousing as her lean, lithe body pressed up against him.

For the first time in more than a decade, Alessandro wanted something with a soul-deep need.

But the same intense desire that was tying him up in knots, that had him shaking like a teenage boy at the mercy of his libido, was also a blaring warning sign.

She unraveled him with her honest words and her genuine concern and her tentative touches. Her fingers on his hand felt more arousing than another woman's mouth on his cock. He swallowed at the filthy images that thought brought on, with her in all of them now. His erection pushed against his trousers. If her gaze dipped below his chest, she'd see it clearly outlined. But it didn't move past his chin.

In the hour that they sat in silence, she didn't look at him again as anything other than a subject, her will as steely as her smile could be soft.

In that first moment of consciousness, Matteo had asked for Sam. Not his mother who hadn't left his side. Not Angelina whose vivacity had gone out. Not their father or Alessandro.

'Sam... I want to see her. I want to tell her that I...' The rest had been lost as he'd slipped back to sleep.

The last thing Alessandro could do while his brother was unconscious in a sterile hospital bed was kiss his girl or his ex or whatever the hell Sameera was to him.

He opened his eyes to find Sameera looking at him but not really seeing him. He, on the other hand, watched her with shameless abandon, lust stabbing through him like an incessant bell.

Her wide lips were wrapped around a pencil while her hair lovingly framed her face. The worn-out crop top showed her navel. He wanted to peel that top off and kiss her all over. He wanted to tongue her belly button and tug at that diamond stud with his teeth. He wanted to dip his fingers into those tight leggings she wore and discover if she was wet for him.

He wanted to make her come on his fingers, mark her skin with light bruises. He wanted to make her smile and laugh, cry and scream, writhe and moan beneath him. He wanted to bury himself so deep inside her that he was a part of the aching loveliness of her spirit and body.

Cristo, he wanted her.

In that moment where his imagination lured him into filthy places, he admitted the truth to himself. Matteo was nothing but an excuse he was using to stop himself.

Because Sameera was not meant for men like him.

If he touched her, he could show her everything she

wanted to taste, but after…he would discard her. He was empty to give her what she needed.

If he knew one thing about the woman who made him realize how empty his life was, it was that she wasn't made to be used and discarded, even if she were a willing participant.

Sam was made for forevers made up of long, cold nights and bright sun-kissed days, filled with laughter and love and joy and connection.

And he'd already had his forever—a flicker flame of joy followed by lifelong kiss of pain.

CHAPTER SEVEN

It was another week before Matteo was brought home and settled comfortably with round-the-clock nurses.

Sam visited him once at the hospital when Angelina had been elsewhere, and he'd been unconscious the whole time. That trip into Milan in a chauffeured car with Alessandro had been unbearable. His extreme solicitousness, as if she were a stranger, had made her want to scratch her nails down his face.

Back home now, Matteo on painkillers mostly slept.

Sam was desperate to tell him she'd forgiven him, that she didn't want to lose him. She wanted to share her confusion about his brother with him, as inappropriate as that sounded. And she wanted to hug him and see him laugh.

More than anything, she didn't want to stay another minute at the villa. Not in Alessandro's bedroom, not in his bed.

Because even when he avoided her, he was entrenching himself into her very thoughts. The morning after she'd begun sketching him, she'd been shown to an airy, sunny room on the second floor where a variety of painting supplies had been waiting for her in pristine, unopened packages. Complete with two new smocks.

Another shock had been when her mom had called two days later, doing a complete one-eighty, asking Sam to live it up and have fun.

Because the great and mighty Alessandro Ricci of Ricci International Finances had personally called to reassure her parents that she was being looked after very thoroughly. In a few minutes of transatlantic conversation, Alessandro had achieved what Sam hadn't been able to achieve her entire life: talked her mom down from the ledge.

He didn't step into her bedroom—*his bedroom*—anymore. There were no more needling remarks to make her gasp, no probing to make her react, no penetrating looks that made her want to burrow into him. Just unrelenting politeness.

He'd put distance between them, distance the blasted man should've kept when he'd found her waiting in his study for his brother. Instead, he'd let her see him, know him. Made her want him.

Yep, she was blaming it all on him.

Unbearable as it was to be subjected to his politeness, on top of Alessandro's aunt's interest in her, Sam couldn't bring up leaving. At least until she was finally able to talk to Matteo.

One bright morning a week after Matteo's arrival home, his parents were arguing in the kitchen in a volley of Italian that enveloped Sam.

Outside the French doors, sunlight shimmered on the lake, and inside the kitchen the scent of coffee and croissants pervaded.

Antonio Ricci—an older, warmer and more smiling version of Alessandro—whispered something to his wife Maria that made the older woman smile softly.

Alessandro's aunt was a lovely woman, but Sam was glad she spoke little English. Maria asked a lot of questions about her and Alessandro. *Girlfriend*, *affair*, *marriage* and *babies* were words she said so frequently in Italian that Sam had been compelled to learn their En-glish translations.

A surge of homesickness hit her as she watched the clear affection between the older couple. Never far behind, as always, was guilt. She had clear memories of her parents like this, arguing with smiles, kissing each other in the kitchen, competing about whose side of her heritage Sam would learn more about. And then, on a beautiful day like this, she'd collapsed and they'd begun falling apart.

God, she wanted them to be happy so badly that her stomach knotted every time she thought of them.

"Sameera, *stai bene, cara mia*?"

Coloring, Sam smiled at Maria. "I'm fine, thank you. Just lost in thought."

"You miss Alessandro, *si*?"

Sam nodded, because it was easier to go along with Mrs. Ricci than explain the twisted complexity of her nonrelationship with Alessandro, who'd been on a trip the last two days.

At least she hadn't been forced to socialize with Angelina who'd been ordered by Alessandro to limit her visits to the villa to see Matteo to mornings. Especially since she came with an entourage of cousins and bodyguards.

If Sam didn't know Alessandro as well as she did, she'd have thought it a lucky coincidence. But he knew she painted in the morning and took an online class in the afternoon and that it kept her out of Angelina's way.

She was glad to sit with Matteo after dinner when Maria's energy lagged. That Maria didn't wonder that Sam spent more time with a sleeping Matteo than an awake Alessandro was just pure luck.

She'd just poured herself a cup of freshly squeezed orange juice when Angelina, thankfully alone for once, entered the kitchen. Sam froze, taking in the simple beige shirt and dark trousers that did nothing to dampen the woman's beauty. She turned toward the doors when Angelina blocked her, her temper in full control of her.

Before Sam could blink, Angelina grabbed the cup from her and threw it in Sam's face.

Sam gasped at the cold slosh of the liquid on her skin preceding the jarring thump of the glass against her shoulder. The sound of it breaking against the marble floor made her falter.

Pain shot through her bare foot as a piece pierced the skin.

A torrent of Italian filled the room as she was bodily lifted from behind. She knew that scent, that body, even the warmth reaching for her. Relief surged through her as she sank into Alessandro.

"*Porca miseria!* Did she hurt you?" Gentle fingers dabbed at her face. "Look at me, *tesoro.*"

"It was just orange juice," Sam said trying to corral her shuddering relief. "I'm fine, Alessandro. She scared me. But it was more…"

He lifted her onto the breakfast table, cutting her words off. "There's a shard stuck on top of your foot"

"Yes and…"

"*Zia*, bring me the first-aid box." He turned around, his back a tense wall. "How dare you treat my guest like that?" His words were soft, slow and yet the quiet rage in them fell like a shroud on the room.

"Matteo is dying because of her." Angelina's voice quivered. "While she—"

"*Dio mio*, Matteo is not dying. Sam is not the reason—"

"She is. She made him crash the bike. He was not happy since she came. You have to throw her out—"

"She isn't leaving," Alessandro bit out in that quiet voice that would've been less scary if he'd shouted.

"Then I will ask my father—"

"*Sam. Is. Mine.*" Each word dropped like a crashing cymbal into the space. "If you touch her again, if you so much as come near her, I'll cut you out of Matteo's life. Permanently." Sam gasped at the vehemence in his tone. "I do not give a damn if your father rules all of Milan. You crossed a line."

"Alessandro, wait—" Sam started before he cut her off.

"You're not welcome in my house anymore. Get out."

Brown eyes filled with shock, Angelina stared at him.

"Alessandro, you can't simply throw her out," Sam said, her words drowned out by his aunt begging the same.

"Stay out of this, Sameera."

Italian flew back and forth between him, his parents and Angelina, but he didn't relent. The quiet rage in his eyes when he checked her face made her swallow.

He felt guilty for not protecting her, she knew. Guilt and pity and politeness weren't what she wanted from him. Still, pathetic as she was, she couldn't help touching him. She bent her forehead to his back, clutching the taut muscles of his biceps. "Alessandro, give her a chance to explain."

"There is nothing to explain," his voice softened instantly, the muscles clenching under her touch. "Papà, get her out of the house. If she makes a fuss, call security."

A thundering silence followed his harsh dictate.

Antonio sent Sam a reassuring glance before he walked a hysterical Angelina out. Still, she cast an astonished look at Alessandro's protective stance around Sam.

The moment she left, Alessandro pushed in to stand between her legs.

Her belly rolled, sensation making her thighs quiver. When she looked up, his face was a taut mask. The man wasn't even aware how provocative their positions looked.

Sam flushed as his aunt approached, a first-aid kit in her hand.

"Leave us, *Zia*."

Maria gave Sam a quizzical look and left.

Deafening tension crackled around them. Sounds from the outside breezed into the room, the table dappled in bright morning light as if the universe itself was orchestrating the moment. That sharp pain persisted in her foot, but the feel of Alessandro's powerful thighs pushing hers wide apart trumped every other sensation. Awareness pulsed with a vengeance between her thighs.

With that tightness to his movements that betrayed his lack of control, he undid the cuffs of his dress shirt and pushed the sleeves back. The sight of his corded forearms sprinkled with dark hair made her think of those arms holding her down, of those long fingers touching her everywhere.

God, everything about the man made her think of sex.

"Alessandro…" she said, suddenly glad for Angelina's stunt. Which made her more than a little twisted in the head. "It was just juice—"

Pushing the wooden bench back, he brought her foot to his thigh. Even the sight of her foot in his large, elegant hands made her core flutter. Not looking at her, he laid out a bunch of things from the kit on the dark wood of the table.

Sam pressed her heel into the hard muscle while he, with infinite care, pulled out the shard stuck in her foot. Her heart expanded to dangerous proportions as she watched him clean up the cut, apply an antibiotic and wrap her foot in layers of gauze.

A muscle jumped in his cheek as he packed up the supplies. "Do you still think I'm overreacting?"

"I never thought that." Gripping his wrist, she whispered, "Won't you look at me?"

Those long lashes lifted, and the cocktail of emotions there made her swallow.

Not because she was afraid of him. Never.

But she'd never seen him at the edge of control like this. The devil in her wanted to push a little more to see what she could get out of it. God, when had she become so conniving? "You're very angry."

"What if it had been hot soup or that ginger chai you drink in the mornings?"

How was she not supposed to feel flattered by the fact that he didn't miss a single thing about her? "It wasn't."

"She could have seriously hurt you."

"She scared me, yes, but she didn't hurt me. What she wanted more than anything was to make herself feel better."

Eyes wide, he looked at her as if she'd lost her mind. Sam was thinking the same. But for other reasons. "How would you know this?"

"I have a cousin like her, a total diva. And I've seen the lingering panic in Angelina's eyes. She's scared that she'll lose Matteo. To something worse than me. I'm the option she can control. If you'd given me a moment with her, I could—"

His scowl deepened. "You're not going near her."

"And who are you to order me around?"

"*Per piacere*, Sam. Do not push me around right now."

"You called me Sam," she whispered, beaming wide. Her foot hurt, her heart was getting entangled in this man, but that he called her Sam was enough to send her on a fizzy trip.

He looked at her, finally. Properly looked into her eyes. And the hook was back in her lower belly tugging and pulling her into those gray depths.

"I don't want to fight with you about her," she said in a low whisper.

A soft, breathtaking smile lifted the edge of his mouth. It was like standing in a patch of sunshine created just for her. "And here I thought you loved nothing more than to put me in my place."

Lifting her hand, Sam almost touched the groove the smile dug in one cheek. "I miss you," she said, her fingers hovering over his jaw.

Every inch of her wanted to touch him, to mark him. To claim every small part of him as her own. Beginning with that smile. If it were up to her, she'd make sure everyone knew they belonged to her. The ones where his gray eyes turned warm and one corner of his mouth tugged up...they came out for her, only her.

He tensed. "You *miss* me?" he said slowly, as if he couldn't quite get the texture of the words on his lips.

Embarrassment flooded her. But she couldn't do coy or smooth or flirty. She'd missed all the stages where she'd have liked simple, easy boys. Instead, life had made her skip them all and brought her here to this man.

This remote, ruthless, yet inherently kind man who was determined to keep her at arm's length. Whose gray eyes betrayed his longing. Who said so much with his actions and nothing with his words.

"I do, yes." She clasped her hands back in her lap. "Between Mom and your aunt, I'm struggling to keep the lies straight. But you know I'm just floating around, half-scared that I'll be untethered any moment but desperately wanting to anyway."

"You want to fly, *cara*?"

"Like you couldn't imagine. Nothing worse than fear that keeps you still."

He watched her for a long beat. Then, as if all her raw vulnerability meant nothing, he grabbed a cold washcloth and pressed it against her face.

His fingers were so refreshingly gentle as he wiped away the sticky remnants of the orange juice from her temples and her hair.

Sam closed her eyes and let the sensations take hold. In a delicious contrast, his warm breath coasted over her skin.

Her spine felt like it was made of those chocolate straws her mom used to buy for Sam to drink her milk with—melting and bendy at his fingers.

With an efficiency that made her smile, he wiped down her cheek and neck. Suddenly, his fingers were at the buttons of her shirt dress. Her eyes flying open, he gripped his wrist.

Jaw tight, he said, "There's more on your neck."

Sam did feel the stickiness between her breasts. "I'll just shower—"

The first button on the shirt popped off. Two more buttons and he would see the scar that was a reminder of how she'd spent her teens. He'd already been avoiding her for the past week. Panic gripped her. "Stop unbuttoning my dress."

He arched a brow, his fingers lingering over the third button. "Why am I not surprised that you're a prude, *bella*?"

"Of course I'm not," she said with a forced laugh. "Just because I don't want to get half-naked in the kitchen."

"Let me carry you to the bedroom, then."

"I can walk—"

"I feel responsible for—"

Sam clasped his jaw. "Alessandro, I don't need your fucking pity."

His fingers lingered on the third button of her shirt. The patch of her bare skin where he touched her burned. "The last thing I feel when I look at you is pity, *tesoro*."

"And yet I'm so easy to avoid, so forgettable, *si*?"

His gaze met hers and held, his fury slowly cycling out and replaced with something else. Long fingers touched her jaw, his grip tender. "You're the least forgettable woman I've ever met. Ever since you…" His exhale was long. The thrust of his fingers through his hair rough, his words gravelly. "What do you want of me, Sam?"

Sam leaned forward and pressed her mouth to his cheek. Her heart beat so rapidly in her chest that it should've scared her, but sitting in the warm cocoon of his body, she felt so vibrantly alive that there was no place for fear.

Hands gripping her shoulders, he went utterly rigid.

"One kiss," she said, the stubble on his chin scraping her lips in an abrasive whisper. "So that I know how you taste. So that I know you want me. One kiss, Alessandro, so that I can live it a million times in my head." Her breath left her in a shuddering exhale as she waited.

All her life, she'd waited for others to make life-changing, sometimes life-threatening decisions for her. From doctors to her parents to the universe, her will nothing but a swaying leaf in a storm. But this waiting…there was pleasure in this.

This was a battle. Her will against his, her need against his control. Ordinary, dull, unexciting Sam against remote, ruthless, strikingly beautiful Alessandro Ricci.

This was a waiting she'd plunge herself into again and again. A choice she would make a thousand times.

If all of her entire being weren't tuned in to him, Sam wouldn't have sensed it. But he moved, and his mouth shifted until it sat flush against hers. A dam of longing, never too far beneath surface, broke through her.

His mouth—oh, his mouth!—was soft and firm as she moved her lips. The man was full of contradictions, and she liked every bit of him. Up and down, messy and damp and a little rough, she rubbed her lips against his, every minuscule motion sending a shocking jolt of molten heat to her sex. Then she licked his lower lip and nipped it.

She stretched her thighs wider so that she could scoot closer, so that she could feel of all him against her. And he let her. Not for a second was Sam unaware that he was granting her this. That his own control was hanging by a thread, that she desperately needed to snap it.

A long, shuddering sigh left her as her chest grazed his, as her belly pressed against his hard one and their hips flushed. She couldn't help but thrust her hips, a soft gasp escaping her. Slowly, every cell in her came awake with a blistering heat as his arousal took shape and form against her core, as it lengthened. The very thought of that hard length inside her made her sex clench greedily.

His curse punctured the silence as loudly as if the bright chandelier overhead had crashed into a million pieces around them. But all Sam cared about was the warmth unspooling in her lower belly, untethering her.

She had done this to him—naïve, unsophisticated, unexciting Sam. Confidence and desire whipped through her, an explosive cocktail. Tightening her fingers at the nape of his neck, she kissed him again.

She traced the shape of those thin lips with the tip of her tongue, nipped at the lower lip with her teeth, licked at him like a lazy cat until he opened to her with a guttural groan that set off vibrations through her. Greedy for more, she licked into his mouth, stroking, tasting, teasing, taunting, stealing his breath for herself.

A rough growl escaped him as his hand wrapped around the nape of her neck. Sam groaned as he bent her back over his arm, and then his mouth devoured her. She finally understood what those flashes of consuming hunger in his eyes meant. There was no sweet exploration, no soft learning.

Alessandro ravished her. He took from her as if she were the last breath of air. Drank from her lips as if she were the last sip of water.

Pleasure flew through her in rivulets, pooling at her sex into damp readiness. The kiss was all him—the licking fire of hard nips, the cooling ice of soothing licks—a spectrum of pain and pleasure in between.

No safety, no soft whispers, only sheer hunger. Within moments, he taught her how to deepen the pleasure blooming between them, when to pull away and when to cling.

His hands moved all over her hips and back and spine and neck and butt, coasting, kneading, touching, learning. Provoking and soothing. Owning. His touch was full of a possessive intent that made her want to submit to everything he did. For every hurt he caused with those teeth, he gave back pleasure that resonated a thousand times more deeply.

Sam groaned into his mouth, the thrust of his hips making his erection hit her exactly where she needed. She locked her legs around his hips, brazenly thrusting against him. Hands fisted in his shirt, she was sobbing, begging for more, begging him for relief.

When he trailed a path over her jaw and neck, she buried her hands in his hair, her body a mass of sensations she couldn't catalog fast enough. But it was her heart that felt full to bursting. Her heart's unfathomable desire for more that terrified her.

"Is this enough to prove I want you, *tesoro*? That I lose control when anyone could walk in?"

If he'd mocked her, maybe Sam could have pulled her senses out of the miasma of longing. But there was no humor in his words. Nothing but a deep hunger for more that she recognized in herself.

She looked up at him, fighting the pull of reality. Fighting the embarrassed heat that was already flowing into her cheeks. "Have *you* had enough?"

One corded arm swung around her lower back, and he pulled her forward.

A filthy curse and a string of Italian met her ears when she thrust up in answer. Then his mouth touched hers in a sweet kiss that stole the breath from her lungs. Wedged hard against him, the heat and hardness of his erection branded her. All she wanted was to move, to rub up against him until the restlessness under her skin found a destination. But his grip was firm on her legs, keeping her prisoner.

"From the moment I saw you, standing apart from the crowd…"

Sam wanted to ask what he was talking about. But he didn't give her a chance.

His mouth and his whispers and his kisses stole rational thought. "Wanting something so much, only…" He drew a trail from the corner of her mouth to her chin to the pulse at her neck, punctuating his kisses with words, breathing them into her skin.

And then suddenly, he stopped.

She sensed the shift in his mood as easily as if someone had dumped a bucket of ice-cold water over them. "Alessandro," she whispered, pushing that one lock of unruly hair from his forehead like she'd wanted to so many times. "What is it?"

He didn't budge. Didn't look up.

Slowly, he pulled the flaps of the dress apart. And Sam knew what had stopped his lazy exploration. What had frozen him.

***

Alessandro stared blankly, his stomach so tight with lust that it took him a few minutes to circle back to what had made him stop.

He had ripped the rest of the buttons until her ridiculous dress had fallen open, baring her chest and belly to him. The clingy material cupped her small breasts, and his palms ached to do the same.

She wasn't wearing a bra. The edges of the dress just barely covered the tight knots of her nipples. He could see the light brown aureoles, the tips pushing at the fabric.

He'd also pushed the dress up her thighs, which were stretched wide. Her skin was silky smooth. Lips swollen, hair half out of her braid, she was the most achingly lovely thing Alessandro had ever seen. So lovely that the image of her like this would haunt him for the rest of his life.

All he wanted to do was bend his head and lick her all over. Up and down, around the swells of her breasts and below, until he could play with her piercing.

It took him an eternity to focus on the scar he'd felt under his fingertips. For a second, he'd thought he'd imagined it and stepped back.

Sunlight illuminated her golden-brown skin and the rough ridge of the scar drew a line down, starting at the top between her breasts, going lower. Deep too, as if someone had taken a scalpel and dug into her flesh not just once but multiple times.

He traced it up and down, fighting for control over his breath. Fighting to not give into the panic inching its fingers all across him, leaving something cold and ugly in its trail. Breath harsh, he pressed his palm against her rib cage, desperate to feel the beat of her heart. The thud of it, the soft gasp from her lips, made him realize how roughly he'd grabbed her. He jerked away, feeling as if he'd been hit in the head and it was still ringing.

Her throat bobbed, sending a ripple of motion down her chest, and his gaze jerked up to meet hers. For once, he couldn't read her expression. Always so open and honest and artlessly direct—her words and her eyes. Yet now, it was as if she'd slammed a shutter down between them.

He traced the scar gently, unable to stop. "What...made this?"

"Heart surgery."

A quiet roar reverberated within him, demanding release. "When?"

"What do you mean, when?"

"When did you have the surgery, Sameera?" he bit out.

"I had three heart surgeries between ages eleven and eighteen. The third time was due to a valve problem." There was a forced lightness to her words that he knew was fake. It was probably the first time he'd seen her fake anything. "But I've enjoyed perfect health ever since the last one."

Her words were soft as if she was determined to manage his mood, manage him.

A part of him, the rational part, warned that she shouldn't have to manage his emotions when she revealed such private information. That the onus of his reaction shouldn't be on her. And yet, he couldn't pin his emotions down, couldn't shove them away so that he didn't discomfit her.

"That's where you met Matteo," he said tonelessly, remembering Matteo going to see their great-aunt who lived in California when she'd had surgery. "At the hospital."

"In the hospital café, while I was still in my horrible ass-baring gown." Her wide smile was the genuine thing. "I'd snuck away from my ward. Bored out of my mind because they said I should stay overnight for a routine checkup. I wanted chips. But I forgot cash. He bought me a bag of chips and flirted with me outrageously right there, while I tried not to flash him my ass."

Emotion rattled him—thick and blinding, familiarly unfamiliar, bringing images to bore down on him like an avalanche. The very thought of Sameera looking small and tiny on a clinical hospital bed stole his breath.

The image was too vivid. Too real.

He'd seen Violetta like that for so long. For four years, he'd spent hours at her side in the evenings, reading to her, playing chess with her, holding her hand.

It was diabolically cruel how easily his mind replaced Violetta with Sam... Sam in an ugly pristine white hospital. Sam with her smile faint, the light in her eyes dim. Sam with her breath thin and faint.

Maledizione! He pushed away from the table, sweat beading on his face. His mind was playing games. Triggering memories from a painful period in his life. Which was ridiculous.

Yes, Sam had reminded him of Violetta from the first. Something about the glowing spirit wrapped in steel that they possessed. But Violetta was gone. And Sam was here, vibrantly alive.

"Alessandro?"

He turned to find Sam watching him with trepidation in her eyes.

"That's why your parents are so protective of you." Everything fell into place, but he'd never wanted more to live in ignorance, had never understood Matteo's love for deluding himself more. "Why you still live with them. Why..." His words became sharp, hostile. "Why didn't you tell me?"

"Why would I?" she asked in a small, baffled voice.

It was like waving a red flag in front of an angry bull. "I asked you point-blank why they were so protective of you."

"So?" Anger painted her cheeks a reddish tint. "I didn't have to share anything with you. Especially now, when you're actively avoiding me." She pushed off from the table, her dress still unbuttoned to her belly button. Her hair was in a disarray, her neck and jaw a little reddened where his stubble had scratched her. She looked glorious. "You think I walk around showing people my scar and telling them my history?"

"Why is that wrong? What if you needed an emergency visit? How was I supposed to take care of you? How can you be so irresponsible and flippant about this?"

She flinched, and Alessandro wondered if he was losing his mind.

Chin quivering, she looked at him as if he'd betrayed her in the worst possible way. "I'm choosing to see this as your concern for me and not…" Her words shook, slender body trembling with fury. "If you ever assume that I don't know my own mind or even insinuate that I'm helpless… I'll never forgive you." She swallowed, and that she had a better measure of control over her emotions than he did right then shamed him. "I have all my insurance information, my medication prescriptions, my monthly checkups already set up. As for emergency, it's no different from anyone else needing to be rushed to the ER."

"I still think you should've shared your—"

"Why? So that everyone can look at me the way you're looking at me now? I can see the way you perceive me shifting in front of my very eyes…" Her words held a question in them.

But Alessandro couldn't think beyond what it meant to

him. Couldn't get perspective. Silence had never felt like it could tear two people apart.

Hurt twisted her smile into a mockery. "Thinking this thing between us was worthy of exploration was a colossal mistake. My age, Matteo, and now my history...you'll find something to reject this. And that's your prerogative. But I'll be damned if I let you make me believe that I'm not—" Tears filled her eyes and she inhaled loudly. "I finally understand why Matteo calls you a machine. But he doesn't know the worst, does he? It's not that you can't feel. It's that you don't want to."

She swept out of the kitchen, holding her dress together, her spine straight, head held high.

Alessandro stayed still for a long time, his mind still reeling. Suddenly, he could see all the reasons their chemistry was more than surface level: because she understood what it meant to not have power over your own life.

But her fears and her very real struggles hadn't stopped her from wanting to live, from wanting to taste everything life offered. From recognizing the same hunger in him, even though he was everything she called him—remote, ruthless, heartless.

Only now did he realize how much more he'd lost than Violetta fourteen years ago. Grief had robbed so much from him—friends, of family, even his brother. Laughter. Simple pleasures. The ability to connect.

It had isolated him until he had gotten used to having nothing.

CHAPTER EIGHT

MORE THAN A week passed before Alessandro went to visit an awake Matteo.

While his brother had been conscious for over two weeks now, he had avoided seeing him. Now his stomach tightened at the prospect of a confrontation that had been coming for months, even years.

Neither did he miss the fact that the trigger was Sam's arrival.

It had been a week since Sam had looked at him with such anger, such hurt in her eyes. The first he could bear, the second not so much.

"Where is she?" he said, barging into the room. "Don't pretend ignorance, Matteo. She doesn't know anyone in this town."

His chest tightened at the sight of his brother. Dark, sunken shadows clung to Matteo's eyes, the ever-present pain already changing the cast of his features.

"Hello to you too, Alessandro," Matteo said. "If you mean Angelina, she's not here. Because you banished her." He sighed. "Aren't you the one always telling me to not piss off Vittorio?"

"I meant Sam, and you know it," Alessandro countered. His words sharpened in direct reaction to how pale and worn-out Matteo looked. It seemed his usual self-possession was nowhere to be found now. "But while we're talking about Angelina, have you finally decided to be a responsible adult and sort this mess out? Will you stop overcompensating for your supposed weaknesses as a child and act like a grown-up instead?"

"*Sì*, something shook loose in my brain during the accident," his brother said, shutting Alessandro up.

Whatever he had been expecting, it wasn't Matteo's sudden somberness. Alessandro felt as if he'd kicked a dog that was already down.

"You should know that I told Angelina everything over the phone. How Sam hadn't yet quite broken up with me when I agreed to go out with her. But that I knew it was coming. That I went out with Angelina to feel better about myself."

"At least you can be glad there's nothing else to break in your body. Not everyone is as forgiving as Sam." It was a big step for his brother to admit how far down the wrong path he'd gone. Fresh anger surged through Alessandro. "Before you decided to come clean, did you think about Sam's safety? Did you not realize Angelina would take it out on her?"

"You have no idea how sorry I am. How awful Angelina feels about her behavior toward Sam." When Alessandro scoffed, Matteo sighed. "No, truly. She hasn't told her cousins or friends or her dad everything I told her about Sam and me. She said it wasn't anyone's business."

For once, Alessandro was surprised too.

Matteo bumped his head against the headboard. "The last thing I want is to hurt Sam more. She's…special."

Hearing her name on his brother's lips made Alessandro want to smash something. Even if she wasn't for him. "Are you still in love with her?"

"I used to think so," Matteo answered, his voice steady. "But when I realized she didn't feel deeply about me, that she'd already outgrown me, it made me resentful. I knew then that our relationship was more about how she made me feel about myself, rather than our feelings for each other."

"Because of her...history?"

"Sam made me feel good in my own skin," Matteo said, regret and something else in his eyes. "As if I were a different kind of man. Like I could be someone even without the Ricci name or the large sphere of your influence. If a fearless girl like her could love me, I was worthy. I never told her about our family wealth because I wanted a girl like her to like me for me...without complications. And her parents were too protective of her to ever let her travel, so... she never saw all of this for herself."

As much as he hated it, Alessandro understood the sentiment. "Is that why you never told us that Sam was a woman? Because you wanted to keep her and our family separate?"

"*Sì*. Even when it was good, I knew it wouldn't last, that it wouldn't survive in the true reality of my world. And Sam hasn't looked at me like I was her hero in a long while."

"And Angelina?" demanded Alessandro.

"Angelina's not ready to call it quits. For now, she's claiming that if she breaks up with me, society will think she's dumping me because I'm not the dynamic, charming prize she wanted in the first place. I think she wants to see who I am beneath the bravado. I'm afraid to tell her I might be nothing."

"Don't say that." Alessandro reached for his brother's hand, swallowing past the ache in his throat. "When I saw you in the hospital bed, I realized I had let small resentments fester. I'm sorry I never told you that I care about you."

Vulnerability shone in his brother's eyes. "I never gave you a reason to. The more you warned me about the consequences of my lifestyle, the worse I behaved." Hope danced in his face. "I will do better, Alessandro. As soon as I have mobility, I plan to start work. Believe it or not, my degree in accounting can be put to some use." He raised a hand, forestalling Alessandro. "I already spoke to Papà. I'll start as a junior clerk in the accounts department and work my way up. I will prove you wrong."

"Apparently, it's been a month of me being proved wrong."

Matteo regarded him thoughtfully. "Are we going to talk about Sam and you?"

"That's none of your—" Alessandro pushed his hand through his hair and blew out a breath. "No."

"So there is something between you two." For a second, old bitterness flashed in his brother's eyes, and Alessandro braced himself. Matteo's mouth twisted ruefully. "I could see it even that first night in your study, the way you looked at each other. It made me…" He shook his head, dislodging his curls onto his forehead.

While the last thing he wanted was to discuss Sam with his brother, Alessandro waited. Matteo needed this. Especially if they meant to begin their relationship anew.

"She's honest enough to admit that you shut it down before it even began," Matteo said finally. "I thought I'd be happy. As much as it's a bitter pill to swallow that she prefers you, I can see you…feel something for her too."

"As much as I appreciate your blessing," Alessandro bared his teeth in a mockery of smile, "I want you to tell me her whereabouts right now."

Matteo sighed. "Sam said she wanted to go out. Angelina took her to a club."

Alessandro scowled. "Angelina threw a glass of juice in Sam's face not two days ago."

"She apologized, and Sam forgave her." Mateo held up

his phone, eyes twinkling. "Do you want to see the pics Angelina's been sending me all evening?"

He took the phone from his brother and looked at the screen.

It was a picture of Sam against the bright lights of the nightclub. In a strapless dress in a shiny material in a rainbow of colors, the asymmetrical strips hugging her torso. It cupped her chest loosely, baring the lush swells in a provocative way that made hunger tighten his muscles. But it was the scar that held his interest.

All these weeks, she'd worn dresses and tops that buttoned up all the way.

Yet, now she showed off the scar proudly, even loudly. He wanted to think that he'd brought that change in her, but that was arrogance talking. Sam was only beginning to own herself.

"Swipe through. There's more," Matteo added.

Alessandro swiped. There were numerous pictures and even video clips—Sam laughing, singing at the top of her voice, swinging her hips. Sam sandwiched between two guys while a slow jazz tune played in the background.

Jealousy and something much darker scoured through him in hot trails, making his stomach tighten. He threw the phone back to the bed.

As he walked out, Matteo said, "Sam deserves the best."

Did Matteo think he didn't know that?

She was happy, Alessandro told himself, reaching for the decanter of bourbon in his study. She was twenty-three, and she was doing things people of her age did.

He told himself that again and again as he called his sparring partner Bruno. If what he needed was to have it beaten into him that he should leave Sam alone, then that's what he would do.

* * *

She didn't need to say good-bye.

But as Sam walked around his study, the only room in the house that reflected Alessandro's personality, she admitted to herself that she didn't want to leave without seeing him. Not after all the days she'd spent taking over his bedroom. Not after everything he'd done, in his own way, to watch out for her. Not after everything they'd shared.

He'd hurt her, and the worst part was that she'd thought he was one man who never would. She'd foolishly assumed that he liked her for who she was. Maybe she was nothing more to him than his younger brother's foolish, naïve ex who wouldn't leave.

She'd walked into the study after Angelina had dropped her off. The very woman she'd been loath to meet from that first evening had now become a good friend. Angelina was a spoiled diva with an explosive temper, but beneath it all she was just like Sam: full of insecurities and flaws and desires.

Now that she had Angelina's offer of accommodation at her cousin's place, she needn't stay at the villa at all. It was late, but once the offer had been made, Sam knew she needed to leave immediately.

For the first time in her life, she'd gone clubbing with friends. She'd danced. She'd sung at the top of her lungs. She'd ingested secondhand smoke. She'd flirted. While none of the guys had made her heart flutter like the heartless man who belonged here, it felt good to know that someone did want her.

Smiling, she poured herself a finger of Scotch. She lifted the glass to her mouth when a rough hand pulled the drink away from her and ended up sloshing it all over her. "Jesus Christ! Enough with spilling my drinks."

"What the hell do you think you're doing?" Alessandro glared at her.

A soft gasp escaped her mouth.

His face was...a kaleidoscope of bruises. The lower lip she was so obsessed with was swollen and cut with crusted blood. A cut under his right eye made his cheekbone swell up, and a blue-green bruise the size of her palm painted his jaw. This was so far from the calm, remote Alessandro she'd known from day one that she forgot her anger. "Are you in pain?"

Leaning against the desk, he threw his legs forward. "Pain was the point of it."

"You look like you took part in a street fight. And lost."

"Ahh, your lack of faith hurts more than all of this, *tesoro*. I promise Bruno looks worse than me."

She rubbed her palms over her hips, just to do something. "I thought you were beyond all this, your control ironclad."

His gaze searched her face and held hers. "I was in a nasty mood, and there were only two ways to work it out of my system."

Heat flushed through her in warm rivulets at his tone.

"What were *you* about to do? Alcohol messes with your medication."

Back to this, were they? "Two sips won't kill me."

He raised a brow, and even with his face all bruised, it was the most arrogant gesture she'd ever seen. It made her blood boil, brought all the anger and hurt back to the surface. Looking away, she grabbed her jacket from the desk. "I was stupid enough to want to say good-bye."

"Good-bye?"

She reached the damned heavy double doors. "I'm leaving."

He stalked toward her. There was no other word for it. "And going where exactly?"

Sam took him in—how the drop of blood on the pristine white of his shirt looked so out of place, the buttons undone to his abdomen showing olive skin sprinkled with sparse chest hair, how his usually immaculate black trousers were rumpled. How he hadn't even waited long enough to change before sparring.

As if all the masks of politeness had been stripped off, leaving him with only pure instincts and wants.

She wanted him even more like this. Wanted this raw, distilled version of Alessandro to want her.

"Angelina's cousin's apartment. I'll still visit Matteo daily. Angelina knows the truth. There's no need for us to pretend."

"Did you have fun at the club?"

The sudden switch in the conversation left her unbalanced. "I did." She didn't even have to force the smile. "Angelina's cousins are a hoot. Especially after she told them that I'd never been to a club before. Had never danced before, never been flirted with before." The twins had been outrageous to begin with, sandwiching her between them on the dance floor, but it was harmless fun.

"Did you like all the attention you got?" There it was again, that feral quality about him. Somehow, he'd stalked her back across the room until she was leaning against his desk. Away from the door. "Did you dance with those two men to make me jealous, Sam?"

"I don't play games like that." She frowned. "Wait, how did you know I was dancing with…" She bit her lip, and his gaze zoomed down. Heat crested her cheeks as she remembered all the crazy things she'd gotten up to. "You saw those videos?"

"Matteo showed them to me."

Whether he knew it or not, he'd pushed her into crawling out of her shell. Into owning her scar and her body.

She'd been terrified when she'd walked into the club. Terrified that her scar would be the only thing people would see, that it'd make them feel sorry for her. But while one of Angelina's girlfriends had openly asked her about it, no one had given it a second glance.

While she was never going to be comfortable in provocative clothes, now she knew that it was her choice. Not one made out of shame.

"You won't make me feel guilty about it. Not about this overtly provocative dress. Not about the secondhand smoke I inhaled. Not about the fact that I enjoyed flirting with two men. Men of my age. Men who found me sexy and interesting."

He cast a long look at the dress in question, his lashes flicking down. But his gaze didn't linger on her scar. It moved over the upper swells of her breasts, the asymmetric hem that barely covered her left thigh and her feet clad in black stilettos. Then it climbed back up over her, and this time it did linger on her scar.

Long fingers clasped her cheek with such gentle reverence that all the longing she'd fought flooded back into her. "Tell me why you want to leave."

"I don't want to let one arrogant asshole's rejection ruin my trip."

He laughed, a deep, hard sound that enveloped her. And then he hissed in pain. The cut in his lower lip had split again, and a drop of blood appeared.

She pressed the pad of her thumb to stanch it. He flinched but held still. "I didn't mean to hurt you more," she whispered, a languid heat spreading through her.

He clasped her wrist and pressed his face into her palm. His body caged hers against the desk without quite touching. "I like all the things you inflict on me, *bella*. Laughter, hurt, jealousy… They remind me that I'm alive." He nuzzled into the side of her face. His chest rose and fell, the tension in his body setting hers alight. "You've no idea how much I loathe myself for hurting you."

The soft press of his lips at her temple cracked open her heart with such violence that Sam couldn't breathe. Word by word, kiss by kiss, he was stealing away parts of her, and she didn't know how to keep herself intact anymore.

"Then, don't," she whispered, tucking her chin into the crook of his elbow. He smelled of sweat and blood and whiskey, and she inhaled him as if he were air. Fingers around his forearm, she clung to him, loving the fierce heat of his body.

"I haven't felt anything for so long… With you, it is futile to resist." His soft words were breathed into her skin, as if he were releasing the shackles around himself. He tilted her chin up. "Tell me what hurt you so much."

"You looked at me as if I was…broken. As if my history makes me damaged. Even Matteo behaved better."

He was shaking his head, regret making his face even more severe. "Ahh…you know just how to hurt me."

Sam shook her head. "I—"

Thumb notching into her chin, he cut her off. "Look at me, Sameera. Listen to me." His warm breath feathered over her face. "In my eyes, you're perfection. From the moment you walked in, I wished you were mine. I burn with jealousy when you talk of him with such fondness. How I reacted…it's my weakness, *bella*. Not you."

His hands cradled her head, and his mouth hovered an inch over her mouth, and Sam thought she might be drowning but she didn't care. "I want you so much, Sam, it's an ache in my body. Even the bruises won't kill it. But the thing is..." he licked her lower lip, and a hot poker of sensation hit her "...I can't offer anything beyond a few weeks. No future, no relationship. This would be an affair to work you out of my system. For some goddamned reason, you're a novelty. But the fascination will wear off."

"How does your brutal honesty make you hotter?" she said, chasing his lips. She licked his lower lip, tasted the blood and then nipped him right where the lip was split.

He shuddered, jerked her toward him until she wrapped her arms around his neck and every inch of her was plastered to him. "All I have to give you is pleasure. But you're the kind of girl—"

Sam buried her face in the hollow at his throat and scraped her teeth over his pulse. "I'm the kind of woman who has filthy dreams about you, Alessandro. The kind that wanted you from the first moment, even though I came here for Mateo. The kind of woman who touches herself thinking of you. The kind of woman who survived three surgeries as a teenager and wants to taste life. If you hated hurting me, then make it better. Make me feel good."

"*Bene.*" He licked the shell of her ear, and Sam shivered. Then his mouth went south, trailing warm, wet kisses across her neck, her shoulders, the swell of her breasts.

She swept her hands over him, the sharp jut of his shoulders, the warm, taut skin of his chest, the hard muscles beneath. That she could touch him with such abandon made her breath falter. She snuck her fingers under his shirt, scoring his abdomen with her nails, then trailed them lower.

"No." His forbidding tone made her belly roll. "My control is so thin, *tesoro*. And my need to be inside you...too high."

"Yes."

Gripping her wrists with one hand, he pushed them above her head with a growl that made dampness gush at her sex. "I want to make it up to you. I want you to forget the men you were dancing with, the ones you flirted with. I want you screaming my name."

Sam twisted, trying to throw off his hold. She felt a soft breeze on her bare breasts before she heard the hiss of the zipper on her dress. Her nipples instantly puckered, brazenly begging.

"Perfection," he whispered, gray eyes heavy with desire.

He watched her as he cupped them. As he swirled mindless circles around her nipples. As he rubbed the aching buds with his fingers. As he played with her relentlessly until her spine was bowing toward him. As he bent his head and flicked at one aching bud and then…feasted on her.

It was greedy and dirty and wet, and she was bent over his arm as he licked and nipped and drew her into the wet cavern of his mouth. Need pooled low, making her thong damp.

She moaned in protest when he released her, afraid he was abandoning her again. Until firm fingers clasped her calves.

Heart fluttering behind her rib cage like a trapped bird, Sam looked down.

He was kneeling between her thighs, his face tilted up. Elegant hands pulled her thighs until her ass was half hanging off the desk. And then for long, breathtaking moments he watched her—from her hair spilling over her bare shoulders, her knotted nipples wet from his mouth, the diamond glinting at her belly button, to her hips where her dress pooled.

His nostrils flared, and there was a harsh, saturnine quality to his expression that made the hunger in his eyes seem devouring. "I wish you could see yourself now. As I see you, Sameera. You'd never doubt what I think of you, then."

The gravelly edge of his voice at the end said something she couldn't catch. "Spread your thighs."

"What?" Heat crawled up her bare chest, up her neck until it crested in her cheeks.

"I want to taste you."

"But…you didn't even kiss me." She groaned inwardly. Could she sound more like a high-school girl with a crush on him?

He raised a brow. That damned brow was going to be the death of her.

He was on his knees in front of her, a position she was sure no one saw Alessandro Ricci in. His face was blue and green with bruises, his lower lip split. His hair messed up by her fingers. And yet he looked like he owned the world. Like he owned this room. Like he owned her.

"You're not comfortable with this?" His palms crawled up her calves, caressed her shins, cupped her knees, stroked the lines that connected her thighs and hips.

Sam flushed. He had to know she was dripping wet. He was showing her how this was going to play out between them. Not with soft whispers. No endearments. No sweet promises. This would be purely sexual. If he thought she'd back down, he didn't know her. "I have a question for you."

"Wondering if it will feel good?"

Alessandro didn't know what devil was goading him. It was clear from her face that he was going far too fast for her. That for all her defiant acceptance of his terms, she was young and had had one boyfriend. Which he couldn't even bear to think of.

He had to keep the boundaries clear in his own head, though. Had to keep this physical. He knew he could never allow himself love again, not after the loss he felt with Violetta.

"I already know it will feel amazing," she said, such trust in her eyes. "Are you doing it to prove something?"

"Ever since you walked in and said I was not..." He didn't want to hear his brother's name in this space between them. Not even on his own lips. He wanted no one in this space between them. "You're not the only one with filthy dreams, *bella*."

Her gaze glittered, as if he'd given her a priceless gift, and her hard swallow sent motion rippling down her chest. Eyes locked with his, she fisted her dress in one hand. The pulse at her neck quivered. Ever so slowly, she lifted her foot, placed it on his shoulder and bent her knee until she was all open for him. A flimsy thong, already damp, barely hid her from him.

Lust and tenderness warred within him, rioting out of control. He was never going to walk into this room and not see her sitting at the desk like this.

A little nervous, eyes darkened, brazenly open for his pleasure. *All his*.

He pressed her inner thighs obscenely wide until his shoulders were wedged under her knees and he buried his face in her mound. She jerked and groaned and buried her fingers in his hair when he notched his nose into her folds and breathed her scent in.

His erection throbbed with a life of its own, his muscles, already bruised and beaten, begging for release.

One hard tug ripped the thong off. Looking up, he let her see his rampant desire as he slowly traced the shape of her folds. "I knew you would be pretty all over. But how eagerly you drip for me..." Holding her gaze, he licked at the tip of one finger and made a humming sound at the back of his throat. "You taste divine."

"You still owe me a kiss," she whispered, her fingers sifting through his hair.

"After," he said, grinning. Under his fingers, her core fluttered. He rubbed his fingers up and down, and all around, without touching her clit. "When my mouth is full of your arousal. Then you can taste yourself on my lips."

Her spine arched into his touch, her hips doing the same. Color high in her cheeks, she dug her teeth into her lower lip. Her small breasts rose and fell with her shallow pants, the tight knots of her nipples beckoning for more. "Why didn't I guess that you would go slow enough that I'd expire from waiting?"

"What do you want, Sam?"

"I want to come. So hard that I black out. So hard that reality beats my dreams of you."

"That I can manage," he said and slowly penetrated her with one finger. She swallowed him like a vise, making his cock throb painfully. He cursed and worked in another finger. "You're so wet and tight for me. I can't wait to bury myself inside you, *bella*."

A hoarse mewl tore out of Sam's mouth. While she adjusted to the intrusion, he draped her wetness all over, up and down, teasing, stroking, building her up.

Her fingers in his hair tugged jerkily. He smiled against her inner thigh and nipped the sensitive skin. Her hips thrust forward, the muscles in her thighs tense and taut.

Burying his smile in her sex, Alessandro took a lick of her. Lingered with his tongue pressed against her opening. Sucked at the dampness.

Arching into his touch, she breathed out in rough pants.

He laved her with his tongue, but he didn't touch her clit yet. Not until her legs were locked over his upper back.

His name on her lips rang around, a soft litany, a harsh curse, begging for benediction. Every time she got to the edge, he retreated, soothed her, played with her. His erection pressed painfully against his trousers.

She was honey-sweet on his tongue, tart like grapes and an aphrodisiac like he'd never known. He'd only done this for one other woman in his life. The memory slammed into him. After she'd read it in some magazine and demanded it of him. He'd done it because he wanted something in return from her.

But with Sam, he'd wanted to from the first moment. Not just this—he wanted to do every thing he'd ever imagined to her. He wanted to mark her, inside and out, so that she'd never forget him. So that she never went to another man and didn't think of him.

A hard tug in his hair had him looking up. Her breasts heaved, her nipples all plump and pretty. And her eyes... dilated and full of a raw hunger for him.

Alessandro reached up with one hand and traced the scar, a strange hollow in his stomach.

"Please, Alessandro, no more..."

He tweaked one nipple, and she arched into the touch. "No more of this, *bella*?"

She cursed. "No more tormenting me."

"That's up to me, *tesoro*." He hooked the fingers inside her and pressed at the soft spot. Her mouth fell open on a guttural moan.

He watched her, his heartbeat thundering, every inch of him taut.

But when she looked at him, there was something in

her eyes that speared him in his chest. "You promised me pleasure."

He latched onto her clit with his lips and sucked.

She fell apart in seconds, her fingers scratching and digging into his neck, her sex contracting around his fingers, her hips chasing his mouth in an erotic tango. A soft cry fell from her lips as another climax followed the first.

When he pushed to his feet, she folded into his embrace—damp and soft and trembling—her arms thrown about his waist, face hidden in his chest. Her tears seeped through the shirt into his skin.

He pushed away damp tendrils from her forehead, tenderness engulfing him. "Sam?"

"Don't look at me. I'm just being naïve and silly."

"Take as long as you want, *bella*."

Gathering her to him, he held her, an indescribable sensation cracking open in his chest. This was no affair he would walk away from unscathed. This woman was doing something to him, and he had no defenses left. No willpower to fight.

"Damn, you're good at that," she whispered, before looking up.

"You're vocal and responsive and greedy," he said, tweaking her nose. "That makes you the perfect lover."

"That is high praise. Just don't expect the same kind of expertise from me, okay? I've barely scratched the—" she pressed a hand to her mouth, her eyes suddenly wary.

The last thing he wanted was a look into past lovers. It didn't matter if it was Matteo or someone else. Even the idea of another man seeing her laughter, her tears, her vulnerability threatened to reduce him into nothing but animal instincts.

"You don't have much experience," he said, with a grumbling sigh. "Shall we leave it at that?"

The wariness fled, and laughter danced in her eyes. "How are you hot even when you're so disgruntled and grumpy?"

He kissed her softly, slowly. She licked his lower lip, brown eyes shimmering. "I want to go down on you."

His cock twitched in his trousers. "Not tonight."

"Why do you get to make the rules?"

"Because I'm an arrogant asshole, and I want things the way I want them. When I want them."

She scrunched her nose at him. "Then, we're going to spend my stay fighting and not f—"

With one quick tug, he had her over his shoulder and made for the dark corridor that led to his bedroom. "So you *are* staying with me, then," he said. "I'm glad I've persuaded you."

She squealed and thumped his back. Sudden fear thrummed through him when she panted roughly. "Sameera, is this okay?"

She stilled for a second, then sighed. "Except for the fact that I'm enjoying being carried around like a sack of potatoes far too much for a modern twenty-first-century woman, yes. The view of your ass is particularly spectacular from here."

He tensed but asked anyway. "Will you tell me immediately if at any time you feel…different?" His fingers gripped the backs of her upper thighs.

Her hesitation pricked him. How did he explain to her that his protectiveness didn't mean he thought less of her when he didn't understand it himself? When he wanted to wrap her in a cocoon and never let her out of his sight? She'd surely hate him then.

"Yes, I'll let you know if I feel unwell. Would you like

to know the signs to watch out for?" she said after what felt like an eternity.

"*Sì.*"

"Migraine. Pallor. Light-headedness."

Relief shuddered through him. "Thank you for telling me."

Her hands moved over his back, stroking, kneading. Then she giggled. "FYI, breathlessness after an arrogant Italian expertly eats me out is not a danger sign. Please keep the orgasms coming."

His laughter echoed in the dark, and he ran his right palm up and down her leg. She nuzzled her face into his back in a gesture of affection that made him dizzy.

The corridor felt like a different reality, one which he didn't want to emerge from. He was smiling in the dark like a fool, and his chest felt lighter, his limbs looser than he'd felt in…forever.

She sighed. And he wondered if she felt the same sense of lightness he did. "Is this flying, Alessandro?"

"No, *tesoro.*"

"Then, maybe I'm dead? Because so much pleasure should have killed me."

He pushed the silky hem of her dress aside and smacked her bare ass lightly. "That's not funny," he bit out. Filthy, greedy man that he was, though, he let his fingers linger over the curve of her ass.

Her outraged gasp shivered down his spine. "Okay, that's not a kink I'm into."

"And what if I was?"

With a growl, the minx grabbed his back and pushed herself up. Her teeth dug into his upper shoulder. *Hard.* As a direct reaction, his cock was so hard now it was uncomfortable to walk. "Something like that work?"

"Maybe," he said, grinning.

Every time he'd imagined them together like this, he'd known it would be new. Different because of everything she inevitably forced him to feel. Passionate. Hot. But this...

He grunted when she bit him again, switched his palm to the other cheek, delivered another tap on her ass, and then while she was biting and cursing him, he walked into his bedroom. Which she'd completely made hers.

He threw her on his bed and climbed over her. Her complaints, her kisses, her demands, she made everything new. Made him want. Made him greedy.

Because the one thing he hadn't expected was laughter.

This joy in his chest every time he watched her. The overwhelming urge to make this moment last forever.

Sam thought she might be floating on clouds. Or was it that her body had never felt more like an instrument of pleasure?

Alessandro's weight on top of her as they sank into the bed...was heaven. The kiss he took while his chest crushed her breasts and his thick shaft perfectly notched up against her bare core left her reeling.

This kiss was a taking. A claiming, even. He didn't explore or tease or play, he simply ravished her mouth with a hunger that told her how long he'd wanted to do that.

Even better than the possessiveness of his kiss was the abandon with which she could touch him. The corded muscles of his neck, the hard slopes of his shoulder, the sparse hair on his defined chest, the ridges of his abdomen... In that moment, this powerful man was fully hers, and it went straight to her head. Eager for more, she thrust up her hips to dislodge him.

Instantly, he lifted his weight off her, his eyes frantically searching hers.

Fighting a smile, she snuck her hands lower, until she

could cup his hard length. He was like warm steel through his trousers.

A soft gasp escaped her as she imagined him inside her, pounding away at her and, best of all, losing control as he chased his own climax.

"Please, I want to touch you."

Something danced in his eyes before he nodded.

Somehow, she managed to undo his trousers and snuck her hand inside. He was hard and hot and...big enough to startle her a little.

"*Cristo, bella,*" he whispered, his mouth buried in her temple.

Staring up at his stark features, she squeezed him and stroked him from root to tip. The bead of pre-cum made her mouth water.

Head thrown back, Alessandro let out a grunt and a filthy curse that pinged against her skin. She did it a few more times, fascinated by the naked yearning in his face, before he arrested her wrist. "It's been a long while, Sameera. I would rather be inside you."

Sam bit her lip. "Has it been a long while out of choice?"

Slowly, he took her hand in his and laced their fingers. Then he moved off her, leaning on his side. They were both half-naked, and it was how he hesitated that made it so heart-wrenchingly intimate. She scooted closer, knowing the pull between their bodies was the anchor right then.

"I discovered, at a crisis point in my life, that I have an addictive nature." His gaze drifted away from the present. "It was either meaningless sex with strangers or...nothing. After I drowned myself in the first for a little while, I got disgusted with myself and stopped completely."

She traced the small scar through his brow. "I'm sorry it had to come to that."

He shrugged and kissed the back of her hand.

"Should I feel extra special, then?" she said, wriggling her brows in an exaggerated manner. Anything to chase away the dark shadows in his eyes.

Matteo had mentioned in an offhand comment once that his brother had lost the woman he had loved a long time ago. Now, all the pieces she knew about him began to form a picture that made her both like him and want to run away as far as possible.

His fingers sifted through her hair while a small smile played at his lips. The pad of his thumb traced her cheek with a reverence that filled her heart. "You're beautiful and witty and spirited. And probably a witch."

Pushing up, she kissed the corner of his mouth. Which he took full advantage of by devouring her mouth, again.

She was panting when she fell back against the bed, her fingers drawing doodles on his chest. The urgency to feel him inside her thrummed but this...this felt even more precious, more real. "I have to make this all very clinical by mentioning boring stuff. So much for a sophisticated summer fling."

He stilled, then nodded.

"I have an IUD." She cleared her throat. "Getting pregnant is dangerous for my heart condition. But when it's peak fertility time, I like to double up, just—"

"We'll use a condom."

Sam buried her face in his chest. "It's silly but—"

"Nothing about your health or your choices or your sense of safety is silly, *bella*. You insult me by suggesting otherwise."

Snuggling closer, she licked the line of his throat. "Thank you."

His fingers wrapped around her nape, before sliding into her hair, tugging her head up.

Smiling, he pressed a kiss to her temple. A hesitation danced in his eyes.

"Ask me whatever you want, Alessandro." She swallowed against that surge of affection she felt for him.

His fingers sifted through her hair slowly as he said, "You aren't resentful of the options that have been taken away from you?"

"Like babies? Or a long-term relationship with someone who might want the guarantee of a happy future?" she said, without missing a beat. "No."

She took a long breath, loving the intimacy of the dark night cloaking them like this. Loving that he was curious enough to want to know things about her. If this was just a fling, what would a real relationship with this man be like? "For a long time, all I wanted was to leave the hospital. Then it was being alone for an hour or two without my mom flipping out. Then came a solo shopping trip, an outing with friends, building to this confidence to go on a trip by myself. To tangle with an Italian stud. Now it's college and a career as an artist and traveling the world at some point." Looking at his stark, gorgeous features filled her with that joy of simply being there, in the moment with him. "I have so much to live for," she said, kissing the bristly underside of his jaw, "and I refuse to spend even a minute mourning the few things I can't have."

Nodding, he dipped his head, and this was a different kiss. It was soft and reverent and so full of promise that Sam couldn't sift through all the feelings it evoked.

The jarring tone of his cell phone broke the spell.

She straightened her dress as Alessandro answered his phone. A volley of Italian followed, bringing an instant pall over his features. Then he pressed a hand to his neck, a gesture that betrayed his discomfiture. "I have to go."

Sam looked out the large windows, out into the dark night beyond. "Now?"

"*Sì.*"

Frowning, Sam got off the bed and followed him into his cavernous closet. Even the sight of her clothes neatly hanging by his didn't throw her anymore.

"I have to go to Florence," he said softly, throwing a change of clothes into a small bag.

"Are you running away from me?" she whispered, giving voice to the crows pecking at her. In the flash of a second, it was as if the intimate world between them had fractured, thrusting him back into a reality she couldn't join.

He stilled. "I'm not a coward, *bella*."

"No, but you do like to control yourself, Alessandro." A long breath shuddered out of her as she claimed her power herself. "And I have challenged it from day one, no?"

Dropping the bag, he covered the distance between them to clasp her cheeks. "I have to visit a friend, an old woman in distress. And I can't abandon that responsibility because I'm desperate to fuck you." He pressed a quick kiss to her temple, then grabbed the bag. "If I get inside you, I won't want to leave."

Hurt found a tender spot in her. But she had power too in this relationship, whatever else he called it. She couldn't forget that.

"Are you saying that for my benefit or yours, Alessandro?"

Shock danced in his eyes before he left the bedroom, leaving her alone again.

CHAPTER NINE

SAM STEPPED OUT of the small, stuffy examination room and into the bright July afternoon. She smiled wide, loving the sunshine on her face. The cardiologist's office was located in a colorful piazza in the city of Como, a myriad of its intriguing lanes leading to grand galleries and beautiful churches.

Hitching her crossbody bag over her shoulder, she crossed the side street into the main thoroughfare and stilled.

Alessandro stood across the street, in his usual white dress shirt and dark trousers, leaning against a tinted Maserati and looking at his phone.

Even from the distance, the force of his presence hit her straight. Had he come to see her straight from the airport?

It had been two days since he'd left in the middle of the night. The next morning, Antonio had informed her that he'd gone straight to Tokyo.

He didn't owe her anything, she reminded herself again.

There was no future for them.

And yet, her belly knotted painfully every time she thought of returning home, of never being regarded again with that intense gaze, of never touching him again.

As if he felt her gaze on him, Alessandro looked up. Heat arched between them like a live wire. Her heart kicked against her rib cage. If it weren't for the fact that the cardiologist had told her she was perfectly fine, she'd have gone back in.

He crossed the street in long strides. But he didn't haul her into his arms or kiss her cheek or even pat her shoulder, as horrifically platonic as that sounded. In fact, he left at least a foot between them. Something told Sam it was a conscious decision, to stop himself. And just like that, her entire mood took a downswing.

She couldn't believe it was the same man who had gone down on her as if she were a feast he was starved for.

"What's wrong?" he had the gall to ask.

"Nothing. When did you get back?"

He jerked his chin at the building behind her. "How did your appointment go?"

"How did you know I'd be here?" she countered.

"Your phone was off, and no one at the villa knew where you were." An edge crept into his words. "Angelina told me."

"It's on Airplane mode. The roaming charges will be astronomical," she said, waving her phone. "I don't want to send my parents into debt again. When I'm at the villa, I connect to Wi-Fi." She sensed his hesitation—no, frustration. How were they starting off on such a wrong note? "Don't freeze me out. Just say what you want to."

"I have a phone and a chauffeured car I want you to use."

"Isn't that overkill?"

"I would like to reach you when I want to, Sameera."

"You say my name like that when you're railroading me into something."

He rubbed his brow with his fingertip, a sure tell that he was employing about hundred filters between his real feelings and what he said. "Is it such a pain to accommodate me?"

Was she imagining the flash of vulnerability in his eyes?

Sam sighed. It wasn't as if she wasn't eating his food, staying at his house, sleeping in his damned bed already. "Okay."

His jaw relaxed. "What did they say?"

"Just a routine checkup."

He ran the pad of his thumb under her eyes. Sam wanted to lean into the touch so badly that she swayed. "You look tired, *bella*."

"Is that all you see when you see me, Alessandro? Someone you have to check up on?"

He flinched at her sharp tone. And that made her feel like gum stuck on her shoe.

Hands tucked into his trousers, he watched her. "I can't seem to stop upsetting you." Hardness crawled into his words, etched into his features. "As long as you're mine, I'll worry over you, Sameera. I will not apologize for being the way I am."

Her mouth fell open. "Is that how you see me? As… yours?"

He frowned as if she was being dense on purpose. *"Sì."*

She should address the deeper issue here, but all she felt was this fizzy feeling, as if she were filled with bubbles of joy. Was this about seeing her as someone who was incapable, or about his needing to be in control?

"I haven't been sleeping well because I've been painting. What I had in mind, it's taking shape on the canvas." *He* was taking shape on her canvas, and she couldn't stop obsessing over it. "I'm at that stage where I just want to keep going, night or day. I don't care about sleep or food—"

Her stomach interrupted them with an embarrassingly loud growl. She'd slept in late and had to rush to the appointment. Which meant she'd missed breakfast. In the scheme of things, it wasn't a big thing. Until her body decided to turn it into a big thing.

Her own stubbornness kept her from admitting she was wrong. "Why aren't you at work?"

"Day off."

"Oh." In the weeks she'd been at the villa, she'd heard Maria complain that Alessandro worked ninety-hour weeks without a break. Even Antonio had asked his son to take it easy. "What were you planning to do?"

"Go to bed and stay there all day. With you."

All the doubts died an instant death, and Sam threw herself at him.

Wrapping her fingers around his neck, she pressed her mouth to his. Despite everything, all she wanted was to kiss him.

She tasted his surprise in his stillness. His mouth was soft and tasted of coffee, and he was hard and warm against her body. When she moaned in complaint, he laughed and opened for her. She licked into his mouth eagerly.

But he didn't deepen the kiss.

Instead, his mouth was soft, exploring, almost…reverent. His emotions buffeted her, carrying her along. This kiss wasn't like the one in his study. Or the one in the kitchen. This wasn't a prelude to sex. No rushing toward a destination. This kiss said he wanted nothing more than to be here with her in this moment.

She buried her face in his chest, loving the thunder of his heart against her cheek. Part of her didn't want to keep acknowledging what he was becoming to her. But part of her knew this moment would be over soon.

Some of the tension she'd felt in his frame dissipated. That he liked her telling him how he made her feel was obvious. Why didn't he reciprocate?

No, she wasn't going to analyze this. He'd taken the day off to spend it with her. That said more than words ever could. "By the way, I'm very competitive when it comes to these things."

He tucked a lock of her hair behind her ear, and she buried a smile that wanted to bloom. "What things?"

Casually, she took his hand and laced his fingers with hers. That infinitesimal stillness came over him, but he shook it off. She dragged him toward the noisy piazza. "Two-point-five to nothing. I want to even that score."

"Two-point-five?"

"Our orgasm count."

His laughter exploded onto the quiet street. The sound dug its very roots into her heart. More than one woman stopped and stared at the stunning picture he made.

Her fingers tightened around his—something dark and possessive blooming in her chest. She wanted to drag him back to the privacy of their bedroom, to cup that laughter and hide it away for herself. She wanted the other women to stop looking at him. "Alessandro?"

"Sì?"

"I know you said this is a fling, but I'm out if you…if you even look at someone else." She sounded particularly bloodthirsty, but she didn't care.

"Okay." His gray eyes were warm when he looked down at her. "How did you come up with the half?"

Sam pushed the stubborn lock of hair from his forehead back. "The half comes from me trying to…" she licked her lips "…to get off to you the other night after you left. I didn't quite manage it."

Naked desire made his eyes pop. "Then, let's go. I want to see how well you keep all these promises."

"I've got another appointment." Something darkened in his gaze, and she hurried to explain. "With Giuseppe, this guy I met at the club."

"The exclusive thing works both ways, Sameera." Pure steel in his tone.

They started walking again. Instantly, he adjusted his pace to match hers. "He's a painter," Sam said.

"What do you know about him?"

"Angelina's already checked him out. She's as overbearing as you."

"Now I know why I always liked her."

Sam laughed at his sarcasm. "I can't ditch Giuseppe. It's a series of…appointments."

"Sounds important."

"He's painting me. Nude."

Alessandro stopped walking. "Going all in on this vacation, *bella*?"

Sam nodded.

He rubbed his neck. "What made you decide to do this all of a sudden?"

"Well, you saw the dress I wore to the club. I met Giuseppe there, and we got to talking about different painting techniques. At first, he—"

"Asked you to go home with him," Alessandro supplied.

"I said I wasn't interested. He said it was bad luck for him. We chatted a bit, then he asked me about the scar. He said he'd love to paint me nude for a series he's doing about imperfect bodies. Usually, I wouldn't have agreed. But it took me a long time to have a healthy relationship with my body. This is a way of celebrating it."

"You should," Alessandro said softly.

"Is it weird that I wish you were a little jealous that another man will see me naked?"

"Oh, I am, *tesoro*. But—"

"We aren't in a real relationship. I know," Sam said before he could.

"I was going to say that's my problem to deal with. Not yours."

"Oh."

"Is he going to sell it?"

"Of course. I wish I could buy it myself. But I've seen his work, and I can't afford it." It had made her feel strange at first, the idea that someone would own a nude painting of her. But she also wanted her body, her courage in this small act, to be a source of inspiration and joy for another. "He's offering me a chunky model's fee, though. It will be displayed at a gallery in a few months. The tickets are already sold out."

Sam eyed the peaceful square. The sunny day, the colorful shops and restaurants and Alessandro's fingers clasped around her, it was a moment out of her dreams.

She wanted the dark intimacy of his desire, but she wanted this time with him even more. She wanted to talk to him, get to know him. She wanted to steal away pieces of him whether he was willing to part with them or not.

"I have a couple of hours before the sitting," she said, managing to sound breezy. "Keep me company until then?"

"If you promise to go to bed on time tonight," he countered instantly.

"Fine." She dragged him to a faded but cheerful yellow table away from the rest, one with a chess board drawn into its worn grain.

When she went for the chair opposite him, he tugged her into his lap. And then he took her mouth with a roughness that made her gasp. On and on the kiss went, his tongue thrusting in an erotic dance that made her cheeks heat.

A little urgency, a lot of impatience and a whole lot of darkly possessive declaration that she was his—despite who saw her naked—the kiss was eloquent.

"Whether I sleep or not is up to you, isn't it?" she whispered, when he released her. "I'm not letting you leave me alone in that bed again."

That raised brow greeted her like an old friend.

It was the warmth he got in his eyes when she argued with him, the hitch of his mouth when he smiled at her, that little tic in his jaw when his control was teetering on the edge that returned that fizzy feeling to her chest.

Alessandro knew he should've waited for her at the villa, waited for her to finish her appointments and come to him. He could catch up on much-needed sleep, try to recoup the time he'd lost because he'd walked away from two more days of business meetings.

But he was done denying himself this small pocket of pleasure.

To leave Sam that night, her soft pliant body, her flushed face, her wide smile had been the hardest thing he'd ever had to do.

Not just because what he wanted was to be buried inside her, because he wanted to discover if having Sam, if losing himself in her body, would rid him of this…obsession. This constant need. This…voracious hunger.

She looked like a sunflower when she teased him. Or laughed with him. Or when she mentioned orgasms and blushed fiercely. Or when she got mad at him. Or when she tried to hide how much he hurt her or how aroused she got around him.

Every minute with her was like standing alone in an entire field of sunflowers. He constantly felt as if he'd miss something precious or that he could spend a lifetime with her and still be unable to take it all in.

The want she made him feel was a drive for life. A fire in his belly. A newfound appreciation for each day, each minute. As if she were introducing him back to himself, one facet at a time. And he was on constant edge, trying to manage it all. Trying to not feel so much. Trying to do damage control for when she left him and suddenly he had no one but himself again. Nothing but a yawning ocean of loneliness in front of him.

The alternative that he could ask her to stay was unthinkable. Unbearable.

"What are your plans for fall?" he said, once their orders were out of the way.

"Starting college for a business degree. Eventually, I want to stretch beyond just oil paintings. They're tedious and time-consuming, but I love them. I need to build passive income streams." She dipped her fork into the pasta and took a big bite. "It would be fun if I can get out of California, but out of state means I'll end up with huge loans. Also, I don't think Mom can take it. A community college is my best bet."

"If you need money for college, I'll pay…" He cleared his throat when she pinned him with a fierce look. "I will loan it to you."

She cast him a sweet look that packed a punch. If he weren't so damned turned on by her temper, by her clever moves in chess, by her voracious appetite, that sweet sarcasm that made her eyes pop would've floored him. "And why would you do that?"

"Because I have more money than I know what to do with, *tesoro*." Irritation coated his words. How did he explain to her that he wanted to remain a part of her life even when he wasn't there? He didn't understand it himself. "Like I said, it can be a loan." There, he was even making all kinds of adjustments for her.

"So we're going to keep in touch after I leave?"

He suppressed the fingers of panic that rose at that idea. "You're being difficult on purpose."

"Just establishing the etiquette for after-fling behavior."

"Sameera…"

"It's bad enough I haven't told Mom everything. The last thing I want to explain to her is where I got the college tuition from."

"You haven't told her—"

"That I've swapped brothers? No."

"Don't say it like that."

"That's what everyone thinks. Even Angelina. Though, she won't say it to my face." She ran the tip of his finger down his tight jaw. "It doesn't bother me."

It bothered him. Not what people thought of him and her, but how they treated her, how they saw her. That his brother would always have a claim on her affection bothered him.

It was the height of hypocrisy after he'd declared that this was nothing but a fling. But he wanted no other man to have such significance in her life. No other man to know her as well as he did.

Cristo, there was nothing rational in this.

"Mom will say you're taking advantage of me," she said, that familiar rancor back in her voice. "At least your aunt puts the blame at my feet."

"*Zia* knows? How's that a good thing that she blames you?"

"Because she thinks I have enough sense to make my own decisions. Even if they're morally wrong. As to why…" she bit her lip "…Matteo told your parents. He's continuing his I-will-admit-all-my-sins phase."

"And as usual, he doesn't think of anyone else. Was *Zia*… rude to you?"

Her smile made him relax. "Oh, she's far too nice to say anything to my face, Alessandro. You know that. But she's been considerably cooler toward me. I caught something in Italian along the lines of...*coming between brothers*, but who knows? To give him credit, Matteo did explain that he'd cheated on me. Clearly that doesn't absolve me of the sin of trapping you when I was done with him."

"You didn't trap me, *bella*. If anything—"

"What, Alessandro? You trapped my poor, naïve, unsophisticated self, is that it? Seduced me away from your brother because I didn't know better?"

He realized then that he could hurt her, in ways he hadn't understood until then. Gripping her chin, he tugged until she looked into his eyes. "Thinking like that means invalidating everything you've endured, everything that makes you who you are today. I'll never again make the mistake of thinking you less than who you are, *tesoro*. All of you."

Shock flared her eyes wide. Swallowing, she looked away from him.

How did he tell her it wasn't their age difference or her health or Matteo that bothered him? That it was his lack of control when it came to her, his ever-growing need to steal her away from the world, to protect her, even from himself, that ate through him?

It didn't matter that this was temporary. That she thought of this as an adventure, that she probably even considered him to be a dangerous, exotic once-in-a-lifetime ride she'd never try again.

Christo, even that didn't dent his self-esteem. On the contrary, he found immense pleasure in the fact that she found him attractive, more so than his own brother.

Whatever he told himself, it didn't change the intensity of his feelings for her. Didn't change the fact that he was beginning to crave more and more of her, even knowing there was no future for them.

Before the moment could be fractured by his incapability to verbalize his chaotic thoughts, his chauffeur appeared at their table with a bag in his hand. He took the bag and handed it to Sameera.

She tore through the packaging and spread the contents out onto the table in front of him. Little jars of oil paints in a rainbow of colors and a variety of brushes and a bunch of other things he'd picked cluttered the table, tinkling against each other. If it were up to him, he'd have bought the entire store.

"There's more," he added, his heart crawling into his throat at her stunned expression.

His first impulse had been to buy her jewelry. He'd discarded the idea immediately. He wanted her to remember him when she left.

Now every time she painted using one of these colors, she'd think of him.

Really, he was a selfish bastard.

Her fingers shook as she picked a glass jar with amber color that glittered in the sunlight. "These brushes and paints...they're super expensive. How did you even know this brand was the..." Then she gasped, eyes going impossibly wide in her small face.

Unable to help himself, he ran his knuckles over the sharp jut of her collarbones, once again marveling at the dizzying complexity of how fragile she looked and how strong she was beneath. And while she'd bash him on the head if he told her, both parts enthralled him.

The strength and the fragility...everything about her called to him.

"It's the best gift anyone's ever given me."

And then she was back in his lap, trailing kisses all over his face, whispering things he couldn't make out, and he thought it was the happiest he'd ever been.

CHAPTER TEN

SAM WOKE UP to find the bedroom bathed in strips of moonlight.

Alessandro had picked her up outside Giuseppe's apartment, having waited for two hours. She'd fallen asleep the moment he'd started the car. By the time she'd showered, he had disappeared.

Blinking, she sat up and found him in the armchair. Legs kicked out in front, fingers clasped on his abdomen, eyes closed. His dark hair gleamed with wetness, that aura of quiet confidence clinging to him in repose too.

Gray sweatpants hung low on his hips, and his bare chest was lean but defined.

She moved to stand in front of him, skin thrumming with molten awareness. For all that he claimed that this was an affair, they still hadn't had sex. If anything, he seemed almost…reluctant. All her insecurities about how inexperienced she was crashed into her.

With Matteo, sex had been another milestone, a rite of passage, even another item in her adulting checklist. She had wanted the experience more than she had wanted him specifically, which was horrible and stupid in hindsight.

With Alessandro, though, all she wanted was to lose herself in him and make him lose all sense of control.

"Sameera?" he said, coming awake. "Everything okay?"

"Why didn't you join me in bed?"

He straightened in the armchair, the soft light from the standing lamp making his pecs shine. "You didn't invite me in."

"What do you think the last few weeks have been about?" she snarled, throat tight.

"You were deeply asleep," he said in that same calm tone. "I didn't want to disturb you."

"You want me or not?"

He spread his legs in a wicked invitation, and her gaze slid down his body. The shape of his long, thick erection, evident against his sweatpants, made her skin prickle. His gray gaze patiently waited for her to come back. "I'm always like this now, *tesoro*. All it takes is a thought of you."

Squaring her shoulders, she moved forward until she was straddling his legs. Putting her weight on the armrest, she climbed into his lap. His thighs were rock hard against her flesh, and his scent of cloves and pine wrapped around her like a tendril of lust.

His palms stroked her hips, her ass, her thighs, over and over. The scrape of his abrasive palms against her smooth skin left pockets of heat behind. Those gray eyes searched hers. "You're nervous, *bella*." His hands drifted upward, spanning the tight curve of her waist, rough knuckles brushing the underside of her breasts but not lingering. "We'll take it slow, Sameera," he said, a ragged edge to his words. His open mouth drew a wet-hot trail over her jaw.

Swatting his hands away, Sam scooted upward on his thighs until his cock speared her, notching perfectly against her clit. "I don't want slow or controlled, Alessandro. I want to consume you, break you apart. Until I know you like no one else does."

Squeezing her hips hard, he jostled her on his throbbing

length, just enough to send dampness pooling at her core. "Why, *bella*?"

Leaning down, she bit his lower lip. "I don't know, okay? I…have never felt like this before."

"In that, we are not apart, *tesoro*." Then took her mouth in their hottest, hungriest kiss yet.

Sam couldn't catch her breath. She didn't want to. He ravaged her mouth, breathing out endearments when she willingly took it and curses when she got aggressive. His tongue thrust into her mouth in a vulgar parody of what she needed somewhere else. He whispered things in Italian she didn't understand but made her shiver.

He stroked and kneaded every rise and dip of her curves. His fingers moved up and down, charting her skin. On every downward slide, they pressed against her breasts, but never touching enough, never following through.

"Please, Alessandro, just come inside me now…"

"No, *bella*. Let's get you ready first, or I will hurt you."

Sam moaned into his mouth, desperate for him to be as mindless as her. "I want fast and furious," she said biting at his lower lip.

He shook his head, his hands busy rolling up the hem of her T-shirt. "Not for our first time, no."

She lost her protest as her shirt came off. Long fingers circled her nipples, which were tight and achy even without touch. His palm flat on her belly, he pushed her until she was leaning back, her hair a silky waterfall down her bare back.

Her balance as precarious as her heart's yearning, Sam bowed back.

Something dark and wicked shone in his eyes as they trailed over her breasts and lower. Much lower where her pink thong was mostly damp and swallowed up by her folds.

"You're so beautiful, Sam. I don't know where to begin. If I'm not careful, I could—"

"I don't want careful, Alessandro," Sam said, leaning forward. "If so, we should stop now before I—"

Another kiss and this one was pure male dominance, with all his expertise pitted against her relative inexperience.

His fingers trailed all over again, tracing her scar, playing with her breasts, drawing circles around her nipples, tugging at the diamond piercing at her belly button, leaving pockets of heat wherever they went.

"God, you're such a tease." Sinking her fingers into his hair, she tugged.

Laughing against her thudding heart, he bent. Tongued her nipple in a wet lash. Did it over and over, a featherlight touch that disappeared too fast for her to pin down.

She looked down, and he looked up as his mouth closed over the taut peak. That simple, searing eye contact was the most erotic thing she'd ever known.

How Alessandro looked at her—as if everything about her was fascinating, as if he couldn't get enough—was just as arousing as what he did to her with that mouth. He thrummed her other nipple with his fingers as he drew the first one into his mouth and suckled, hard.

Rivulets of sensation zoomed down to concentrate at her core.

Fighting his hold, she moved up on him, and they both groaned. He sucked and tugged at her nipples until she was so sensitive that she couldn't take it anymore. She writhed on him, trying to find the right angle, while release hovered just out of reach.

Sinking her fingers into his hair, she tugged hard. "Give me what I need. Make me come. Now."

"I told you I like you best demanding and clingy." With

that, he ripped her thong off. His thumb found her clit and stroked, slower and gentler than she needed, fingers dipping into her wetness.

"*Cristo*, you're so wet," he said and then dripped her dampness all over her clit. Over and over, up and down, he played with her folds, flicked her clit but not enough to get her off.

Sam bent her spine, buried her mouth in his neck and bit him.

His laughter joined the symphony of sensations sizzling across her skin, a kaleidoscope of pleasure urging her on and on. Then slowly, ever so gently, he penetrated her. One finger, then two.

The fit was tight and burned, and Sam never wanted him to stop.

"*Maledizione*, you clench me so tightly. What will you do to my cock, Sameera?" He thrust his fingers in and out, stretching her, his long fingers pressing and nudging a spot inside of her that made her shudder.

Sam rocked in tune with his thrusts, every inch of her coalescing at that spot.

On and on, he caressed her, urging her on with his filthy words. Never shifting his gaze from hers. She was chasing his mouth at her nipples for a deeper pull, his fingers inside her for a better angle, but it was his eyes that made her fly.

One second it wasn't enough and the next too much. Pleasure fluttered its wings across her body, spiraling down and down, until it splintered. She moaned and rocked into it, desperate to hold on.

Alessandro lavished openmouthed kisses over her neck and shoulders, his fingers still wrenching the after-tremors inside her.

"You come so prettily, Sam. The sounds you make..." he

said, his mouth at her temple, his fingers pulling out of her with a squishy sound, leaving her feeling achingly empty. "I need to feel you bare, *bella*."

Then he was pushing down his sweatpants onto his corded thighs, pulling her up onto his abdomen until his shaft pressed up against her sensitized clit. The heat from his skin burned her, the slide of that thick length against her folds making her arch into him.

"Inside me," Sam whispered. As long as he made her feel like this again. As long as he looked at her as if he wanted to consume her. "Now, Alessandro."

She was a rag doll in his arms as he lifted her up, tore open a condom packet and rolled it down his length. And then the broad head of his erection notched at her entrance. The sight of him playing with her folds, draping himself in her wetness…made new embers heat through her.

Sam watched in growing fascination and spiraling alarm. He was big, and it had been so long for her. It was going to hurt. Just as she braced herself to not betray too much, he cupped her hips, lifting her.

Panting, she pushed down her weight, hands on the slopes of his shoulders. "No, here. Now."

"Even if you've come, it will hurt like this. You're fragile." His refusal was steel even as his gray gaze was hazy with lust.

It was the wrong word to use on her. She wanted no accommodation, no second-guessing on his part. She wanted him to take her without apologies.

She went for his mouth. She licked and laved at his lips, nipped and bit, stroked her tongue against his until his hands wandered away from her hips to cup her breasts. He cupped and played with them, the tips of his fingers flicking against her nipples.

He groaned as she pushed up to her knees, took him in her hand and dipped the head of his shaft inside. One inch, then two. She hissed as even that stretched her impossibly. The burn of it made his kiss that much keener, sweeter.

With one downward thrust, she impaled herself on him. His hips thrust up instinctively, as though he couldn't stop himself. Which meant he stroked into her fluttering channel in one hard thrust, until he was lodged all the way in.

His palm on her shoulder held her down from jerking away. He went so deep that Sam wondered if he'd ever not been a part of her.

The pain came then. A flash of sharp, achy burn that meant she couldn't keep from crying out. His long, filthy curse accompanied it. Sam breathed in a long gulp and breathed out.

Fingers gripped her chin roughly, tilting her head down. His eyes were stormy, the black at the center swallowing up the gray like a dark cloud. "You're the most infuriating, outrageous—"

Sam stole another kiss. She wasn't experienced enough to seduce him—not yet, but she knew him now. Knew what he liked. Knew he wanted her more than he let on. Knew to tease him and taunt him until his control shattered.

So she swallowed his anger. Cajoled with her mouth. Petted him with everything she had in her. Begged him. Told him how much she wanted him to move inside her. How she'd struggled to shed her inhibitions before. How she wanted no one but him.

He pulled away with a harsh exhale, brows tied. "You're not naïve at all, *tesoro*. You're conniving and manipulative, and I could have really hurt you."

Sam nipped his lower lip, the harsh edge of his voice

curling around her spine. "What I am is determined, Alessandro, to have you. In every way possible."

The fire in his eyes refused to thaw. "You should've let me take you slowly—"

She caught his upper lip with her teeth this time, and he groaned and took over the kiss. For a few seconds, there was nothing but the sounds of their mouths tugging and licking.

A fervent urgency filled her, and she trailed her mouth down his jaw to that hollow in his neck that called to her. She licked him, tasting the salt and sweat of his skin, breathed him in, and still it wasn't enough.

It amazed her that she could touch him like this, warm muscle and sinew and skin. She wished she could touch his heart too. Wished she could write her name on it, like a name tag to claim possession.

"Do you know you say a lot of *you should*s to me? Also, every time you say Sameera in that forbidding tone, it makes me want to defy you, just on principle."

His hands, finally, moved from where they'd had clamped around her hips to stop her from moving. Mouth buried in her neck, he touched her breasts, pinched her nipples and dragged his hands down to play with her clit until she was dripping again and the intrusion of him burned less.

"I promised myself that I would never hurt you, Sam."

"And I told you to not treat me as if I were fragile, Alessandro. This momentary pain, which is already gone by the way, is nothing for me."

Sam shifted her hips experimentally. Jesus, it felt good. More than good. It felt amazing. So she did it again, and his answering thrust came a breath later. Their groans rippled through the air around them. Her channel still felt unbearable achy and full, but that only amplified every little twang of pleasure.

Before she could build a rhythm, he pushed up to his feet, and the movement sent sensation rippling where they were joined.

Her back hit his bed, a cool embrace in contrast to the wall of warmth at her front. She grimaced when he slipped out of her.

Climbing up after her, he didn't miss it. The night lamp she'd turned on bathed his naked body in strips of light. Straddling her, he bent down and kissed her. "Shall I take what I want, then, Sameera?"

"Yes. It's all I want. If you hurt me, you'll make it better. Don't you get what this is all about, Alessandro? I trust you. I want you. I'm here with you because you make me want to take risk after risk."

His forehead pressed to hers, he drew in a sharp, shuddering breath.

He said nothing with his mouth after that. Oh, but his lips, and kisses and nips and licks and hands and caresses and grunts said everything…

He built her up all the way to the edge before he thrust into her. Except for a pinch that lasted a few seconds, it was that achy, stretching fullness when he was inside her. Even then, he gave her time to get used to him.

Kissed her, licked her, laved her…and then he picked up his pace as he angled her body the way he wanted it, pushing her knee into her chest. Every thrust hit a spot inside of Sam that seemed to hold it all tightly together.

And then there were his fingers at her clit, and his thrusts hit that spot again and again, and she was nothing but spiraling sensation, and on the next breath she exploded into a million fragments and screamed his name and clung to him, and he shifted her again and then he was pounding into her, hard enough to make her see stars, hard enough for her core to take a battering, hard enough for the heavy bed to creak and moan, and then he pinned her down with his hips, arresting her movements, using her body for nothing but his pleasure, and his release when it came made him shudder in her arms, and a roar fell from his mouth, and it was the sweetest sound Sam had ever heard.

Alessandro watched as Sameera slipped into a deep sleep, one arm thrown around him, feet tucked in between his own. His heart beat like it was on steroids, even though his release had been hours ago.

She had been sore after but wouldn't admit to it when he'd carried her into the shower. Had seen the marks he'd left on her skin and liked them. Had understood finally how much she trusted him.

And yet, that trust didn't feel like a weight, like his other relationships. Her expectations that he take everything he wanted from her was like undoing a shackle he'd wound around himself.

She asked for nothing and yet somehow took everything he had.

It felt like discovering a patch of sunlight after living in shadows and darkness. Like a gift he wasn't sure he deserved.

As dawn's pink and orange light illuminated the room, he gathered her closer. Marveled at how easily he could get used to sleeping with her wrapped around him like this. To wake up with her like this for a million mornings.

Sated in body and mind, he couldn't stop his heart from wondering about the shape of a future with her.

CHAPTER ELEVEN

ALESSANDRO DIDN'T GO into work for two whole weeks. The day after the weekend, his cell phone blew up enough for Sam to know how unprecedented it was.

The first three or four days, she ate and slept and woke to have sex. For his part, he fed her in bed, drew her rose-scented baths, cajoled her into a game of chess and, when she was in that sleepy, lazy state, played the piano for hours. Only coming to bed when she dragged him to it, pulling at his stiff fingers.

He was insatiable. She was even more so. For years, she'd wondered if sex would ever be something she craved. If her history had somehow inhibited her ability to simply let go, to live in the moment. She definitely had frustrated Matteo on more than one occasion with her lukewarm responses and halfhearted interest.

But now, she knew the taste of that mindless craving.

Alessandro and his kisses, caresses, lazy lovemaking and sudden bouts of have-to-be-inside-you put paid to any and all doubts she'd ever harbored.

On day four, they ventured into his study through the secret corridor to pick up something to read. Because her body needed a break and he needed a distraction, he'd declared.

She'd discovered she had muscles in places she hadn't even given a thought to. They'd spent hours lazing in separate recliners, discussing Jane Austen and classical music. Then they played chess while eating cheese and fruit.

On the way back, she'd kissed him in the darkness, feeling that urgency of having wasted too many precious hours. That itch beneath the skin that wanted to touch him, lose herself in him. He'd offered token protest, groaned when she'd bit him, picked her up, propped her up against the wall as if she weighed nothing and then thrust into her.

She had been ready. He'd checked. Still, the first thrust had felt raw and rough and painful but oh so glorious. When she'd been unable to hide her grimace on the second thrust, he'd pulled out, sunk to his knees, whispered apologies and soft kisses into her belly and then made her come again with the featherlight flicks of his tongue.

She'd been sobbing at the end, alternately begging for more and for him to stop.

By the time the next weekend rolled around, he'd thoroughly trounced her at chess, in so few moves that all her competitiveness spilled out. When she had attacked him on the bed, outraged that he'd pretended to lose to her until now, he'd let her straddle him and then, while he was inside her, he'd confided that she'd beaten him the other times because he'd been far too distracted imagining her in all kinds of positions.

On the eighth day, he worked from home while she painted in the studio he'd arranged for her. Tongue in cheek, she had said she could bear it if he went in to Milàn for work, but he'd insisted on staying near her. He'd ruined her concentration by coming to his knees in front of her, punishing—or rewarding—her for teasing him.

They were both people used to silence, who craved solitude and yet somehow to find it with each other too. As if their silences had their own language to communicate with.

They spent hours together not talking, her painting, him working, then coming together in a flash of biting kisses and rough, needy sex.

Sam didn't understand the magic of their togetherness and decided against trying.

As remote and untouchable he was, Alessandro said hello when she called her cousin Kavi who never coddled or was condescending to her. He'd been shirtless and looked thoroughly debauched, and when Sam had ambushed him because Kavi begged to see *who Sam was tapping*, he played along with his arms wrapped around her while Kavi gushed over his good looks and teased Sam with horribly intrusive questions. Alessandro had then informed Kavi in that deep voice that Sam had seduced him with her stubbornness… It was the moment Sam knew he had her heart. Faulty and courageous as it was, it had gone over into his keeping.

And she also knew the inevitability of it shattering into so many pieces soon and of being able to do nothing to stop it.

They were like a newly married couple on their honeymoon, Angelina told a stunned Sam when she'd come down for breakfast on the second weekend. Sam hadn't been expecting all of the Riccis to be right there in the kitchen having breakfast.

Alessandro still worked from the villa, and Sam had started painting him with oils. They escaped one evening to a museum, which had of course been emptied of people for him. Because he didn't want the world to intrude on her time with the art, he'd said.

Dismayed, Sam stared down at her short shorts and old T-shirt of Alessandro's. It wasn't indecent, but it was an undisputed announcement to a kitchen and backyard full of family, cousins and close friends.

How was she to know that her sudden cravings for carbs would result in all of the Riccis bearing witness to her walk of shame? Was it a walk of shame if she wasn't ashamed of all the things she'd done with him?

Sam filled her coffee cup blushing beetroot red no doubt and said hello to people Maria insisted on introducing her to. Several male cousins winked at her. A couple of aunts looked her up and down, as if to see what all the fuss was about. One, introduced as Lucia, muttered something about violets.

Looking away, Sam took the picnic basket a beaming Maria handed her, piled with enough food to last them another week, and tried not to run. But even in her haste, she didn't miss the fact that Alessandro's aunt had loaded it up with protein bars, the kind she liked, and yogurt cups.

She'd almost teared up on the stairs. Yep, she'd finally reached the stage where her body had been through such a wringer that facing reality felt like a hard crash.

She had half finished a protein bar by the time she returned to his suite.

Alessandro was at the piano. Back bare, spine erect, sweatpants sitting low on his hips, playing another heart-wrenching tune.

Sam stood at the door and listened, loath to disturb him. Even to her untrained ears, it was clear that he was a gifted pianist. It was his one addiction he didn't smother. The music soared through her, filling her, saying things she knew Alessandro would never put into words.

She loved seeing him like this, knowing him in this moment. More intimate than sex. Knowing without doubt that no one else crossed the barrier he put between himself and the world. Not even his family.

And yet he had let her in.

Despite all his warnings, he'd opened himself to her. He'd made the last few weeks the best time of her life, even when they'd been fighting, even when he'd been rejecting this thing between them.

"Sam?" he said, turning around.

"FYI," she said, swinging the basket onto the coffee table, "not my fault if people ask you later about planning a wedding."

The shutter fell down so hard in his eyes that he might as well have slammed a door in her face. "Sameera..."

"It's a joke, Alessandro." Her laughter released with a hard edge she couldn't hide. "I wouldn't be able to tolerate your controlling personality beyond this tawdry affair."

Something tightened in his face, giving his features that saturnine cast. "I did not realize this was *tawdry* to you."

And she realized, with dawning dismay, that she had just hurt him. Worse, she had done it to see if she could. "Okay, maybe *tawdry* isn't the word. But I definitely fit the label of a *mistress*. You have spent a fortune on just my painting supplies, and we rarely go anywhere."

"All you had to do was ask to go somewhere, *bella*. And you're not my mistress," he said, looking down his nose. As if the very word was offensive to his entire being. "What put you in such a mood?" he said, his anger already under control. As if she were still that puzzle.

Sam sighed. "Your entire family, extended included, is in the kitchen, overflowing into the patio." She tugged at the neckline of her T-shirt. "They're celebrating Matteo's progress to the wheelchair."

"He'll tire himself out."

"Angelina's watching him like a hawk." She gathered her tangled hair and redid her messy bun. "I wish I hadn't walked into the kitchen looking like this. Honestly," she said and something ugly and hot crawled into her throat and refused to dislodge, "I don't like attention, and I definitely don't like being looked at as though I—"

"How do you think you look, Sameera?"

"Disheveled. Like I just crawled out of bed after a weeklong sex session. Like I'm not good enough for you."

"Maybe it's the other way around, *bella*. Maybe they think I'm too old, too jaded, too much of an arrogant asshole for someone like you. As for how you look..." his lashes fell and rose "...you're beautiful." It wasn't what he wanted to say. "As to my family, they have no boundaries."

She shrugged, that angry itchy feeling persisting under her skin. "If you want to join the party, please go ahead. I might catch a nap."

"Not interested."

"Won't they expect you?"

"Not even if I didn't have you here with me," he said, a small smile wreathing his lips. "I'm not into parties or crowds either. I don't go to clubs. I don't spend hours with friends. I'm...sort of a loner."

She nodded, struck again by how alike they were. "I met your great-aunt Lucia. It was interesting."

Sam was sure his aunt had said Sam could never be Violetta. And that was it—the source of her sudden, unnamed distress.

The woman had Alessandro had loved and lost. The one that Angelina had accidentally dropped into their conversations more than once. The one he clearly still loved after all these years. "I think she also mumbled *Indian*, *too thin*, *too American* and something else before she turned up her rather beaky nose at me. Apparently, no aspect of me lives up to her standards."

Violetta...the name pinged around in her brain, hitting

the walls, out of control, the echoes increasing and spiraling and amplifying until it was all she heard. She even raised her hands to close them over her ears. As if she could shut it out.

And Sam knew, like she'd known that first moment when she'd seen him that something was changing within her, with that intuitive certainty, that Violetta had meant everything to him. That the Alessandro Sam had got was the after-Violetta version. That she'd only got a part of him, not the whole.

Loving Violetta and losing her had changed him. And suddenly, it felt unbearable that he still belonged to that ghost from the past. That he wasn't hers completely. Even the splintered version of his heart that was left wasn't hers.

He wasn't offering it to her.

But she wanted it.

"Aunt Lucia is an old crone who doesn't approve of anyone. She calls my cousin's wife a crow to her face."

"So the fact that I haven't been assigned a bird is a compliment?"

"You want compliments, Sam?" he said, spreading his legs as if to make space for her. "I will give them to you."

"Don't patronize me," she said, feeling wonky in her own skin. Even at her sickest, she'd never felt this disoriented. As if she was falling endlessly.

"You're upset." He frowned and swept his gaze all over her. "Come, Sameera," he said in that calm, quiet voice that sent shivers down her spine. "I will make you feel better, *bella*."

"I don't want what you're offering. Not today," she said, her own voice breathless and shallow.

He didn't call her out on her bad temper. Instead, he leaned his elbows against the piano, pushed his legs forward and waited. As if he were offering himself to her.

Afternoon sunlight poured through the window, over the olive-toned skin stretched taut over lean muscles. With that much light dappling over him, she could see the small imperfections that made him so gorgeous—the small scar under his chin, the slight bifurcation in his right brow, the too-tight jut of his cheekbones that gave him such a severe profile, the spot on his neck that he'd missed while shaving last night because she'd distracted him…

God, she was becoming dizzyingly addicted to running her fingers through the hair that coated his chest, the slight flare of his nostrils when he wanted to have sex and the predatory stillness that followed because his first instinct was to control the impulse, the warmth of his eyes that betrayed how much he liked her… She wished she could capture him with her brushes in this moment.

But more than that, she wanted to stay in this moment with him forever. And that was a terrifying thought that had been returning with an unerring frequency.

But right now, something else trumped fear. Right now, she felt bloodthirsty, possessive, feral in a way she'd been before. She wanted to claim him as hers.

The moment she reached him, his hands slipped under her T-shirt and slid to her hips and tugged her toward him. Sam fell into his warmth with a soft gasp as the hands that glided over piano keys so smoothly now played with her nipples. He pinched them with just enough pressure. "Tell me what would make you feel better. I'll give it to you," he said, right before sucking her nipple into his mouth along with the shirt.

A jolt of pleasure shot up her spine as his teeth tugged at the aching knot in a rough movement that made her core clench greedily. "Tell me where you would like my mouth so that…" One hand drifted down and snuck under her panties.

Sam closed her eyes as his fingers delved between her folds, played with her clit before the broad pad of his thumb notched into her opening. Dipping in and out, thrusting farther in with every motion while the pad of his palm pressed up against her clit... Her knees shook. Her entire body began that shuddering ascent, mindlessly in search of the freefall.

"Stay here with me, Sameera. Look at me. Kiss me," he demanded, as he always did when she was getting close. As if it was her vulnerability in that moment when she was tumbling, her greediness for whatever he gave her got him off. He always made her come when he was inside her even if it meant postponing his own release, even if that meant revving her all the way up again.

Fingers sinking into his hair, Sam almost climbed into his lap. But that arrogant possessiveness in his gaze arrested her. Bending, she scraped her teeth over his jaw roughly. His gravelly moan gave her a foothold to fight the need for her own pleasure.

Nope, today she wanted to own him. Today, she wanted to be the one that made him mindless. In this moment, she wanted her name on his lips, in his heart, vibrating through his entire being. Not the ghost of another woman.

It was nearly impossible to stop when release was a shimmering starburst one breath away, but she did it. Clasping his wrists, she went to her knees.

From this angle on the floor, he looked like some otherworldly god she could never hold on to. Could only have in flickers of finite moments. And those were dwindling faster and faster.

"Sam? What's going on in your head, *bella*?" A hint of frustration seeped into his words.

She lay a hand on the band of his sweatpants, her cheeks on fire. His abdomen clenched under her touch. A thrill shot through her at how sensitive he was, even to that simple contact. Licking her lips, she trailed her finger along the line of hair that thickened below his belly button and disappeared under his pants. "How come you never ask me to do this?"

Dark color crested his cheeks. His throat rippled, and Sam caught the flare of excitement in his eyes that he tried his best to suppress. And it lit a conflagration in her body. "Do what, *bella*?"

He was stalling until he could better control himself, she knew. "Go down on you."

His palms scraped along her forearm as he caught her mouth in a gentle kiss. "Because…we're still new to each other, *tesoro*."

"Yeah, but it's not like we have months for me to ease into it."

Their gazes held. All of time and space should have stilled around them. And yet, Sam could hear the laughter from the patio rise, the chitter of some insects, felt the cold marble floor against her knees, felt her heart go boom in her chest.

She slid her hand down his abdomen. His erection twitched in her palm, thick and hard. "I want to experience everything with you—"

"Tell me what has you so…perturbed."

She shook her head. "You're distracting me, and I won't be."

"*Bene*," he said, inclining his head. A king letting the peasant come to their knees.

He jerked his hips up, his sweatpants came down. Her breaths became a struggle as he took her palm and wrapped it around his shaft. A shuddering hiss filled her ears.

He was steel cloaked in velvet as she pumped up and

down slowly. Sensation fizzed around in her body, thrill and power and arousal colliding like fizzy bubbles.

His fingers pulled her hair away from her face, a dark humor in his eyes. "Open up, then, Sameera. Let's see what you can do today then, *sì*?"

It was her turn to swallow.

His mouth curved into a sardonic twist. "Not time yet to swallow, *bella*."

"Don't mock me, Alessandro."

"I wouldn't dare."

Leaning forward, she licked the head where a bead of pre-cum glistened. He was salty and musky, and Sam went back for more. But for a breath before that, she looked up at him.

Head thrown back, the thick veins in his temple and neck stood out in stark relief. That didn't last for long, though.

As Sam continued to lap him up, up and down, over and under, his thighs turned granite under her fingers and his gaze locked down on her. As if seeing her do this was more arousing than the sensation of her mouth on him. Every new thing she tried, he let out a long growl, thrust his hips up as if he couldn't help himself.

Opening her mouth wide, Sam took as much as possible of him, and that wasn't much. His head barely touched her throat.

He cursed, long and filthy. "Slow down, *bella*. Breathe through it."

When she did it right, he went a little farther. In and out, she followed his command, hollowed her cheeks out, until the head hit the back of her throat. But he always pulled back before it became too much.

"You're such a good girl here, Sameera," he said, his words husky and gravelly. "If I had known you would submit so prettily to whatever filthy demands I make of you, I'd have made you go down on your knees the first time."

Sam looked up, eyes blazing, heart pumping fast, his taste an explosion on her tongue. "Well, now you know," she said catching a breath.

His grin was wicked, harsh, full of arrogant need. The floor at her knees was rough, his grip in her hair was rough, her mouth began to ache, but she had never felt more gloriously alive.

"*Basta*, Sameera!" he said, pulling out of her mouth.

"No, I want you to finish in my—"

Lifting her into his lap, Alessandro smiled against her mouth. She kissed him back sloppily, breath out of rhythm, cheeks aching, lips sensitized, but God, she wanted him to know how she felt. "Come in my mouth," she said with a pout. Between their bodies, his erection notched tightly against her belly.

He was shaking his head, tugging her to her feet. "Whatever you're trying to prove, Sam," he said, tightly clasping her face in his palms, "you don't have to. You're more than enough for me."

Words burst out of her. "Prove it, then."

A teasing glint appeared in his eyes as he played with her lower lip with the pad of his thumb. It was a gentling of sorts… "Prove it how, *bella*?"

"I don't know… I just want you mindless, like you make me."

"Come with me, then." A wicked glint shone in his eyes.

Sam followed him as he brought her to a vanity table. New sensations skittered across her skin as he got her naked within seconds. His legs kicked hers out wider, and pockets of heat broke out all over.

While she watched their reflection in the mirror, he thrummed her all over. Her skin was flushed damp, she was panting and vibrating with need when he finally bent her over and stroked into her without hesitation and Sam had no rational thoughts left.

Everything on the vanity went flying as he slammed into her. "Look at me, Sameera," he whispered, his chest falling against her back. Watching her, moving through this moment with her. Binding her to him.

Sam looked in the mirror, and there he was. Dark and broad, eyes shot with lust, skin damp, desire etched into every pore. "See how mindless you make me, *bella*. See how I do not care that you're all swollen and puffed up down here. See how much I mark your tender flesh. See how desperate I am to come inside you, over and over."

A dark smile edged his lips. "You ruin me every time you let me do these things to you, Sam. And somehow you remake me too." His mouth came to her shoulder.

Sam braced herself, her core fluttering, clenching and releasing, around his thick length. But there was no escape from him, inside and out, and she didn't want that. Tingles raced down when he dug his teeth into her shoulder just as he stroked out and in.

Her body bowed, her legs shook, and her scream remained locked behind his rough fingers. He took her roughly, with barely any rhythm but a madness he was chasing, molding her body into what he needed.

As his thrusts became faster, his free palm moved from her chest to her clit. When climax broke her apart, when he groaned at his own release, when he picked her up and carried her to the tub and washed her body as if she were infinitely precious, Sam didn't have any thoughts or words left.

All she wanted was more days like these. More moments like this.

Her greedy heart wanted forever with the man who made her feel gloriously alive.

A few days had passed in a hazy, dreamy blur along with hot, steamy nights when Alessandro walked to Sam's studio on the second floor and stalled at the threshold.

For once, she wasn't at the easel, covered in paint like he usually found her. Found her and then distracted her whether she was done or not.

He'd had the room emptied and tidied because three walls were all-glass doors and the lighting in here was perfect. It had once been his mother's craft room, Papà had informed him. But he had no memory of her, neither did it hold any kind of sentimental value for him.

Now he could think of it as nothing but Sameera's studio. And when she left… The thought ran around in his head like a bullet ricocheting against the walls of an empty chamber, looking for a target.

But there was nothing to pin down, he reminded himself. He was able to feel this much, take all of what she gave because this was only a small pocket of time. If she were truly his for the rest of their lives, he didn't think he could survive the intensity of his feelings. Nor would she.

Months, or maybe years from now, the memories associated with this room, memories of Sam during this time, would simply fade. She'd become an interesting highlight in his past.

He knew why he was thinking such morose thoughts too. The banquet that was held for the cancer research foundation he'd established in Violetta's memory was tonight.

Though, tonight, he didn't want to think of the woman

that had slipped away from his life. Tonight, as much as he couldn't skip the banquet, his mind constantly dwelled on Sam. As it had done since her arrival.

She was standing on the small balcony that the French doors led to. The smock she'd tied around her neck left her back bare except for the strap of her bra. The low-slung shorts hugged her bony hips and curvy ass, the only place she wasn't skinny, which she'd flashed and jiggled and rubbed up against him since she'd discovered it was his weakness, the cunning minx.

The shimmery orange of dusk's rays picked up the golden highlights in her hair, the result of a salon visit with Angelina.

Their friendship, as strangely as it had begun, didn't surprise Alessandro. For her youth—well, relative youth, he corrected in his head because she didn't like it when he called her *young*—Sam had an innate ability to empathize with people that made everyone like her.

Her elbows resting on the sill, she looked thoughtful.

"Sam?"

She turned and blinked, but he didn't miss the sheen of tears in her eyes.

"What's wrong?" he said, cutting the distance between them with long strides.

Leaning back against the balcony, she swept her gaze over him, a tremulous smile coasting her lips. "Every time I think you couldn't be any sexier, you prove me wrong. You know what the tuxedo makes me want to do?"

"What, *bella*?" he asked, knowing that she was distracting him. It was a miracle that they'd managed to learn anything about each other at all. She was as secretive as he was. As stubborn as he.

"It makes me want to rumple you up. But then I think,

nope the world can have this sophisticated version of you. The hungry, savage version is mine."

The raw, naked claiming both excited and tethered him, as always. "Give me a few hours and I'm all yours."

Reaching her, he pulled her until her back was against his chest and he wrapped his arms around her waist.

She fought a little first—a symptom of her clear upset, but he didn't relent.

It was strange how he was the one who had resisted touching her like this, outside of sex, and yet, now she was the one who fought any kind of tenderness or affection. Initially, he had worried that he had scared her with his unrestrained need at all hours. Nearly three weeks hadn't remotely dampened the intensity of his sexual hunger.

But no, she demanded release, she demanded every tender and filthy thing he could do to her, as insatiable as he was.

Still, something had made her spirit dim just a little, and he could not bear it. While he continued in the same vein outwardly, a quiet panic was beginning to build inside. That she was changing, that she was leaving soon. That she...

"Whatever it is that has been upsetting you these past few days," he said, holding her a little too tight, "we shall fix it, Sam. Together."

"How sweetly you make that offer, Mr. Ricci," she said, turning to look at him. Her fingers traced his lips while her gaze did the same to his features. "But we both know life doesn't bend to our whims. Not even to arrogant, powerful Italians whose kisses are pure sin."

He nudged his nose against the arch of her neck and shoulder, and finally she settled against him.

He loved holding her like this, as if he could capture her in this moment and space, as if he could control the tornado she was sweeping through his life. Even though it was nothing but an illusion.

He rested his chin in the crook of her neck and shoulder. "Please, Sam. Tell me what has upset you so."

"How come you didn't invite me to this charity banquet?" Her arm swept out between them, signaling to his formal attire. "Angelina told me all of Milan's high society will be there. Apparently, it's the social event of the year."

He rubbed a finger over his brow, his stomach strangely tight. "You wouldn't enjoy it."

She gave a slow nod, her eyes wide. "Is it that, or are you worried of what people will think when you bring me? You aren't ashamed of being seen with me, are you? Because I'm too young and naïve and fragile for your crowd?"

"That's the most ridiculous thing you've ever said to me." Ire coated his every word. He took a beat to breathe through the tight fist in his gut. "The evening is basically rich people showing off with their donations, courting me. And I do the whole song and dance because the charity means a lot to me. If you came," he said, his hesitation betraying him, "you would be bored by all the showboating."

"You like to keep me separate from the rest of the world, is that it?"

"*Sì*," he said with enough force that the calm around them fractured. "Is that so wrong? Is it wrong if I don't want the world to cast its eyes on you and speculate on our affair? You were distressed by it when it was just my family. I do not care what the entire damned world thinks of this thing between us, but you might be hurt. And I won't subject you to that."

"Okay," she said, running her hands over his collar, soothing him. Rubbing at a spot on his jacket with her finger. And then she gave up on the pretense and simply patted his chest with her palms.

He liked it when she touched him, but today it was different. Today there was a hesitation. As if she were gathering all of her courage to ask whatever it was. It filled him with tension. "Just ask, Sam. Whatever it is."

She looked up at him, surprise making her brown eyes impossibly wider. Then she sighed. "This banquet, the research foundation, it's all in her name, isn't it? Violetta."

He nodded. It was strange to hear Violetta's name on Sam's lips. But not as jarring as he'd imagined it would be. "How do you know?"

"One can't be your plaything and escape her name being thrown in one's face, Alessandro. But I want to know about her," she said, a wariness to her mouth. "Especially when it's clear that she was—*she is*—a big part of who you are." She swallowed slowly. "I mean, Angelina told me most of the details."

"What else is there to know?"

The sky was suddenly overcast, dark clouds rolling in. Like his mood.

Alessandro didn't know if he preferred the light or the dark for this conversation. Only that he didn't want to hurt Sam by saying the wrong thing. But stopping her when she set her mind to something was impossible. He'd learned that when he'd tried to stay away from her.

"I know that she fell sick a month after your engagement. That she endured a long fight with cancer. That you stayed by her side for four hellish years. That you—" She faced him then. Tears welled in her eyes, but she blinked them back. "I'm so sorry that you lost her, Alessandro."

Words escaped him as he beheld her. As she stared back at him, communicating all the pain she felt for him. For the future he'd lost. For the woman he'd loved as if she were his own breath. Acknowledgment of all he'd endured shimmered in her eyes. And yet it felt like benediction, not pity. Not comfort. Like acceptance without expectations that he move on, become normal again and be happy.

It felt like she was entering that space where he was most tormented and she was holding his hand through it. Telling him he wasn't alone.

Emotions whipped him around like a leaf in a storm. It shook him again how this woman was so fragile and yet so strong, so stubborn about venturing where she knew she'd be hurt and still plod along anyway because that's what life demanded.

"Then, you know everything, Sameera," he said, in that forbidding tone she teased him about but couldn't help.

"The thing is," she said, her breath an audible hitch, "everyone talks about how you lost her. How you changed after she was gone. How her death changed the very course of your life and I...hate that."

He felt as if one of Bruno's fists had connected with his solar plexus, punching his very breath out of him. Stunning him, tilting the axis of his life yet again.

"I want to know what kind of a woman she was. Tell me what made her angry, what made her laugh. Tell me about what...made you fall in love with her. Tell me about her."

"She was ambitious," Alessandro said, words rushing to his lips like a torrent unlocked. "She wanted to own the world as much as she wanted to change it. We were at school together. At eight or nine years old, she decided she wanted to be a doctor. She wanted to help people. She beat me at every competitive exam we took. She...called me on every bit of my arrogance." *Like you*, he didn't say. A laugh burst out of him. "She was the life of the party. She was petty about small things, could hold a grudge like no one else and was generous where it mattered."

"She sounds lovely," Sam said, and he could tell it wasn't a platitude.

"She was," Alessandro said, as sudden darkness completely blanketed them.

Sameera shivered, and he gathered her to him, although it was for his own comfort. He swept his palms all over her—the bare midriff, the toned arms, the silky skin—and as he warmed her up, he told her all about Violetta.

He talked about things even he'd forgotten. Things he'd buried so far deep in his heart that they had ceased to exist. Everything Violetta once had been came roaring back to life in his words. Wrenched forth by this woman who was made of sunlight and laughter. It was as if Sam had reintroduced Violetta back to him as something more than a dying woman.

When it got too cold, when his chest felt so light as if someone had shifted a heavy weight from his shoulders, he swept Sam into his arms and brought her inside.

Moonlight rendered her exquisite for him, just for him. He sat with her in his lap on the chaise, and he kissed her, the moment as fragile and tenuous as the joy in his heart.

And despite the fact that he was about to break his own rules, he made love to her. Uncaring that he was late. Uncaring that he'd look less than perfect. Uncaring that she had become a weakness that could and would shatter him soon.

He stripped her of every inch of clothing and hugged her trembling, silky form to him, pretending that she needed him as much as he did her.

He worshipped her with his mouth, his fingers, with everything in him. He wrenched an orgasm out of her, swallowing her cries and mewls, before he buried himself deep inside her. He drove into her like a possessed man seeking freedom, uncaring of her fragility.

The dark amplified her groans and his hunger. And yet, it was slow and lazy and soft when his own orgasm broke, a balm to his shattered heart.

He wrapped her up in a blanket and lay down with her on the chaise longue until she fell asleep. And then he kissed her temple, traced that scar that he knew better than his own hand now, listened to the steady beat of her heart and left for the banquet.

It wasn't until hours later that Alessandro noticed a drop of dark red paint on the lapels of his pristine dress shirt. A bright pink streak on his neck. A yellow dot on his chest. She'd done it on purpose, he knew.

Rumpled him up. Splashed color onto the empty canvas of his life. Changed him, made him hers, even if for just a little.

He liked it. And for the first time in fifteen years, his heart didn't feel heavy at the thought of Violetta.

For Sam had helped him remember all the glorious things about her. All the stubborn things. And more than anything, she'd helped him remember that Violetta had loved life. To the last moment. And that he wanted that for himself too.

Sam woke alone a few hours later, her skin cold, her limbs sort of frozen, and pulled the blanket Alessandro had wrapped around her tighter.

When she stretched her legs tentatively on the chaise longue, her core ached, instantly reminding her of how possessively he had taken her before he had left.

How reverentially he had kissed every inch of her skin. How his fingers had left brief divots in her flesh.

Her body ached and throbbed while her heart, her foolish heart, soared at yet another new experience. Uncaring of the crash it had signed up for.

She had fallen in love with him, with the man whose heart would always belong to a dead woman. She knew it as well as the stuttered beat of her heart, her warm breath and her aching body. Knew that this trip, this adventure that she had so desperately wanted, had changed her. Irrevocably. More than anything ever could.

She also knew that she could not share this vast, brilliant truth with him, that Alessandro wouldn't want it. That she wasn't strong enough to face his gentle, polite but irrefutable rejection of her love. That she couldn't bear to compete with Violetta's memories.

She deserved better. She deserved him, fully, wholly, unconditionally. She deserved that deep, vast, kind heart of his that could feel so much.

Sighing, she untangled herself from the chaise and got to her feet. Her knees quaked, and a sob surged up through her chest, nearly breaking her. God, she loved him so much and she always would. One look at her and he would know, and the one thing she couldn't bear to see was his pity.

He'd given her the taste of an entire lifetime in a few weeks, and that had to be enough.

She was gone.

Alessandro had known it even as he'd walked up the steps into the house, returning in the early hours of the morning after the charity banquet.

As strange as it sounded, he'd felt it from the moment he'd stepped out of the car in the courtyard and knew it with a certainty even before he reached the bedroom.

Their bedroom…

It was free of all the hundred things she'd scattered about.

Now it looked sterile and empty, like a damned coffin for all he could breathe in there.

She'd left without good-bye. She'd left before her vacation was up. There was at least another week left. He knew, because he'd been counting the days like a lovesick fool.

He rushed to the studio, and that was as empty as his heart.

Matteo found him in the studio, the creek of the elevator doors and his wheelchair alerting Alessandro.

"She didn't discuss this with you?" Uncharacteristic gravity filled his brother's voice.

Alessandro shook his head. He doubted if he could form words even if he tried. His chest felt like it was collapsing on itself, an ocean of pain drowning him.

He'd imagined how it would feel once she left. He'd prepared himself for the sudden emptiness, for that stark silence of his life again. He'd get used to it, he told himself. He'd pick the pieces of his life back up again, like people did after a storm blew over.

But the reality was so much worse. Everything in him felt blank, silent, oppressively empty. As if she'd taken all of him with her. Given him back his ability to feel, such searing joy and crushing sorrow, and then taken it back.

The alternative was unthinkable. If he pursued a future with her, if he even indulged in the idea of it and then lost her…the pain would be unbearable. Worse than when he'd lost Violetta.

Because despite everything, he had barely been on the cusp of manhood when he'd lost her. He hadn't known himself fully before he had become part of a couple, only to lose her. He'd been angry, resentful that the world didn't bend and sway at his command, and he'd simply shut himself off.

This thing he felt for Sam…it defied definition. Refused

to be caged into words. The love he felt in his heart was all encompassing, so vast that it turned all his assumptions into dust. It humbled him, restored his faith in everything around him.

Losing her was worse than any pain he had imagined from loving her and living with the fear that her heart might give out. Much worse.

But what did she feel for him?

Doubts unlike he'd ever known engulfed him.

Had it been easy for her to leave without saying goodbye? Had he truly been nothing but a part of her summer adventure?

"She said something's up with her parents and she needed to be there. She also said…she did what she came to prove, to herself and her parents. That she was ready to leave, Alessandro. Nothing could've stopped her. She asked me if I could book her on an immediate flight. I didn't know she hadn't…"

Alessandro flicked a glance at his brother.

Whatever Matteo saw there, he swallowed and looked away. He wheeled closer to Alessandro. If not for the fact that his heart was shattering in his chest, Alessandro would've laughed at the role reversal.

His brother, it seemed, really had grown up. For he didn't offer platitudes or suggestions. He simply stayed there in the darkness and kept him company as Alessandro fell apart silently.

He wanted that joy of laughing with her again, that glorious feeling of being alive when they fought, that sense of purpose he found when she let him look after her, that soul-deep connection when he slid into her welcoming heat.

He buried his head in his hands, feeling a desolation unlike he'd ever tasted.

How would he have borne seeing her walk away from him? How would he have felt knowing that she was moving on with her adventures, with her life, while he stayed stuck, standing still without her by his side?

Could he love her without suffocating her with his own fears? Without stifling her glorious spirit? Without making his love a shackle?

He wanted to love her for the rest of his life. And that meant being the bravest version of himself. For the woman he loved had the most courageous heart, and he wanted to be its equal.

CHAPTER TWELVE

Six weeks later

SAM THREW HER backpack under the console table in the small foyer of her parents' house and kicked off her single sneaker with unwarranted violence.

Which made the grocery bag in her arms shake in her grasp. The salad she'd picked up at the deli fell to the tiled floor with a quiet thud. Which meant there was now lettuce and carrots and grape tomatoes scattered all over the floor with the dressing splattered and staring back at her. Which also meant her dad would have to clean it up because Sam couldn't bend her left leg right now.

Sudden, indulgent tears filled her eyes, and she pressed her forehead to the door.

Her right hip ached with how much extra load she'd been putting on it to compensate for the giant bruise on her left hip. God forbid she be of use to anyone else. For once in her life, she wanted to be the one who didn't need looking after.

But it wasn't just the frustration of the accident she'd had since returning or the anger over how exhausted she was by the end of the week after juggling classes, her portrait commissions and schlepping home every evening from the campus.

It was *him*.

She wasn't sleeping because she missed him in her bed.

Missed being held by him. Missed his gaze on her, relentlessly digging and probing. Missed the warm curve of his mouth as he pressed it to her skin.

She wasn't enjoying her college experience because everything felt colorless without him.

She had no appetite, but she forced herself to eat anyway because that's what grown-up people did. Even when their heart was torn into pieces. Especially grown-up Sam because her damned heart couldn't be trusted to not fail on her if she didn't look after herself.

Just another week before she was free of the cast on her foot, she reminded herself.

This too shall pass, she repeated to herself, as if her life depended on it.

She'd wanted adventures and life, and that meant heartbreak too.

Apparently real life for her meant falling in love with the wrong brother in a matter of a few weeks and running away without even telling him how she truly felt because she was terrified of seeing his irrefutable rejection of her love.

But she'd get over him, as she did with all hard things in life, and be stronger for it. Just not yet. It would take her all of her twenties probably. Maybe some of her thirties.

By thirty-five, she'd be ready to throw herself into another red-hot affair. And maybe she would target a man from a different continent this time, just for variety.

That ridiculous plan for the next decade felt like control when nothing else was in her grasp.

Stepping around the wilting lettuce and sodden carrots, she walked into the house, only noticing then that it was too quiet for a Friday evening.

Her mom's favorite Indian soap opera—hers too, now—should've been playing loud enough to drive Dad bonkers.

The thought broke her dark mood. Even her dad's old excuse that he didn't understand Hindi didn't stand anymore. In the vein of all soap operas across the universe, the show moved so slowly and so dramatically that even he could understand what was happening.

"Mom, what's happening? Did Rishika discover the truth about her evil twin? Has she—"

Her breath emptied out of her in a loud, long exhale.

Alessandro was standing in their kitchen, a bottle of her dad's favorite beer dripping condensation all over the granite counter next to him.

White dress shirt and black trousers. His hair needed a cut. His mouth was set in that tight, forbidding line she knew so well. And his eyes... God, his eyes. A rainbow of emotions flickered through them as they roved over her hungrily.

From her hair in two braids to the Band-Aid on her chin to her crop top and low-slung shorts to the large blue-green bruise showing on her hip and her foot in a cast.

His gaze lingered at several points, mainly her foot and the bruise, and then crawled up to her face. Tension thrummed around him, as if he were creating a strange force field around himself.

He should have looked so out of context here in their kitchen, in their house. At least that's how she'd survived the last few weeks. By compartmentalizing him in her head, like a fantasy. A temporary illusion that had felt incredibly good.

In silence, she walked into the living room where her parents were on the couch, and Alessandro followed. On the big plasma screen on the wall, Rishika was running around the streets of Mumbai chasing after her amnesiac lover who was being stolen away by her evil twin.

Sam registered this on the periphery of her senses, as if

they were a background track for her suddenly very vivid life. Someone muted the television.

Her mom finally broke the silence. "Why didn't you tell us you were dating Matteo's older brother?"

Sam's eyes widened. He'd told them? What, exactly?

"For God's sake, Sameera, he's eighteen years older than you. I can't decide if he's worse than Matteo or not. Because *he* should know better." This she addressed to Alessandro with an almighty scowl.

Heat rushed into her cheeks, but Sam couldn't break away from that gray gaze. Dad's *Hush, Geeta, let them sort it out* fell into the tense silence.

Alessandro raised an eyebrow.

Fluent in his facial language, Sam understood him instantly.

He was asking whether she wanted him to answer her mom's inquiries.

The gesture was so familiar, had haunted her so much, that raw longing flooded her body. For a wild, crazy moment, she wanted to say *Go for it*. She wanted to let him take on her mom and see the fireworks. She wanted to see what he'd say about them now that they were... Wait, why was he here at all?

"Sam?"

She turned to her mom, hearing the worry in it. "Whatever it was, it's over now, Mom." She heard the catch of pain in her voice but had no energy to fight it. "So let's not argue about the irrefutable fact that I'm an adult, and while you're allowed to express your opinion, you have no say in how I live my life, hmm?"

"Then, why is he here?" her mom continued. "He's been here all afternoon and grilled us about you for hours."

Her belly swooped. He'd been waiting all afternoon?

She turned to Alessandro. "Are you going to just stand there and look at me, or explain why you're here?" she said, her stomach twisting. Did he have any idea how hard it was for her to see him here like this and not touch him? To fight being pulled back into his gravity? "If not, Mom will continue to talk about you as if you're not standing there taking up all the space." Sudden anxiety flooded her. "Wait, is Matteo okay? Angelina didn't say anything about—"

"Matteo is fine."

No one could have missed the jealousy in his tone. *No one.* Sam blinked.

"Are you in pain?" he asked, tilting his chin at her foot.

"It's just a hairline fracture," she said, clumsily wiggling her foot.

That he'd ask her that of all the hundred things he could've said...her heart felt like a fragile piece of glass. Liable to shatter at one wrong word. And because she would hate him to reach the wrong conclusion, she elaborated. "This...teen kid was driving a moped and almost crashed into a delivery vehicle. I tried to get him out of his way, right outside. I ended up twisting my foot and falling," she finished slowly.

He didn't nod at her explanation. His gaze didn't relent, as if his intensity had been dialed to the max. "Pack a bag. We'll go to my hotel suite." He rubbed a hand over his temple. "Do you need help?"

Her mom's outraged gasp punctured the silence. God, she couldn't give them a moment, could she? And what was Alessandro doing, ordering her around, in front of her parents?

Despite it all, Sam was tempted. Beyond tempted to simply follow him.

He could have said they'd go to the end of earth or a different dimension or a parallel universe and she'd still have followed him. If he'd asked for a few more weeks, or days or even one last night for closure…she'd be all in. Again. She'd put aside embarrassment, her self-respect, her pain—everything if he'd just kiss her one more time. If he'd hold her. If he'd make love to her. She was that desperate for him.

But if she did go, she wasn't sure she could break away again. The thought of his rejection was the slap of common sense she needed.

"I have an early morning class, and it's my turn to make dinner tonight," she said, uncaring that it sounded like an excuse. It wasn't.

He came toward her. A strange dizziness came over her as he took the bag of groceries in one hand, grabbed her waist with the other and simply lifted her and carried her to the kitchen.

Sam breathed him in like an addict.

"I will help with dinner. We can eat and then go. I'll make sure you get to class on time in the morning."

Sam simply nodded instead of telling him she was not going anywhere with him.

To his credit, he did help her in the kitchen. But her heart couldn't simply settle down in his proximity.

Since she'd lost the salad, she heated up leftover rice and used the vegetables he'd chopped to make fried rice.

Her parents watched from the living room as if two aliens had taken over the kitchen.

Sam set the table while Alessandro scrambled the eggs until they were golden and fluffy and just…perfect like everything he did. It was such a domestic yet extraordinary moment that she didn't know what to think.

"I didn't know you could cook," Sam said, when the four of them settled down around the table.

"You don't know a lot of things about me," he said, a soft

twinkle in his eyes. "You ran away before I could tell you." The last part was a whisper just for her ears.

"I didn't run away," Sam retorted.

He didn't argue back, but the tight set of his jaw said more than enough.

If the fried rice was too spicy for him, he didn't let on. He ate two helpings as if it was the most delicious dish he'd ever tried, and a fierce kind of joy stabbed through Sam's middle.

Mom stayed quiet, but Dad and Alessandro chatted about computers and business and the Ricci branch in California without an ounce of awkwardness.

Soon they'd piled up all the dishes around the sink and she'd cleaned the dining table. Her heart started rabbiting in her chest.

"I'll see to these," Dad said, gesturing to the dirty dishes while Mom filled the kettle and turned it on. Sam didn't know what to do with herself. Or the sudden tremors that seemed to overtake her at the thought of him leaving.

Alessandro thanked her parents for their hospitality and did it with such genuine regard that even her mom cracked a smile. Then he turned to her. "Ready to go?"

Sam followed him into the living room so that they could have some privacy. Not so much that she'd lose the little sense of self-preservation that was holding her back. "I'm... exhausted, to be honest. It's been a long week."

He crowded her until their chests grazed. "I can see that, *tesoro*. You can just sleep. We don't have to talk." His knuckles traced the dark shadows under her eyes. "I just... need to hold you."

Sam stared, in shock. She hadn't imagined the slight catch in his tone. Hadn't imagined the bob of his Adam's apple. He sounded on edge. Stepping back, she looked up into his face, and something slid into place. "Wait, did Angelina tell you about my accident?"

"Does it matter, Sam?"

"Yes, it does," she said, her voice rising, aware that her parents were staring at them. "Where's your blasted honesty now?"

"Fine," he said with that infuriating calm in the face of her temper. "She was at the house yesterday. She mentioned that you had a short stay in the hospital two weeks ago. I flew here overnight."

She felt as if she'd been punched in the gut. Pushing away from him, she'd have stumbled if not for the wall at her back. "Did you come because you thought I was dying?" Tears pricked, never far these days. "As you can see, I'm perfectly fine, and you can fuck off with your pity. I don't have—"

She never finished. Because the blasted man picked her up in his arms all the while being extremely gentle with her foot and walked up the stairs.

Sam buried her face in his chest but didn't protest. Or fight. Or say anything. She was too busy crying, falling apart, to put up a fight. And it felt like her heart was breaking all over again.

To leave him once had been heartbreaking, but to do it again…she wasn't strong enough.

Alessandro deposited Sam onto the small bed in the attic room. While every cell in him wanted to crowd her into the bed, kiss her and generally railroad her into submission, he backed off. This wasn't a small thing, and the last thing he wanted was to restart their relationship with him minimizing her complaints.

He looked around the small room. Pictures of Sam greeted him from a bulletinboard, from all ages and sizes.

Framed art hung from the wall, some her own pieces and some not. Her room was a kaleidoscope of colors and sunlight and shimmer. Just like her.

Seeing a familiar face on the board, he went closer for a better look. It was a picture of Matteo and Sam with his arm around her, younger and grinning into the camera.

He backed away, that prick of jealousy as fresh as always. But before he turned, one last thing caught his attention. It was a sketch of him, rendered in nothing but dark lines. That dark void that had opened up within him since she'd left ate it up hungrily.

Finally, he turned to find Sam glaring at him, her face etched with exhaustion. "Go to sleep, *bella*. You clearly need..." He swallowed the rest.

"As soon as you leave."

"I'm not leaving, Sameera. Not until we talk. It's not too late to go to the hotel. We'll have privacy and more room," he said, eyeing the single bed. There was no way he could sleep next to her on that.

"There's nothing I want to do with you that requires privacy."

He crawled onto her small bed, nuzzled into her temple and whispered, "I do."

She sniffled, and a tear made a track down her cheek. He wiped it away with his sleeve. "That's gross. I have tissues," she said.

"I've licked things off of your body, *tesoro*. This is nothing."

Pink crested her cheeks, and a tentative smile curved her mouth. When he reached for her hand, she gave it reluctantly. He laced his fingers through hers, and something in his chest settled. Like a key sliding into place, turning tumblers, unlocking a whole new world of joy and contentment for him.

It had started turning from the first moment. He'd been too numb inside to see it happening, to appreciate it.

"Why did you leave without saying good-bye?"

"My cousin Kavi…remember her?"

"The one that called you a stubborn goat? *Sì*. I like her."

He felt her surprise rather than saw it. Did she think he'd forgotten a single moment of the time they'd spent together?

"She finally told me what was happening here. She always tells it like it is. Mom and Dad…are pregnant. That's what set her off to a near breakdown. She…she's forty-six, and she was terrified the baby might have the same genetic heart condition I have. They were doing all these tests to see if it was even viable. Her blood pressure was out of control. A little baby brother… Can you imagine?"

Fresh tears filled her eyes, and he tucked her face into his shoulder.

Relief made him shudder when she stayed there. "Anyway, they're having this baby, and I told them I'd cut them off completely if they kept secrets from me ever again. Or if they treated me like a child anymore. I love the idea of him so much already, Alessandro. I think I understand some of her overprotectiveness with me."

"She and the baby are healthy?"

"Everything's good. Perfect." She pulled back to look into his face. "After Kavi told me, I wanted to be here for them. But of course I had an accident not two weeks after coming back."

"I'm sorry you were hurt, *tesoro*."

"That's not the point."

"What is?"

"I wanted to look after her. Not the other way around."

"But this is just an unfortunate accident, and you saved a kid from getting hurt worse. It's got nothing to do with your abilities." He lifted her knuckles to his mouth and kissed them. "As for looking after you...why do you automatically assume that it's a burden? It's abundantly clear how much she loves you." He gentled his tone. "You didn't tell me she's a lawyer. She grilled me for hours today. It's natural that she...worries about you. It doesn't mean she doesn't think you capable, Sameera." With a bracing breath, he added, "Some people have a hard time dealing with boundaries when they love someone. You say you understand her need to protect you a little now? Then, give her some grace, *no*?"

Sam stared at him. She'd been at odds with her parents ever since she'd returned, even though they'd finally gotten their act together. But one look at her face and Alessandro seemed to understand exactly what she needed to hear. It was why he'd helped with dinner too. Because he understood it was important to her.

"Why didn't you at least call me?" he said.

There was something in his words that tugged at her, but she was too exhausted to figure it out. Neither could she manage flippancy. "You know I hate confrontations."

He tensed. "Good-bye would have been a confrontation?"

"Yes, because I couldn't have stopped blurting out that I'm in love with you. And you'd have given me a hundred reasons for why we don't suit, super politely and then—"

Sam squealed as in a blink he'd flipped her onto the bed and covered her body with his. The delicious weight of him pressing down made her eyes roll back. His mouth hovered over hers, his gray eyes roiling with such emotion that it made her chest ache. "I wish you'd stayed and confronted me. Then I'd have told you I'm in love with you too, and then it wouldn't have felt like my heart had been trampled when I found you gone."

Sam wondered if her heart might jump out of her chest. Tears gathered in her throat and trickled down her eyes onto the bed. "I…"

Shifting to his side, he pressed his face into her neck, one hand palming her all over. "I rushed here after Angelina told me, *sì*. But I'd have been here anyway in a couple of weeks, *bella*. Some of the arrangements were taking time. Especially with Matteo still in recovery and my father grumbling about coming out of retirement."

"What arrangements?" Sam finally whispered.

Her chest still felt too full of wonder and disbelief. Too vulnerable about this sudden happiness. She couldn't believe he was saying these words to her. That he was here, touching her, kissing her and looking at her as if she meant everything to him. It was the stuff of her wildest dreams.

"Moving headquarters from Milan to California is quite an upheaval."

"You're moving to Cali? Why?"

"I want to be near you."

A vast ocean of happiness opened up in her, sucking her in. "Why?"

Gray eyes held hers, but this time Sam needed words. And he seemed to know that. He kissed the corner of her mouth, rubbed the tip of his nose against hers, as if he needed to brace himself to say them. "Because my life is colorless without you, *tesoro*. It is unbearable. Every morning, every evening, every moment in between…it's empty. And because I'm an arrogant asshole, it took me too long to realize that my happiness is a choice I have to make. That it lies with you."

Sam tried to smile but more tears rolled down her cheeks.

"I'm not going anywhere, Sam," Alessandro said, kissing her with such reverent tenderness that she wanted to burrow into him. His hands traced the seam of her top, careful to not touch the bruise on her hip. "I know that you have all these plans for your new colorful life, like college and raves and… I just ask that you let me be a part of your life. Even if all you can give me are weekends and—"

"So you want to be my weekend boyfriend? Am I allowed to date other men during weekdays?"

"I was hoping you'd agree to the exclusive thing again," he said oh so politely, as if his gray eyes weren't full of a stormy bleakness. "All I want is to love you, Sameera. To show you how much you mean to me."

"I…but you love Violetta. I can't—won't share you with anyone, Alessandro. Not even the past."

He didn't mock her or talk down to her. A harsh sigh left him. "I understand the feeling. Every time you mention Matteo with that affection, I want to break his pretty face." He shook his head. "A part of me will always love Violetta, *sì*. But that's a tiny part, Sam. Until you made me talk about her, it wasn't even her I remembered. It was the pain, the loss and the powerlessness of losing her. She became nothing but a reason I used to shut myself off. You…"

His breath rattled and his voice broke, and it was long moments before he spoke again. "You are laughter and joy and pleasure and fragility and innocence and stubbornness and fear and… I want to spend the rest of my life loving you, kissing you, laughing with you, playing chess with you, fighting with you…" He rubbed at her top where the scar lay, and Sam knew he wasn't even aware of it. That it had taken him everything to fight the fear of losing her. "That I feel this much for you, it scares me. The *what-if*s that go around in my head… But I won't be a coward anymore. I won't deny myself this chance with you. Not a day, not a moment. This happiness…it's a choice I'm making, even though it terrifies me, Sam."

"You do know that I can't have children, right? And that my life will—"

His hand covered her mouth. "I was a shadow, living a half life until you blazed into it, filled it with colors and emotions again. All I want is a future with you, whatever its shape, *tesoro*. Please, don't doubt my faith in this, in us."

Sam grabbed his hand and pressed a kiss to the center of his palm. "I've been hurting all over," she said, wanting to bask in their closeness, "so make me feel better, Alessandro. Give me all of you," she demanded, pushing up on elbows to press her mouth to his.

He didn't need to be asked again. Whispering her name as if it were a benediction, Alessandro kissed her with such tenderness that Sam felt like her heart was coming back to life again. Her bed was tiny for his frame, but she loved that because it gave him no room to move away from her.

He trailed kisses down her cheek to her neck, and before she knew it, her top was gone and his lips left blistering warmth all over her breasts and her midriff. There was no inch of her that he didn't touch or kiss or nip. And yet all of that frenzy calmed down in a matter of breaths as his fingers tugged at the seam of her shorts.

"I hate seeing these bruises on your body," he said, and then let out a curse. "Don't be mad, Sam." Slowly, softly, he kissed the perimeter of the blue-green bruise. "I told myself I would not stifle you or suffocate you or make you think you're incapable. I just… The thought of you in pain or anything happening to you…turns me inside out."

Sam buried her fingers in his hair and tugged until he looked up at her. The naked love in his eyes made her hiccup like a child, as if he were a fantasy that might disappear the moment she opened her eyes. "It's okay. I want to know these things you feel. And you're already doing better."

And then she was naked, and he was kissing her all over, his fingers pulling and tugging, and she was like those piano keys he played so deftly. One more breath and she'd fall away and...

"My parents," Sam exclaimed and then giggled. She cast a look around the room and groaned. "Every little sound carries down from this room. I don't think I can ever face them again."

Alessandro nipped at her right hip, hard enough to leave a small mark on her skin. "Will you listen to me next time when I say we need privacy?"

"*Sì.* Absolutely."

He grinned and buried his mouth in her inner thigh. Another nip at the silky flesh, revving her up all over again. "Didn't you hear them? Their car left a while ago."

"What?"

Alessandro rubbed her lower lip as if he couldn't stop touching her. "I spoke to your dad earlier when your mom took a nap. I wasn't sure if you'd..." He flicked her nose. "I wanted you all to myself tonight. I told him there's a room in their name at the Four Seasons in case he wanted to take your mom out for the night, and in case you refused to come to the hotel with me. I wanted all bases covered to have you to myself."

Sam bit her lower lip, but the smile broke through anyway. "I'm not going to encourage you going behind my back and conspiring with my parents of all people...but in this case, I excuse you. I guess my dad likes you."

Alessandro grinned. "And he knows you better than your mom does." That wide, wonky smile winked at her. The change in him—the sheer happiness in his expression was like a balm to her heart. She did want his words, but nothing spoke more eloquently than his gray eyes.

"Although, I'd prefer to not talk about him right now."

In reply, Sam snuck her hands in between them until she could wrap her palm around his erection. "Come inside me, please," she said, cheeks heating at the length and feel of him. Her core clenched, greedy and damp. "I won't break, Alessandro, not because of a couple of bruises and a broken foot. And that's the only way this relationship will work."

He opened his mouth, shook his head and then closed it. She laughed.

Between kisses and laughter, somehow, they managed to push his pants down, and then he was notched at her entrance. Then there was no reason for words.

He thrust into her, slowly, softly, stretching her impossibly wide, whispering so many words she didn't understand into her skin. And when he was lodged all the way in, he told her how she felt, how he'd been thinking of this moment, how he'd never stop wanting her.

Sex with him had always been a study in vulnerability and boundaries and falling off the edge when those boundaries were crossed. But this time, it was different. Their hands clasped, their eyes holding each other, joy suffused every movement, every word.

The blasted man took his own sweet time. And when Sam begged him to let her come, he tilted their angle and went deeper and faster, and she unraveled. Even their climaxes felt different, felt so much more than simple release. When he'd have pulled away, Sam held him, loving the weight of him on her and said the words she knew he wanted to hear. "I love you, Alessandro. You make me want to take risks, you make me come alive, and you…"

He took over and kissed her and whispered more words in Italian, and Sam knew she had found her grand adventure and her resting place all in one man.

***

It was dark in the room when Sam woke.

She turned to find Alessandro leaning his head on his elbow, studying her, his fingers drawing lazy circles over her belly. She flushed as she realized he'd not only cleaned her up but dressed her back in her shorts. "I didn't mean to fall asleep."

"I like looking after you." He grinned, something wicked and naughty flaring in his eyes. "Plus, I know how much you dislike being all sticky."

She flushed, heat rushing to her cheeks.

"I love when you get that expression in your eyes, *tesoro*. Reminds me there's so much more we still have to do with each other. To each other."

Moving onto her side, she faced him. With him around, she needed to get used to feeling warm and gooey and wanted and satisfied. A state of being she liked very much.

She didn't miss the thoughtful look in his eyes or the tension that drew his upper lip into that taut line before he covered it up with a grin. And Sam had a niggle what had put that look in his eyes.

She ran her hand over his chest, adoring the feeling of his skin stretched taut over lean muscles. He was hers. It was going to take time to get used to it. He was also a man who felt deeply, a man who suppressed every need and desire he felt first.

Sam wanted to be what he needed. Give what he wouldn't demand. "If I ask you something, will you give me an honest answer?" she said, unable to hide the gravity in her voice.

His gaze flicked to hers. "Ask me."

"I can't tell you how much I appreciate you moving to California. Because I can't leave Mom and Dad right now. I want to be here when the baby comes. But after…when things have settled down, we can go back to Italy, if you want. I know you're leaving at a hard time for your family too."

"I made these plans before I knew about the baby or your accident, Sam. I want to be where you are."

She nodded, her heart bursting to full. She pressed her mouth to his chest, the thundering din of his heart soothing her. "Will you tell me what is truly in your heart? What do you want from this?"

He gathered her to him and buried his face in her hair. Hiding the vulnerability he felt, she knew. When he spoke, his voice was hoarse. "I promised myself that I won't railroad you. That I'll let you choose the shape of our future. You have all these dreams and plans, and I don't want to take over your life and...your mom's complaint that I'm too old for you...it's not unfair."

"Not the answer to my question."

He looked at her, and those gray eyes captivated her. And that she had the power to grant all the wants in them was a trip of its own.

"I would marry you tomorrow. I would wrap you in Bubble Wrap and steal you away to my bedroom. I would..."

A soft gasp escaped her. He pressed a hand to his eyes, and shook his head. "I knew it was a bad idea."

"No. Listen, Alessandro. I... What about one out of the two?"

His head jerked up. "What?"

"The first one...the marrying part."

"But you want to go to college and—"

"And I can't if we marry?" Sam clasped his jaw and willed him to believe her. "Before I met you... I wanted what I thought was a normal life. College and parties and raves and dating...all the stuff I missed out on. But I hate parties, and the whole idea of dating terrifies me, and I wouldn't touch anything at a rave. I think men in their twenties are mostly immature." She clasped his cheeks, her heart overflowing with love. "Everything fades into gray scale when I think of my life without you. You're my grand adventure. My excitement. The one man who sees me...all of me. College and painting and building my own business... I can still do all of them with you in my life, *si*? We will just fight as husband and wife instead."

He laughed, kissed her, swirling his tongue against hers with a possessive urgency. "Then, marry me tomorrow. Be my wife. Give me all of you."

Sam burrowed into him, her mouth at the hollow of his throat, her heart running away. "You have all of me, Alessandro. And yes, I'll marry you. As soon as you can arrange it."

Sam cried again, and Alessandro gathered her to him, and they fell asleep like that, all tangled in each other, waiting for the new dawn that would tie them together forever.

* * * * *

Were you blown away by
Italian's Last-Minute Mistress?
*Then why not explore these other dazzling stories
by Tara Pammi?*

Contractually Wed
Her Twin Secret
Vows to a King
His Forgotten Wife
Baby Before Vows

Available now!

CONVENIENT WIFE CONDITIONS

REBECCA HUNTER

MILLS & BOON

To the best author crew—Addie, Adrianne, Amy, Anne, Dafina, Elizabeth, Jackie, Kilby, Ro and Shannon—for all your love and support on my path to Harlequin Presents. SBC forever!

CHAPTER ONE

"The wedding will be scheduled for two months from now," said Giuseppe d'Avalos, third-generation head of his family's far-reaching empire. "That is the soonest it can take place without suggesting more urgent reasons for this marriage."

Massimo Carandini took a drink of his grappa to hide his scowl at the hint of scandal suggested in the man's words. He swallowed, letting the liquid run a warm trail down his throat, then leaned back in the leather armchair and gave d'Avalos a tight smile. "Agreed. And I will defer to your daughter on the location and details of the event."

Massimo glanced toward one of the library's window seats, where Catarina d'Avalos quietly listened to the conversation. She was angled toward her father, so all he could make out was a long tangle of chestnut tresses, white trousers and a satin top the color of the sea. He thought he saw her nod, an acknowledgment that she was in agreement with their plan, but the bursts of sunlight filtering through the yellows, oranges and reds of the tall stained-glass window made it difficult to be sure.

The window lit the room, casting a warm glow on brass lamps, rows of old books and museum-quality relics of the past. Arched alcoves lined the interior walls, featuring old portraits of self-important men and women, undoubtedly evidence of the family's pedigree. If the property itself wasn't enough. This was the kind of estate that marked the legacy Massimo Carandini's grandfather had sacrificed his life for. And then his father had squandered it.

An engagement was the last thing Massimo wanted to waste business hours on this afternoon. And yet, here he was, missing a key meeting to spend an hour in the library of this sprawling home, just to close this deal with Catarina d'Avalos. Because the desire to restore his family's name once and for all far outweighed his distaste for marriage.

Massimo's aversion to this arrangement was not personal. His future bride was lovely by all accounts. Before he had approached Giuseppe d'Avalos with his offer, Massimo's assistant had provided him with photos, one from a fundraiser, where she wore a rich red gown and a demure smile, her glossy brown hair swept into some sort of twist at the base of her long neck. Another showed Catarina alongside her parents after the opening night of one of her mother's performances. She was attractive, if not beautiful. Massimo supposed it would be helpful to find his fiancée attractive, even if it wasn't his primary concern.

He had studied and then dismissed two other equally attractive but less suitable potential candidates. The first, minor nobility, had a well-polished image by day that belied her preference for much wilder nights. The second he'd rejected when his assistant had discovered the topless photos someone had taken of her at a party. He didn't condemn a taste for wild nights or topless photos on principle, but his own purposes were very specific. If it had only taken a few strokes of the keyboard to dig up those pieces of evidence, what would the paparazzi uncover when their marriage came under closer scrutiny? Massimo wasn't interested in finding out.

Giuseppe d'Avalos must have also seen his daughter's nod or somehow gotten the response he was looking for because he returned his attention back to Massimo.

"Yours is not the first offer of marriage that a business associate has proposed," the man said.

Massimo didn't mistake his casual tone for anything that neared offhandedness.

"I have no doubt," he murmured. There was an empire behind her, generations of money and acquisitions, and as the only child, it would all fall to Catarina.

"But yours is the first I have seriously considered," the man continued. "You have a reputation for following through on your commitments, despite…"

D'Avalos waved his hand through the air dismissively, as if it was unnecessary to detail the train wreck of Massimo's father's business failures. As if the whole world knew enough about the rise and fall of the Carandini family legacy that he didn't have to put it into words.

Massimo gritted his teeth, resisting every steely retort that came to mind. How long would the sins of his father be used as a lens to analyze every decision he made? Hadn't he shown that he was not the kind of man who would, for example, spend investors' money on a "company" yacht simply because his wife demanded it? But this was a business deal, like any other, he reminded himself. Except, in this case, he couldn't leave the velvet-cloaked negotiations to his brother. He had to deal with this one himself.

"Trust is the foundation of this deal on both sides,"

he said smoothly, as if references to the disgrace that marked his father's legacy simply rolled off him.

The marriage would secure the future of both the families' businesses, but most importantly, a stable, appropriate marriage would prove to the world that the scandals that had plagued the Carandini family were firmly in the past. No more wary investor meetings; no more whispers about that one terrible night on the yacht. So while he wanted a wife who would be a suitable companion at high-profile events, he had instructed his assistant that his first priority was for the woman to have absolutely no controversy attached to her name. She should be a blank slate as far as the media was concerned so as to lend a stable, calming presence to the Carandini name. This was harder to find than one might think in the age of social media, where people regularly and willingly—*willingly*—offered documentation of their private lives for the world to see.

In this area, Massimo would not compromise. Truth be told, compromise never had much appeal, nor much use, in his life. Ever since coming of age, he and his twin brother, Alessandro, had worked single-mindedly to restore the family's fortunes and reputation, both of which his parents had so quickly and thoroughly ruined. Massimo and Alessandro had made it their lives' work to restore their grandfather's crumbling shipping empire that had fallen into ruins and make it bigger, better, grander than ever. None of their accomplishments were built on compromise.

However, public opinions were unpredictable, fickle and not nearly as controllable as the business itself had proven to be. So while their profits had increased, the stench of their parents' public drama still clung to the family name. It was holding them back.

After a lifetime of living with their parents' public fights, their preoccupation with each other at the expense of everything else, neither brother was interested in marriage. However, during one of many endless strategy meetings with PR firms and specialists, the solution became unavoidable: They needed to show the world that this generation of the Carandini family was not cut from the same cloth as the last. They needed to prove that a marriage—because everyone assumed the brothers would inevitably marry someday, no matter how often they discouraged this idea—would not result in the same downward spiral that had caught hold of their parents and never let them go.

Of course, Alessandro had argued that Massimo should be the one to go through with said marriage.

"How convenient for you," Massimo had responded in his driest tone. "Though I can't help but point out that you're far more suitable to find a wife than I am."

"If you're referencing my reputation for understanding what women enjoy, then yes," Alessandro had said in that lazy voice of his. He used it to close business deals as often as he used it to charm the women that seemed to flock to him.

"But we are discussing a marriage that will not spur hungry paparazzi to dig through their archives for old speculations to rekindle. A marriage that does not attract scandal," his brother had continued. "That is your territory."

Massimo had scowled at Alessandro, the way he always did when his brother was right. Alessandro's public reputation was only saved by his carefree facade. He had all but publicly declared his permanent playboy status, and women knew this when they entered into anything that could be mistaken for an entanglement. His brother's image wouldn't work for a marriage that inherently implied stability. Massimo, on the other hand, had no qualms about showing himself as the relentlessly calculating businessman that he was. His public persona quite accurately aligned with the relationship he expected: a marriage free of the illusion of love, strictly for convenience.

"I'm already doing my part to sway public opinion in our family's favour, one woman at a time," Alessandro had added with a smirk. "You, on the other hand, are determined to force your iron will onto the rest of the world. If anyone is in the position to change our family's reputation, it's you."

He said all of this with a lazy, knowing drawl that got under Massimo's skin. Especially since, once again, his brother was right. If Massimo showed that his steely reputation would not be bent with marriage, that would certainly settle any lingering doubts that this generation of Carandinis would not make the same mistakes as the last.

D'Avalos looked in the direction of Catarina again, and Massimo sensed the man was gathering his words. He waited, observing his future father-in-law. D'Avalos was impeccably dressed in a well-tailored shirt and dark wool slacks. His hair was streaked with silver, and his brow creased with evidence of heavy sorrow and loss. The man had rarely smiled even before the untimely death of his wife, Marie Nordland, the so-called Nordic Siren, and now, *rarely* had swerved closer to *never*.

When d'Avalos looked back at Massimo, his gaze was almost wistful.

"I have never claimed to understand my daughter," he

said in a low, serious voice. "However, Catarina's future is more important to me than anything else in this world."

D'Avalos's steely gaze flickered with hints of emotion, but just as quickly, all traces were gone.

"My wife's last wish was for me to make sure that Catarina is taken care of for as long as she lives," he continued. "I have arranged this marriage for her because I am not a young man. Catarina was a surprise and a blessing to both my wife and me. I recognize I will not always be here to carry out my promise, so I would be trusting that to you."

"Your trust would not be misplaced," Massimo replied.

Though there were plenty of things this marriage would not be, providing for Catarina was straightforward. She would have his money, and his residences, plane, cars and boats would be at her disposal. She would be able to live the lifestyle she was accustomed to. Massimo wasn't sure what d'Avalos saw on his face, but it seemed to satisfy him. The man stood and turned once again to his daughter.

"Catarina," said d'Avalos in a voice that was both gruff and tender, as if, even after twenty-four years, he still was not quite sure how to talk to his daughter. "I will leave you to make your final decision."

The older man retreated from the room, and the door closed with a quiet snick. Through the rays of light, Massimo thought he saw Catarina's back straighten. Her shoulders rose and fell, as if she was fortifying herself with a deep breath. He felt a stab of sympathy for this woman, whose future was determined in backroom business deals. Then she lifted her chin, stood and turned to him.

Massimo couldn't explain what came next, except that

she met his gaze and something happened. Something *must* have happened, he would later tell himself, because he was unaware of anything else except the feeling that the entire world had suddenly stopped. All he could do was drink this woman in. Her eyes were a shade darker than her chestnut hair, and they were wide, curious, with an openness he had no idea what to do with.

Her lips parted slightly. They were full and pouty, as if they were made for pleasure. And then he was thinking about pleasure in detail. Hers. His. An electric jolt of desire ran through him, shaking him out of this strange stupor. Massimo blinked, and much to his dismay, he found that he was standing, too, though he had no memory of rising to his feet. He gritted his teeth and shoved all thoughts of pleasure to the dark recesses of his mind.

Massimo knew how to handle attraction, satisfyingly for both parties and without any lingering sentiment. That was exactly how their marriage would be conducted. He wasn't the kind of man who had time for wants and needs, not his nor anyone else's. Clear expectations should be set from the beginning. But first, she needed to agree to this marriage.

"It's a pleasure to meet you," he said, giving her a charming smile. Charm was a skill like any other, something that he had mastered with ruthless efficiency and exercised when necessary. Most often it wasn't necessary, he had found. Today was an exception, he told himself.

"The pleasure is mine."

He hadn't fully understood Marie Nordland's moniker, the Nordic Siren, until this moment. Without a doubt, the famous soprano had passed her voice down to her daughter. Massimo was sure of it because Catarina's voice floated inside him, light and beautiful and somehow pushing away all other thought. It hummed in him, filling his senses with a song that could bring a man to his knees. Here, in the quiet, subdued library, filled with dark shelves and leather-bound books, her voice rang like a bell, echoing through his well-tempered senses. Massimo steeled himself against the rush of pleasure the soft music of her words conjured. It was no wonder that Giuseppe d'Avalos kept his daughter practically locked up in this estate. How many men would be pounding on the door if they heard her voice? The thought was an ugly thing that he shoved somewhere deep inside.

"You must have been told many times that you have your mother's voice," he commented, keeping his own voice mild.

She gave him a hint of a smile. "But not my mother's taste for the stage. To my parents' eternal disappointment."

Her tone was so light, so airy, as if ignoring family expectations could be brushed off. A sudden wave of resentment washed over him, the resentment for the position his parents had put his brother and him in, the duty the brothers were bound to. What a privileged life Catarina had lived that she could simply choose not to follow her family's wishes because they didn't suit her. And still, her father was looking after her, smoothing out her future. She had been protected. Coddled, even. But the usual resentment bubbling inside him was overshadowed by something else, something darker. He pushed aside this strange feeling in his gut.

These privileges were the very qualities that made her a perfect wife for him, he reminded himself. She was not hungry for attention, for money, for the temptations that a life as his wife might present. She could rise above whatever they faced. He couldn't forget that he was closing a business deal, like any other. So Massimo quashed the last of his simmering bitterness and focused on the woman in front of him.

As Catarina walked toward him, Massimo couldn't ignore the grace with which she moved. Her brown hair spread out in waves over her shoulder, and her azure blouse moved like the placid waters of the Mediterranean. He could see why her mother had insisted on her being cared for in her dying wish. There was something ethereal, something otherworldly, about her. She was lovely, a perfect choice, he told himself, ignoring the faint warning bells ringing deep inside him.

He watched her as she seemed to glide across the room, taking slow steps, her eyes focused on him. Her expression wasn't deliberately seductive, the way countless women approached him when they wanted some combination of sex, power or money from him. Instead, it was as if she held a secret, one just for him. The warning bells rang louder.

"It's a strange thing, meeting the man my father has arranged for me to marry," she said softly. There was that openness in her gaze again, a curiosity.

Massimo gave her a smile, calculated to put her at ease, resisting the sizzle of attraction that grew hotter with each of her steps. He could do this, he told himself. He was in control of his emotions. He wasn't his father. "I hope I meet your expectations."

"Of course," she said, and her lovely cheeks turned a golden red. "My father will always look out for my best interests."

He thought he detected a hint of wryness in her voice, but her placid smile simply suggested contentment.

Catarina came to a stop in front of him, close enough that he was tempted to brush his hand against her cheek, just to test the softness of her skin. He found himself studying her dark eyes, those long lashes. The electric pull took hold of him again, and something white-hot arched between them as she rose onto her tiptoes. Her scent was everywhere, roses and the salty kiss of the sea, swirling around him. She brushed her lips against one cheek, then the other.

It was an everyday greeting, nothing more, but Massimo felt as if something echoed between them, reverberating deep inside him, something strange and new. It was as if the brush of her lips on his skin called to the deepest, most hidden part inside him. And he *wanted*. He wanted badly. That part of him roared to life, the part he had spent every day of his adult life burying, beating into submission. *Give in*, the siren's song called. It grew, expanding inside him, then exploded to life, roaring a single word: *mine*.

The word clanged through him like an alarm, its screech too loud to ignore. This was the force his father had given in to, the seductive pull that had dragged down Massimo and Alessandro in its wake. Never would he succumb to it. Massimo would never be his father. So he shoved all these feelings back down, deep inside him, once and for all.

CHAPTER TWO

CATARINA HAD SEEN Massimo before. It was in a lush ballroom somewhere in Milan, lit by sparkling chandeliers. She remembered a chocolate fountain, a black Steinway piano in a corner that she'd admired and an army of waitstaff, dressed in all black and buzzing around with bottles of champagne. She remembered the silk of her gown, blue and whisper-soft against her skin. She remembered the stylist's expert hands in her hair, testing one updo after another as her mother sat beside her, blue eyes warm and so very alive. Her mother had always been the sun of the family, lighting it up, and Catarina was content to be an outer planet, kept in close by gravity, deferring to larger planets as long as her mother's steady warmth and energy were near.

She remembered the hall with its red velvet curtains and the murmur of the crowd over the hum of the string quartet. And she remembered Massimo, at the center of it all. At least, he'd seemed to be the center to her at the time. Massimo Carandini didn't notice her, of course. At sixteen, she had been a shy, wide-eyed girl in a demure gown, all but hiding in the shadow of her mother's glowing presence.

But she'd noticed him. How could anyone not be

drawn to this tall man with captivating brown eyes, a bespoke suit and silky black hair that she'd inexplicably wanted to touch. In a room full of men in elegant suits just like his, Massimo Carandini shouldn't have stood out, but he did. There was a hardness about him, something distant and forbidding that made her sixteen-year-old self feel things she hadn't recognized at the time. *What made someone hard like that?* she had wondered. Why was she struck by the strange desire to run her hand over the hard line of his jaw, the stark planes of his cheeks, searching for hints of softness?

But that was years ago, back when her life had been a series of questions, girlish and ultimately inconsequential. Would she rather attend an all-girls boarding school in England or in the Alps, closer to home? Would she rather spend the fall in Taipei learning Mandarin, or did she want to work for her mother? Back then, gaining freedom from her father's controlling hand hadn't crossed her mind, and her mother was still around to temper his tendency to turn concerns into rigid rules. So each time, she had chosen to stay closer to home. She had chosen with her heart, and now, in the devastating aftermath of her mother's death, she was grateful that she had. At sixteen, Catarina had known that the choices she had been given were privileges and that life was unfair that way, but her life simply *was*. She hadn't questioned it, much less considered how she would feel if her life were to upend, suddenly and irrevocably.

Now, every day, she lived with the bone-deep understanding of what the loss of her mother meant for her. Catarina was alone. At first, she hadn't quite noticed the narrowing of her independence, or if she did, she attributed it to her loss, her solitude. It had taken a long time before she was aware of the way her father's worries had turned into restrictions.

Still, when her father came to her with a proposal for marriage, she hadn't contemplated any deeper questions, such as: Should her father even be involved in her plans for marriage? Catarina had focused instead on the freedom she would gain when she escaped her father's watchful gaze. When he'd floated the name Massimo Carandini specifically, she'd asked herself a second question: How had this man made her feel back in that ballroom when she was sixteen? He had made her shiver with what she now understood was desire. From across the room, no less. That feeling had been private, unattached from her famous mother. And it had felt like the opposite of being alone.

Then there was the fact that, despite his oppressive impulses, she trusted her father implicitly, so why wouldn't she comply with his wishes? Why wouldn't she do her best to make her father happy? She'd promised that much to her mother in her final days, that she would look after her father's happiness.

Now, in her favorite room of the house, surrounded by books that had buoyed her through darker times, Catarina stared at the stranger in front of her, reminding herself of all the rationales for this arrangement that had floated through her mind.

She thought she had prepared herself for the moment she'd face the object of her teenage crush, for the inevitable conclusion of her mother's last wish and her father's relentless determination to fulfil it. It was a decision that would bring to rest the uncertainty of the past few years since her mother's death. But nothing inside her was at ease. Instead, it was as if the hum of an electric current ran through her, unexpected and shockingly intimate.

As she gazed at the man in front of her, she could see she had made a grave miscalculation. Her father had always treated her as if he was a little baffled by her, like she was another species, a favorite dog, perhaps, content with pats on the head and endless treats. So although her best interests were always at the forefront of her father's mind, why had she assumed that Giuseppe d'Avalos would know who would make a good marriage partner for her? How could her father possibly know what she needed in a husband, what she could handle? Because the man in front of her was far too much to handle. Just the sensation of being close to Massimo threatened to overwhelm her.

Up close, it was clear that her memories didn't do justice to this man. His lean, muscular frame was starker than she remembered, more imposing, more *everything*. She could see the outline of the well-defined muscles of his shoulders under the crisp white of his shirt. The top button was undone, showing a hint of dusky hair against bare skin, so shockingly intimate, so sexual and not at all in line with the inscrutable expression on his face. That perfectly fitted shirt followed his broad chest, his tapered waist and disappeared into charcoal-gray wool pants.

Was she really focusing on this man's pants? Her gaze flicked back to his face as her cheeks flushed. She was not ready to identify all the feelings that were running through her. Instead, she met his eyes. But none of her memories captured the piercing intensity of his dark brown eyes as he watched her. They drew her in, pulling her toward him. She wanted to touch him. She wanted to test the softness of his inky hair between her fingers, the smooth line of his jaw. She inhaled, and his scent filled her, spicy, masculine with a hint of pine that sent her thoughts to her house deep in a remote Norwegian fjord. This was the scent of freedom, and she wanted more.

Catarina couldn't help herself. She lifted up onto her tiptoes and brought her lips to one cheek, pressing them against his soft skin. Just a greeting, she told herself as she took another breath of his scent. Nothing more. But her heart slammed in her chest, beating out its message, *liar, liar, liar.* Still, she moved to the other cheek, greedy for more. When her lips met his skin again, she heard the quietest of groans from somewhere deep inside him. It was electric. *Magical.* The word resonated inside her, as part of her battered heart opened up in what felt very much like hope.

Catarina was scared to move. She was scared to breathe. If she did, she might disturb this feeling inside her, the feeling that there was hope, that maybe she didn't have to spend the rest of her life alone. Maybe her mother wasn't the only person she would ever grow close to, who would understand her. Maybe this marriage wouldn't simply be a compromise she was forced to make, her father's satisfaction for fulfilling her mother's dying wish in exchange for the freedom of a life out from under her father's scrutiny, not dictated by his misguided maneuvers. Maybe this marriage could be more than a business arrangement. No one would ever replace her mother, and that was the last thing she wanted, but maybe there was a chance that Catarina had found another connection.

Then something shifted. Massimo's expression seemed to shutter, leaving only a distant stillness. She stared at the man in front of her, so remote, searching for the connection she had felt just moments before. It had to be there, somewhere inside him, because it was still bubbling inside her. It had been there before, and she would find it again.

Catarina could feel her determination grow. She had spent too much of her life buffeted by her mother's awful twist of fate, by her father's autocratic decisions. This man in front of her was an opening in her future. Clinging to that electric pull she'd felt, that groan of pleasure she swore she'd heard, she took a deep breath and squared her shoulders at this imposing man. *Just a man*, she reminded herself.

"Massimo?"

Just his name, nothing else, as she tried to capture into words the questions that reverberated inside her. *What is this overwhelming pull between us? Don't you feel what I feel right now?*

Massimo closed his eyes, his long, dark lashes resting on his cheeks, and she thought she detected a faint shudder or a grimace or some reaction that she couldn't read. Then, when he opened his eyes again, her blood ran cold as that last spark of hope, the one she was clinging to, drained from her body. In front of her was the man she had seen in photos, a self-contained, arrogant man with a coldness that was unmistakable. It was as if he had just turned off every emotion, so methodically and thoroughly, leaving absolutely no trace of the man whose cheeks she had brushed her lips against, the man whose eyes had flashed with desire and something else.

Or maybe he hadn't turned off his emotions. Maybe this was who Massimo Carandini really was, and what she had mistaken for a connection had been just a facade for her father's benefit that he'd let linger. Maybe this was the true face of the man underneath it. The man she would marry. Catarina swallowed.

"Miss d'Avalos." Her name rolled off his tongue, velvet-soft, both a caress and a warning.

"We are to be engaged," she said, pulling her thoughts in order. "Surely first names are appropriate."

He frowned, disapproval radiating from him.

"What I require of a wife is someone who will maintain an impeccable reputation," he said, his gaze fixed on her, impenetrable as the silky tone washed over her.

How could his voice leave her so aware of the way her shirt brushed over her breasts each time she breathed? Catarina tried to focus on the fact that he didn't seem to find her comment worthy of a response.

"I will require you to attend dinners where we will entertain business clients," he continued in a cool, imperious tone. "We will make regular public appearances to ensure that the world understands the stability of our partnership. Our priority is to portray the image of stability."

He enunciated that last word slowly, as if she might have missed all the implications of the values he was laying out. Catarina resisted a frown. She tried to read his face for some hint of emotion, but she found it impenetrable, a wall of stone. If this was the kind of interaction he wanted, she had a lifetime full of practice with it. Growing up with her mother in the spotlight, she had learned early never to show her emotions. Hopes, dreams and disappointments were saved for the privacy of her own home, for her family. That was the nature of having the Nordic Siren for a mother. Any hint of discontent would be picked apart by the paparazzi, each observation fueling a spiral of further interest and speculation. Catarina would never subject her family to that. But at home, away from crowds and prying eyes, she could finally exit the stage, and she had found relief in that freedom. How foolish she had been to so quickly slot Massimo into the role of family. The loss of the warmth of her family had been a gaping hole inside her since her mother's death, and she could not expect marriage to Massimo to fill it. Still, she needed to clarify the terms of this engagement.

Catarina kept her face serene, tilting her head to the side. "This proposal sounds an awful lot like a business negotiation."

His eyes grew even darker, more distant. "I was given to understand that you were clear about the nature of our agreement."

"I am," she said lightly, as if she wasn't negotiating her entire future. "I suppose I just wondered if there would be any ceremony to this, perhaps a ring or a proposal on one knee, just for tradition's sake."

She gave a little laugh, the kind that had amused and enchanted the crowds that her mother drew.

Massimo did not smile. "I kneel for no one."

"Noted," she said mildly.

His eyes narrowed as if he was searching for sarcasm, for any hint of rebellion. But he wouldn't find it. She had learned long ago, in her endless dealings with her father, that challenging a man like this directly was not the most effective strategy. Instead, she changed tactics.

"I will, of course, require time for study. I put off university to be by my mother's side." Catarina hadn't actually applied for university or even thoroughly considered this path, but it was one of many roads to freedom she had entertained before her father had dropped this marriage into her lap. Her comment was a test of sorts, she supposed, one that she had the uneasy feeling Massimo might fail. Too late, Catarina realized she should have asked for the results much earlier.

Massimo didn't react to the mention of her mother, let alone offer the condolences that usually followed any reference to their family's devastating loss. Instead, he waved a dismissive hand. "You can schedule that with my assistant to ensure it doesn't conflict with the functions we will attend."

Catarina smiled pleasantly at him as she digested his words, trying to ignore the heaviness that weighed in her gut. This man was as autocratic as her father, but a future with him would be much worse. Giuseppe d'Avalos loved her, and regardless of how ham-fisted his attempts to steer her life had been, she had never once doubted that his intentions were true. He only wanted the best for her.

But Massimo Carandini didn't care about her happiness. That much was clear. This man hadn't sworn on her mother's deathbed to take care of her. Instead, he was looking for an expensive, showy decoration, paid for with the kind of upscale exchanges that were made in a study filled with the scent of grappa and cigars. None of the fruits of those deals would come her way if she married this man. Massimo would treat her like a prop, brought out when he needed her and put away afterward. Catarina had been stuck in her father's gilded cage for the past two years, as they'd struggled to find a way forward in a world without her mother. But Massimo's cage would be much smaller, and he wasn't even pretending it would be gilded.

Catarina had told herself she would go through with this marriage for her father's sake, but staring at the cold, implacable man in front of her, she was no longer sure she could. And yet, she had to. Her father had rested the future of his business on this union. And no matter how different they were, she loved her father and wanted to please him. She wanted to allow him to rest easy. But how could she promise her life to a man like Massimo? There had to be a solution. It was just so hard to think rationally when he was so close. His body seemed to call to hers.

She smiled pleasantly at Massimo as he glared at her, and she found herself searching for a chink in his armor of demands and control. This was a man who didn't even think to downplay his arrogant commands on their first meeting, before she had even agreed to their marriage. Clearly, Massimo didn't have enough people in his life who said no to him.

"I do so look forward to our next meeting, but I am afraid I have business to attend to this morning," she said. "Unless you were expecting a romantic walk through our gardens first…"

She followed her delicate jab with a bland smile. A flash of surprise crossed his face, as if the last thing he'd expected was this poke at him followed by a dismissal. It disappeared immediately, but the glimmer of satisfaction inside her lasted longer.

"We will have plenty of time to talk about future expectations," he said, his low voice rich and ominous.

That voice slid through her, leaving her breasts heavy and heat pooling between her legs. This was what made him so dangerous. Her body didn't seem to care about cages, gilded or not, even if they belonged to closed-off men with iron wills. Despite everything he'd said, she still had the inexplicable urge to run her fingers over his full lips, so improbably sensual against the hard set of his jaw. Though she'd all but told him to leave, a part of her ached for him to protest, to close the distance between them and press her mouth against his lush lips. If just his cheeks were enough to spark heat inside her, what would his lips do to this feeling inside her?

But Massimo didn't kiss her. He just stared at her with that cold, assessing gaze, as if he was calculating her use to him. Then, without another word, he turned and walked out the door.

Catarina stood in place for a long time, in the middle of the library, the shelves of books glowing red and orange in the light from the windows. But she wasn't thinking about books. She was thinking of Massimo and those deep brown eyes that, for a few moments, had seemed to be a window into a more private part of him.

No. She must have imagined those few moments, imposing her own spin on the distinctly less charming reality of her life. It wouldn't be the first time. She'd spent enough of her childhood entertaining herself with her imagination to know how easily ideas could turn fantastical.

Later that evening at dinner, Catarina smiled pleasantly across the table through course after course as her father ticked off characteristics that made Massimo the perfect husband: money, family name—tarnished but redeemed—and multiple estates for her exploration. She didn't miss his unspoken assumption that this list should make her happy, and she didn't say a word, just murmured in assent and let her father talk.

As he continued his expounding, Catarina found herself thinking about her mother. How would her father's ideas about marriage have played out if Maria Nordland had lived? Even before her mother's death, her father's overprotective tendencies had been stifling at times. That he loved Catarina had never been in doubt, but he had never quite figured out what to do with her, swinging wildly between indulgent and strict. Her mother had protected her from her father's efforts to raise the society girl that he had always assumed someone of their station would become. In that path, Catarina had no interest. She had only sporadically attended the all-girls boarding school, tucked away in the Italian Alps, staying just long enough to learn languages and anything of interest before she took off to be by her mother's side for their next adventures. A flurry of tutors had ensured she'd passed all her exams, but many of the finishing school lessons this academy prided itself on were lost on Catarina. After eighteen, she had resisted her father's more pressing calls for an appropriate future and assumed the position of her mother's full-time travel companion. Her life might have glided on like that for years, but her mother's stage-four breast cancer diagnosis five years ago had changed everything.

From that day on, Catarina's life had been turned upside down. Her mother had been her only real friend, and when they traveled, it was as if the two of them had existed in their own little world. At the age when she might have entertained the idea of university or some small stretch of independence, she grew even more attached to her mother. At every single one of those last performances, she and her father had sat, side by side, in tears, bonded by their mutual love and impending loss. During those last months, the world had closed. It was then that her mother's last wishes were uttered, the wishes that had haunted both Catarina and her father since that day. She had eavesdropped outside the heavy door to her parents' bedroom, unwilling to miss a moment of what was left of her mother's voice.

"Protect her," her mother had said to her father. Her mother's voice had been so soft, so weak, so unlike the larger-than-life music that had shaped Catarina's world. "She will be lonely when I am gone. Make sure that she is protected for the rest of her life."

If Catarina hadn't eavesdropped that day, she never would have understood what was behind her father's clumsy attempts to push her in one direction, then the other. But when he announced the plan for her marriage across the heavy dinner table, surrounded by portraits of generations of the d'Avalos family, a rare smile had teased at her father's lips. He had found his solution, the way to fulfill his promise to his beloved wife, and that decision was final. Her mother would have been horrified. This was decidedly not what Maria Nordland had meant, and yet to point out that Catarina knew her mother's intentions better than he did would devastate him. So she'd said nothing. Not yet. Not until she got her head around a solution that would untangle the mess that was winding its way around her life.

Since the day her father had announced the marriage

proposal, Catarina had buried herself in her books and traveled, trying desperately not to think about this rapidly approaching future. She'd visited her mother's family in Oslo, just to hear them speak the secret language she and her mother had shared. But her cousins' homes were haunted by her mother's ghost, so she'd left them and retreated to the towering place her father had built for her mother, with its mix of Scandinavian sensibilities and an Italian flair for luxury. It was perched on the mountains that rose up from the deep blue Norwegian fjords, dramatic and immovable.

As she listened now to her father wax prosaic over the future that Massimo would bring her, Catarina found herself thinking once again about that place. It was her and her mother's retreat from the world, the place that truly felt like home. It felt like freedom. Catarina alone had inherited it, as her father never had any interest in the stark beauty of his wife's home country. As she nodded at her father's long soliloquies, an answer to her predicament came to her, an answer that would free her from the vise that seemed to be tightening around her chest.

Late that night, long after her father had disappeared down the hallway of the master suite, Catarina packed her bags full of soft wools and fleeces and slipped out of the house. She alerted the pilot of their family's jet that she needed to make a quick trip to Norway, confident that her years of impromptu trips with her mother would mean the crew wouldn't suspect anything out of the ordinary. Definitely not something that her father should be alerted of.

Catarina wasn't running away; at least that was what she told herself on the taxi ride to the airport. She was simply making some space to think. Her father would find her, of course, but with any luck it would take a few days for him to catch up. Knowing her father and his aversion to snow, he was more likely to send someone else to collect his daughter. By then, she would have a plan, because as much as she wanted to please her father, her mother's voice would always speak louder.

"Someday, my little songbird, you must fly on your own." The words still rang in her head. Maybe this wasn't exactly the sort of flight her mother had had in mind, but it was only now that Catarina fully understood why her mother had spoken these words, now that a marriage to Massimo Carandini threatened to take this possibility away.

Catarina had always been a quiet, obedient daughter for her father, but at her core, she was her mother's child. Tomorrow morning, when he found himself alone at the breakfast table, he would be reminded of that fact.

CHAPTER THREE

"I SAID I was not to be disturbed," Massimo said impatiently into the speaker of the phone that sat in the middle of his desk. In front of him lay three newspapers, all featuring speculations of his engagement. While his family's contentious history with the paparazzi had done much damage to both the Carandini name and the brothers' childhoods, Massimo found that some amount of the inevitable publicity could be used strategically. Like, for example, the shot of him pulling up at the d'Avalos family home that he was currently looking at. Massimo was in the middle of reading the article, appropriately flattering thus far, when his assistant's voice had interrupted him.

"Giuseppe d'Avalos is on the line," she said.

Massimo frowned. Was his soon-to-be father-in-law calling to praise the effectiveness of his public relations campaign publicizing their upcoming engagement, or was he calling to manage it? Either way, Massimo wasn't interested in this conversation. He leaned back in his leather chair and ran a hand through his hair. He looked in the direction of the tall windows that opened for a view of Milan's terra-cotta rooftops and green hills in the distance, but he wasn't thinking about the view. Instead, the memory of Catarina's lips on his cheek inexplicably resurrected inside him, followed by the bolt of desire that had pulsed through him, bringing his rational mind to a standstill. Massimo scowled, forcing that thought away.

"Put him through," he grumbled, picking up the receiver of the phone.

"It's Catarina." Giuseppe d'Avalos's usually controlled voice was urgent in Massimo's ear. "She's gone."

Massimo's entire body stilled, and his hand tightened around the phone.

"What do you mean, *gone*?" His voice was as cold as the icy dread that ran through him.

"Catarina did not appear at breakfast, and I found that my pilot had logged an entry for our family's jet last night."

Anger thundered through him. This was not acceptable. Yesterday evening he had spent an hour with his assistant going over the detailed plans of how best to position the release of their engagement. The speculation that had appeared in the morning papers was just the start. There were supper reservations this evening at the iconic Ristorante Emmanuel Rossellini, for example, where their first public appearance would certainly be noted. He had planned to present whatever ring his assistant had purchased to Catarina over dessert. Everything was not only in place, but also set in motion.

Scandal. The word blazed through him. Massimo had spent his entire adult years building up an empire so that he could avoid these kinds of disasters. Now everything he and his brother had worked so hard for could be destroyed in one fell swoop.

"Where did she go?" he asked, keeping his voice under tight control.

"Norway. Her mother had a place in the mountains outside of Tromsø, and she left it to Catarina."

Norway. The flight would be a few hours. Massimo massaged his temple with his free hand. There was still hope of fixing this...situation.

"Have you spoken to her?" he bit out.

"There is a problem with that," said her father cautiously. "Currently, the phones are out of service. The area is prone to strong weather, and this happens more often than not during the storms. I have spoken to the pilot, and I am waiting for the plane to return so someone can gather her up. Discreetly."

The line was silent. Massimo glanced at the Patek Philippe watch ticking away on his wrist. It was just after noon. If he took his own jet, there was still just enough time to bring her back and make their eight o'clock dinner reservations, if he could maneuver through any delays.

Finally, he let out an irritated sigh. "I will go and bring her back myself."

Of course, it would mean canceling all his afternoon meetings. *Like your father used to do*, whispered an insidious voice in the back of his mind.

He flinched, recalling his parents' loud arguments during the intermission of *Tosca* with a flare and drama that had rivaled the action on the main stage. If the theatrics had stayed discreetly between the two of them, maybe his father could have clung on to his family's name. But how many deals had fallen through because his father had canceled a key business meeting to join his wife on a last-minute reconciliation trip after one of the countless times she'd threatened to leave him due to his "neglect"? Of course, he and Alessandro had not missed the fact that neither of his parents had dropped anything when the brothers had gotten kicked out of school.

Massimo gritted his teeth as he tried Catarina's phone number and was immediately directed to voice mail. This engagement was supposed to be a conduit for business, not a hindrance. He would handle Catarina the way he handled everyone else who got in the way of his plans: by making it clear that it was in her best interests to follow the paths he presented to her. Because he knew how to make sure that the people at his command did what he asked them to do. Massimo told himself that this was like any other business crisis he had handled in the past. He would deal with it swiftly and efficiently. And he absolutely would not lose his temper.

Massimo's private jet was ready within the hour, and as the plane flew north, he contemplated his options. Her weakness seemed to be her father, and their marriage agreement was connected to the man's business. He was debating the efficacy of taking a harsher approach with her when his phone rang, and his brother's name appeared on his screen.

"I saw the newspapers this morning," said Alessandro. "Not wasting time with your plans. Efficient as ever."

"There's been a complication," he muttered. "My lovely bride-to-be appears to have fled to Norway."

His brother's laugh traveled through the phone, further grating on his nerves. "You always were a charmer."

The jab irritated Massimo more than usual because of the reality it exposed. He had walked into the library of the d'Avalos estate fully intending to be charming, or at least his best version of it. Somehow, his plans had fallen apart the moment her voice sang through him. And when her lips had brushed against his cheek...

"It's nothing I can't handle," he barked. "We'll return in time for supper at Ristorante Emmanuel Rossellini, as planned."

"I have no doubt," said Alessandro, and Massimo could hear the smile in his brother's voice, crawling farther under his skin. "But I can hear your scowl through the phone line. Maybe you want to work on that before you talk to the woman again."

"I don't need relationship advice from my younger brother," he growled because he was, in fact, a minute older than Alessandro.

This comment only made his brother laugh even louder.

"By all means, use your own...expertise," he said, and Massimo didn't miss the sarcasm that his brother infused in that last word. "As long as this marriage boosts our family's reputation, I don't care how you make it work."

"It will work," he said with finality. "Just take care of anything that is burning this afternoon."

When he ended the call, Massimo reminded himself that he loved his brother. He did, truly, in the same way he loved his grandmother. The two were the only relatives he associated with happy memories from his childhood. When his parents were too busy with their latest dramatic fallout or reunion to be bothered with two young boys, Massimo and Alessandro would spend weeks at their grandparents' sprawling estate on Lake Como, climbing trees, staying out of their thunderous grandfather's path and clinging to their grandmother, elegant, stern and loving. In those earliest memories, neither he nor Alessandro had thought their parents' absences were strange, nor did they think twice about the tempestuous fights that echoed through the house when their parents occasionally graced them with their presence, not when their grandmother would appear with fresh vanilla cake and cold lemonade.

She had protected them, Massimo later realized. His distant grandfather had, too, in his own way, when he'd left the business to the two boys when they came of age, to govern alongside their impulsive and distracted father. The subsequent twelve years since leadership had come into their hands had been spent reviving the business while putting out their parents' fires. Massimo would not allow Catarina to become yet another fire he needed to put out. That was the first message he would make clear when he found her.

As the plane landed on the tiny runway of the Tromsø airport, heavy flakes of snow were falling everywhere, melting on the windows and settling on the snowbanks left by a season's worth of plowing. By the time he walked down the steps and onto the tarmac, the snowfall had shifted from flurries to a storm.

One of his assistants handed him gloves and a change of boots. He waved them off. "I won't need those," he said, picturing the well-groomed path from his car to his favorite resort in the Alps. This would be simple. Quick.

"The storm warning has been upgraded, sir," said the assistant.

Massimo frowned.

"I won't be needing your services until I return," he added, dismissing his staff. "Stand by for my call."

Bringing Catarina back to Milan was a delicate matter, best done alone, no matter how much he trusted his staff. He might even need to adjust his strategy slightly, though first, he needed to figure out why she ran away when the deal was all but signed. He flashed to the smile she had given him just before she had ushered him out of their family's estate, and an unfamiliar wave of uneasiness washed through him. She was not quite the biddable, naive young woman he had taken her for, but this just meant that his new strategy likely needed to involve a more nuanced effort, including some of that…charm his brother mentioned. There was no reason for the wariness this idea seemed to invoke. His intense reaction to her was likely just surprise at his unexpected attraction, nothing more.

A thick layer of snow had settled on the ground as Massimo drove through the narrow streets of Tromsø, passing buildings painted in bright reds and yellows, topped with mounds of white. He crossed a bridge, following the GPS coordinates Giuseppe d'Avalos had given him, and began climbing up the side of the mountain. As he ascended, the lights from the town disappeared, and the only evidence of civilization were the car tracks that guided the way through the newly fallen snow. Great walls of it lined the uphill side of the road, and the downhill side disappeared into a white abyss. The higher his car climbed, the less visible the curves of the mountainside were, as thick, wet flakes hit his windshield. He had rarely driven in more than a centimeter of snow, but he was Massimo Carandini. He could do anything he set his mind to.

When he heard an ominous rumble from the mountainside, he followed his instincts and put his foot on the gas. The SUV fishtailed around the curve, skidding dangerously close to the edge, but he focused on the road in front of him. The GPS told him he was close to the spot where Catarina's mountain home sat, perched on a remote cliffside, so he ignored another rumble from the mountain and sped up. Out of the corner of his eye, he caught a glimpse of movement in the haze of white, uphill from him. It looked as though an enormous snowbank was racing toward him. He slammed his foot on the gas as snow pelted his roof, bumping over mounds as more came crashing down all around him. An avalanche. There was nothing he could do but keep driving, so he raced onward. Too late, he realized he was driving much too fast for the growing layer of wet snow on the road. But he would make it. He was sure of it. The snow was everywhere, covering the windshield now, blocking all hope of seeing what was in front of him. Massimo slammed on the brakes, and the car skidded and spun until it hit something solid. Then everything slammed to a stop.

As the storm picked up, blowing its wind in swirls, what Catarina felt was relief. Phone service was already down, and with any luck, the roads would close soon, too. Planes would be delayed from the heavy spring snow piling on the runway, falling too quickly for the plows to clear.

Catarina sat on a bar stool at the island counter of her kitchen, dressed in her favorite cashmere sweater and leggings, birthday presents from her mother years ago. She warmed her hands with a mug of tea as she looked out the tall windows. In one direction was the barely visible road, and in the other, there was only a hazy white, where on a clear day the fjord would stretch out below her. Today wasn't anywhere near clear.

Thank goodness she had a stocked refrigerator to wait out the storm. On the plane ride from Milan, she had called Signe, their longtime cook, who had filled the refrigerator and cabinets with her favorite Norwegian delicacies as well as ingredients for the meals she would fix after Catarina had settled in. Somehow, Signe had managed to bake cinnamon rolls between the time Catarina had called and the time she had arrived, and she really hoped that Signe hadn't done that in the middle of the night. If she had, at least their family paid her a generous full-time salary for what was very part-time work, so Catarina hoped this made up for the last-minute, late-night inconvenience.

She shivered and shifted her gaze to her third attempt at a fire that was currently smouldering in the fireplace that rose from the opposite side of the great room. This one seemed to be headed in the same direction as the other two. She couldn't get the logs to catch fire properly. It took a while for the central heating to find its way through the many rooms of this house, so for now, she was a bit cold. But at least she was free.

Catarina avoided letting her gaze pause on the piano. There had been a time when music had been her constant companion, playing through her mind. When her mother had entered the last stages of life, that music had faded. Catarina didn't notice until a few weeks after her mother's death, when she sat on the familiar bench, but the music no longer played. She had reached for the keys, playing a few measures by rote, but grief overcame her.

After weeks of this, she gave up, and it had been years since she had bothered even to try.

But she wasn't here to think about that time in her life. Instead, Catarina focused on the fact that she'd arrived in the darkness and fallen into bed, burying herself in the billowy layers of down for the most peaceful sleep she'd had in a long time. This morning she had awoken to a breakfast of boiled eggs with caviar, pickled herring on crisp bread and an assortment of fruit, the Norwegian breakfast she and her mother had always eaten when they were here. Now she was working her way through her first cinnamon roll of the day. On her last visit, the ache of loneliness and loss had both pulled her here and then driven her away. Even four years after the funeral, it had felt as if her mother's death took up too much space for anything else to exist in her life.

But this time was different. This time, the ache was tempered by the relief of getting away from her father's autocratic decisions, away from an even more autocratic fiancé. It was a reprieve, a chance to come up with a plan that fulfilled her mother's last requests, both for her father and for herself. Because while her father seemed to believe that a strategic marriage was the path to her happiness, Catarina was sure her mother would agree that there was no happiness in the arrangement Massimo had so clearly laid out for her. As the snow continued to pile up on the windowsills, covering the bushes and trees outside and surrounding her in a soft blanket, thick enough to keep the world at bay, she would come up with a new plan, a plan with her freedom at the center.

She was not ready to think about the dreams that had filled her sleep, dreams of the way Massimo Carandini's gaze had burned into her. But touching him had fully entranced her, the electricity that had skittered over her skin as her lips met his cheek. Her dreams erased the moment everything had shifted to coldness. Instead, in the fantasies born in the deep recesses of her mind, Massimo had angled his head and brought those full, sensual lips to the sensitive skin of her neck, then lower...

Catarina gave herself a little shake. There was no reason to think about this fantasy world her mind had created. Instead, she stared out the window, *not* thinking about Massimo's lips nor his broad shoulders nor any other part of him, parts that she had already imagined in exquisite detail.

These not-thoughts were interrupted by a low rumble from outside, and the floor began to shake underneath her. She grabbed the countertop as she saw the great blanket of snow on the mountain crumbling, dissolving, moving. An avalanche, inevitable in these parts when new snow piled on the thawing layers. Close, but not a threat. More relief flooded inside her. Maybe this one would cover the road for days, giving her more time to come up with a plan.

There was a flash of black that burst through the white haze of the road. An SUV, covered with snow, careened much too fast around the curve of the road. Who was driving in this weather? The car skidded and spun until it hit the snowbank at the base of her driveway with a crunch of metal that reverberated through the triple-paned glass of her kitchen window. The sound was a punch in the gut. Someone was in that car. And she was the only person around for miles.

Catarina abandoned her tea and cinnamon roll and

raced to the entrance of the house, the one that had been shoveled and groomed when she'd first arrived but was now covered with snow. She grabbed her pillowy down parka and pulled on the furry boots that covered her calves, then opened the door into the storm. The wind blew the thick flakes in swirls around her as she made her way down the steps, slick with new snow from the storm. She ran down the driveway until she came to the vehicle that was now wedged between the snowbanks, blocking her path out.

She detected no movement inside the car except a haze of white dust that drifted inside, probably from the airbag. Catarina knocked on the window. Nothing. She knocked again, her heart pounding. Still nothing. Then the door creaked until it was wide enough for a person to move through.

When she looked up, her breath caught in her throat. Massimo Carandini appeared out of the dust. He climbed out from behind the airbag, stepping into the snow, raising himself to his full height. He was standing so close to her, the snow dancing around him, landing in his tousled hair and on the shoulders of his woollen coat.

Then she saw the blood. His hair had hidden it, but a stream of red was coming from his forehead near his hairline. Catarina meant to speak, but her voice died in her throat as the intensity of his stare hit her. His eyes were dark, and she felt that fire from those first moments after they met buzzing between them. He gazed at her with something she might have called *wonder* if she didn't know better. Still, a rush of desire ran through her, unwanted and ill timed.

Massimo continued to gaze at her with a strange,

searching expression, like he wasn't quite sure what to do with her. He stared at her with a focus in his dark brown eyes that made her feel as if he truly saw her. It took her breath away, so she found herself looking everywhere but his eyes, at his silky black hair that was collecting wet flakes of snow, at his charcoal-gray jacket, appropriate for a cool night on Lake Como rather than a blizzard in the remote mountains of Norway. And then there were his hands, those lovely, long fingers, completely bare. Who drove into a Nordic blizzard without a hat or gloves?

Massimo Carandini did. Only an arrogant man with the confidence of a king would assume that he was above Mother Nature. Also, he had just crashed his car, she reminded herself.

"What are you doing here?" she whispered, and her cheeks burned in the cold air.

The sound of her voice seemed to startle him, and whatever openness she had seen closed. The intensity of his eyes turned to something more ominous.

"You forced me to follow you to the Arctic and now the car is..." He gestured at the airbag.

She blinked. "I *forced* you to come?"

This was rich. He blamed her for following her and seemed to be on the verge of blaming her for the state of his car. This was the man who had just recklessly driven to her cabin in the middle of a snowstorm, and yet he made it sound like she was somehow putting him out.

He checked his watch, then glared at her impatiently. "We still have enough time to make our supper reservation at Ristorante Emmanuel Rossellini if we leave now."

"In Milan?" Catarina was aware that her usually tempered voice betrayed hints of incredulity. "And how do you suggest we make our way through the avalanche that you just barely escaped?"

"A helicopter could land somewhere in this open space, for example," he said, gesturing into the white swirl of the snowstorm.

"And how do you suggest we call one?"

His answer was a glare that suggested further irritation. He pointed to her house that towered in the nothingness of the white snow that was coming down increasingly harder. "You must have some way of getting out of here."

Catarina took a deep breath, trying to control her exasperation. "I'm afraid I don't, as we are currently in the middle of a blizzard. I am going to interpret this magical thinking of yours as a possible consequence of the head injury you have sustained."

He glared at her. "I have no idea what you are talking about."

"You're bleeding." She hadn't meant to soften her voice, but every time she caught a glimpse of the red on his forehead, something tugged at her gut. *He's just a man.*

"I'm not bleeding," he snapped.

She ignored his comment and reached up to touch the trickle of blood. This was a mistake. When she touched his skin, the electric pull between them sparked back to life. His eyes narrowed, as if he had felt it, too, and was blaming it on her yet again. She swallowed, shoving away the uncomfortable heat inside, and turned her hand to show him the blood. He didn't speak. They stood in some sort of silent battle until she could no longer ignore his bare hands, exposed to the wind and cold.

"You need to get out of this weather," she finally said, then indicated up the hill, in the direction of her cabin. "You might as well come in. Do you have anything in the car that you need? Perhaps clothes or toiletries?" she asked.

"I brought nothing. We are not staying."

"Indeed," she said. Had he actually suffered from a concussion, or was he just so arrogant as to assume that even a snowstorm was not an insurmountable hurdle for following through with the plan he had engineered? Though Massimo was undoubtedly well-traveled, clearly, he had never been to a remote fjord, far from cities and servants at his beck and call. This remoteness was what her mother had loved best about the place and, quite possibly, what had made her father stay away. Here, the forces of nature did not bend to money and power, and her father preferred to stay in the realm where it did. Massimo was likely the same, and he would understand his predicament soon enough. She knew better than to press the issue.

"Someone should call about my car," he said, nodding in the direction of the mess of crunched metal and shattered glass that was the front of the SUV.

Someone meaning...her? Catarina resisted an eye roll because twenty-four years of managing her father had taught her to keep her tone unfailingly polite. Even when the situation did not call for it. "Unfortunately, as I mentioned, the mobile towers are down at the moment."

She waited for his reply, but it didn't come. He simply gazed out into the blizzard.

"Shall we go inside?" she asked, giving him another one of her patient smiles.

He ignored her suggestion and gestured again at the endless white landscape in that imperious way of his, as if the entire world was at his bidding. As if, even here, in the middle of a blizzard on an empty mountainside, all it took was a mere flick of his finger to set into motion whatever he willed. As if he expected her to respond to him the same way.

"The road," he said. "Where does it lead?"

It was the oddest question to ask. He didn't choose the obvious one, which was, why did you leave so suddenly in the middle of the night, on the eve of our official engagement? Actually, she was expecting something more demanding, something that started with *how dare you...?*

Catarina sighed. This interaction only validated her decision to flee. How could she marry this arrogant, imperious man? Still, she drew on her years of patience and ingrained manners and answered him. "There's not much that way, just a smattering of houses close to the border of Sweden."

Massimo frowned, but said nothing more.

"Let's go inside," she said gently, coaxing. "It's quite chilly out here."

He looked a bit startled by her last comment, and she could feel the intensity of his gaze return fully to her. Then Massimo unfastened the top button of his coat. He moved on to the second one.

"What are you doing?" she asked quickly.

He looked at her with a kind of exaggerated patience, as if his actions were perfectly obvious. "You are cold, so I am giving you my coat."

His gaze was almost a glare, as if it hadn't crossed his mind that her concern about the cold wasn't for herself.

She wasn't sure what to do with that, so at odds with the rest of their conversation.

"Keep your coat on," she said urgently. "Please."

She pressed her bare hand against his long fingers. Her breath caught in her throat as the electric desire buzzed across her skin. She pulled her hand away, refusing to meet his gaze. It was dangerous to touch this man. Despite the cold, the rush of heat shot through her. She would avoid it at all costs, she promised herself, even if she was snowbound in her cabin with him.

Catarina turned away and said over her shoulder, "Follow me."

CHAPTER FOUR

MASSIMO HAD EXPECTED TEARS. He had expected demands for tokens of affection, perhaps the ring she had mentioned at their meeting the day before to solidify their engagement. But Catarina didn't throw strategically selected pieces of her family's heirloom porcelain, nor did she collapse into a breathless display of distress on her favorite chaise longue, the way Massimo had seen his mother do the moment his father walked in the door. He had at the very least expected to find Catarina looking distraught. However, for a moment she had looked almost…irritated at his appearance in her driveway. That couldn't be right.

But that inexplicable expression had so quickly disappeared, replaced by the veneer of politeness she so expertly wielded. Was she just disappointed that the unfortunate crash of his car hadn't allowed for her best, most dramatic performance? That seemed the most likely explanation. Catarina had claimed that she didn't crave the spotlight, but plenty of his mother's performances had taken place out of the public eye. Catarina could simply be reconsidering her approach.

Massimo found that his temper was rising at yet another unexpected complication. She seemed to excel at creating these complications, he thought bitterly, particularly for someone selected for the lack of complications she posed. He followed Catarina along the driveway as he scanned the area for possible ways to leave. Though this entire situation that she had forced him into was frustratingly inconvenient, he would not let Catarina destroy the plans he had so carefully orchestrated.

Snow had seeped into his leather shoes, leaving them cold and wet, and each slippery step in the new snow sparked the temper that still threatened to flare inside him. His temple throbbed, and he brought his hand to the spot where Catarina had touched his forehead just moments ago. He could still feel the echo of her fingers against his skin, the soft brush that shimmered inside him. He took away his hand and frowned at the traces of blood on his fingers. Another wave of uneasiness washed over him. Had he misread her middle-of-the-night disappearance? Did she flee not to get his attention but to escape the marriage? That would be…inconvenient. The thought triggered the unsettled feeling in his gut that had persisted since his phone call with d'Avalos. He needed to get them back on track, which meant figuring out what she was after.

As they walked up the driveway, the house took shape, rising up in the blowing snow. Though no one would call a place of this size and grandeur a chalet, the building had echoes of its humbler version of the mountain cabins he had passed along the road. But this was a home, stately, clad in varnished wood with long windows and a towering peaked roof of metal, clearly made to withstand storms much worse than this. The design was clean and deceptively simple. Catarina led him along a snow-covered path and up the steps to a covered porch at the entry of the house. She opened the thick wooden door, and he followed her inside.

The front hallway opened into an enormous room lined with windows, with a stone fireplace at its center. The diffuse light from the snow outside came in through the tall windows, giving the place an almost mystical glow. He frowned and scanned the entryway, focusing on the only part that stood out, an abandoned pile of luggage, handbags, scarves and other miscellaneous items in the corner. His gaze moved to Catarina as she took off her outer layers and hung them in some sort of metal box in the corner of the hallway, leaving her dressed in a cloud of a sweater that hugged her breasts and accentuated her narrow waist. His body reacted. Her lush curves were on full display, and suddenly Massimo was all too aware that they were stuck together in a remote place.

"You can hang your coat in this drying closet," she said as she turned the knob, and the appliance came to life. Then she frowned at his shoes. "Though I don't think it can do anything about those."

Massimo hung up his coat, shoes and soaked socks in the closet, then followed her through to a large room that spanned the entire length of the house. A dining room table was positioned at one end, and across the broad space was the fireplace, with a grand piano in the far corner. The exposed beams across the towering ceiling were offset by the white walls and wide-planked wooden floors, covered with rugs patterned in reds, blues and whites. She gestured to the floor-to-ceiling windows.

"When the snow lets up, the sofa provides a view across the fjord and up the mountains on the other side," she said, as if he was a weekend guest stopping by for a tour.

She pointed him toward the kitchen, then disappeared in a different direction. The tile was cool under his feet as he took in the sleek white cabinets, accents of light wood and sparkling steel appliances that surrounded him. On the counter, there were glass containers of baked goods, cookies and buns of some sort, and a few dirty dishes were abandoned by the sink. No shards of family porcelain were in sight, nor was there evidence of domestic help. Massimo didn't know what to make of this scene, but he braced himself for the inevitable onslaught of her emotional upheaval, whenever it came.

Catarina returned to the kitchen, her cheeks flushed from the cold, her hair tousled, and the scent he remembered was everywhere, roses and something from the sea. A bolt of lust flashed too quickly to resist, and the warning that chimed through him was just as strong. But Massimo was not his father, who so eagerly responded to his mother's every whim. He would make that perfectly clear.

She was holding a flat metal first aid box, a pair of thick, navy-blue socks and a hideous Christmas-themed jumper. She placed all three items on the island counter and smiled at him with a glint of challenge in her eyes.

"I'm afraid the place hasn't fully warmed up yet, so I brought you an extra layer from my father's closet," she said. "And in case you're concerned, none of it has been worn."

He gave the jumper a disdainful glance. "I can't imagine why."

She rested both hands on the island counter and leveled him with her gaze.

"Why did you come?" she asked. Her voice held a hint of temper.

This reaction he recognized. This he could handle. Massimo took a step forward, and he bit back a smile when her breath caught and her cheeks darkened with heat. His own body stirred in response, but he didn't allow his attention to stray to her lush lips that begged to be kissed, nor did he let himself tangle his fingers in her silky hair. Not yet, at least. Because he had her exactly where he wanted her. "Should I not follow my runaway fiancée?"

She swallowed and raised an eyebrow. "Are we engaged? I guess I must have missed the moment I said yes, among all the fanfare of your proposal."

Her tone had returned to unfailing politeness, the way it had the night before, and there was no mistaking the cutting sarcasm laced in these words. The comment triggered a bizarre urge to snap back at her, to make clear that their arrangement was supposed to be settled. It was also supposed to be convenient, a descriptor that she was doing her best to defy.

"Did your father keep you in the dark about the nature of my proposal?" he said, keeping his voice silky smooth. She looked away when he mentioned her father, so he continued. "Did he promise you something that I did not deliver?"

"Of course not. You were exactly what I should have expected." She managed to make this sound like an insult.

"And yet, something did not meet your satisfaction,"

he continued. "Maybe you were still hoping for a fairy-tale marriage?"

Her cheeks flushed, and he could see he was on the right track.

"You have nothing to worry about," she said, and the corners of her mouth turned down. "I have no illusions of a happy ending between us."

"There will be plenty of happy endings between us, *cara*," he said, letting his voice turn rough with the fire that blazed through him at these words. "That is a promise. But I am a far cry from Prince Charming. As you might have noted."

Her eyes flashed with unmistakable heat, and he felt a surge of satisfaction. He had found his way under her polite facade. But Massimo's body surged with anticipation, and he flashed back to the moment her lips brushed against his cheek back in her library. Her touch had been dangerously electric. He held back the urge to frown and focused on the plan he could not lose sight of.

"As soon as this—" he glanced out the window, into the haze of snow "—is over and we have phone service, I will call a helicopter, and we will fly home then head directly to the restaurant, where I will propose appropriately, with all the fanfare you require. And, if you choose, we can begin right away with the happy endings you claim you are not interested in."

Catarina appeared wholly unmoved by his plan. She lifted her chin, exposing more of the slim column of her neck.

"While we are setting expectations," she said in that prim voice of hers, "I should warn you that restoring phone service will likely take days, as will clearing the road from the avalanche."

He tried to tamp down his frustrations. "I am leaving for Tokyo tomorrow, and that absolutely cannot be postponed."

"I apologize for the inconvenience," she said, and a hint of exasperation laced her polite tone, "though I cannot help but point out that coming here was entirely your choice. In fact, you might note that I left in a manner that suggests I did not want to be followed."

The idea rattled through him, triggering another wave of uneasiness. Her words stirred up a strange mix of emotions that felt a little too close to disappointment for his liking.

"Though I am always pleased to see you, of course," she added sweetly.

"Of course," he bit out.

Had she truly not wanted him to come? It should have been a relief that she hadn't shown any signs of the showy hysterics and demands that his mother made. He told himself it was proof that he had, in fact, made the right choice in marriage partners. This was a woman who avoided the spotlight, something she herself had emphasised. She wouldn't turn dinner parties and galas into a forum to demand his public fealty to her. This, above all, was most important. Still, he couldn't help but note the way she was provoking him, which led him to another possibility. Maybe she was playing the same games as his mother, though with more cunning and restraint. If so, she had succeeded in getting his attention, he thought with a frown.

"Why did you run?" he asked, his voice low and deceptively calm.

"I didn't run. I retreated to gather my thoughts." Her eyelashes fluttered as she stared up at him, defiance shining in her eyes.

"We had an arrangement, which you backed out of." His voice was low and ominous. "I would hate to think that this is how you approach your commitments. Your father was certainly displeased."

The polite smile fell from her lips, and for a moment, in its place was something that looked like pain. Massimo felt an unwanted twist in the gut. He told himself he didn't regret his comment. He was entering negotiations, just the way he had intended. And yet, her expression made him feel distinctly...uncomfortable.

Catarina took a deep breath and added, "I needed time to consider my options. I still have options at this point, don't I?"

"Everyone has options, *cara*," he said, keeping his voice smooth. "Some lead down easier roads than others."

She licked her lips. It was an unconscious action, and yet his body responded to it. "Maybe I found that I am less interested in easier roads, no matter how smooth they are. We all choose roads that lead us to the desired destinations, do we not?"

"That assumes you have a map. But no one can be certain of where a road will take them," he said wryly, "no matter how carefully they choose it."

The events of the past day had reminded him of this lesson.

"Thank you so much for this piece of wisdom, which I

will, of course, consider thoroughly. However, I'm afraid neither of us has many options at the moment," she said crisply. "In the meantime, let me bandage your forehead."

She reached up toward his face, but when her fingers came close to touch him, the hum of attraction that he had been ignoring surged. Catarina pulled her hand away, as if she had felt it, too, and for a moment, uncertainty flashed in her eyes. She swallowed, and he had the distinct impression she was silently talking herself into something. Then she added, "Signe would never make my favorite cinnamon rolls again if she had to clean trails of blood through the house."

She waved her hand around, as if the entire ground floor of this enormous place was at risk. Then she got to work.

Massimo studied her as she opened the first aid box on the granite countertop and sized him up, like she was taking in his height. Catarina frowned, then dragged a chair over from the table. He sat, which put him in the unfortunate position of being eye level with her breasts. They were pert and full beneath the soft cloud of a jumper she was wearing, and he found himself imagining the way they would feel in his hands. In his mouth. A stir in his groin cut through the cool sting of the alcohol wipe on his forehead. This was certainly not how he had seen this day playing out. And yet, he had to admit his situation had sparked a note of curiosity in him. Also, he didn't mind the view.

"You still haven't told me what you want," he said, softening his tone, noting the way her pulse at the tender base of her neck skittered each time he spoke.

Catarina swept a hand around the expansive room,

filled with the kind of understated luxury that left no doubt about her singularly privileged upbringing. "This is all mine. I want for nothing."

There was a wryness in her voice, an irony that suggested there were, in fact, things she wanted. And Massimo found himself wondering what those things were and how he could tease this information out of her. He flashed her an indulgent smile. "Indeed. You have planes and houses at your disposal, though there appears to be an oversight in the domestic worker department."

His gaze flickered to the dirty dishes, then in the direction of the front entryway, where she had left her belongings in a heap. When his gaze returned to her, he caught a hint of amusement in the curve of her lush lips.

"Maybe I prefer to be alone," she said tartly as she patted his forehead with the alcohol wipe.

"Maybe. But you could have simply attended our engagement dinner first," he said, his voice deceptively calm. "Surely you didn't disappoint your father just for one extra day of 'me time.'"

The amusement disappeared from her expression, and despite the fact that he was trying to get under her skin, he found he didn't like this change. Once again, it was the mention of her father that triggered another flash of discomfort. This time, she didn't try to hide it.

"You know nothing about me," she said, her jaw tight as she reached for a bandage.

"How fortunate that we have the rest of our lives to learn as much—or as little—about each other as we choose," he said, a smug smile tugging at his lips. "I am certain that we can come to an understanding that allows for plenty of alone time, if that is what you desire. You'll find that I will not require your presence too often."

"What a relief," she said, not bothering to disguise her sarcasm. She let out a huff of a breath. "I've patched you up, but I probably should check for a concussion."

"I do *not* have a concussion." He and his brother had gotten into more than enough fights in the back halls of their boarding school to gauge that this was far from a concussion. "But feel free to continue your...inspection of me." He found that he was enjoying all her focused attention.

She took a step back, and her gaze traced his face until he could almost swear it settled on his lips. The stir of desire surged inside him, and he allowed himself to lean into that feeling. Massimo had not forgotten that moment in the d'Avalos library, when she'd looked at him like she was overflowing with innocent desire.

Her long, slim throat was exposed, and the pulse at the base of it was even faster than before. The vulnerability with her father was difficult to wield and certainly contained many unknowns. This baser kind of vulnerability he understood completely. He knew from a lifetime of watching his parents that passion could override everything else. He'd watched his father make decisions that put that reckless desire before his sons, his future and his family name. Maybe desire could make Catarina reckless, too.

Her eyes begged for things she probably didn't even know how to name. There was naked, raw want in her gaze, want that was already overriding her desire to keep her distance. Massimo told himself he knew exactly how to handle this, to keep it under control and use it as a tool. Even if the situation had veered much too far from his control today. But he could sort that out later.

Instead, he focused on the tempting heat that sparked in her gaze. He leaned forward and let his eyes dip to her mouth, watching the way it parted slowly as he lowered his head. Her eyes widened as he closed the distance between them, but she didn't move away. Instead, she leaned closer, bringing those lush lips only inches away from his. Her soft breaths came faster, brushing over his skin, kicking his own desire up a notch. But this was nothing he couldn't handle.

"What are you doing?" she whispered.

Though she was innocent, Massimo had no doubt she knew what he was doing. He let a satisfied grin spread across his lips.

"You treated my wound," he said, his voice rasping deeper. "I'm thanking you properly."

And then he closed the last distance and let his mouth press against hers. He had meant it to just be a brush of his lips, a temptation of sorts to hint at the untapped pleasure between them that could lure her into submission. But the moment his lips touched hers, they were suddenly back in her library, with Catarina's voice ringing inside him, so lovely and captivating, and the smell of aging leather contrasting with roses and the salty sea-like scent that flooded him when she was close. His last coherent thought was that she had somehow managed to turn the tables on him, that he was losing control. Then everything came together in a resounding chorus that rang inside him once again, the song he had been resisting since she had appeared surrounded in a halo of snow: *mine*.

* * *

His mouth brushed over hers just once, but the caress of his lips triggered an earthquake of unsettling heat that raced through her body. Before she could steady herself enough to fully register these sensations, the heat turned to an ache that pooled in her breasts and between her legs. *Just a man*, she tried to remind herself. And yet, as this imposing man hovered over her, these sensations threated to overwhelm her body. There was no *just* about him.

Since Massimo had stepped out of the car, she had watched a combination of frustration and confusion flicker across his face, but she had also seen hints of what she could have sworn was curiosity. Interest. Maybe she had misjudged him…or maybe this was her imagination, triggered by the idea of fairy-tale marriages. And happy endings, she reminded herself. That had set off a molten cascade through her that gathered deep in her belly. Now, standing so close, she wasn't prepared for the way his eyes narrowed imperceptibly with desire, the way they turned dark, filling with a bottomless hunger that called to her. She wasn't prepared for the craving it awoke in her, the way it cut through marriage bargains and stifling expectations, calling to a part of her that couldn't resist feeding that hunger.

She pulled back slightly, taking him in. Up close, Massimo was breathtakingly beautiful. Until now, Catarina had not fully registered the way this man made it feel as though the ground under her feet was unstable. The cut she had attended to wasn't his first injury, she noted. Above his left eyebrow, a thin white line marred the bronze skin of his forehead, jagged and long-since healed, and his nose had a rugged look to it, as if it had been broken at some point. The remains of old injuries only served to highlight the beauty of his face, the sharp angles of his cheekbones, the square line of his jaw, the impossibly long lashes that softened the brooding intensity of his eyes. And then there were his lips. They were two sensual, carnal promises that lit her body and left her fingers trembling with an ache to touch them. God, she wanted to touch them. She was caught between temptation and warning, because though she did not know exactly what those lips promised, she knew she wanted it. Maybe even needed it.

Catarina had been on dates, of course, with appropriate men, and on the whole, she found these dinners exactly what they were supposed to be: entertaining and civilized. Somehow, she had mistaken these experiences for attraction. But what she'd felt during those well-mannered evenings had nothing in common with this sensation that her body was not enough to contain the heat that rushed through her. When he was sitting on the chair, looking at her as she tended to his wound, Massimo's nearness had felt uncomfortably intimate. But now, as he towered over her, she felt a different kind of intimacy, a different promise that made her shiver. It was a promise too much to even contemplate and she instinctually knew she needed to stay far away.

Catarina was so aware of how close they were and how alone they were, so far from the structures of her life. This house in the mountains was a place that was her own, a place that had always meant independence, but right now, she was so far from the freedom she craved. And though she tried to tell herself that she would run again from him if she could, she knew that this was a lie.

Back in her library, she had still been in the thrall of her fantasies, partly rooted in the fairy tale of a man she had seen from afar at sixteen, and partly rooted in the freedom that she assumed would come from that marriage. But here in the mountains, without her father nearby, watching to assess the probable outcomes of a favorable marriage contract, Massimo Carandini was viscerally real.

She wanted to move closer. Her whole body was alive with a craving that narrowed her focus to this man in front of her. What would happen if she kissed the hollow at the base of his neck, the place where his heartbeat ticked its relentless reminder that he was a red-blooded man whose physical presence called to her?

He was hovering right above her, his lips just out of reach, and a sudden panic welled up inside her. Would he pull back? Would *she* pull away if she thought any of this through? Before doubts could take over, she slid her hand down his cheek, feeling the smooth, soft skin, where it met the roughness of the stubble. The heat of him shot through her body, and she felt more alive than she had in years.

This was that craving that had swept through her in her library, a room filled with the oppressive weight of her mother's death and her father's overbearing designs on her life. This was the craving she had felt when she had kissed him, that gentle brush of her lips against his skin. She was alive and not alone, and even if this feeling only lasted for this fleeting moment, she would not back away. Catarina cupped her other hand to his cheek, holding his face in her hands, and urged his lips back to hers. Just one more time, she thought, just so she didn't doubt it was real, the way she did last time. Just so she didn't regret letting this moment slip away. Because whatever regrets she had over the past twenty-four hours, his kiss definitely wasn't one of them.

Her heart pounded in her chest as she rose to her toes. It was hard to breathe when she was this close, and yet it felt impossible to pull away. His eyes narrowed, as if warning her away, then widened when she didn't retreat. She focused on his lips. They seemed to call to her, so she answered, pressing her mouth against his. He didn't move. He didn't respond, and for a moment, she thought he would push her away. But suddenly, before she could sense the shift in him, his arms slipped around her neck and into her hair, and he was kissing her back. Sensations rushed through her body, flashes of heat that lived just under her skin, addictive and demanding. He parted his lips, and she gasped as his tongue swept against hers, so intimate and sexual. A craving was building deep inside her, a longing, a chasm that had opened inside her. She *needed*. Massimo let out a low rumble, somewhere between pleasure and frustration. Then his strong hands moved through her hair and pulled her closer. He tilted his head to deepen the kiss, and all semblance of thoughts disappeared.

Then, suddenly and achingly abruptly, he pulled back. His hands braced her shoulders, as if he was physically forcing himself away, despite the connection that sparked and sizzled between them. There was a wild look in his eyes, something new and so out of control that it made her breath catch in her throat. The sound seemed to break the connection. The wild look disappeared, morphing into something more familiar. It was triumph.

"What are you playing at, *cara*?" he said in a lazy drawl.

She blinked in confusion.

"Playing at?" she finally whispered. Her voice shook, and she was so far from under control.

"You tell me you didn't want me to follow you here, and then you kiss me as if you're inviting me into your bed." His eyes flared with lust as he spoke those words, as if he, unwillingly, was thinking about their kiss again, and exactly where it could lead. He shook his head, and that sheen of desire disappeared from his eyes.

"Which is it, Catarina?" he said, his voice low and seductive. "What do you really want?"

She stared at him. What *was* she doing? As a child, her mother had encouraged her to follow her desires and passions, but what would her mother say if she saw Catarina now, awash with a hunger that had pulled her under for a few blissful moments? All the details about this man, details she had been trying so hard to ignore since he arrived, bombarded her: the way his shoulders stretched against the seams of his well-tailored shirt; the hints of laugh lines at the corners of his eyes; the traces of whiskers on his clean-shaven skin; and the scent of him, with hints of pine, masculine in a way that felt undeniably sexual. Now that she had kissed him, she couldn't stop thinking about this. This was something elemental, as if a part of her was opening, a part that she never knew existed. Also, she was snowbound with Massimo inside this house. There was no way they could leave tonight, which meant they would be spending the night under the same roof. Just the two of them. The night before, when she had fallen into bed alone, this towering house had felt as if it echoed with emptiness. Now Massimo's presence made it feel stiflingly small.

Everything about him felt sexual, and it lit her body on fire in a way that she could not ignore. And yet, she had to. This was the man who wanted to take away her freedom, she reminded herself.

Massimo raised his eyebrows expectantly, as if daring her to answer him. But she was in control of her voice. Her voice was one of the tools she had learned to use, a skill, if properly honed, that had the power to cut through the forces that steered her life. Her mother had taught her this lesson. A voice was power, a power that could be wielded within the confines of Catarina's position. Though she had none of her mother's ambition to sing on stage, she had learned to sing in her own ways.

Catarina felt a sudden urge to laugh, but it came out as a bitter, humorless sound of exasperation. "What am I playing at? I recommend you reassess the situation."

She didn't even know where to start with how wrong his accusation of *playing* was. Yes, she had continued his kiss, but only after he'd kissed her and looked at her in a way that made her feel like he was going to devour her. What was his expectation? That she would sit back and wait for him to take the lead on everything, starting with the terms of their marriage all the way down to how and when they kissed? How very arrogant of him, to assume that even that last space between their lips should have been under his control, that she should act according to his unspoken parameters. It was almost as if he did not consider her as a person, with her own will. This was her worst nightmare. So why did her body burn like he was exactly what she wanted? She pushed that question out of her mind.

Her breaths were still coming fast from the kiss as she looked up into his dark eyes, full of recrimination.

"You kissed me." She had meant it as an accusation, but her voice had taken on a husky tone that made this statement sound more like an invitation. She should hate this man for whatever game he was playing or manipulation he was trying, but her gaze flicked down to his lips again, and a shudder of pleasure ran through her. He saw it, too, and he released her and stepped away, as if she were made of fire and he had just been burnt.

"We will save this discussion for later, when you can be more rational about this," he said darkly.

This last sentence seemed perfectly designed to spark her temper, despite all the years of perfecting the art of holding it in. It was yet more evidence that he had mistaken a quiet, media-shy daughter for an obedient ornament. But just because she didn't love attention didn't mean she lacked a will of her own. It didn't make her an unformed piece of clay to mold into whatever shape he chose.

She had to get away from him before she made any further mistakes—because the kiss had, in fact, been a mistake. But Catarina was better at dodging problems rather than confronting them head-on. It was how she had ended up in this mess in the first place. She had run from her father instead of confronting him about the marriage arrangement. But it was too late for regrets in that department. She needed a better plan. She needed space to cool down and think.

"Why don't I show you to a room," she said, then added, "You can attend to some of your *important* business."

He was watching her in that calculating way he had, as if assessing her motives. Before he could say anything more, she took a deep breath and forced a long-practiced calm she didn't feel into her voice. "We are stuck here for the foreseeable future. The house is big enough for us to stay out of each other's way, and the generator should keep us warm for a while."

His eyes narrowed, and she answered with a placid smile, then turned away and started for the staircase. At the top of the steps, the hallway spread out in two directions. She turned to the right and walked the length of the hall to the end. Next to her, Massimo loomed. She wasn't even facing him, and yet Catarina had never been so aware of another man.

Turning the handle, the door swung open and Catarina walked into the bright room, lit with the fall of the snow. "Everything you need should be here."

A king-size bed in rough-hewn wood was the centerpiece of the large room, and it was surrounded by a dresser, small tables and a rocking chair in the same wood. Over the bed hung a large painting of their fjord, the deep blues of the water and sky contrasting with the peaks of the forest of pine trees and stark gray rock. In the middle of the wooden floor was a soft white carpet.

Catarina had not entered the guest room in years, and as her gaze swept across the room, she caught a glimpse of the single framed photo on the rough-hewn wooden table next to the rocking chair. It was of Catarina and her mother, sitting on a stretch of bare rock at the top of a mountain not far from the house. Catarina's aunt and two cousins had visited from Oslo the summer before her mother's diagnosis, and the five of them had wandered up paths and stopped for a picnic lunch to take in the panoramic views. Her aunt had meant to capture the stark beauty of the landscape, but what the photo captured for Catarina was a sense of *before*, a time that sometimes felt like it no longer belonged to her.

Massimo's gaze was on the photo, too. Then he looked at her with an expression that she couldn't read.

"I trust you to make yourself at home," she said quickly and turned for the door.

"If I need anything, I'll find you," he said, and his voice stirred inside her, sending a hot lick of desire through her body that echoed far too long.

CHAPTER FIVE

She really should check on him, Catarina thought as she laid her book on the side table, the one she had been staring at unproductively for too long. Instead of reading, she had found herself thinking about how silent it had been in Massimo's room. Her mind flitted to her previous worry that the accident had caused a concussion. The right thing to do was to check on him, she told herself. For his own good. Not because of this desire he sparked in her. Not because of the memory of his fingers against her scalp as he wove them through her hair and then the startling heat of his mouth as he took hers. The word *took* was the only way to describe what he did with his hands and his mouth. Catarina had thought she'd known the meaning of that word, but his kiss had destroyed her old understanding and rebuilt it into something new, something that enticed her as much as it made her wary. Because she had wanted him to take more.

But she was checking on him out of concern, she repeated to herself as she headed out of her room and down the long hallway. She knocked on the door, and the sound echoed through the quiet house. He didn't answer. Catarina knocked again, and when he didn't answer immediately, she rested her hand on the door handle. But as she turned the knob, the handle was yanked out of her hand.

Catarina's breath caught in her throat. Massimo was standing so close, and a spark of electric heat shot through her. The stark planes of his face were tight, and his gaze was inscrutable. A bump had formed on his head, and Catarina detected dark shadows under his eyes, as if he hadn't slept well, even though his broad shoulders suggested a kind of power that wouldn't budge for such worldly obstacles as a car crash. Or a snowstorm. Or a wayward almost-fiancée.

"Yes?" He used that same sultry tone he had in the kitchen, and his deep voice sent another spark of awareness through her.

"I was just checking to see if you were—" she hesitated. *Conscious* didn't seem to be the right way to finish this sentence "—warm enough?" Belatedly, Catarina registered that he was wearing the tacky Christmas jumper she had left for him, along with the socks. He lifted a brow, as if daring her to comment further on his attire.

"Right. You look fine," she continued quickly. "Also, our cook stocked the refrigerator with food when you are hungry. And if you need anything else…"

"For example?" His voice was so distracting that, for a moment, she wondered if he was…flirting with her? The idea was a spark inside that she knew she should ignore. And yet, she didn't.

"Perhaps more Christmas attire?" she asked archly.

She could have sworn the corners of his mouth twitched up in amusement. "Very generous offer. I'll keep that in mind."

She felt his penetrative gaze bore into her as she walked away.

All afternoon she found herself distracted by this conversation. He couldn't have been flirting with her, could he? Their first meeting the day before suggested that Massimo Carandini was constitutionally unequipped for such frivolities, and yet that spark inside her wouldn't go away.

Not even later that night, when she closed her book again. The house was quiet. In fact, she hadn't heard a sound from Massimo's side of the hall in a long time. She flashed back to his tall frame in the doorway of his room, the hint of amusement teasing his mouth…and the bandage on his forehead. This man had been in a car accident, she reminded herself, which probably meant she should have checked on him more carefully earlier instead of getting so distracted by, well, everything. He had, of course, appeared to be the pinnacle of health. Still, now that she thought about it, she definitely should see if he was all right, especially considering the warnings she was remembering about head injuries and sleep.

Catarina rose from the soft comfort of her reading chair and crept into the hallway until she reached the door to Massimo's room. She stopped and gave the door a gentle tap. Just to make sure he was fine, she told herself. The house was still and silent. She tried again, this time more forcefully. Nothing. If he was asleep, then she really should wake him, just to make sure. Catarina knocked one more time and was answered with silence, so she took a deep breath and entered the bedroom.

The snow lit the walls in a silvery glow, and the light from the windows cast shadows that emphasized the cut of his cheekbones, the angle of his jaw. At rest, he looked so much more peaceful. The intensity of his gaze was gone, as was the frown he gave her so often. The glimmer of the snow brightened the white duvet and shimmered on Massimo's bare skin. So much of his bare skin was exposed. Her heart took off in her chest, sending a wave of tingling desire that settled in her core, racing toward what Catarina had spent too much time pushing away. *Don't get distracted this time*, she chided herself as she crossed the room. *Just wake him, then exit.*

Up close, the silvery light highlighted the curves and shadows of his muscular stomach and chest. He lay on his back, shirtless, with one arm tossed over his head, revealing a patch of silky hair under his arm that somehow made him look both aggressively masculine and also vulnerable. He had another patch of dark hair across his chest and a third trail that invited her gaze down to where the covers began, as if begging her to contemplate what lay beneath. A shiver of desire ran through her, hot and electric. *Just a man. A man who could have a head injury*, she reminded herself sternly.

Her mind was suddenly flooded with things she wanted to do, perhaps trace the hair on the torso to test its texture or maybe bring her lips to his skin just to see how he tasted. But one did not do these things to a sleeping man, even if said man was slated to become one's fiancé. *Wake him and exit*, she repeated to herself.

But she was wary of touching him. Every inch of his body felt aggressively sexual. With an unsteady breath, she settled on the bed next to him, her hip so close to his chest. Heat from his body radiated through the silk of her pajamas, reminding her once again that this was not a dream. She watched the gentle rise and fall of his chest as he breathed, and she studied the harsh planes of his cheeks and nose and forehead, softened in his sleep. She studied the defined muscles of his shoulders, taking in their hard solidity as more electric heat zapped through her. Her breaths came faster as the need grew inside her. She had the urge to press her body against his to soothe this ache in her belly, between her legs.

Which was completely inappropriate. Massimo was *sleeping*, for goodness' sake. Catarina raised her hand to her chest, as if to steady the flutter of her own heart, but when she moved, she could have sworn that his muscles tensed. She froze.

"Massimo?" she whispered.

Nothing. She was imagining things again. Just her own guilty conscience, she decided.

She swallowed, steeling herself for her reaction to the feel of his smooth skin under her fingers. Maybe, she thought wryly, this could also act as a dose of self-styled exposure therapy to tone down the way her body reacted to this very real, very physical, man in front of her. She let out a huff of exasperation. *Just wake him and leave, Catarina!* His biceps lay at rest, cast so invitingly over his head. There was nothing inappropriate about touching his arm, right? Her fingers trembled as she reached across and brushed her hand over the bulge of his muscles.

All at once, those muscles came to life. Before Catarina could react, Massimo moved, and she found herself on her back with him over her, pinning her down. She no longer had to wonder about what was under the covers because a long, thick erection was pressed hard between her legs. She let out a moan before she could stop herself.

"*Dio*," he muttered, his voice a husky rasp. "What are you doing?"

Her senses were overloaded with the heat of his body,

the scent of him so much more intimate, cologne and something that smelled like pure masculinity.

"I... I..." Catarina struggled to respond, struggled to focus her brain when he was everywhere. But she had gone over her answer too many times to forget it. "I was checking on your concussion. You're not supposed to sleep the full night with a head injury."

For a moment he studied her, as if he was weighing her answer, but then something that could have been dark humor settled in his gaze.

"Are you sure?" he said softly. "If you wanted to see me naked, you just had to ask."

Her entire body was exploding with heat with his words, with his warm, muscular torso pressed against her. Her breaths were coming in short pants, which was only making his case about her intentions stronger.

"I'm talking to a man arrogant enough to try to outrun an avalanche," she muttered. "Of course you would assume I'm here for sex."

"How quickly you jumped from seeing me naked to sex," he said, his voice full of lazy desire. "Interesting."

Embarrassment flashed heat to her cheeks, but Catarina tried her best to glare at him. "Next time I won't bother checking if you are still alive."

"Already planning for next time?" A smile teased at his lips. Then, slowly, Massimo lowered himself onto his elbows, bringing his body to hers. His lips were so close, and she told herself she should resist. Instead, she arched to meet his mouth.

Catarina was everywhere. Her hair spread across the pillow, a backdrop that highlighted her bewitching brown eyes and lush mouth, and her voice rang inside him like a song. Her pert breasts skimmed his chest, and her thighs had parted the moment he had taken control, welcoming him. That scent that emanated from her now was mixed with something blatantly sexual that hijacked every breath of his, urging him to bring his face to her neck and inhale.

This woman was going to be the death of him. He had awakened the moment she entered the room, but had kept still, using his well-honed restraint to put aside temptation and try to discern what she was after. What was her angle? At first, he had assumed she was trying to get the upper hand by crawling into bed with him. That he could have handled.

But instead, as he lowered his mouth to hers, he saw a raw, open longing in her eyes that threatened to take over all rational thought. And before he could weigh whether or not this could still be a complicated game of manipulation, she pressed her lips to his. Massimo groaned as an electric current seemed to arc between them, making every inch of his body come alive. He took his time, tasting her sweet mouth, opening for the soft slide of her tongue as his suspicions faded to the back of his mind.

He wanted this woman. Every inconvenience she had caused him dwarfed in comparison to the want that coursed through him. She shifted, spreading her legs farther, adjusting to fit perfectly under his, and Massimo struggled to keep his sanity as her soft gasps stoked the fire in him higher. The promise of more pleasure was within reach. Just the thinnest scraps of silk separated them from the ecstasy he couldn't stop thinking about. He could have her over and over if he played this right, he reminded himself. If he kept himself under control.

So he forced himself to pull back. Catarina let out a soft whimper that triggered another surge of heat, threatening to overwhelm the thread of control he was hanging on to. He had missed the opportunity to use her desire against her earlier in the day, but now with her below him, the path forward was clear. She wanted pleasure from him, too, making this fire between them a tool. If stoked high enough, a fire had the power to bend even a will of steel, to forge what he ultimately wanted: the convenient fiancée he thought he was getting, who understood the necessity of both their roles in this partnership. Ultimately, he needed a wife who would not, under any circumstances, distract him, preoccupy him or do any of the things that had continued to ruin his father's life and tarnish their family's name. Because even if Catarina was not his mother, he could not ignore the burning need that suggested he was, in fact, at risk of becoming his father.

His cock was notched between her legs, and he flexed his hips experimentally, to see how she reacted. She let out a quiet moan and flexed her own hips, sending a new ripple of pleasure through him. Yes, she definitely craved this.

"Why are you here, Catarina?" He moved more deliberately this time, slowly dragging his cock between her legs, drawing out the pleasure, biting back the drive to finish that was burning in his throat. "Did you come to my room to learn what this feels like? Did you come here so I could show you?"

Massimo did it again and again, moving against her, pressing against that spot that drove her wild. She closed her eyes, as if she was losing herself in the pleasure, and he let her for one more stroke, another, listening as her breaths came faster, turning to soft moans. The music of her voice threatened to overwhelm him, but he resisted. He would not get carried away again. He would stay in control and bring this to the end. He gritted his teeth and dragged his cock against her one last time, then stopped.

Catarina's eyes fluttered open, and she swallowed visibly. Her eyes begged him to continue, and his own body clamored for him to respond. He resisted. He ignored her soft, lush lips, begging to be kissed, and reminded himself of his goal and the promise of future pleasures it brought.

"Answer," he rasped, his voice heavy with the pleasure that threatened to spiral out of control. "Why are you here?"

Her eyes were wide as she blinked up at him, silently begging for more. Though he had told himself he would withhold what she wanted, he moved his iron-hard length between her legs yet another time, and she gasped, as if she was on the edge of ecstasy. As if all it would take to bring her to a climax was one more tilt of his hips. Massimo found that he wanted to give this to her. The drive to please her called from deep inside, casting an ominous shadow over his thoughts.

He waited for her answer, but she didn't reply. Instead, she closed her eyes and moved her hips against his. He glared down at her, telling himself to pull away, but the sound of her gasp held him in place. She moved again and again, using his body to take her own pleasure, testing his sanity until she let out a cry and came apart. A burst of primal satisfaction flooded him as her song of ecstasy threatened to topple the balance that tipped inside him. He fought against the need that pounded inside him. He knew where that path led, and he would not follow it.

CHAPTER SIX

CATARINA HAD ONLY the haziest memory of being carried back to her bed, boneless and still half-delirious from pleasure. The whole encounter was a jumble of dreamlike sensations: the press of Massimo's hard torso on hers; the delicious bliss of his erection between her legs; the rasp of his voice in her ear, taunting, demanding, each word setting off more fireworks inside her. All these came together in an irresistible crescendo too tempting to resist. In the exquisite bliss that followed, he gathered her into his arms with a gentleness that went against everything she knew about him. As she nodded off, clinging to him, the pit of loneliness that sat inside her did not seem as unfathomably deep.

But her memory sharpened the moment Massimo laid her down in her bed. The moment he let go, she looked up at him, silently begging for more, but his expression was an impenetrable mask. Then he was gone. Moments before, she had felt sated, but alone in her bed, the ache inside came back. So quickly and worse than before. In the empty silence of her room she wanted him enough to wake her up after fitful bursts of sleep.

Still, in the light of the morning, Catarina couldn't bring herself to regret it. Though her late-night adventure had probably made the day in front of her more difficult, the vulnerability quickly faded the moment she realized that, for the first time since her mother's death, she wanted to play the piano. The piano had been the one place in her life where she was allowed free rein to sort out her feelings, a space where she would be left alone because she was using her time "productively."

And then, when her mother died, the music stopped. Every time she sat on the piano bench, a tsunami of grief overtook her. The emotions that had always flowed so freely through her body to her fingertips suddenly buried her in a sea of loss.

But today she had awoken with a giddiness, a feeling that her skin was too small to contain the feelings that were running through her. Quickly, she threw a soft sweater over her silk pajamas and rushed downstairs to the grand piano that shimmered in the bright morning light. Here, she could make sense of these sensations that ran through her. Here, she could get them under control. She opened the lid, bracing herself for five years of grief to wash over her. The grief was still there, hovering, but it didn't cascade onto her the way it had before. Instead, the sensations from the night before came back, punctuated by a burst of hope. Freedom, she told herself. That was what this was; a taste of the long-elusive freedom she had been searching for.

Catarina stared at the keys, suddenly wondering what Massimo would hear as she played. Would he detect these strange layers of old grief and new possibility mixing inside her? Would he know that it was his body, his touch, that had awakened this strange brew of emotions? Everything about this man seemed to be designed to leave her vulnerable. Catarina sat with her back straight and her hands ready, listening to the music that finally played again in her mind and through her body, letting all these thoughts swirl around her.

A creak from the staircase startled her out of this purgatory and into a different one. Catarina swung around, and her heart jumped in her chest. She was entirely unprepared for how it felt to see him again in the clear light of day. He was wearing just a white T-shirt and his perfectly fitted dress slacks that showed off his muscular thighs, the flat planes of his chest and the well-honed contours of his biceps that she had studied so carefully the night before. Massimo had been devastatingly handsome in his white button-down shirt, the sleeves rolled up to expose his corded forearms, just a suggestion of the physical nuances of his body underneath. But the T-shirt put these nuances into sharp focus. Catarina couldn't ignore all the ways Massimo filled out the shirt, stretching at the shoulders and pressing against his hard biceps. In these clothes, the businessman disappeared, leaving just the man, and the bandage that peeked out from behind the silky locks of his hair gave him a rougher appeal.

Her breath caught in her throat. Last night had been so very physical, so very real, and something about that had stripped her layers of protection away, leaving her raw. Vulnerable. She called on her years of practiced distance and found those walls far less sturdy than she remembered.

"Do you play?" Massimo nodded to the piano.

"Not recently."

He tilted his head. "Why?"

This question made her vulnerable in an entirely different way, but she resisted the urge to look away. Powerful men like him were well versed in rooting out people's vulnerabilities as weapons. The best way forward was frank honesty.

"I haven't played since my mother died," she said with a lift of her chin, then braced herself for further prying.

He studied her quietly, and his expression softened to what she might, in another man, call gentleness. After a moment, he gave a hint of a nod and asked, "And before that? Did you perform?"

She gave a little laugh. "Only when my parents cajoled me to play a few pieces for guests in our home."

"The first day we met, you said you didn't have a taste for performance."

Catarina was surprised that he had been paying such close attention to what she'd said that day, not between all his orders and demands. A twinge of hope inside her pushed her to continue.

"My father was thrilled at my interest in at least one of the high-value talents that well-bred women of our social standing were supposed to possess," she said wryly. "And my mother encouraged any and all forms of musical interest in hopes that it might lead me closer to a life of performance, the kind she had enjoyed and excelled at. But I've always seen the piano as something for me."

Somehow, the way he was looking at her now felt just as intimate and dangerous as the unguarded desire in his eyes when she was in his bed, underneath his hard, naked body. This thought was a mistake, because a new jolt of heat ran through her body and made her breaths uneven. Massimo's eyes narrowed with desire.

"I trust you slept well," his deep voice called to her as he came closer, sending a new flash of lust through her.

The inquiry was of the most banal nature. Innocent on the surface, but the wicked quirk of his eyebrow made the bubbling heat inside her rush to her cheeks as she flashed to the memory of the delicious weight of his body over hers as she fell apart in his dark bedroom.

Catarina swallowed and gave him what she hoped was a challenging smile. "Are you looking for praise?"

She felt a surge of satisfaction when his eyes flashed with a mix of surprise and humor. But as he came to a stop next to her, his expression shifted to something both arrogant and sexual.

"I was there, Catarina," he rasped. "I know you enjoyed yourself."

She rolled her eyes, trying to ignore the heat that flashed through her body. "Don't let it go to your head."

He let out a low chuckle. "Are you worried I'm making plans for the next time you show up in my bedroom?"

He said it in that low, seductive voice that suggested he had already thought through said plans. In detail. Her heart pounded in her chest, the way it had the night before. He oozed sensuality, especially when his gaze fixed on her. It was too much. Even under the cover of darkness the night before, she had felt like she was drowning. But in the daylight, there was nowhere to hide when his eyes flashed with undisguised desire. It was like a burst of direct sunlight, and she felt its burn, a warning that suggested the irrevocable harm he could do.

She wanted to create some distance between them, but standing only brought her closer to him. She could simply run away. Part of her wanted to. And yet, something was keeping her in place. Something that kept her there against her will, she told herself. Because wasn't it freedom she was after? And this, right now, felt like the opposite of freedom. So why wasn't she running? Catarina searched for an excuse, for something to say that would break this spell.

"I should get you a change of clothes," she said in a voice that she hoped passed for breezy. "I'll search the Christmas jumper drawer."

Massimo simply looked at her, and she felt his gaze penetrate her, as if he was searching for her vulnerabilities and was on the brink of discovering all of them. He parted his lips, and her first thought was that he was going to kiss her. Instead, he spoke.

"You never answered my question last night, *cara*. Why did you climb into my bed?" His voice was soft and low, coaxing and sensual. A new shiver of desire spread through her. It was simply his physical nearness, she told herself, and the fact that she had never been so close to a man like this, snowbound with no escape. "What do you want?"

This time, the silky veneer of his voice turned into something harder.

And that was enough to shake her out of the haze of desire. She had been taught all her life that it was pointless to take on men like this head-on, that it was better to maneuver, but there was nowhere for her to maneuver. And why wouldn't she simply tell him her purpose? Surely, he had already assumed worse. Maybe a straightforward answer would end this conversation once and for all. She tilted her chin up and said, "I want freedom."

His expression looked thoughtful, and for one short

moment, she believed that he had heard her, really heard her and was considering what she said. Her heart soared in her chest, and for that one breathless moment, she believed that there was a way forward, that she could get the freedom she wanted, and that he was not like her father. That despite all the signs to the contrary, he could and would compromise. And she couldn't help that her gaze traveled down to those lips, because if there was hope for compromise, maybe there was hope for even more. Maybe the ache that she had felt all morning was possible to satisfy, too.

But the moment her gaze dipped down to his lips, the pensive expression on his face slowly changed into something else. His eyes narrowed, and his lips took on that twist that couldn't possibly be called a smile. It was something far from humor. It was a warning, but his body was so close that she couldn't bring herself to care.

"The truth, Catarina," he said. "Just the truth."

But there was no time for indignation or outrage or protest, not when his lips brushed against hers.

Massimo had wanted to believe her. Her eyes had been so clear when she spoke, and it felt as though the words had come from her whole heart. It would be so much easier if all she wanted was freedom. Of course, only someone never burdened by responsibility truly believed in freedom, but that illusion could fit with his requirements for a marriage of convenience. He had almost been convinced, but then her gaze had dipped to his mouth. That look of carnal desire had flashed in her eyes, a look that had nothing to do with freedom. Massimo knew exactly what it meant. It was a cage he would recognize anywhere, and yet he had been startled to suddenly find himself outside the door of it.

Desire thrummed in his blood. He had waited for this moment since he awoke, and he found his own gaze drawn to her lips, so soft and sensual. He wanted to taste those lips again. He wanted to provoke her, to kiss her until she begged for more. He told himself that this was necessary, a lesson for her and a reminder of how easily he could become a victim of his own desire.

As his eyes dipped to the high flush on her cheeks and the way her full lips parted, as if in anticipation, Massimo thought about the difference that he had seen in her since the first day, the change he had not quite been able to put his finger on. Here, on the mountain, he realized that there was a wildness to her, an untamed part of her that he hadn't seen in Milan. She hid it behind her demure facade, but he had caught more glimpses of it this morning when she sat behind the piano. In this house, surrounded by the endless snow, she was no longer hiding it, and Massimo couldn't shake the feeling this was somehow at the center of why she had fled from him.

But that thought slipped away when she licked her lips. There was nothing between them. There was only the deep brown of her eyes, open and curious, and the bow-shaped mouth that he hungered for. The word *mine* rang through his head, the toll of a bell that called and called in his mind. For once, he did not have to restrain himself from this call. For once, he didn't have to weigh how the decision would affect his business, his family name. Because for once, his wants were in line with his most strategic and expedient move. This moment was born by circumstances that he never would have chosen, but right now, he was no longer angry that she had run because it allowed him to seduce her into granting him the marriage he needed. This moment was a short reprieve from a life of sacrifices. He would take what he craved and give her what she so nakedly asked him for, then hold it up for her to examine.

Slowly, he lowered his head. Her eyes widened, as they had in her kitchen, when he had given in to this urge. Her breath hitched, a sound that shot through him and landed directly in his groin. Purpose faded as he lowered his mouth to hers, lush and red, and he told himself it didn't matter, that this was not the same as giving in to the temptation of her parted lips.

Massimo brought his hands to her flushed cheeks, testing the heat that burned between them. Her skin was soft, and her silky chestnut hair drifted over his hands as Massimo pressed his mouth to hers. The scent of roses overwhelmed him, triggering the memories that had haunted him since the day in their library. Gently, he tasted her again, coaxing her lips open farther until he felt her giving in. He teased her, tilting his mouth for a better angle, and she answered, exploring his mouth tentatively, then with a growing confidence. A surge of satisfaction coursed through him as she came alive under his touch. He fisted her hair and moved his tongue over hers in long, luxurious strokes. With his mouth he promised what he could do with her. For her. He showed her the way that he would please her and she would more than please him.

As he took control of the kiss, she seemed to simply let go, to give in to him. Yes, this was the right way forward. That he could give in to this feeling, just a little bit, just to tempt her further. But soon, his hunger grew stronger, roaring to life. He had it kept tamed so well over the years that he had sometimes even forgotten that it was there. Now it surged, threatening to take over.

Massimo gasped and pulled away. Her mouth was still so tantalizingly close, and she was watching his, but she didn't move closer. She simply stared at him, her eyes both wild and startled, like he was a revelation, and that idea satisfied something inside him. He ignored the warning that clamored because he had her exactly where he wanted her.

"There is no freedom in a kiss like that," he said, letting the wild hunger roughen his voice. She needed to see the dangers of this kind of desire.

Her eyes were bright, and her breaths lifted her chest, pressing against him. "What do you mean?"

"Fires like this burn until they leave everything in ashes." If she did not understand this, she would continue to taunt him with desire. She would tempt him and ruin them both.

At some point, she had reached for him, and her fists were full of his T-shirt. She stared down at her hands for a moment, then let go, smoothing the material with a trembling hand. She took a step back. That hunger inside him roared to life, resisting the distance between them. He had the urge to pull her against him again, but down that road led to disaster, so he gritted his teeth and forced himself to still.

"And we are the future ashes in this scenario?" Catarina sounded more curious than rebuked.

"Not just us," he said gravely.

Massimo watched her carefully as her breaths slowed and her expression returned to that placid, docile mask that somehow provoked a surge of frustration inside him. Because she was proving to be anything but docile.

Massimo flashed to the first moment he saw her this morning, when Catarina sat on the shining black bench of the grand piano, dressed in pajama pants that hinted at the fullness of her thighs and a soft white sweater. Her hair fell over her shoulders in a mass of silken waves that made him ache to weave his hands through it. The keys of the piano were exposed, and sheets of music were arranged in front of her, but her hands were still. On her face was an expression that Massimo could only describe as wild astonishment. He realized with a start that he recognized this expression. She had given him a version of it in her library, and he had written it off as too starry-eyed, full of the unrealistic hopes that he had felt the urge to tame. Just moments ago, when she had given him another version of this same look, he saw something else. He saw dangerous, untamed passion.

But now she wore the mask of the biddable wife again, and Massimo told himself that this was what he wanted. Not the challenge that stoked the fire between them until it threatened to burn out of control.

Catarina tilted her head, as if weighing his words. "Then I suppose that means you shouldn't kiss me anymore. Though that's an interesting take on marriage."

Massimo frowned. "That kiss was a warning that—"

"Yes, yes." She cut him off with a placating smile. "Disaster ahead if we feel passion. I understand."

Massimo stewed over the way she mocked his warning. Clearly, she didn't understand. Which meant that here, in the confines of this home, Massimo needed to demonstrate the danger that lay ahead on this path.

He needed to take her to bed.

It was the answer that his body had begged for ever since she'd entered his room last night, clamoring for attention. But the purpose of taking her to bed was not to satisfy his own needs, he told himself. It was to teach her the lesson that he had learned over and over throughout his life, that passion was a silken noose, so soft and temptingly sensual, that slowly slipped tighter and tighter until it suffocated. Better to teach this lesson now, when they were stuck here together, so she would learn it quickly instead of drawing it out over the years.

"But you still want to play with this fire?" he asked softly. Another warning.

"Are you trying to protect me from myself?" She looked almost…amused. "How sweet."

Before he could answer, she walked away.

Massimo stared out the window at the thick wall of snow that held them here, trying to tame the frustration and desire that brewed inside him. *Dio*, this woman was driving him crazy. He wanted her in a way that defied rational thought. But he had controlled this want, he reminded himself, and he would continue to keep himself in line. But wasn't his whole life's work perfectly suited to this task? From the moment he and Alessandro had taken over the family's company, he had learned to put his own needs aside to lead others down a path that, in the end, was ultimately to his benefit. He had done it in far more high-stakes conditions, he told himself, and yet there was a dark rumbling inside that told him that never had the stakes been higher. But he would master this control. And if she refused to respond in an acceptable way? Massimo could end their marriage arrangement and find a more biddable bride. The idea turned over inside him uncomfortably. In fact, he found that even thinking about this option provoked a strong distaste.

No. He would make this arrangement work. And it *would* work as long as he didn't mistake his own lust for anything more than a tool to be wielded carefully and precisely, a tool to help negotiate a marriage that would show the world that, contrary to his father's example, Carandini marriages were a stabilizing force in the dynasty. Emilio Carandini was the colorful exception, not the rule. The problem wasn't the family's temperament, as some tabloids had suggested when Massimo and Alessandro were kicked out of school. Massimo Carandini was not his father, as he had reminded himself so many times, and he never would be. Though less attraction between them would be ideal, if she could master it, they could craft an acceptable form of marriage. Every bit of his investigation suggested she knew how to calculate her best interests. Tonight he would nudge her to apply this skill to their relationship.

Catarina d'Avalos was sheltered, her visions of marriage no doubt as fanciful as those in the books that lined her extensive library shelves. She had made it clear that she'd wanted a bit of romance, and though this was far outside his natural inclination, Massimo had a few ideas to work with at the moment. The fire that sparked between them had made her curious, so he would flame it.

He would spend time softening her, opening her for seduction, which eventually could make her pliable, amenable to his will. To make this work, he would likely need to be more approachable, less intensely…himself. Temporarily, of course, until she agreed to the marriage bargain. Strangely, he felt an unfamiliar hesitancy with the ruthlessness of his plan of using her softness, her curiosity, against her. He felt a confounding aversion to the idea of taking advantage of her vulnerability. After all, he had chosen her precisely for these characteristics. But he pushed this hesitation away. He would simply get what he wanted from her, so they could come to an understanding that she could soon realize suited them both. And then he would move on from this distraction. They would live separate lives the way the most levelheaded members of society did, coming together occasionally only to slake any lingering desire. Children would, of course, put them in closer proximity, as he had no intention of neglecting his children the way his parents had. But that was a problem for long in the future. For now, he would draw her out with passion and bring her back to those first moments in the library, when she had been prepared to marry him.

CHAPTER SEVEN

AFTER A DAY of slinking around, trying to avoid Massimo *in her own house*, Catarina gave up. Her breaking point was the scent of garlic, olive oil and spices that seeped under her door and swirled in the air. Was Massimo…cooking? It was an image she couldn't quite conjure in her mind, and yet, as she rounded the corner to the kitchen, she found Massimo in front of the oven looking as if he belonged there. He was wearing a new T-shirt that fit in all the right places, and the sweatpants sat temptingly low on his hips. In one hand he held a dish with an oven mitt, and with the other, he squeezed a lemon in his large, capable hand. Dark, wavy locks of hair hung over his forehead as he worked, obscuring the bandaged cut. Catarina found her gaze pulled back to the way the muscles on his forearm flexed as he held the pan. He looked focused on the task in front of him, shockingly at home in the kitchen in a way that she herself had never been. The scene was captivating.

Catarina didn't realize he was aware of her presence until he turned and gave her a smile dazzling enough to momentarily stun her. "I hope you're hungry."

"I thought Alessandro was the charming one," she said. "Did you do some sort of twin switch with your brother?"

"I contain multitudes of layers, Catarina." He said it with his usual self-important seriousness, but followed the statement with a wry smile. Was he laughing at his own intensity level? "I hope you like fish."

"Much better than my plan for shrimp, mayonnaise, dill and cucumber sandwiches."

He arched an eyebrow. "Interesting choice."

His tone suggested he was glad he knew how to cook.

"It's a Norwegian tradition that reminds me of summer." Summers with her mother.

He nodded. "Then that's understandable."

"How gracious of you to say so," she said with mock sincerity. "The country is grateful for your approval."

His eyes danced with humor, and she had the same off-kilter feeling she'd had a moment before. He was so much more approachable all of a sudden, as if he wanted to please her. This was enough of a change to make her suspicious. Or maybe she was just irritated by the fact that he had taken over her kitchen.

"Please..." he said, then gestured to the table.

"Make myself at home?" She flashed him a wry smile. "Thank you."

Catarina turned to the dining room area and noted what she had somehow missed in her dazed walk from the stairs to the kitchen: The table had been transformed. Massimo had pulled out one of the many linens her grandmother had monogrammed and laid it across the far side of the long table, creating a more intimate space. On it, he had placed candles at the center that he had gathered from various shelves. Two places were set, facing each other, using her grandmother's silver, and to the side of the candles was a chilling bucket for wine. Catarina eyed the platter of olives, figs, olive-oil-soaked goat cheese and a selection of crisp crackers, some of which she didn't even know she had, and she wanted to make another comment along the lines of making himself at home, but the voice stuck in her throat. The table was beautiful, and he had somehow transformed the emptiness of this house, with its ghost that still lingered, into something inviting. She approached the table and sat in one of the tall-backed chairs where her former life had played out, bracing herself for the familiar rush of sadness. But instead, Catarina felt a small burst of something else. Was it hope?

The thought made her want to retreat to her room, and maybe she would have if she hadn't been so incredibly hungry and if the scent of the food he had prepared hadn't been so intoxicating. *That's not the only reason*, said a voice somewhere deep inside. She felt Massimo behind her, stirring the heat that seemed to grow stronger each time he was near.

"I hope you approve," he said.

"It's lovely," she acknowledged softly, hoping her voice didn't betray a hint of the wistfulness she was trying to tamp down.

But Massimo's words from her father's library returned, mocking this optimism. *I was given to understand that you were clear about the nature of our agreement.* She absolutely shouldn't pin hopes on this man. He had made that perfectly clear.

He set another plate on the table, this one a grilled antipasto platter of zucchini, carrots and red onions with a creamy dip that gave off hints of garlic. She had been entranced by this man from the moment she walked toward him in the family library. His raw sexuality was overwhelming. But this Massimo Carandini, who'd created a multi-course meal from the ingredients Signe had brought and no recipe? He was even more dangerous. This softer, more approachable man intrigued her, even when she knew better than to trust his motivations. And underneath it all was still the thrum of their electric connection that sparked and sizzled inside her.

Catarina took a long breath. The kiss this morning had been a lesson, probably even a warning of what lay ahead. That he had meant it as such had been clear. Was he right that there was no room for freedom in a kiss like theirs? It certainly wasn't freedom she had felt when she'd clung to his shirt as if it was a life raft in the storm of their kiss. She knew cages, and this didn't feel like one. It was something new, something that she needed to understand, especially if she were to marry Massimo.

Was she still considering this marriage? When she fled to this mountain refuge, all she could think about was escape—from her father, from the marriage, from Massimo. She had put aside the feeling in the library and left, and maybe she could have hardened her resolve if he hadn't followed her. But now she knew the way it felt when his stern gaze darkened with desire, when his solid frame pressed against hers, his soft lips coaxing hers open, his hard length between her legs, the intent unmistakable. Everything about him preoccupied her to the point of distraction. Maybe she could make sense of this feeling that giving in to her desire for Massimo could cost her everything. It was their situation, this inescapable closeness, she told herself, that sparked this intense flame between them.

Through the windows, the snow continued to fall. The

light from the candles reflected on the walls and warmed the hue of Massimo's bronze skin as he opened the bottle of wine and poured her a glass. He took his seat across from her and raised his. "To unexpected pleasures."

She raised her glass and smiled. "Pleasures like avalanches and head injuries?"

"My head is fine, but thank you for your...concern last night." His eyes darkened, as if he was remembering the scene.

Her face flushed, but she gave him a mild smile. "I think the bare minimum of my host duty is to make sure my guest doesn't lose consciousness."

His laugh was deep and sensual. "You can consider your duty well-done."

"I'll take that as glowing praise," she said primly, but as embarrassment heated her cheeks, she found herself smiling, too.

As Catarina took a sip of her wine, she studied Massimo, aware that he wanted something from her, even demanded it from her at their first meeting. That day, the demand had felt too much like obedience for her to ignore it. Was he trying a softer tactic to the same end, or was this softness an opening to another possibility between them?

Explore it, her body begged traitorously, so willing to ignore the wariness this implacable man stirred inside her. Or maybe this flutter in her stomach was something far more tempting than wariness. Maybe this was why her father had kept her hidden away, she thought darkly. Because Giuseppe d'Avalos knew the power that one person could hold over another. He lived with the loss of it every day. Had he arranged this marriage to help her avoid the same kind of devastation? The idea was a revelation. She could see the merits of this approach, but it was not possible with Massimo. Not when it felt as if he was a gravitational force, and she was helpless to resist the pull.

The table gave her a little space, enough to remind herself that she, too, could play Massimo's game. She could use this situation to better understand this man who was determined enough to pursue her that he'd ignored avalanche conditions. Despite the fact that he had shown so little interest in her own wants and needs back in Milan. In his bed last night he had shown a completely different side of himself, and now he had prepared a meal for her. At the very least, a little prying could help her make a decision about their future.

"Have you visited Norway before?" she asked.

"I have stayed in Oslo for business, but I have never seen this." His large hand indicated the windows that lined the room, all clouded in endless snow.

"Impressive, isn't it?"

Massimo looked out into the white abyss, and she wondered if he was contemplating the storm that had the power to bring even him to a halt? When he turned back to her, he gave a subtle nod in assent and took a drink of his wine.

"But I imagine you've traveled to plenty of other far-flung places," she said.

"My travel is almost exclusively to cities for work."

"But as a child...?"

"When my parents traveled, Alessandro and I did not come." There was a flicker of a frown on his lips when he mentioned his parents, but he smoothed it over with a smile. "Though a few of our boarding schools could qualify as far-flung."

"In Italy?"

"The far-flung schools were in Switzerland, but the last one we attended was in Milan." He chuckled. "Our grandparents wanted to keep a closer eye on us."

Catarina was intrigued by this emerging sketch of Massimo's background. Multiple boarding schools suggested a teen who exercised far less of his current iron control.

"It must have been a comfort to have your brother with you," she said a little wistfully, thinking back to that strange feeling of isolation at a new school.

Massimo laughed. "Alessandro was often more trouble than comfort."

And yet, the warmth in his voice suggested a closeness to his brother.

"All those years at boarding school, and yet you cook? I must say it's a little unexpected," she said. "Even for a man of all your accomplishments."

Massimo flashed her a devastatingly handsome smile, threatening her last defenses. "You may want to reserve your praise until after you try it."

She gestured to the bandage on his forehead, just barely visible under his thick locks of hair. "I have heard many strange reports of survivors of car crashes, people speaking with ghosts or waking up with full novels in their head that they had to write down. But I have never heard of a crash that left someone with professional-level cooking skills. Truly, it's a miracle."

Massimo's stark features lightened, and he laughed, his eyes crinkling in the corners in a way that made her heart stutter. He had been called a lot of things in the press—driven, obstinate, demanding—and their first meeting had more than confirmed those descriptions. But right now, Massimo looked almost…at ease. She was wary of the way she felt herself softening toward him.

"I am afraid the explanation is rather prosaic," he said, the humor still dancing in his voice. "My grandparents did not grow up wealthy. When my grandmother saw the direction my father was taking the business, she decided to arm her grandchildren with more practical skills."

"How very sensible of her," she said. "I wish I could give her my compliments."

"She would be delighted to know her efforts were not wasted," he said, though Catarina doubted his grandmother had worried about Massimo's determination to master whatever the lesson had been. Even in the little time Catarina had known him, she had gleaned that anything that Massimo did, he would relentlessly pursue excellence.

Massimo looked out the window and added, "Her lessons have proved useful in many ways."

"Indeed. My father tells me that you and your brother rebuilt your family's business from the ground up."

"We had the Carandini name to redeem. It was our duty," he said with a mixture of pride and self-deprecating humor.

Massimo was the third-generation holder of the Carandini family legacy, and though his father had done plenty to ruin it, he and his brother had so quickly and thoroughly rebuilt it. It was why Catarina was being offered up to him, the prize her father so readily turned over: because he would protect her with his name. Marrying into this family would ensure her future. And yet, she sensed that his efforts were about more than a duty to the Carandini name.

She couldn't help but notice that when he laughed, he looked almost…younger, like a different person, one who had been taken away at birth and lived a much more comfortable life. It was a strange thought.

She lifted her glass and met his gaze, and she could feel the humor in his eyes shift into something different, something that stirred the want bubbling inside her.

"Your mother's death must have been difficult," he said, watching her carefully. "I saw the photo of the two of you together in my room."

She looked away. Her pain was something private, something that no one, not even her father, could understand. And yet, she felt strangely soothed by his tone. "It was. I traveled with her quite a bit. My father occasionally met up with us, but often it was just my mother and me."

"I'm sorry," he said softly.

"Thank you," she said, taking a drink of her wine, busying herself with anything besides meeting his gaze. She didn't want him to see the rawness in this topic. Still, after four years.

In many ways, the man across from her was who she had hoped to find when Massimo had walked into the library. That day, she had decided that man was an illusion, a figment of her imagination. But today, in the glow of the candlelight, she felt the tempting stirrings of hope.

She took a bite of the exquisite fish, decorated with herbs and lemons and asked, "Where does your grandmother live?"

"In her country home in the mountains near Lake Como, though she still stays in Milan from time to time."

"And this country home is where you learned to cook?"

"Among other skills," he said. Then his gaze turned darker. "Neither of my parents could be called anything close to practical, but my grandparents enjoyed running an estate of that size, even as their health declined. My grandfather passed away a few years ago, but running the estate is still a part of my grandmother's daily life. They want Alessandro or me to take it over someday."

He took a drink of his wine and continued. "When the two of us were kicked out of our boarding school in Montreux and our parents were away on one of their many reconciliation vacations to Seychelles, we were shipped back to Lake Como. Our grandparents decided that a practical connection to the world was in order. They felt that they had spoiled and corrupted their only son, and they were determined not to let the same happen to the two of us. The result is that I can cook and tend to animals and an orchard, build fences and make fires, to name a few. In retrospect, that summer was the happiest of my childhood."

There was a warning in his tone that told her not to ask more, but she ignored it. This was her chance to learn about him.

"I would not have guessed that you were the type to be kicked out of school," she mused. "Though you did mention trouble with Alessandro…"

"I took away a lot from the experience that summer, including that serious, hard work soothed a lot of my anger," he said. Then, unexpectedly, he laughed. "My brother seemed to have taken an entirely different lesson from it."

Alessandro Carandini was as well-known as Massimo, which was why her father would never have considered him as a candidate for marriage. He was, in crass terms, a playboy, someone with a charm that had drawn in princesses and commoners alike. But none of his attachments lasted for longer than a few weeks. Massimo's reputation was the opposite of charm, though she was starting to understand that he was perfectly capable of it. Instead, he seemed to have made a deliberate decision not to use it.

But she was listening closely to the tone that Massimo's voice had taken when he doled out these little hints of his background. He loved his grandmother, that much was clear, and maybe Catarina had expected that, but what she hadn't expected was the depth of emotion she could hear he had for his brother. If one were to read the tabloids, one might assume that the two brothers were at odds, their warring personalities pulling them in different directions.

But most notable was the icy bite he reserved for his parents and the warning she sensed as he moved the conversation away from the topic. She knew the basics of his parents' very public excesses, but now she wished she had probed further at these stories. She wanted to ask more but was almost sure her questions would be shut down. She needed to take a subtle approach.

Catarina had intended to quickly eat and then withdraw to her suite, but he was keeping her here, not with coercion but with the intensity that seemed to radiate from him, sprinkled with unexpected humor. At times, his eyes sparkled with amusement as he spoke, but under his smile she felt there was something carnal lurking, something her body seemed particularly attuned to. Those moments reverberated inside her, leaving a tingling sensation running through her limbs.

As the white landscape darkened, she could feel the lure of this man across from her grow stronger. But if she were to marry him, she needed more, she reminded herself. Would he lower his guard for her even further? It was hard to be strategic when she wanted to run her hands through the silky waves of his hair. To trace the sharp angles of his cheekbones, of his jaw, the hard planes of his chest that had tempted her the night before.

She reminded herself that Massimo had arrived so unceremoniously at the bottom of her driveway determined to take her back to Milan. He had been so sure he could bend her to his will and make her do something she didn't want to do, and the only thing that stopped his plan was a literal force of nature. Catarina knew she was still the bird in this arrangement and Massimo held the cage. Even if he gave her the illusion of flying right now, he could just as easily show her the bars, gilded or ironclad. Not once had he *asked* about what she wanted, which suggested that either he hadn't considered this angle or he didn't care. She wasn't sure which was worse.

That first day, he had shattered her imaginings of him as a sort of fairy-tale prince, someone she had seen across the room and projected her own ideas and dreams onto. Why had she been surprised when he made it so unmistakably clear that he was not the person she had invented on that first day? And yet, despite the fact that she knew better, Catarina could feel her dreams come to life again. This conversation was a glimpse beneath his harder exterior to a man vulnerable and hurt by the past in a way that resonated deep inside her. She had no idea what to do about it.

But whether or not she chose to marry Massimo, she knew she wanted him. She wanted to know what it was like to give in to the desire that had been building all day, just to see what it felt like to be free to follow what her body begged her to do. All day, she had told herself that the growing want inside was simply physical attraction and curiosity, natural for someone with as little experience as she had but also something easily disrupted with distance. But as she watched Massimo across the table, she had the growing suspicion that this feeling inside was more complicated.

It felt like music.

Every comment was a prelude to something distinctly intimate, each exchange a crescendo. But unlike the scores that she had listened to and played countless times, this piece was unwritten. She could not simply choose an etude from the shelf, depending on her mood. She could not use a concerto to invite particular feelings to wash over her and then let them come to their predictable end. This time, she had no idea where the music would lead her. She had no idea which emotions it would expose, and there was no way to preview the score before she sat down on the bench to gauge whether the piece suited her. Too late, she found that this concerto was playing faster than she could keep up with and, too late, she was realizing that this was no longer her score alone to play. It was Massimo's, too. She felt the crescendo between them growing. *Give in*, it sang. *Give in*.

Maybe she would. As long as she remembered not to mistake the desire that reverberated inside her for anything more.

He found Catarina far too intriguing. Her dark eyes were so soft as she'd listened to stories about his family, and there was empathy in her voice when she responded. That was the only explanation for why he found himself offering too many details about the past he had worked so hard to leave behind. It was the only explanation for the overwhelming need to know more about her, to understand her. The knowledge was strategic, he told himself to calm the unease stirring inside. These were details he could leverage to craft their marriage.

"What would make you happy, Catarina?" This was a different version of the question that he had thrown at her since he'd set foot in this house, a question she had dodged and answered with what he was certain were half-truths. But this version seemed to get through. Her eyes widened in surprise, and then she tilted her head, as if she was truly considering it.

"For a long time, I thought the only thing that would make me happy was if my mother was alive. Not possible, of course, but that's what I wanted. And I still want that." Her voice wavered at those last words, and something twisted in his gut. "I want children, though maybe not right away. But my family has always been at the center of my life, and I cannot imagine it otherwise."

She paused and looked away.

"I was being honest when I told you I wanted freedom," she continued, her voice steadier. "In hindsight, I can see I lived a very sheltered life under my mother's wing, and life was easier that way. But I don't want to go back to that. I want to discover what is meaningful to me. That's what I meant by freedom."

"You deserve to have this." His words came out more forcefully than he'd intended.

Catarina's laugh lacked the humor that had laced their conversation until the topic turned to her. "Few people in this world get what they deserve."

Massimo found that he didn't like this answer. Right now, she looked so lovely, so self-contained, as if she could weather any storm gracefully, and Massimo told himself that this was exactly why he had chosen her. And yet, the idea that she viewed her own life through this lens was...dissatisfying.

"But there must be things you've dreamed of doing," he pressed.

"When I was young, my parents and I watched a movie with scenes in a hospital, and after this, I declared that I wanted to be a nurse," she said. "Of course, my father laughed, and said, you will have plenty of opportunities to take care of someone. And now, here we are."

She glanced at the bandage on his head. Her voice held that light, airy tone, but he couldn't miss the undertones of irony.

"Is that the university path you were referring to when we were in the library?" he asked.

She raised her eyebrow, and he got the sense that she was surprised he remembered this piece of information. Then she waved off his comment.

"That whim has come and gone," she said lightly. "Those are not the kinds of skills I was taught at boarding school, though my mother and I did go through CPR and first aid training. My father insisted when we began traveling alone. I'm so glad to have the opportunity to put these skills to use."

There was a flicker of emotion in her eyes, and then it was gone.

"I supposed you could always pursue a career in top secret witness extraction or the like," he said.

Catarina blinked at him, then did the most unexpected

thing. She laughed. Nothing had prepared him for the sound of her laugh, musical and intimate. He could hear that it was a real laugh, one that slipped from behind the polite mask that she wore so diligently. It was a laugh just for him. Even more improbably, he felt the corners of his own mouth tug up in answering humor.

She shook her head. "You didn't have to work too hard to find me. Thanks to my father's guidance, of course."

It wasn't bitterness in her voice but something that sounded like betrayal. He discovered he did not like that sound.

"I would have found you anywhere." His smile faded as much baser feelings surged through him.

Her eyes flared with heat, and she stood suddenly. He rose and circled the table. Her breath caught. She was close enough to touch, and he needed to be closer. He wanted to lean forward and press his mouth against the slim column of her neck, to the hollow where her heartbeat raced. She stared up at him with those wide eyes, and those beautiful red lips parted, waiting for his. He tottered on the precipice of control. He wanted to take her right there on the table, so driven with this disturbing need to make her his. Because he wanted her. He needed her like he needed his next breath.

Under no circumstances could Massimo lose control. He could not lose sight of the seduction as a path to marriage. Catarina was an innocent, and she wanted more than a man who could not and would not ever give her the love she deserved. *Deserved.* He had no idea where that thought came from, but the words rang in his head, and he took them as the warning that they were.

So he resisted every urge inside him and stepped back,

leaving her room to pass. His own retreat shocked him, right at the moment he was getting what he wanted. It was strategic, he told himself, even if the thoughts of what she deserved echoed ominously inside him. Catarina paused, her eyes searching his, maybe even pleading. Then she looked away and left him standing alone in the room.

As her footsteps on the staircase echoed in the room, Massimo drank the last of his wine, focusing on its cool trail down his throat, forcing his thoughts to the crisp floral notes of the Vernaccia di San Gimignano, reminding himself that his driving desire for this woman did not rule him. Reminding himself that this seduction was a calculated risk, that any end game had winners and losers. And he never intended to find himself in the latter category.

The rational choice was to back out of their marriage deal altogether, to weather this runaway fiancée scandal to avoid the risk of a much larger one, a scandal born in this weakness that had the power to lead him down the same path as his father. And yet, Massimo knew he was not going to let her go.

Until they returned to Milan, he would focus on securing this marriage. He would highlight the kinds of sensual promises he could give her. These promises weren't a lie, he told himself. Not exactly. In the future, he would need to slake this burning thirst for her from time to time. But he would limit their interactions when they returned to Milan, of course, until this dangerous urge to possess her wholly was under control. At that point, far, far in the future, they could negotiate children.

For now, he would satisfy the need that sparked between them, both his and hers. Tonight he would give her the passion she craved. Though this spark between them threatened to flare out of control each time she was close, experience told him that it would eventually fade, most often sooner rather than later. And any power she held over him would be lost.

But this remote fjord felt so far away from his business and the weight of his family name. It seemed to whittle his thoughts down to something baser, something much more compelling. For now, his next move was not to subdue this fire. His next move was to show her all the ways to stoke it higher.

Massimo slowly made his way across the great room. He was in control. He focused on the most efficient, expedient route to his goal. He headed for his room and searched his wallet for a condom, shoving it into his pocket. Then he strode to the opposite end of the hallway and entered her bedroom.

The lights were off, but moonlight echoed off the snow and through the window, casting a dreamlike glow over the room. Her bedroom's design was much like the rest of the house, with vaulted ceilings, exposed beams and plush carpets scattered over the wooden floors, but this room had a more feminine twist. Clouds of pillows were scattered over a puffy down duvet, and the wooden dresser and mirror were carved with flourishes. Matching bookcases lined the other side of the room, and he wondered what books she held here in her private library. But that thought faded as his gaze drifted to the window. Catarina stood next to a reading chair, and the long shadow of her profile cast a graceful image across the floor. She was dressed in a long gown that covered her form, and yet it was made of a material that the moonlight rendered translucent. It highlighted her soft, rounded thighs, the generous swell of her rear, the tight buds of her breasts. Massimo hardened as he traced each curve with his gaze. Catarina turned, looking over her shoulder at him, and he couldn't decide if he had startled her or if she had been expecting him. Maybe it was both.

His fingers ached to trace each curve, to feel the weight of her full breasts, to tease the hardness of her nipple, and his groin throbbed, begging him to do it. *You can give in just this once*, he reminded himself, just to show her what this could be like. Somewhere in the back of his mind, he registered that this need for Catarina complicated their situation. She would be an indulgence, one he would strictly limit before the siren call of attraction grew too strong. But by then she would be his forever. Or maybe it was the reverse. Maybe it was he who would be hers. But Massimo was long past caring.

He didn't remember deciding to move, and yet he was crossing the room. She said nothing, just watched him. He stopped in front of her, close enough that her warm breaths brushed over his skin, close enough to see the plea in her eyes, both pushing him away and calling him closer. The lure was irresistible.

"Surrender," he rasped, and the words were as much a promise to himself as they were a plea to her. "Surrender to this."

CHAPTER EIGHT

CATARINA BLINKED UP at the man in front of her, letting his features come into focus. The moonlight highlighted the contrasts on the sharp planes of his cheekbones, bringing the harsh angle of his jaw into relief. His brown eyes were obscured in the darkness, but she could see his mouth—a harsh, grim line. Tension radiated from his body in hot waves. Yesterday she might have mistaken these signs for anger. Maybe there was some of that, too, but today she understood he wanted her. Perhaps it was because she was also thrumming with a need that wound her up and begged for release, but there was no mistaking his intent, despite her innocence. Her body knew. *Surrender.* The word whispered through her, echoing in his deep rumble of a voice that created friction inside her, one she was desperate to soothe.

After reasoning through this all day, debating whether she should give in to this need, right now she could see that reasoning was irrelevant. With him so near, the lure of his sensuality was too powerful to resist. *Surrender.* Whatever else happened between them, at least this experience would be hers.

Slowly, she lifted her hand to his face. The brush of scruff on his chin scraped her tender skin, adding another sensation to this cauldron that was bubbling inside her, a tonic that felt almost otherworldly. Massimo let out a groan, and then the tension in him seemed to snap. His mouth came down on hers for a devastating kiss that was nothing like the one earlier in the day. That kiss had been a slow seduction, a temptation. This one was lush and indulgent and greedy. It was everything she had spent a lifetime training herself never to be. And yet, here with his heat and his masculine scent surrounding hers, she finally let go.

Catarina explored his mouth without shame, took without worrying about giving, but every one of her sighs was matched by his groans, louder and deeper. Massimo was taking what he wanted, too. His hands found her hips, then moved up her body, the whisper-thin material of her nightgown brushing over her skin, so deliciously sensual, setting her insides on fire. He angled his mouth and took their kiss deeper, and she found herself gasping for air, trying to get enough, trying to get closer. She pressed her body against his and felt his hard length, so solid and so *there*, a stark, tempting reminder of what could come next. And oh, how she wanted it. Underneath all her dreams and fairy-tale endings lay something so breathtakingly raw, something she had never imagined and yet somehow, her body still knew she had wanted it the whole time.

Massimo pulled away from the kiss and swore under his breath. The lines on his face were so harsh that, for a moment, he looked almost angry. But then all thoughts left her because he was kissing her again, taking with a hunger that made her weak and sending pulses of need between her legs. She grabbed onto the hard muscles of his shoulders, steadying herself.

His kisses traveled down her neck, over her chest, and then he cupped one of her breasts. His mouth covered it, and she drew in a frantic breath as pleasure burst through her. Before she had time to recover, he sucked on her nipple, and it was as if there was a direct line from her breast to the sensitive bud at her core. Her insides burned and her legs ached as his tongue circled, coaxing. The room echoed with cries, and she was suddenly aware that they were coming from her. She was losing all control.

Massimo lifted her, and in a few quick steps her back was against the wall. One thick forearm held her against him so that her core rested on one of his hard thighs, and between his legs, her own thigh was pressed against his long, insistent length. Cool air drifted over the wet material of her gown, pressing against her nipple, bringing a shiver of pleasure through her whole body. Massimo swore again, then took her other breast in his mouth and, with a shift of his large hand, rubbed the bud between her legs against his thigh. It was too much. She came apart in a spectacular crescendo of pleasure, her cry hoarse as she shuddered and shook. If he hadn't been holding her so firmly, she would've collapsed, but he held her body snugly between him and the wall as she simply let go, let the waves of pleasure wash over her.

His breaths were rasps in her ear as he lifted her, his soft touch against her back so at odds with the harsh look she had glimpsed on his face and the thick, insistent pulse of his steely length against her thigh. He carried her over to the bed and gently set her there. Her nightgown was askew, and Massimo was staring at her with a look that could only be described as thunderous. He took a step back, and a whiff of panic startled her out of this languid purgatory of pleasure. He was going to leave. She was sure of it.

"Don't go." She meant it as a plea, but her voice was an invitation filled with pleasure.

He swore again. Massimo Carandini, who had bent the entire world to his will, wanted her. The thought was a powerful aphrodisiac that sparked new desire inside her, opening her curiosity. If he could bring so much delicious pleasure with just his mouth on her breasts and his thigh between her legs, what would happen when he used more? The *more* in question was on display, straining against the material of his sweatpants. She ached to explore it.

"Surrender," she whispered, echoing his word that was still ringing in her head; the word that had brought her to this point of uncharted pleasure.

Massimo closed his eyes, and he shuddered. Then he grasped for the hem of his T-shirt and pulled it off, exposing the hard muscles she had thought about all day. But nothing in her imagination could have prepared her for the way they moved with each of his breaths. It was clear that he was no stranger to physical work. She had felt his hard biceps as he held her, and she could see the ripples of strength across his chest. In front of her were the ridges of his abs and the trail of hair that disappeared into his waistband, so close and on blatant display. She wanted to get on her knees to explore him, but before she could even think to move, he was stripping off the sweatpants and his boxers, and then he was naked in front of her, his erection proud and so much larger than she had imagined.

"Stand up. I want you closer."

His voice was gentle, almost tender, and she responded to it immediately. He closed the distance between them and lifted her nightgown until she was naked, too. And whatever had been satisfied inside her just moments before turned back to want. This want felt so much larger, so much more overwhelming because he was now bare before her, and somehow, the promise of pleasure for both of them made it even stronger. Catarina reached for his chest and touched him tentatively, and she felt his muscles tighten under her hand. He let out a sound too raw to be called a laugh.

"Careful." The word echoed with an unmistakable warning.

But Catarina was done being careful. She was done being the person her father wanted, and she had long been cast out from the sheltered life that revolved around her mother. Every moment, every move, was now hers. Though she had no idea how this would play out, she knew she wanted it. So she slid her hand up his chest, feeling the thump of his heart, relishing in his desperate breaths and the electric power of touching his skin.

Just a man, she reminded herself, but she found this was no longer a comfort, now that she had had a taste of what this man could do with her. To her. Catarina explored, and he stood still, letting her, using his well-known control. Except this control seemed to be teetering on the edge of something else, something she wanted desperately to understand. A rush of satisfaction surged through her. *She* had this effect on him. But as she moved her hand lower, to the trail of hair on his stomach, he grabbed her wrist. Before she could register what was happening, he cleared the bed of her billowy duvet and pillow with his other hand, and then she was on it. He leaned down for something, and she heard the rip of a package. A condom. He rolled it down his length, and she watched, entranced. He climbed on top of her, nudging her thighs open, and settled there so easily that it felt as though his body had been made for hers. He propped himself on his elbows, his body skimming over hers, his muscles flexing under his weight, and his hardness, thick and full against her core, moving over it with delicious friction, setting off a fresh wave of pleasure. He didn't seem to notice any of that. He was staring at her face.

"Surrender," he said in a voice so stark, so final, that at once she could feel that he was not simply asking for sex. He was demanding something much more devastating.

Then, the nudge of his hardness pressed against her, and all other thoughts disappeared.

Holding himself on the brink of ecstasy, Massimo stared down at Catarina. Her thick brown hair spread over the pillowcase in waves, her lush lips were parted and her eyes were innocent and wide, as if she was on the verge of a discovery so unexpected, so earth-shattering, that she didn't know what to do.

But Massimo knew exactly what to do. He knew what she needed because he felt that same need pulsing through his own body. He was no longer going to lie to himself, not after seeing her response to his touch; not after tasting those tight buds of her nipples in his mouth; not after the way she drove him wild with her cries. He needed this like he needed his next breath. All the havoc that this feeling could wreak on his life he would contemplate later, but now was the time to answer this siren's call. To surrender to it. Both of them.

He stroked himself along her soft core one more time, gritting his teeth against the overwhelming urge to let go, instead focusing on the hitch of her breath, the moans and sighs that sent rushes of pleasure through him. Then he positioned himself at her entrance and nudged in, straining at the tight fit, slowly easing himself into the hot, welcoming place he craved. His desire spiked higher with each of her breaths. She was so soft and wet from her pleasure that when he came to the point of resistance, he almost forgot to stop. He almost lost control.

But suddenly, her muscles tensed, jolting him back from the edge of ecstasy. He felt a resistance, and wariness now clouded her eyes.

"I'll take care of you," he whispered, stroking his hand over the silky skin of her cheek. "I promise."

He had meant to comfort her, but her eyes inexplicably filled with tears. He froze, then pulled back, searching her gaze for what had gone wrong. But she shook her head and pulled him closer.

"Please," she said in a voice that was husky with need. "I want this."

I want you. Satisfaction soared through him. It should have been satisfaction that his seduction plan had worked, but the pleasure that ran through him was complicated in a way that he couldn't begin to contemplate. So he didn't. He lowered himself to kiss her, pressing his mouth to hers, and that magical thing that seemed to happen each time her lips touched his happened again. He lost himself in the kiss as he slowly, slowly, continued to push. He felt the moment where the resistance gave, felt her flinch. He soothed her with more kisses until she moved, urging him deeper and deeper until finally, *finally*, he was inside her completely.

"*Catarina.*" Her name slipped out of his mouth, his voice a rasp of insatiable hunger that lurked inside him. As sensations threatened to overwhelm him, a sudden thought darkened the bliss of that moment: This was something he would never come back from. The idea swirled inside him, an uncomfortable mix of fear and satisfaction that he tried to push away. Then she moved again, and he moved, too, focusing on reining in his control, pleasuring her, holding himself on the edge of abyss. Each stroke, each cry, took him further into pleasure, building it until the whole world fell away, and it was only this connection between them. With another hard thrust she fell apart in his arms, shuddering with cries that broke him. He came with a long, guttural groan that reverberated through his entire body. Ecstasy flooded him in wave after wave as her body responded, drawing out both their pleasure. He held himself over her, his lips pressed to her neck, breathing in her scent, until the world took shape again.

He rolled onto his side, bringing her with him, and she held on to him with an intensity that was almost too much to bear. The small gasps of her breaths echoed through the quiet room, in this house so far away from the ceaseless demands of his life. But for once, he just let the weight of history and the future be. He stayed inside her as the sharp ecstasy of pleasure turned into something warmer, something fuller. She was his now in a way that reached beyond business deals and marriage contracts. The thought gave him a surge of visceral satisfaction. Because he was closing in on his goal, he told himself. Though he would rarely indulge himself like this in the future, he would do so enough to ensure that she was his forever.

Catarina stirred. She opened her eyes and looked at him, the wonder in them still laced with pleasure. Her hair was mussed, her lips swollen. An echo of the word *mine* reverberated through him.

She smiled at him, and the smile was not a mask for polite company. This one was full of intimate pleasure. Before he could stop the thought, a future played out in front of him, a possibility of having something far more than he had ever imagined. It was a future where she smiled at him like this across the breakfast table, even when there was no paparazzi there to watch. It was a dangerous thought, so he pushed it away.

"I hope you are feeling all right," he said gruffly.

"Much better than all right." Her voice sang with humor and a touch of wonder that swelled inside him.

He should move. He should take care of her somehow. He was not in the habit of deflowering virgins and, frankly, knew little about what she might want next. Gently, reluctantly, he slid out from her, and it was then that he felt something was wrong. He froze as an icy chill ran through his veins. The condom had broken. He had spilled his seed inside her.

He stared down at the condom, then looked up at Catarina. The smile on her face faded into confusion, her eyes searching his. Then she looked down, too.

"Oh." It was just one word, so soft he almost didn't hear it. But he could feel the shift in her, and this shift sent another cold shock wave through his veins.

"We must get married immediately," he bit out instinctively. Even as the words came out of his mouth, he knew they weren't the right ones, and yet he couldn't stop them because all he could think was *scandal*. Her father had alluded to this kind of scandal on the first day when discussing a well-timed wedding, but that concern paled in comparison to the threat that filled him. The Carandini family could not have a child born out of wedlock. It was one thing for him to weather a scandal alone but quite another for him to subject the next generation to one before the child was even born. He would never allow that. Never.

But children were supposed to be an issue they'd sort out far in the future, long after this electric connection had died out. Not now, when everything inside him felt so…volatile.

By the time Catarina's gaze met his again, there was an unreadable mask across her face, and a cold politeness rang in her lovely voice. It did something strange to him when she spoke. "We absolutely do not have to marry."

"I will not allow my child to grow up under scandalous conditions," he snapped, louder than he meant to.

"We don't even know if I'm pregnant." There was an incredulity in her voice that almost covered the shakiness. Almost.

A feeling was rising in him, a souring brew of all the emotions that the past hour had stirred in him. This recent turn of events bound them together in the most disturbing way. Massimo rolled off the bed and reached for the clothes he had tossed aside. His thoughts were too… tumultuous to continue this conversation, too chaotic to even hear one more word of protest out of her mouth, so he headed for the door. When he reached it, he turned around. Catarina hadn't moved. She was on her side, her hair cascading over her shoulder, half covering the breasts he still longed to take in his mouth. Still, despite everything. She wasn't looking at him. She was staring out the window with an expression that looked too much like resolve for him to contemplate further.

"We will get married," he said, his voice steady despite the tremor that resonated deep inside. "I will do everything in my power to make sure of it."

CHAPTER NINE

Catarina was as still as death as Massimo's footsteps disappeared down the hallway. She didn't move as she heard the creak of his door. But when the door slammed shut, she rolled onto her back on the bed, a place that was supposed to be her own. This room had always been a refuge, but as she took a deep breath, his intoxicating scent still lingered everywhere. Catarina wanted to scream. She wanted to cry. Most of all, she wanted to run far away from this man who made her weak.

I'll take care of you. Massimo's words had taunted her with a promise she so dearly wanted, and now they haunted her. It had taken her a moment before she realized that he was simply referring to sex, nothing more. He seemed completely unaware that they were the words that her father had used in their marriage discussion. He was simply clarifying that he would make sure this first time would hurt as little as possible, and he had shown her a tenderness that had evoked that stubborn hope that she couldn't seem to shake, the hope for *more*.

Catarina balled her fists in frustration. Even if his promise had only been for this one act of intimacy, it was still a lie because right now, everything hurt worse than she ever dreamed it could. Worse than it should have. Massimo had shown an unexpected passion, and somehow it made this ending even more heartbreaking. She had been so very right to be wary of his autocratic statements because the moment the evening took an unexpected turn, the tenderness disappeared, and the cold demands returned.

But his demands weren't the most disturbing part of the awful ending of their encounter. The hardest part to digest was the fact that, as he walked away, she'd had to bite her lip to stop herself from calling out to him, begging him to come back. Her body craved his. She craved his touch, his warm, hard chest against her, his big hands splayed across her back, holding her close, and the long, hard length of him deep inside her. She *needed* him again. There must be something wrong with her, she decided, to want someone who had completely and treacherously turned on her.

Because the last thing she wanted was to start a family with a man who clearly could not—no, would not—love her. Who would not give her the respect she deserved.

Catarina blinked up at the ceiling as outrage competed with the intoxicating memory of his mouth everywhere. She needed to sleep. Everything would look better in the morning. She pried herself out of bed to wash the tears from her face, then returned to bed, burying herself under the covers until somehow she fell asleep.

Her sleep was fitful, her dreams, vivid, erotic and haunting, but when she awoke in the morning, the music returned. It was playing through her head with the clear ring that she used to awaken to every day. But the tune that played was one that had captured her imagination in her teens and then haunted her dreams in the days after her mother's passing, Rachmaninoff's Prelude in C-sharp Minor. Now it called to her with an intensity she could not ignore.

Yesterday she had sat on the piano bench, the familiar cool wood under her welcoming her back as the music filled her, but she had not been ready to let it out, to reveal the emotions that brimmed inside her. Today was different. Today they would not be contained. They seeped through her defenses, through her carefully constructed facade and made her vulnerable.

And in the same way Massimo's kiss had taken over yesterday, consuming her, she felt consumed by the need to play. Something deep inside ached, something that, if she was honest, had ached for years, begging to be free. She had been an obedient daughter and ignored this wild intensity inside, but last night something had shifted. She might carry a child of her own. She could no longer sail through her life, allowing the winds around her to guide her course. Catarina owed this child her protection, the protection her father had not given her, despite his good intentions.

Catarina didn't bother to dress or wash her face or do any of the things that she was taught to do to make herself presentable. She simply rose from her bed, brushed her hair from her eyes and descended the stairs, her gaze fixed on the piano.

Outside the window, the wind had let up, and the fjord was just visible through the fat flakes of snow that fell like feathers, drifting back and forth in the gray morning. A soft, diffuse light lit the piano as she approached it, as if it were calling to her.

Catarina opened the bench and rustled through the music until she found the right piece. Her heart pounded as she propped it on the music stand, took a deep breath and played the first notes of the Prelude that had haunted her. The music seemed to swell inside her. She began with the heavy chords, feeling the foreboding that echoed in each one. When the chords changed into arpeggios, picking up speed and turmoil, all in that haunting minor key, she was swept away into the turbulent progressions up and down the keyboard until they came to the end in a clatter of chords. She entered the final lines, heavy and absolute. Breathless, her hands hovered over the keyboard. She expected to find herself crying. That had been her worry the previous morning, that her music and her sorrow were inextricably intertwined. But what she felt was more complicated than sorrow.

The room came back into focus, and Catarina was suddenly aware that she was not alone. She looked over her shoulder and saw Massimo, standing at the base of the staircase, his expression inscrutable.

Awareness shuddered through her, that now-familiar lick of hot desire, along with the protective urge to suppress all signs of it. The best course of action was to put all of these thoughts aside and examine them later when they had returned to Milan and she was in the safety of her room. She could sort them out the way she always had, alone. But even the thought of returning to her father's house, back to safety, was no relief.

She attempted to school her features, to push down her feelings the way she had spent years practicing, but Catarina found that she…couldn't. Something had broken free inside her, something she could no longer suppress.

"What were you playing?" he asked, his voice so much gentler than she'd expected.

"Rachmaninoff's Prelude in C-sharp Minor," she said, and she could hear that her voice was still tinged with the dizzying turmoil of the music that had started to untangle the mess of emotions knotted inside her. "It is said that the composer wrote it after a dream of his own death."

"That was...stunning," he said, and his eyes now seemed to be filled with open admiration.

Her breath caught in her throat as the knot tightened inside her once again. Would he simply talk to her like this, as if nothing had happened? Yesterday he had dangled a different kind of future in front of her, a future that included long evenings of food and conversation and unspeakable passion, and then, when the condom broke, he had so viciously yanked it away. And now he was complimenting her on something she held so dear. What was she supposed to do with this man?

"The piano holds no judgment of me for the times my thoughts are less palatable to those around me," she replied, and her voice wavered with emotion. Why couldn't she say this in the careful tone she had practiced her whole life? How could she have let herself get this out of control, exposing herself, making herself so vulnerable in a way that she could no longer take back?

She had meant her comment as a subtle reference to her less than generous feelings toward him, but if he understood this, he didn't take offense. In fact, in his gaze she found something that looked like understanding. Real understanding. Maybe he was looking for a way forward, a way to talk through the possible consequences of the broken condom. The flicker of hope wasn't nearly as strong inside, but it was still alive.

The room was quiet, and he said nothing, just gazed at her. And in that moment, a roller coaster of emotions raced through her, one that seemed to mirror what she saw in Massimo's dark eyes. She saw hope. Fear. Joy. Frustration. And with every peak and valley was that insistent desire that never seemed to go away with Massimo. The air seemed to charge between them, but before she could think through this, he looked away.

"The storm seems to have abated," he said, gesturing out the window. "I imagine I will be able to contact my helicopter soon, and we will return to Milan. I expect that things will be clearer then."

She could hear the implication behind these words, that the moment she faced her father and the trappings of their lives again, she would soon bend to his will. Frustration took over, and Catarina looked away, trying to hide any traces of the sinking feeling that she had been mistaken. Even misled. This conversation, this connection, was simply a lead-up to the next step in his plan. And her job was to fall in line.

"I find that things look perfectly clear from here," she said tartly as she tried to shut off every other complicated feeling that had been building inside her.

Both of them knew how much easier it would be if she simply gave in. This was why she had fled to her house on the edge of the vast fjord, wasn't it? Because being in Milan in her father's house, she felt the weight of her obligations to her parents and their vision of what her life should be.

Then Massimo had followed her here, and her private hideaway no longer eased this problem. Or maybe the safety of her mother's mountain home had only been an illusion. The struggle lived inside her as it always had, but Massimo had triggered these long-simmering emotions to erupt, and the problem cut deeper than the expectations laid on her. *She had chosen* to shape her life around these obligations. It was time for that to end. She took a deep breath. "I will return with you to Milan when the storm clears, but I will not marry you simply because there's a chance I am pregnant."

The unreadable expression on his face turned glacial. "Everyone has things that they need, Catarina," he said, his voice a low, unmistakable warning. "Some of us want to preserve our family name and others want to please our fathers, for example. These can be powerful motivators, and I find that people go to great lengths to ensure those needs are met. These most basic drives are impossible to ignore."

"Of course, you are speaking from experience," she said.

"I am."

Catarina found her temper flaring higher at the cold control in his voice, while her own wavered with emotion. Was he truly the same man who had lit up with passion, who had called out her name and looked at her like nothing in this world would pull him away? Yesterday must have been a lie, all of it. He had toyed with her emotions and satisfied his own desire. The only piece that she had to hold on to, the only thing undeniably real, was that desire. Catarina clung to the naked want she had seen as he moved over her, driving them both crazy with pleasure. If he was using his desire so recklessly, then she would use it, too.

Catarina stood and took a step toward him. Another. She caught a flicker of surprise in his eyes before the hardness returned, so she continued. He retreated, the wall now at his back, as his gaze traveled down her body. Awareness tingled in her breasts and between her legs.

Just the brush of his gaze was enough to harden her sensitive nipples, and she felt the sensual scrape of her silk pajamas against them. His gaze momentarily fixed on her breasts, and she caught a flash of the heat that she had seen the day before.

Yes, this was the road forward. This was the only way she knew how to get through to him. She had tried to use her voice, and he was shutting her out, but she could use this, show him that he could not freeze her out, that he would not control her. Catarina took another step and another until she was almost flush with him. Her body exploded with heat, and her breaths were coming one on top of the other. There was no mistaking her intent, but he did not move. He had schooled his face back to that impenetrable mask, and yet passion flared in his eyes. Massimo had started this battle of wits, and he was waiting for her to back down. She would not. He had done this to her, made her vulnerable, opened this Pandora's Box of her emotions. He had set them free, and now he would see the results.

"If things are as you say," she whispered, letting him hear her desire. "If I will, indeed, give in and marry you on your terms once my father is at the negotiating table, then I see no reason to hold back right now."

She lifted her hands to his cheeks. He had showered but not shaved, and the rough stubble contrasted with the soft fullness of his lips. She knew that she would lose herself soon again. That was inevitable. If he had entered her room this morning, she wouldn't have turned him away. She desperately ached for this man, and he had given signs that he might ache for her just as desperately. At least this could be a place where they met on equal ground, she told herself as she urged his face closer to hers.

He gave no resistance. His gaze did not lose its hard edges, but he didn't pull away. Her breath caught in her throat, and her heart took off in soaring arpeggios, higher and higher. The ache between her legs throbbed insistently, and no amount of logical thinking could make it stop. Instead, it grew and grew into something too strong to control. So when his mouth neared hers, she parted her lips, welcoming him. And when his lips descended on hers, she lost her mind.

This kiss was a trap. Something had shifted in her. Her expression was different, new. Back in his room just moments ago, his temper had been fully reined in, and his purpose, clear and unshakable. Massimo would pursue the marriage he had bargained for with the same relentlessness as he had pursued everything else in his life.

Then he had heard the music, and he'd found himself opening the door, moving closer. Catarina was playing the piano, and the slow succession of minor chords was so haunting that it took his breath away. It was as if his inner torment had been embodied in a piece of music. He only had a passing interest in piano, but he knew enough to hear that this feeling was about more than simply the notes. It was just as much about the skill and passion of the musician who was bringing the piece to life.

Massimo's thoughts jumped back to the image of Catarina the previous morning on the piano bench, sitting still, her face marked with traces of passion, and maybe even ecstasy. Something had twisted in his gut, something that he did not want to acknowledge.

And then the music was over. Massimo was conscious that he had descended the stairs, moving closer as she played. He'd tried to summon the righteous indignation that he had felt since he had left her room the night before, as he had built the story in his head, turning Catarina into his mother, but it didn't come. He was struck with the uncomfortable knowledge that, with his anger stripped from him, a powerful want took over, relentless.

When Catarina finally turned to him, her hair was a wild tousle of waves, and her eyes flickered with unfiltered passion that he had seen as she fell apart in his arms the night before. He could sense the power inside her, growing and transforming. She was blooming, and he couldn't bring himself to dislike it, even though she was turning this newfound power on him. Massimo was caught between the dual instincts to watch her break free of the cage that she kept herself in but also to pull her in so tightly that she would never escape. She was dangerously enchanting.

As she urged her lips closer, he reasoned that he could not turn away from this passion now unleashed inside her. If he resisted, would she turn this passion elsewhere when they returned to Milan? The question rattled him to the core, shaking every piece of the stony hardness that he had used to brace himself. As he felt the last of his resistance crumble, he could not bring himself to care, not when her lips were on his. He would make her his.

Satisfaction surged inside him as she seemed to soften to him. He no longer had to resist the maddening pull between them that had kept him awake all night. He brought his lips to her mouth, and the relief of touching her again was usurped by something far less tamed. She responded immediately, opening for him, kissing him with wild abandon. Her hands tangled in his hair as she drew him closer, taking from him greedily, stoking this fire that burned so brightly between them. Her lips were velvety soft as she kissed him with a desperation that spiraled so quickly out of control. He pulled her against him, his hard length meeting her softness. The moment their bodies connected, he left behind the notion of control and negotiation.

"I don't have another condom," he bit out roughly.

"That's okay," she said.

Massimo shuddered with a surge of possession that overtook all other thoughts. Last time the broken condom had been a mistake, but right now, he was suddenly gripped with the thought that he could throw all this uncertainty away and make her his. This time for sure. And though the idea of a baby rattled him to his core, he suddenly wanted this irrevocable bond between them more than he feared the consequences. It defied every last rational thought.

But then she was lowering herself to her knees, and he realized that she had an entirely different idea in mind. Not sex without a condom. Not giving in to the voice that thundered *mine* inside him. But before his mind could fully register his own shocking reaction, she had made quick work of his belt and pants, and now her slim fingers fumbled with the last layer between his length and her mouth. If he were a better man, maybe he would have resisted the mix of lust and innocence in her eyes. It made him wonder if he would survive this with his sanity intact, but he didn't stop her.

Catarina took him out. She looked up at him through dark lashes, then back at his thick length. *Dio*, this was too much for any man to resist. Her lips parted, and she tasted him. Pleasure rippled through his body, but he gritted his teeth, letting her explore. Then, finally, she took him into her mouth. He let out a deep groan. Her hands searched, inexperienced, and he moved them, showing her how to hold him, guiding her fingers to the places that brought him most pleasure. She eagerly followed his lead, then continued with new explorations that were all her own, leaving him shuddering on the brink of bliss. She took him deeper, deeper, as he slowly lost his mind. His hands came to her hair, and she eagerly pleasured him until he couldn't hold back. The ecstasy came on so quickly he almost missed warning her, but when he bit it out, she didn't back away. She took him in one more deep stroke, and he released, calling her name.

Massimo collapsed against the wall as aftershocks racked his body. In his haze of bliss, she stroked him gently, then straightened his clothes, caring for him with a tenderness that was heartbreaking. Then he found himself on his knees, too, easing her onto her back on the soft rug at the base of the steps. He moved her silken panties off her lovely hips, moved between her knees and worshipped her. He worshipped her until she was panting, then moaning, then finally calling out his name. She moved and shook and came, and he drew out every ounce of pleasure with the slow caresses of his mouth. He felt a surge of satisfaction in her pleasure. Time had stopped. Nothing mattered except this moment.

She blinked once, twice, as if falling back into reality, then lifted herself to her elbows and looked at him. Her eyes were unfocused, half-lidded with drunken pleasure. The thrum of the word *mine* pulsed through him, threatening to overtake everything else. He wanted to carry her to the bedroom and discover all the uncharted pleasure he was only beginning to imagine between them.

He needed to share a bed with this woman every single night. And then another image came to him, unbidden: This was the woman whose belly could grow round with a baby. His baby. The unsettling idea hit him, shaking him with the feeling that he refused to identify this time. Still, he couldn't now unthink the picture in his mind of Catarina pregnant, nor could he forget the word that continued through the murky cloud of his thoughts: *mine*.

He shoved this word deep down inside as he gathered the last threads of his self-control.

"We will marry," he said, and he was relieved to hear the hard, implacable edge to his voice.

She rolled her eyes. "It's kind of cute you still think this method of persuasion will work on me."

The sarcasm in her voice was cutting.

"We have to," he insisted, but it came out more like a plea.

"Why?" Her voice was softer now. "You have heard me say I don't want this path. Why do you keep insisting?"

Massimo swiped a hand over his face, trying to control this rush of emotions that threatened to destabilize him. How did he explain the harm his parents' lives had infused in every part of his for far too long? He didn't have the strength for that, not now. So he fought for control over the hurt and need and leveled her with his gaze. "Be ready to leave when the helicopter lands."

Catarina sat on the soft red rug in the great room, her body alive with the pleasure that still pulsed through her. He had given in to the temptation of her kiss quickly and eagerly, and so had she. Tasting his hard length, so erotically tempting, and the intense satisfaction in Massimo's gaze as he'd pleasured her, had tipped her over the edge into bliss. The heat between them was undeniable, but she was no longer sure if she had wielded it or if this electric connection had taken on a life of its own. After playing the scene over a few times in her head, she found herself thinking about the moment when she had answered Massimo's comment about the condom. The look on his face had been so strange and wondrous, and she might have written it off as excitement about the prospect of the pleasure she was offering, except that it changed when she got to her knees. He looked almost… disappointed? In that moment, she had had the strangest feeling that he had *wanted* sex without condoms. That he had wanted the possibility of a baby.

This defied all her assumptions. Up until that moment, she had assumed that he saw the possibility of a baby as an unfortunate outcome of their actions, an assumption backed by the evidence of his cold declarations about illegitimate children and the duty to his family name. But the glow in his eyes made her wonder if she had missed something important.

Slowly, she got to her feet. Her knees were still weak. Her whole body was weak. But as she started up the steps, Massimo appeared on the landing. He was fully dressed, as if he had just emerged from a business meeting and not from the abyss of sex. His chiseled jaw and sharp cheekbones looked even more sculpted in the morning light. He looked like the man she had seen in her father's library, a hard, exacting man who used his authority ruthlessly, so far from the man who had looked at her with overwhelming hunger. And yet, his full lips taunted her, reminders of the pleasure they could bring. Catarina crossed her arms, unwilling to expose the path of her thoughts, but Massimo's gaze had already drifted down to her breasts, and there was a sudden burst of lust in his eyes before the ice-cold veneer sharpened again across his face.

"The phone service is back, and I have called a helicopter to fetch us," he said in a voice that was hard and final. "It will arrive in fifteen minutes."

He didn't wait for her answer. He turned and disappeared into his room. Catarina stared at his door, trying to process this new piece of information. They were no longer snowbound. She should be relieved. She *was* relieved. But her treacherous body protested, suddenly not ready for it to end. Not like this.

Massimo hadn't bothered to ask if she planned to leave with him. Of course, this made her want to insist that she would not, to put her foot down with this autocratic man. Her next instinct was to flee, but Catarina had already learned that he was a force she could not outrun. Not when the pull to stay near him came from inside herself.

Should she protest? Insist that she stayed here? Certainly, he would not carry her out to the helicopter against her will…would he? A part of her wanted to test him, just to see how far he would go to bend her to his will. Or maybe she already knew the answer. That was what disturbed her. But staying meant waiting for the avalanche dig-out, then the plow, then a tow truck to take his car, which was still buried in the snowbank at the end of her driveway. And after that, she'd need to summon the family jet, which her father had certainly called back to Milan. All of that would take time, and she wasn't sure she wanted to be alone in this house when she discovered whether she was pregnant.

Pregnant. The idea rattled around in her, almost too big to contemplate. She craved the closeness she had felt with her own mother. What would this relationship feel like from the other side? It was a responsibility she wasn't sure she was ready for. But if a baby was already on the way, she had to be.

She showered and gathered her belongings, and fifteen minutes later, Catarina found herself walking through the deep snow, toward the landing spot Massimo had managed to scope out. She was thankful for the loud thump of the propeller, then for the driver listening through the headphones because it meant that she didn't have to speak to Massimo beyond a bare minimum on their way down the mountain.

On arrival at the airport, she managed to summon a few polite words of thanks for the pilot, ingrained into her as deeply as anything else. As she walked up the steps to his jet, she reminded herself that in a few hours, she would be free to sort through these strange emotions stirring inside her. She would be free to fall apart again if she needed to. But for now, she just needed to get through this flight back to Milan.

Catarina settled in a plush leather armchair and turned to face the window. Massimo could have chosen any other seat on the jet, but he chose the one across from her, so that if she looked forward, she would get the full effect of his demanding gaze. Even out of the corner of her eye, she was aware of the strong jawline she had traced the night before, the broad, muscular shoulders that had held his powerful body above hers as he sank deep inside her. Her cheeks heated. Just Massimo's nearness usurped the carefully cultivated persona she had always presented to the world. Catarina reminded herself that she was above anything as petty as telling him to find a new seat or moving herself, so she focused studiously on the sparkling blue sea that spread out underneath them as the plane climbed into the air.

"I will arrange for a marriage within the week at the church," said Massimo as they leveled to cruising altitude. "I understand that you want an extravagant celebration, but we must ensure that the timing leaves no doubt about the legitimacy of this child."

"You have no idea what I want," she snapped.

Massimo raised his eyebrows, and his eyes flashed with heat. "Are you sure about that?"

His tone was unmistakably carnal, and her body simmered with the truth of these words. She swallowed and looked out the window, trying desperately to escape his gaze, to rein in the heat and temper that pulsed inside her.

"*If* there is a baby," she started, putting the emphasis on *if* and ignoring the feeling that the word *baby* created within her, strange and unexpected, "this child will be loved and cared for regardless of our marriage status. That holds far more importance in my mind than your worries about what you call legitimacy. No child of mine would ever be made to feel illegitimate, whatever decisions *both* their parents decide to make."

Catarina slowed on the word *both*, and she said it in the measured voice that she endlessly practiced over the years, all without taking her eyes from the vast blue of the sea passing below them.

Even without looking, she sensed Massimo did not react well to this answer. When he finally spoke, his voice held a chill that made her shiver. "A Carandini heir will not be born under threat of scandal. We *will* marry."

She turned to him and narrowed her eyes. "You might want to think back to what happened the last time when you demanded the terms of what I will or will not do."

He looked away, and the lips that had been so soft against hers now formed a hard, thin line. Catarina flashed back to the look in his eyes the last time he demanded marriage. It was almost…bleak. *He was in pain.* Her reaction was visceral, the memory twisting in her gut. Something about their relationship scraped at his wounds, wounds that seemed to be somehow caught up in the Carandini family name and history. This understanding settled inside her, shifting her frustration into something more complicated.

Catarina took a deep breath and tried again. "If you want me to reconsider, you need to give me reasons. Why must we marry? Why is your family name so important to you? Talk to me. *Please*."

Massimo flinched at this last plea, but he said nothing. She returned her gaze to the jagged coastline that marked the European mainland, but before she could fully look away, she caught a glimpse of an expression she had seen before, the one she could only call tumultuous. Was this the expression of a man determined to bend her to his will, even if it meant breaking her, or was this something more?

The cabin of the jet was silent. Massimo must have somehow indicated to the flight attendant not to disturb them because there was no sign of anyone else. There was only Massimo across from her, his imposing body too present to ignore. The longer she sat close to him like this, the longer she could feel her body softening, longing to touch him again. It was torturous to know that he was capable of such passion and tenderness, and yet also capable of cutting it all off so coldly and suddenly. All because the condom broke. All because of the threat of an unplanned pregnancy. All because he wanted an obedience she would not—could not—give him. Not without breaking.

She caught her first glimpse of the Mediterranean, sparkling in the distance out their window. The flight was almost over.

When Massimo finally spoke, his voice was grave enough to make her turn. "Do you know the story behind the bankruptcy of our family company?"

"Only vaguely."

"The company had been on a long descent since my grandfather's stroke forced him to step back from the day-to-day running of the business. But the turning point was on the eve of our parents' anniversary when they invited friends and business associates for a weekend on the 'company' yacht. They had anchored on a reef off a remote island and their day unfolded in its usual chaotic way. Just this close-up view of their relationship would have likely been enough to end some of these relationships." Massimo grimaced, and Catarina could see that recounting this story was causing him pain. "The night escalated to throwing glasses and plates and culminated with my father's demand to return to the mainland immediately. After a shouting match with the captain about protocols, my father got his way. It was only when they had returned to the wharf that some poor crewmember was allowed to point out that they had left two people behind—the president of a major shipping company they were in negotiations with and his wife. The crewmember remembered spotting the two alone in the dark waters, taking what they had intended to be a quick and romantic skinny dip. Later they learned the couple had been forced to swim over a kilometer to shore and, upon coming to land, had stumbled along the rocky beach, naked, until they had found a small fishing hut. They had spent the subsequent few days hospitalized with hypothermia."

"That's awful," she said, almost to herself.

"Even without that terrible end, business relations would have likely soured after that evening, though neither of them ever seemed to understand that. To this day they blame the crewmember for not speaking up sooner." Massimo's expression flashed with disgust. "The disaster on the yacht was just the exclamation mark at the end of a long and winding story of the downfall of my father's reputation and, thereby, the Carandini family's. The day the news reached my grandfather, he had a second stroke."

"Oh, my." Catarina wanted to reach for him, but he felt so very far away right now.

"Alessandro and I have dedicated our lives to rebuilding the company. We have sacrificed everything for it. And yet, we cannot shake the suspicions that we are one step away from self-destruction. Business partners, the paparazzi…" Pain slashed across Massimo's face again. "Alessandro is better at handling the pointed humor than I am. But it still haunts both of us every day of our lives."

"A baby out of wedlock would trigger more suspicions," she added, understanding falling into place. His expression softened as he met her gaze, and for a moment she felt their connection before he looked away. His actions over the past few days were finally starting to make sense. Massimo carried the burden of his family's past on his shoulders, and it was crushing him.

His gaze was solemn. "Maybe Alessandro, with his well-known flings, could get away with it, but not me."

"It must be hard to live like that. Always vigilant," she said softly. "Your parents must be grateful for everything you've done."

The corners of his mouth turned down.

"The most generous interpretation of my parents' relationship with my brother and me is that the intensity of their fights and passionate reconciliations doesn't leave them the energy to consider their impact on their children. The likely truth is that they simply don't care." He kept his eyes on the window, and his expression was stark.

"I'm so sorry," she said.

"I've had a lot of time to think about how two people could become so careless, and I still haven't come up with anything other than selfishness. I will do everything in my power to make sure no child of mine has that experience."

There was an anguish in his words, a despair that suggested his demands were about so much more than his getting his own way. He had alluded to his parents' absence over dinner as the background to the summer he and Alessandro spent at their grandparents' estate; but this time, she heard devastation in his voice. And why wouldn't it be there? He had been a boy once. Vulnerable. Catarina had lived her entire life around her mother, and this loss was still a gaping hole, even four years after the funeral. His parents were still alive yet forever out of reach.

Just a man.

"I'm so very sorry this was your experience," she said quietly. "But I'm sure you know marriage doesn't have to be like this."

"This is a risk." He gestured between the two of them as the dam of his emotion threatened to burst. "For the last two days I could think of nothing but you. And the idea of a baby…" He shook his head. "Everything could fall apart again."

Catarina thought back to those first moments in the library of her home. There had been a connection between them, and he had tried to quash it. *Just like he was doing right now.* She wanted to reach for him, to comfort him, and yet she was almost sure he would turn her away. Where did she go from here?

"I should know within a week whether or not I am pregnant," she said. "We can decide what to do from there."

He was silent.

"If there is a baby, another week won't matter," she added.

"We cannot ignore the engagement dinner I scheduled." Just a few days ago, she may have mistaken this stillness, this blank look, for detachment, but right now, she understood that there was a well of emotion behind it. But that didn't take away from the fact that he was still pushing the engagement, despite everything she had said.

"We can *discuss* it," she replied. "But first, I need a little space to think this through."

He must have heard the determination in her voice because he didn't push further.

Catarina had little memory of the landing or the silent car ride back to her home in Massimo's Ferrari. He didn't even look her way when she climbed out of the car, and she told herself that it didn't hurt, that this is what she had wanted. Space to think. She climbed the front steps of her family home and entered through the intricately carved doors. Gianluigi, their butler, greeted her with a deferential nod as she walked through a vast hall, with its high, vaulted ceilings and plaster flourishes, along the deep red carpet that trailed down the center. She passed one heavy wooden door, then another, pausing as she came to the doorway to her father's office, then continuing through the familiar halls until she came to her suite. She opened the door and found everything exactly as she'd left it. The delicate covers and pillows were neatly arranged on an antique bed, and her collection of childhood books sat on the corner shelf, next to her reading chair. It was all achingly familiar, and yet the room didn't bring her the relief she'd expected. It felt as if it belonged to a distant version of herself.

The past few days with Massimo, she had argued with him, slept with him, stood up to him and, most painful of all, fallen for him. But somehow, this journey had all become a discovery of herself, too. She couldn't stay here. In fact, she should have moved out long ago, she realized.

So she closed the door to her room and walked through the hallways, thinking of all the people in the world who lived in cages of one form or another, cages that were imposed on them by others. She was not one of those people. It occurred to her that, at this point in her life, the cage she was in was actually self-imposed. The risk of disappointing her father had coaxed her to avoid conversations with him about what truly would make her happy. She had made that decision herself out of fear, out of wanting to please and honor her parents. But as she walked through the hallways, she vowed not to stay in this cage of her own making any longer. Had it always been this easy to push open the door and fly? Or had the hindrance been less about flying itself and more about what she wanted to do once she was free?

Catarina came to a stop in front of the door of her father's office again. This time, she knocked.

"Come in." Her father's voice was a familiar gruff bark, and when she opened the door, she found that he did not look the least bit surprised to see her.

"Massimo told me you would be arriving shortly," he said, treating her to a hint of a smile that so rarely came these past few years. "I hear wedding plans will be sooner than expected."

Massimo had clearly called her father, just another move to ensure she acted according to his will. Even after she had told him she was open for negotiations. Why did his betrayal surprise her? *Because you're still hoping for more from him.* But this betrayal cut too deep. He was pushing her too far.

"I have not agreed to the marriage yet, Papa," Catarina said, and her voice was stronger than she expected. "I want to move to the flat in Milan this afternoon."

Her father blinked at her, as if this was the last thing he had expected her to say. He opened his mouth to speak, then closed it, and she felt the bars of the gilded cage around her rattle. The sun hovered behind him, casting shadows on his face, and she noted the lines and wrinkles, the gray streaks in his hair that seemed to multiply daily. She used to see him as a man who outsized the world, but since her mother's death, he had grown smaller. He was growing older. She felt an intense love for him, a closeness despite the fact that he would probably never understand her.

"I know you want what's best for me," she continued. "It must have been hard to watch me struggle with Mama's death."

He turned away, as if even hearing these words was too much, but not before she saw hints of devastation he was trying to hide from her. Her mother's death had left her so afraid of the grief-shaped hole inside her that she had retreated from her own life. It was no wonder her father had grasped at something, anything, to try to help her.

"You are all I have left, my love," he said, and finally, he turned back to her. For the first time since her mother's funeral, she saw tears welling in his eyes. Her own lips trembled.

"I'm going to be all right. I will make sure of it." As she spoke these words, she could feel they were true. Even though everything hurt right now. Even though she had no idea what her future looked like, she would make sure she was all right. For the baby, if there was one, and for herself. "I need to do this on my own."

"Whatever you need, it is yours," he finally said. "I will alert the staff to your arrival."

As she walked out of his office, her hand came to her stomach. For the first time, she was on her own. Being alone had become her worst fear, and she had to face it before she made any more choices about her life. Especially since a pregnancy would mean she wouldn't be alone for much longer, no matter what happened with Massimo.

CHAPTER TEN

MASSIMO STARED AT the photo on page ten of this week's edition of *Gente* magazine. Someone had taken the picture on the tarmac of the airport where they'd landed, and it showed Massimo escorting Catarina into his Ferrari. He hadn't even thought to scan the area for paparazzi. He had been too focused on Catarina, and the look on his face in the photo was undeniable proof of the level of his distraction. It was obscene. Never had Massimo looked as much like his father usually did, fawning after his mother.

The conversation on that plane ride had dragged up emotions that should have stayed buried. And yet, he had found himself reopening old wounds for her, leaving him raw enough to let himself look at her like *that*. He needed to secure this marriage and then stay far away from Catarina. This was no longer simply strategy; it was the only way he could hold himself together. Clearly. And the baby? He had nine months to figure out how to handle that. For now, he needed to focus on the present.

For the past three days since their return, his assistant had combed the press, searching for any leaks of their broken engagement dinner. There had been mild speculations, of course, but this was different. This was much worse. The magazine arrived at the conclusion that there were clandestine motives at work, and he didn't bother reading further. To quiet whatever rumors circulated, he and Catarina needed to appear publicly as soon as possible. She had tentatively agreed to their engagement dinner, and following through on it would solve this current problem. Except Catarina had not responded to the seven messages he had left on her phone this morning.

Massimo tossed the magazine onto his desk and paced back and forth in his office. He glanced at the phone on his desk, tempted to call her once more. Instead, he stormed out the door and into Alessandro's office. He found his brother holding a different magazine, folded back to a page with the same photo. Massimo scowled.

Alessandro looked up from the magazine and studied him long enough to make Massimo squirm. He did not like to be studied, and certainly not by his brother, who seemed to be able to read his thoughts too well for comfort.

"She won't answer her phone," he thundered.

"You said she would contact you when she knew more." His brother's voice was maddeningly calm. "I agree your powers in this world are vast, but as far as I know they do not extend to speeding up the natural revelation of a pregnancy."

"Nor do I expect that," Massimo bit out. "But at least she could…"

His voice trailed off as he tried to capture the frustration that plagued him. Though Catarina had been correct in pointing out that waiting another week would not cause any more or less scandal, neither of them had foreseen this new development.

"It's quite a romantic candid shot of you," said Alessandro, his voice filled with irony. "You do, in fact, look...what's the word they used?" He glanced down at the magazine. "Ahh, here it is. Devoted."

Massimo could hear the censure in his brother's comments. The proposed marriage was supposed to quell speculations about the brothers' personal lives, not stoke them. Clandestine getaways with reclusive heiresses hardly presented a stable front. And if the paparazzi heard whispers of a pregnancy out of wedlock? They were doomed.

"Fix this, Massimo." His brother's voice was insistent. "There are other ways of getting in contact. You could go to her." Alessandro must have seen the way he stiffened because his brother added, "Or you could call her father."

Massimo had the urge to snap that of course he could do these things, but the truth was that he hadn't even considered them as real options. He hadn't considered much of anything that was rational, truth be told. So he gave his brother a grunt of acknowledgment that made his brother's lips quirk up into an ironic smile. But thankfully, Alessandro kept his mouth shut.

Massimo charged out of his brother's office and returned to his, slamming the door behind him. He came to a stop at a long window and looked out on the rooftops of Milan, the city spreading out in front of him. How could all his money and prestige and power count for nothing right now? What was the point of all this if he was still stuck here in agony? Because he ached for Catarina. He told himself he just wanted her in his bed, but even the thought of talking to her was enough to ease some of this relentless need. Just like his father. Massimo scowled, but he still picked up his phone.

Giuseppe d'Avalos answered on the first ring.

"Is Catarina at home?" Massimo's question was rough and abrupt, but it was the only way that he could stop himself from asking the question that pressed in his mind: Why hadn't Catarina returned his calls?

"She's gone."

"Gone?" Everything seemed to collapse inside him, and he didn't bother keeping the dread from his voice. "What do you mean?"

"She left for our flat in the city," d'Avalos said slowly. "I believe her words were something about dealing with this on her own."

Massimo heard the man's pointed emphasis on the words *on her own*, so he clung to the last thread of politeness and ended the call, then asked his assistant to find the address of the d'Avalos home in Milan.

Suspicions lurked in the back of his mind. Had she indeed left for their Milan flat, or was this story just a cover for yet another disappearance, this time more remote and difficult to track? The thought stirred a familiar frustration mixed with something far more dangerous, far more desperate.

Massimo left immediately, stalking through the streets of Milan, trying to shake off some of the ominous thoughts that raced through his mind. He glared through the crowds of people on the sidewalk, all lost in their own worlds, so blissfully unaware of the torment that reverberated through him. His plans, his family's name, his sanity—Catarina was jeopardizing it all.

Massimo arrived in front of the tall building where she was supposedly staying, and the scent of roses blew by him in wisps, taunting him. The building was older and newly renovated, with gargoyles, stone flourishes and ostentatious columns as if to mark the legacy that the residents held in the city. He frowned as he walked through the marble corridor, muttering a few words about his fiancée to the doorman, who had his magazine open to the same article Alessandro had been reading. He looked at the photo of Massimo in the paper, then back up to the man in front of him. With a nod, he walked to the elevator and keyed it to the top floor.

The elevator groaned and creaked as it slowly made its way upward, trying his patience. The walk hadn't helped with his growing unease. Instead, a steely determination had grown as he'd stormed through the streets of Milan. He would demand that she answer his calls.

You might want to think back to what happened the last time when you demanded the terms of what I will or will not do.

Her words echoed inside him, laced with the soft temptation of her voice, and he felt the last shreds of his control fraying. He had spent his entire life making sure he would not be ruled by his emotions, and yet this appalling raw ache inside him was driving his every thought.

The elevator rattled to a stop and the doors slid open. Massimo barely registered the polished marble floors or the plaster flourishes that decorated the hall as he stalked to her door, raised his hand and knocked. He listened impatiently for her footsteps. Was she in the flat, as she'd said? Or had she fled yet again? Fleeing was exactly what his mother would do, he thought bitterly. How often had his mother left at a critical moment, giving only clues about her destination, expecting Massimo's father to chase her? He had to tame these brushfires of emotions and shake this feeling that was too much like despair. Because if Catarina had left, he knew he would scour the earth to find her. Which meant he was living out his worst nightmare. He was, indeed, his father's son.

Massimo was shaken out of these disturbing thoughts by the sound of soft steps behind the door, then the turn of the lock. The door opened, and she was in front of him, so breathtakingly beautiful his chest hurt. She was barefoot and wore a sundress in a pale shade of green that came down in a V, showing off her deliciously full breasts and cinching at her narrow waist. Her dark hair fell around her shoulders, and there were no traces of makeup on her lovely face. Catarina did not look like the proper society woman he had contracted to marry. Instead, she was a version of the woman he had seen in the Norwegian house, the one who wasn't keeping herself under careful control. He wanted *this* woman, he realized. He stared at the creamy skin that her dress revealed, thinking of the opportunities he had missed to taste every inch of it. Before he called the helicopter, he should have taken her to his room and let the fire between them burn one more time. He had squandered his chance.

Now he could not touch her. From the beginning, her touch had caused earthquake after earthquake, each one rattling him to the core, shaking the foundations that he had built his life on. He had given in to the temptation when they were alone, telling himself it was part of a careful seduction strategy, but in his heart, he knew that was a lie. Massimo had given in because no one tasted like Catarina. And when she had touched him, even the possibility of a baby born out of wedlock had not mattered. In that moment, he had *wanted* for her to be pregnant with his baby, regardless of the fallout. Which was madness. The last thing he wanted was to bring a child into the world while the Carandini name still carried the stain of the past. Children were not supposed to factor into this marriage until far, far in the future. And yet, in that moment, he had wanted a baby with Catarina, deeply and irrationally. Which was why he needed to stay away from her. But the siren's song of her voice and her body and every other element of her was irresistible, so the only option left was to tie himself to the mast of this marriage plan as they moved forward.

Catarina's eyes were wide, and she looked a little startled to see him. A burst of unwanted lust flared inside him, followed by frustration.

"Why did you ignore my calls?" he demanded.

The wonder dissolved from her face, and he silently cursed his heavy-handed outburst.

"Was I supposed to be available to you whenever you needed me?" she asked, and her achingly beautiful voice was cloaked with icy politeness. "I apologize."

He scrubbed his hands over his face. Why was he so hotheaded with this woman? He had never once struggled to maintain control with anyone else. It defied reason. Belatedly, he was aware that they were having this exchange in the hallway. In his experience, curious eyes and listening ears were everywhere, so ready to feed the next slice of juicy gossip about the Carandini family to the paparazzi.

"I'd like to move this discussion inside," he said. "Please."

The word *please* was a concession, along with the fact

that he had resisted his instinct to order her, to demand what he wanted, an instinct he was increasingly understanding as desperation. And maybe she understood this because her polite expression softened just a fraction. After another breath, she stepped aside and indicated for him to enter, then closed the door behind him.

The hallway was bright and unexpectedly modern for the era of the building, but there were traces of its original form in the patterns of the wood floor and the intricate plaster flourishes around the doorways. Massimo noted each of these details, trying to divert his attention from the way the soft material of her dress so perfectly highlighted the roundness of her full rear. He ached to close the distance between them, to hitch up her skirt, plant his hands on her hips and take her against this carefully arranged wall, full of priceless art. He ignored the inconvenient stir in his groin and followed her into the living room. Catarina took a seat in a white armchair by one of the large windows that overlooked the city. At the far end of the room, sunlight reflected off the deep ebony of her piano, with books of music propped, one on top of the other, in front of the open keyboard.

He turned to her and focused on the reason he had come. "I called your phone several times. You didn't answer."

She sighed. "My phone is in the kitchen, and the ringer is off. I needed some time to think."

Logically, he was aware that the harder he pushed Catarina, the more she seemed immune to his frustrations. Yet, it still was a struggle to soften his tone. "And did this thinking lead you to any conclusions?"

"No conclusions, but things are becoming clearer, as you promised," she said with a polite smile.

He recognized that smile from the first day they had met. Her words were perfectly agreeable, though he was sure her thoughts were very far from that. The idea that this woman held in her hands a decision that would affect his life, a decision that he had no control over, was too disturbing to contemplate. Massimo had built an entire life around never having to be at someone else's mercy. His life was his own to control, and yet this control had slipped from the moment Catarina had entered his life.

And if she was pregnant… That thought was a clap of thunder that threatened to shatter his thin veneer of calm. But there was still a chance that she was not, he reminded himself. There was still a chance he could walk away from this whole mess. Find another bride who actually understood the *convenient* part of this arrangement. But just thinking about leaving Catarina for someone else made his stomach feel as if it were in freefall.

"I would like you to answer my calls," he said slowly, grasping at the last threads of his self-control.

"I'll take that under consideration," she said crisply. "Now, please tell me why you are here."

When Massimo handed her the latest edition of *Gente*, Catarina's first instinct was to laugh. The idea of this stoic man spending the morning leafing through a notorious gossip magazine was absurd. But as she focused in on the photo he pointed to, all the humor inside her shifted into shock. She stared at it, frozen in place. Catarina remembered the exact moment the picture was taken, and her face flushed at the thought that someone else was watching. Heat traveled through her body as she recalled the gentle pressure of his hand on her back, the tender caress of his touch when he had helped her into the car, so at odds with the cold distance in his voice. At the time, she had told herself that the gesture was nothing more than politeness.

Catarina had spent the past three days trying to be rational about what had happened between them during the snowstorm. Massimo wanted a convenient marriage to an obedient wife, and he had used the spark of attraction between them to get it. It was that simple. He was definitely attracted to her, but he had made it clear on the plane that he would never let himself become close to her, not after he had seen his parents destroyed by what they thought passed for love. She could understand his frustration, as she had, in fact, agreed to a marriage of convenience. But that was before she had spent days with Massimo. Talked with him. Done those unspeakably hot things with him in bed. On the floor. And then learned what it felt like when he turned to ice afterward. She could no longer accept a distant marriage. It would be a prison, and he was determined to be her warden.

Yet, the picture in the paper gave her evidence to the contrary, evidence she could not look away from. The photographer had zoomed in, likely to validate their identities. But he had caught more than that. Catarina's own face was turned, focused on the step into the passenger seat of the Ferrari, but the shot showed Massimo's clearly, and it was full of raw emotion. He was looking down at her as if he was in love with her, despite his efforts to fight it.

Shock and confusion rattled her. She had spent the

past three days trying to accept the fact that he desired her but did not—and would not—ultimately care for her. If she was pregnant, she needed their relationship to be on stable ground, which would mean putting her own feelings aside and making good decisions that kept their baby's best interests at the center of everything. She told herself that, under the right conditions, an accidental pregnancy wasn't the worst twist of fate. After all, she herself had been an unexpected baby, and her parents had never once made her feel like the pregnancy was a mistake. As long as their baby grew up surrounded by love, regardless of the parents' relationship.

Their baby. The words had played in her head over and over, threatening to overwhelm rational thought. Unlike Massimo, who had been brought up in a household where wealth was a substitute for parental attention, she had been surrounded with love, imperfect but wholehearted. Her parents had given her this, and she would give it to her baby. But the family she wanted right now was about more than children. She wanted a family with Massimo, this impossible, imperfect man who was capable of so much passion. He had shown her glimpses of tenderness, of the kind of connection she craved, and she wanted more.

Yet, his words on his jet had shaken her to the core. He seemed to believe that wholehearted love meant a self-centered destruction of everyone in his orbit. When she had arrived at the flat, she had spent the day scouring the internet for articles about his parents. As she read story after story in black-and-white, she could see that Massimo had, in fact, downplayed the dramatic public fights and equally public make-up scenes that his parents endlessly played out. What she hadn't fully calculated was how young Massimo was when this had all started.

Catarina understood where Massimo's conclusions about love came from. Maybe she would believe the same in his shoes. But that didn't change the problem at the heart of their relationship. Was she trying to fit a square peg into the nice, round fairy-tale ending that she wanted for their story? Maybe it was futile to convince him to embrace this passion between them. Maybe it was better to put her energies toward a compromise, so that by the time the baby came, the path was smooth. Over the past three days she had debated her choices, her heart and her mind at odds. Now, as she stared at this candid photo of him in the magazine, his expression so raw and open, it felt as if she were looking at a mirror of her soul.

She was falling in love with him. But if she said those words, it would only drive him further away from her. The thought was devastating. Catarina swallowed, then looked up at Massimo. As he gazed down at her, she searched for cracks in the facade of his hard expression. She found none.

"The photo is unfortunate," he said in that commanding voice he used with her, the one that frustrated her. But it also did strange things to her insides because she couldn't stop hearing the pain behind it, too. "We cannot wait a week for our dinner. To that end, I would *like* to make reservations for tonight."

At least he was attempting to ask and not simply commanding her presence. She tilted her head, studying him. "Surely, you don't imagine one public supper will smooth over all speculations. Won't it simply fuel more?"

There was pain in his reaction, a grimace, so small

she might have missed it. But it was there. She took a step toward him. His eyes widened, and she felt a surge of satisfaction. This was what had cracked his hard exterior before. This was how they connected. And though touching him scrambled her own mind and softened her will, it was better than the cold reserve between them. Catarina lifted her hand to touch his face, but instead of giving in, he stepped back. His retreat felt like an arrow in her heart, but she told herself to ignore it. She told herself this was to be expected. Even if the photo told her Massimo felt the same as she did, he would resist it with all his being.

Catarina attempted to paste on a breezy smile. "I doubt this evening will be a PR success if you move away when I reach for you."

"There's no need to touch," he bit out, his voice rough and full of frustration.

She didn't back down.

"We are not your parents," she said softly.

His hard exterior seemed to crumble at her words.

"This—" He gestured to the remaining space between them. "This is madness. It can be twisted and manipulated and used for harm at any time."

Catarina's own frustrations took over then, laced with the heat and the heartache she was trying desperately to keep under control. "How can you say that? How can you ignore how good this feels?"

Massimo's eyes narrowed, and his expression was thunderous. "You're using sex to provoke me."

The accusation was a slap, and it traveled through her body, finding its way into her soul. It was useless to accuse him of the same because it only proved his point.

"I am trying to get through to you," she said, trying to keep her voice calm, even though her heart was breaking. Because she would absolutely not give him the dramatic meltdown he was expecting. "You shut me out the moment you sense a threat to you or your precious family name. You've built this—" she gestured at his tall, imposing figure, his hard expression "—this image of Massimo Carandini, made of impenetrable steel. You're not giving us a chance."

"This is who I am," he said in a voice that was hauntingly final.

"You are more," she whispered, but her words sounded like a plea.

He frowned and turned his back to her and started for the door. "I will pick you up at eight."

CHAPTER ELEVEN

Catarina stepped out of Massimo's Ferrari, into the misty Milanese night. The evening rain had left a sheen that glistened on every surface. The city felt alive, washed clean and bubbling with car engines, laughter and the last of the rain spilling out of gutters, all mocking the tempest that had brewed inside her all day long. She wanted to show Massimo that they could be something different together, but the cold distance between them was too much to bear. The urge to turn away, to flee, to escape this pain, nagged at her.

The valet whisked the Ferrari away, and she was left standing next to Massimo. He wore a suit that emphasized his broad shoulders and narrow hips, and the collar of the crisp white shirt was unbuttoned, showing a glimpse of the dark hair on his chest she couldn't erase from her mind.

Sensations threatened to overwhelm her, the silk of her dress caressing her, and the cool night air on her bare legs. The warmth of her soft cashmere coat and scarf. The flare of desire that roared in Massimo's eyes when he opened her car door. All of these sensations contrasted with the hard, inscrutable expression he wore as they approached the restaurant. The well-dressed doorman opened the thick wooden doors, and she ached for the exquisite tenderness of his touch on her back, guiding her through the entryway and into the dark warmth of the restaurant. It never came.

Massimo said a few low words to the host, then gestured to the staircase that led to the second floor of the elegant restaurant, past curious onlookers. As he nodded to familiar faces, Catarina was reminded of just how much she disliked being in the spotlight. Her mother had always been the object of interest at high-profile appearances, drawing attention away from her, but here, she felt on display. She felt exposed right at the moment her defenses were down. But she had a plan, one that had kept her from listening to the old voice inside begging her to flee, run far away from the rawness she felt when she was near him.

Massimo led them to a circular table next to a window that curved out above the street. Though the distance from other guests gave them a bit of privacy, the table was visible to anyone who entered the second floor. Just the kind of audience Massimo had wanted, thought Catarina. It shouldn't bother her, this public theater of their relationship. After all, this was exactly what they'd planned, exactly what she had signed up for. And she did want to ease some of the gossip about their relationship that the photo had stirred up, at least to give them some space until they had an answer about the pregnancy. Still, it bothered her. Where was the man who had cooked for her and then worshipped her body with his? She wanted another glimpse of the man she had opened her heart to back in the remote cabin in Norway; the man who had shown her his pain on the plane ride home. Massimo seemed determined not to be that man.

He pulled out her chair from the table, making sure to keep his distance. The silver and glassware glistened under the light of the candles, and through the window the Duomo twinkled in the darkness. Just a week ago, she would have been perfectly satisfied with this evening, ready to play this role in exchange for the kind of freedom she had craved. Now everything had changed. Now that she knew what was possible between them, she could no longer settle for less.

The server came to present the evening's menu, and Catarina found her mind wandering to the impassive man across from her. She had absolutely no idea what he was thinking. When the server left the table, Catarina took a deep breath, then met his gaze.

"A few days ago, you asked me what I wanted," she said. "I have a new answer."

Her words had played through his mind all day, singing *You are more* in that silken caress of her voice, tempting him with a promise he knew wasn't real. The fire between them was a living thing, sparking to life at unpredictable times, taunting him to forget everything that he had spent his life building. Massimo should have felt suffocated by the oppressive heat of it. Instead, he burned hotter, the temptation growing stronger.

These dangerous feelings were starting to feel as inevitable as the tide, an unstoppable force of the ocean that flowed high on the banks of his self-restraint each time she was near. Now these vast, tumultuous waters were never out of sight.

A cloud of foreboding had hovered over them since he had picked up Catarina. He hated the calm facade she had masked herself with throughout the silent car ride. How maddening it was that he had sought her out for precisely this skill that was haunting him. Two competing desires warred in him: He craved the passion she had shown him every time they touched, and yet he absolutely could not tolerate the idea of a passion that threatened what was now and would always be his first priority, the redemption of his family's name. And even more maddening was the threat that lingered every time he considered this war of opposing forces inside him: He knew what happened when passion won this struggle. He had seen it play out for his entire life. And yet, he was still tempted.

But he would manage this point of vulnerability. He had successfully managed his parents until they were no longer a weakness but an obstacle he had overcome on his path to success, something to draw strength from. Though this success no longer felt like the balm it always had been. Still, Massimo had spent the evening telling himself that there was absolutely no reason to be uneasy. This supper was simply a formality, and yet he couldn't escape the feeling that something fundamental had changed since he had left her apartment earlier in the day. Now, as she sat across from him, her chin lifted in a hint of defiance and her lovely brown eyes clear, the foreboding cloud grew darker.

But Massimo Carandini had never backed away from a challenge. He and his brother had rebuilt an entire empire on their single-minded rebuke of their father's course in their quest to redeem their family's name.

He set aside these feelings, lifted an eyebrow and responded to her comment. "Just days ago, you said you had everything you needed. Has something changed?"

"Weren't you the one who questioned my desires?" she said mildly, though her eyes flashed with heat, as if she, too, was picturing the scene in the bedroom when he had held himself over her, taunting her with the question of what she wanted. Her heavy lashes fell for a moment, and when she looked at him again, the heat was gone. "I should think you would be happy to learn that I have reconsidered."

He dismissed the wisp of unease that ran through him, reminding himself that he was, in fact, happy that she had finally given in and come to the bargaining table. She would put forth her demands and he would reiterate his. Maybe the possibility of a baby was bringing out the practical side in her. *Their baby*. The words joined the unsettling mix of feelings that brewed inside him, but he kept them under control. "I eagerly await hearing of your desires."

Catarina straightened in her chair and leveled him with her gaze.

"I want a husband who loves and respects me," she said in a voice that was soft and yet devastatingly final. "Whether or not there is a baby…" Her voice wavered at this last word. "I want a family where love is at the center of all the choices we make together. Though I am far from ready for a baby, I will do everything to be the mother that our child needs, and I want the same from you. A child should be surrounded by love."

Her chest rose and fell, as if she was steeling herself for her next sentence. Massimo was frozen in place, unable to look away. It felt as if he was watching this slow-motion train wreck from the outside. For a moment, her gaze faltered. Her chest rose and fell again, as if she was shoring up strength. When she met his gaze again, her eyes were clear. "That is what I want from you, Massimo. Love."

A maelstrom of desperation and fury thundered through him. "And you are not willing to compromise on that at all?"

She shook her head, and he could see the determination in the set of her jaw and her unflinching gaze. This was not a negotiation at all. It was an ultimatum.

Massimo unclenched his teeth and kept his expression blank. "How can you speak of a life devoting yourself to the needs of your child when you are unwilling to compromise? I have already made far more concessions than I agreed to when I entered this bargain."

She swallowed, the movement in her long, slim neck betraying hesitancy.

"None of this has been what I agreed to," she said. "But I know now that there is no other way forward for me. Not with you."

He hated the waver in her voice, underlining the truth behind her words. And there was a part of him that needed to give her what she wanted. But she was asking for far too much.

It was as if she had pried open the most vulnerable part of him, exposing it for them both to view, right here in the restaurant. The bone-deep need to fight back against this feeling was overtaking him. He knew exactly what he needed to do right now. He needed to lie. He could promise her something vague, like that he would grow to love her. Just a few simple words that she needed to hear.

And yet…

He couldn't do it. Massimo stared across the table as the rush of emotions he had been fighting the entire evening hit him. He couldn't find enough air as he drank her in, paralyzed by her beauty, by the sound of her voice as it sang through him, by the overwhelming need to touch her again. He was paralyzed by *her*. She deserved what she wanted, and yet it would crush him if he gave it to her.

He swiped a hand over his face. "You are asking for the one thing you know I cannot give you."

Catarina did not try to hide the hurt that slashed across her face. "Then I suppose this conversation is over."

Massimo had little memory of what they ate or how they got through the excruciating meal. He no longer cared what observers at the tables around them detected, nor did he care about what might be written in next week's edition of *Gente*. The dignified lift of her chin was a devastatingly sharp knife that twisted each time he met her gaze, silently reminding him of what he knew he could not give.

The ride home was silent, and she didn't look at him as they crossed the entry hall of her apartment building for the elevator. When the doors opened at the top floor, the only sound was the clack of their shoes on the polished marble floor. She stopped in front of her doorway, and he could hear her shallow breaths as she turned the key and opened it. The relentless charge between them sparked and surged, twinged with desperation. She was so temptingly close.

Catarina didn't step inside her flat. Instead, she turned and looked up at him, giving him another searching look.

But this time, there was heat behind it, too. Massimo's body roared with the need he had contained all night. Frustration, desire and desperation conspired against him until he couldn't resist any longer. He leaned over and pressed his mouth against hers, tasting hints of wine and chocolate and, underneath, Catarina. Her hands came around his neck and slid into his hair. She was pulling him closer, kissing him the way she had kissed him in the snowbound house, with the passion and abandon that he couldn't get enough of. He kissed her like she was an oasis in the desert, one he couldn't bring himself to leave. She moved closer, pressing her body against his, and the need to take her right there, in the hallway, to make her his, to remind her of everything that he could give her, overtook him. *This is what you want*, said something deep inside him, ominous and clear. Massimo would never get enough of this woman. He would crave her for the rest of his life. Maybe this was his own twisted version of love, but he could not be a slave to it.

He clung to the last of his sanity as these instincts threatened to overwhelm him. The desire to take her to her bed and spend the rest of the night making love to her would bring him to his knees. But he knelt for no one. It was a matter of survival. So Massimo Carandini used the last of his famous willpower, the strength that he had spent his entire adult life building, to pull away.

He looked into her eyes, half-lidded and hazy with desire. Her hair was mussed, and her lips were parted. He thrust his arms to his sides and clenched his fists, forcing himself not to reach for her again. Not to promise her everything she wanted just to spend the night in her bed.

"This hurts, Catarina," he bit out, his voice raw. "It's torturous. How can you want this?"

She lifted her chin, even as her eyes welled with tears. "I deserve love. I will not settle for anything less."

For once in his life, Massimo Carandini had no idea what to do next, so he did what his entire being was begging him not to do. He walked away.

Two days later, Massimo still had no idea what to do, which was how he found himself in his Ferrari, racing into the Italian Alps, ignoring the awful feeling in his stomach, as if he was in freefall.

He came to the familiar gates, then continued up the winding driveway, coming to a stop in front of his grandparents' towering country estate. Three rows of windows marked the floors of the main house, a symmetry interrupted by tangled vines of rambling roses that climbed the facade. As Massimo walked up the stone steps, he inhaled the familiar scent, then flashed to Catarina, to the same scent that lingered wherever she went. His mind finally made the connection it seemed to have resisted until now: Her scent reminded him of the only place that had ever felt like home.

Massimo looked up at the center window of the second floor, where his grandmother was almost certainly sitting in her reading room, awaiting his arrival. He climbed the remaining step and banged on the door with the brass knocker, a ghost of a smile playing on his lips as he took in its familiar lion's-head shape, knowing the housekeeper had likely been forewarned that his grandmother would answer the door herself. He waited, imagining her slow, regal steps down the grand staircase, her aging hands resting on the banister.

Finally, the door swung open.

"My boy," she said without a hint of irony, despite the fact that Massimo had so clearly left boyhood long, long ago. He bent over to kiss her soft, familiar cheeks.

Isabella Carandini had dressed for the occasion. Her hair was in a neat gray bun at the base of her neck. She wore a well-tailored dress in widow's black, a tradition she still held to after thirteen years. Around her neck was a simple strand of pearls with matching earrings that Massimo's grandfather had given her as a wedding gift, before he had made the kind of money that bought them family estates. During his lifetime, Massimo's grandfather had not been the easiest man, and yet Massimo never doubted the man's love for his wife.

"Constantina made her famous vanilla bean cake," she said, leading him through the long hallway, back to the solarium, where his grandmother spent her days tending to her plants. A table was set in the center of the bright room with her favorite porcelain set. There was a silver pot of coffee with creamer and the sugar bowl Massimo used to steal from as a child. The cake was dusted with powdered sugar, and on a silver tray at the side was a thin bottle of limoncello and two aperitif glasses.

He visited his grandmother less frequently than he should. When the thought crossed his mind, he told himself that it was his busy schedule, but there in her solarium, Massimo was reminded that his feelings about this house were complicated. This was the place where he had taken refuge when he was a vulnerable young teenager, and visiting it meant acknowledging a part of himself that he had left behind. Yet, he had cleared his schedule this afternoon to come. Massimo wasn't ready to contemplate what this meant.

His grandmother gestured for him to sit, and he inquired about her health and the health of her plants as he savored the slice of cake that she had neatly cut and served for him. When they had finished their coffee, she poured him a glass of limoncello and smiled indulgently as she handed it to him.

"I must admit your photo was the last thing I expected to see as I was reading my favorite gossip magazine this week." She lifted an eyebrow. "Maybe Alessandro's but not yours."

Massimo may have taken this as a provocation from anyone else, but there was sympathy and understanding in his grandmother's voice. She knew the depth of hurt that he had once felt from these kinds of headlines.

"Does your visit have something to do with the whispers I heard of an engagement?" she asked.

The words were perfectly polite, and yet he could still hear the rebuke behind them. He had planned to notify her of his engagement before his original supper plans, of course, but that was before the situation had careened out of control.

"I apologize for not calling you sooner," he said. "The situation has developed in unexpected ways."

She tilted her chin in acknowledgment, but he knew better than to mistake it for forgiveness. "Do you love this woman?"

Massimo grimaced. This should have been the easiest question to answer. Overwhelming passion, burning, aching need, possessiveness, even protectiveness—Catarina had wrenched each one of these feelings from him. But he was not capable of the kind of love she deserved. What he felt for her was already tearing him apart. Massimo had no idea what to call this pit in his stomach, this unwieldy heat, this voice that raged inside him, shaking him bone-deep with the word *mine*.

"I love her," he finally bit out. "And it will lead us both to our downfall."

"Don't be so dramatic, Massimo," she said with a wry laugh that pushed away some of the dark clouds that hovered over him. "Have you told this woman that you love her?"

"It's complicated," he muttered, looking away.

"I see," she said, and he had the distinct impression she did, in fact, see far more than he wished. She tilted her head a little, assessing him skeptically. "You must allow yourself happiness."

Massimo swallowed back a new and inexplicable twist of pain. Her words about happiness were so simple, and yet something inside him revolted against them. "And if I am not capable of this? If this feeling is devouring me from the inside?"

"Now you have convinced me that you are, in fact, in the throes of love." She gave him a smug smile.

"The kind of love my parents have?"

His grandmother's glass was halfway to her mouth, but she stopped. She set her limoncello back on the table and turned to him. All traces of her smile were gone.

"I know your father better than anyone in the world, and that includes your mother. He is my son…" She paused, and Massimo registered the grief in her voice.

"And I can tell you that you are nothing like him. I should never have taken for granted that you understood that."

Her tone was breathtakingly serious. He stared at her as she lifted her glass and took a sip. When she looked at him again, there was a hint of challenge that sparkled in her eyes. "Anything you have learned about love from your father you can unlearn. You have defied his example in every other way. Why would love be any different?"

CHAPTER TWELVE

Catarina stared down at the wand, lined up next to three others on a tray on her bathroom sink. Late at night, long after Massimo had left her aching in her lips, in her breasts and in her heart the previous night, she had awoken with cramps in her lower back. She had not allowed herself to analyze the sensation. Her body was speaking to her, but she was tired of listening to it.

Now the message was staring up at her, confirming her body's signals with a finality that she could no longer doubt. The tests were negative. She was not pregnant. Catarina sat down on the floor, allowing herself to fully register the familiar tenderness in her breasts, the familiar cramping. These sensations that she had experienced over the past few days, the ones that she had interpreted as signs of pregnancy, were simply the usual signals of the end of her cycle. Nothing life changing. There was no baby.

Catarina waited for relief to set in, but it didn't come. Instead, a strange stillness was settling inside her body, a numbness she was not prepared for. She had spent the past week worrying about the possibilities of a pregnancy she was far from prepared for, but with these possibilities came glimpses of a larger hope, not just for a baby but for something more, a hope for building the family that she craved. A family with Massimo.

Catarina took a final look at the row of pregnancy tests staring up at her, the single pink line unmistakably bright. Then she turned away and returned to the living room, sinking into her favorite armchair. On the table in front of her sat an enormous bouquet of red roses that had been delivered early in the morning. They seemed to sprout from the wide white vase, spilling over the edges with an excess that she couldn't stop staring at. The scent had filled her flat, intoxicating her, but the card was blank except for a large *M* scrawled across it. How fitting, she thought, to send something so intoxicating, excessive and yet withholding. Still, she ached for Massimo. Even when she should know better. She told herself the flowers were probably the work of his assistant, just another step in his well-calculated plan to make their marriage go through. And yet, her breath still caught when she looked at the bouquet. Her heart had swelled when her doorman delivered them. Wasn't this the kind of romantic flair she had wanted?

She reminded herself that Massimo had told her in no uncertain terms that he could not—or, rather, would not—love her. He refused to give her what she needed, and she knew that anything less would destroy her.

The threads that had held this marriage arrangement together had frayed. All she had to do to snap them was call Massimo and deliver the news that their pregnancy scare was over. And yet, she could not bring herself to do it. Not over the phone. But if she went to him, stood before him and once again welcomed that tempting pull that threatened to drag her under, would she be able to walk away? *Just a man*, she reminded herself. A man like the mountains that rose behind her house in the fjord, unmovable and impossible to ignore.

Catarina had no idea how long she sat in her living room, staring at the overflow of red roses, but finally, the swirl of anxiety and want that mixed with hope, that stubborn companion that dogged her, became too much. She left her apartment, not bothering to call her driver. Instead, she walked. Massimo's address was in a newer part of town, and the building was an impressive show of glass and steel. Catarina stopped outside the doors and stared up at it. It was infused with a starkness that she took as a reminder of everything Massimo Carandini was: powerful, impressive and remote. The truth of this visit hit her, paralyzing her in place: This was likely the last time she would see him.

"Catarina?"

His voice echoed through her, rich and deep, and the relief of hearing it was almost too much to bear. How was it that just his voice was enough to set off this electric current of desire that made her breasts heavy and her heart ache? She turned and found Massimo exiting his Ferrari, walking toward her with purpose in his eyes as the valet left with his car. As he came closer, the fire inside her jumped higher. His hair was combed back from his face, exposing the faint scar that healed on his forehead, and his eyes were dark and penetrating as he focused his gaze directly on her. She stepped back, trying not to be burned by it, but it was too late. It was as if something inside her was now linked to him, responsive to him in some deeper way. *It will always be like this*, said a voice inside her. This was a man who had made it clear that love was not on the table, who had stated he was done compromising. And somehow, this was the man she wanted. This was the man she had fallen in love with. It defied reason, and it was breaking her heart.

Catarina vaguely registered the people who passed them on the sidewalk, pausing to stare. A man in a three-piece suit holding a young girl's hand. A well-dressed woman with a fluffy white dog. Massimo must not have noticed them because she knew he would retreat from even this small hint of public display of emotion. His family's name and image would always come first. This last thought was the push she needed to speak.

"There is no baby," she said, keeping her voice low and clear.

His eyes widened, and Catarina wondered if he, too, had not fully considered their path forward without a baby to bind them together. The surprise in his expression was followed by a glimpse of something else, something that made her wonder if Massimo felt just as lost as she did.

"Please, let's talk about this in my flat," he said with a roughness that was heartbreaking.

Catarina shook her head. If they were alone, she wouldn't be able to resist him.

Massimo frowned down at her. "Perhaps we can move off the street? Just to the building's courtyard?"

Catarina swallowed. Anywhere public, he would never risk showy emotions, she reasoned. He would never reach for her or lean forward for one of his devastating kisses, the kind that seemed to stop time and erase all rational thought. So she nodded.

Massimo led her through the lobby, all glass and shining surfaces, but when he opened the door to the courtyard, her heart gave a painful squeeze. His building took up the entire block, and in the center of it was an oasis of green. It was as if they had been transported away from the noise of the street and into the walled grounds of a castle. There were plants everywhere, towering trees, fresh herbs and flowers on the ground and vines that clung to the fences and archways that separated the space into smaller, more intimate areas. It was as if she had traveled through his remote, carefully controlled layers and found the part of him she had longed for.

She knew she shouldn't hope, and yet she still did.

Restlessness had dogged Massimo the entire morning. After putting out a few fires, he had rushed to the jewelers' and paid the woman a diamond's worth to size the ring correctly while he waited. On the drive home, he played out potential scenarios, but when he stepped out of his car and found Catarina standing outside his apartment building, all his plans fell away. A powerful feeling shuddered through him, a surge of emotions too strong to ignore. His grandmother's words still echoed in his mind. *You must allow yourself happiness.* As he looked into the depths of her dark brown eyes, those words had stopped him in his tracks. His parents had caused so much pain in his life, and he was still letting their actions shape his. He had been on the brink of letting the fear of this pain take away his chance at love.

Now that Catarina was seated on the sofa of his courtyard, her shoulders straight, determined, he registered that this scenario was not one that he had considered. He had been prepared for arguments, contingency plans and reminders of everything at stake, but not the possibility that there was no baby.

Massimo was stunned by a bone-deep feeling of loss. At first, he thought it came from the loss of his plans, or maybe the idea of the baby, but as Catarina stared at him as if she was preparing to say goodbye, the truth hit him, a thunderclap that rattled his entire being. What if he was too late? He was losing *her*, and he absolutely could not let that happen. The desperation from this coming loss overwhelmed him, and in the chaos of his thoughts, one idea shone clearly: He could not lose Catarina out of the fear he had been running from his entire life, that in loving someone he would become like his father. The only clarity in front of him was that this fear was nothing in comparison to the devastation that would stay with him if she walked away. He could not let Catarina go.

"I was wrong about all of this," he started. Those simple words seemed to open a dam inside him, and all the feelings he had tried to repress tumbled through his mind. He loved her. Intensely. Desperately. But it wouldn't be his downfall; instead, it would be his salvation. As she looked up at him from the sofa, her eyes wary, he searched for a way to convey this seismic shift inside him.

Massimo slowly lowered himself to one knee. He pulled the jewelry box out of his suit coat pocket, then reached for her hand. Her breath hitched, and for one heart-stopping moment, he thought she'd pull away. But when her gaze met his, the wariness in her eyes was fading, and in its place, he found hope and a connection that reverberated inside him.

"I've fallen in love with you, Catarina," he started, not bothering to temper the raw emotion in his voice.

"You deserve so much more than what I've offered you in these last days, but I will spend my life making it up to you. I want to surround you with the love you deserve if you will let me. Please, be my wife."

Catarina blinked at him, like she couldn't quite register what was happening.

"I thought you said you knelt for no one," she finally said.

"I kneel for *you*, Catarina," he rasped. "I kneel only for you."

These were words he never thought he would utter, and yet they felt like the truest thing he had ever said. Catarina's lips trembled as he opened the jewelry box. She looked at the ring, and then back at him. "You're carrying an engagement ring? In case the need arises?"

"My grandmother would be appalled at your reaction to this family heirloom," he said with a hint of humor.

Her eyes flared with longing, but she turned away. "You want someone who will play the role of a wife."

"I did say that," he admitted. "I've said a lot of stupid things."

"You did," she said evenly.

"Because I didn't allow myself to want more," he said softly. "I didn't think happiness was possible for me. Not with parents like mine."

He reached up and gently guided her chin so she was looking at him. She needed to see the truth he spoke. "I want you. I want to learn to be the husband you need. I want to love you the way you deserve."

Her gaze turned hot, and it blazed through him.

"You're all I think about," he continued, letting the thoughts he had so desperately tried to resist pour out of him. "I have spent the last week trying to find a way to deny this desperate ache for you, trying to tell myself that feelings this strong are toxic, but I'm done with that."

"This is going to hurt sometimes, Massimo," she said softly. "You said it yourself."

He ran his thumb over her lips, reminding himself that it wasn't too late to change. Not when he wanted to be with her like he wanted his next breath. "I'm going to need to learn to deal with the hurt. Someone much wiser than me pointed out that I have learned everything else out of sheer determination. Why would love be any different?"

"How sensible. Was this wiser person Alessandro?"

"*That's* your first guess?" He chuckled. "No. It was my grandmother."

Her gaze flickered with emotion, but she didn't speak. He told himself Catarina had every reason to hesitate. How many times had he distanced himself, driving her away? It was all in the name of denying this feeling of restless passion that had grown into something much stronger. And yet, despite all the ways he had pushed her away, she was still here. She saw him clearly for all his faults and shortcomings, and still, she was here.

Her eyes were soft, and finally she spoke. "You're not afraid of…?" Catarina gestured to the building around them, all the windows that gave a view of the most pivotal moment of his life.

He raised an eyebrow at her. "I had planned to do this somewhere private."

A hint of a smile twitched at the corners of her mouth, and his heart surged.

"But I am here, down on my knee, in front of anyone who is watching, because my love for you is far stronger and far more important than any fear. I do not want to live without you."

His heart felt as if it was going to burst as she reached for the ring and slipped it on her finger.

"Yes, I will marry you, Massimo." Her voice sang in his body as she brushed her palm over his cheek.

He closed his eyes, soaking in the softness of her touch, the heat of her nearness, the desire that would never go away. And in this beautiful moment, he let himself simply feel all of it. When he looked at her again, he saw a hint of tears in Catarina's eyes, but she was smiling with a kind of joy that made his heart feel as if it were expanding inside his chest. She leaned closer and kissed him with the lightness and hope she had on the first day, in her father's library. This time, he would not squander the opportunity she promised with it.

"I love you, Massimo," she whispered.

It was as if these words reached into his soul, then grew, permeating every part of his being. He could feel the truth that resounded in them, speaking to a truth inside himself. There had been joy and an overwhelming relief when she had agreed to marry him, but these words of love were different. They were everything.

He kissed her the way he had ached to kiss her from the moment he had seen her. The kiss was full of promises and dreams and the satisfaction that they had all the time in the world to explore. It tasted of the future.

Massimo pulled back. "Now will you come up to my flat?"

Her eyes were wild with heat. "Your neighbors will talk."

"Then let's give them something to talk about." Massimo slid one arm under her legs and the other around her body. She laughed as he lifted her and started for the elevator. There would be time to talk about their future later. But for now, it was just the two of them, and there was nothing else on earth he wanted.

EPILOGUE

Catarina looked out at the sparkling fjord and the beach that spread out in front of them, a long, empty stretch of white sand below the green hillside and rocky cliffs. They had hiked down the winding trail from their house to the shore in search of the perfect picnic spot to celebrate their second anniversary. The sun was warm on her skin, and the sky was a bright, cloudless blue that her mother would have loved. The thought of her mother no longer held the sharp pain it had before she met Massimo. The ache of her loss was a larger part of the passage of time in her life, and time had brought her not only great sorrow but also great joy, particularly in the form of the man who now held her hand.

"Here?" he asked, gesturing to their favorite spot, just above the tide line.

Catarina nodded, and Massimo set his pack in the sand. She shook out an enormous beach blanket, and they unloaded an assortment of small containers of food that Signe had prepared for them with strict instructions not to peek, as well as a bottle of wine and one of sparkling water.

When their picnic was neatly arranged, Massimo sat on the blanket and lifted off his shirt. Catarina couldn't keep her eyes off the movement of his well-honed muscles. His bronze skin glowed in the sun, and she felt a bolt of familiar desire spread through her. Massimo flashed her a wicked smile, as if he could read her thoughts. His hair had gotten a bit longer, and it hung over his forehead with a casualness that still surprised her. He was so different from the man she had met in her father's library. And over the past couple of years, she had felt more truly herself than she ever had.

"I'd like a swim first," she said. "Join me?"

Massimo leaned back on his arms and stretched out his long legs. "Not a chance in this cold. But I'd love to watch."

She stripped off her dress, revealing a new tiny bikini, and she could feel the heat of Massimo's gaze on her.

"Don't take too much time," he added with a roughness in his voice as she headed for the water.

As she crossed the sun-warmed sand, she thought about the first years of their marriage. They had proved better than she had imagined. Massimo had suggested that she could find a role in the family business, but Catarina had decided she wanted to do something that was truly her own. When she told him as much, he had surprised her with how he immediately deferred to whatever she chose. What he wanted in return was something she was willing to give freely: her love. And in that balance, a bond had grown between them, one that would last, regardless of the path she chose. This had been the key to her parents' success in marriage, after all—the fact that they both genuinely had wanted the other to flourish. Massimo had spent every single day of the past two years showing her that he wanted the same for her.

On the topic of a baby, when they'd first gotten married, they had decided to wait. While she had been thrilled with that possibility, she'd also wanted time for the two of them to strengthen their relationship and figure out how to best live their lives together. And after some consideration, Catarina had decided to pursue a career in music education. While the piano remained a private pursuit, she was excited by the idea of spreading her love of music to others.

"I'd like to have our own children after I know myself a little better," she had told him.

"Whatever makes you happy," he had responded, leaning in for another salacious kiss. "I'm enjoying getting to know every part of you, over and over again."

But now she had graduated from the music education program, and things were changing again...

Catarina waded into the sea until the cool water lapped at her waist. Then she dove under, focusing on the weightlessness of her body, the refreshing chill against her hot skin. She swam out into the endless blue of her favorite place on earth, then turned back to shore. Massimo's gaze was still fixed on her. She swam in and crossed the sand as his gaze dropped to her barely covered breasts, then to her slick, wet thighs. Passing up the towel he offered, she instead lowered herself onto him, straddling him, feeling the satisfying hardening against her core. He laughed as she pressed her body against his sun-kissed skin.

"Happy anniversary to me," he whispered in her ear with a deep rumble of humor and lust. "Is there something you're not telling me?"

He took the weight of her breasts in his hands, as if he could already feel the way they would soon start growing fuller.

She bit her lip. "I missed my period a week ago, but I was waiting to be sure."

He paused and pulled back a little. His eyes were filled

with the kind of hope he was still learning to show. "Are you feeling okay?"

The corners of her mouth tugged up. "Much better than okay."

His eyes burned with that intense heat she couldn't seem to get enough of. "Now we have something else to celebrate."

He urged her down, against his warm body, and she tasted the salt on his lips, as he kissed her in that way that always made her forget everything else.

"Maybe we should wait until we are back at the house?" she said with a breathless laugh. "What will the gossip magazines say if someone finds us here?"

It still amazed her that they could now laugh at something that used to haunt his life. But love worked the kind of magic that still surprised her every day.

He pressed his lips to her neck. "They will say I am hopelessly in love with my wife, the way they always do these days."

*****

Did you fall head over heels for
Convenient Wife Conditions?
Then be sure to check out the next installment in
The Carandini Legacy duet, coming soon!
And why not try these other Harlequin stories
from Rebecca Hunter?

Pure Attraction
Pure Satisfaction

Available now!

MILLS & BOON®

Coming next month

HIS FORCED SICILIAN BRIDE
Jackie Ashenden

'That's why you took me, isn't it?'

Caterina's pointed chin lifts, her expression half defiant, half imperious. 'So you could finish the job you started twenty years ago?'

So, the little *gattina* remembers me. I wasn't sure if she did.

'If I wanted to do that, you'd be dead already,' I observe. 'But you were right back there in the cathedral.'

Her long, thick black lashes flutter as she blinks rapidly. 'You kidnapping me, you mean? Oh...' Understanding dawns. 'I'm a hostage.'

I give her a slow smile, because I do like an intelligent woman. 'Excellent answer. Ten points to you.'

'My father will—'

'Your father,' I interrupt, 'is irrelevant, no matter what he will or won't do. I'm afraid, *gattina*, no one is going to save you this time.'

The delicate bow of her mouth, highlighted by some kind of shimmery, pink lipstick, compresses into a line, and fear flickers briefly in her eyes.

I expect her to cower in her seat, but she doesn't.

Instead, she stares back at me, undaunted despite her fear.

'So? I'm going to be your prisoner?'

'No, *gattina*,' I correct her gently. 'You're going to be my wife.'

Continue reading

HIS FORCED SICILIAN BRIDE
Jackie Ashenden

Available next month
millsandboon.co.uk

Copyright ©2026 Jackie Ashenden

COMING SOON!

We really hope you enjoyed reading this book.
If you're looking for more romance
be sure to head to the shops when
new books are available on

Thursday 23rd April

To see which titles are coming soon, please visit
millsandboon.co.uk/nextmonth

MILLS & BOON

FOUR BRAND NEW BOOKS FROM
MILLS & BOON MODERN

Indulge in desire, drama, and breathtaking romance – where passion knows no bounds!

OUT NOW

Eight Modern stories published every month, find them all at:
millsandboon.co.uk

TWO BRAND NEW BOOKS FROM
Love Always

Be prepared to be swept away to incredible worldwide destinations along with our strong, relatable heroines and intensely desirable heroes.

OUT NOW

Four Love Always stories published every month, find them all at:

millsandboon.co.uk

LET'S TALK
Romance

For exclusive extracts, competitions and special offers, find us online:

- **f** MillsandBoon
- **X** @MillsandBoon
- **◉** @MillsandBoonUK
- **♪** @MillsandBoonUK

Get in touch on 01413 063 232

For all the latest titles coming soon, visit
millsandboon.co.uk/nextmonth